Tangled Up

MORE FROM ERIN NICHOLAS

The Sapphire Falls Series

Getting Out of Hand
Getting Worked Up
Getting Dirty
Getting in the Spirit (Christmas novella)
Getting in the Mood (Valentine's Day novella)
Getting It All
Getting Lucky
Getting Over It
Getting to Her (novella)
Getting to the Church on Time (wedding novella)
Getting His Hopes Up (a Hope Falls Kindle World novella)
Getting Wound Up (crossover novel with Jennifer Bernard)
Getting His Way

The Bradfords Series

Just Right
Just Like That
Just My Type
Just the Way I Like It (novella)
Just for Fun
Just a Kiss
Just What I Need: The Epilogue (novella)

The Anything & Everything Series

Anything You Want
Everything You've Got

The Counting On Love Series

Just Count on Me (prequel)
She's the One
It Takes Two
Best of Three
Going for Four
Up by Five

The Billionaire Bargains Series

No Matter What
What Matters Most
All That Matters

The Boys of Fall Series

Out of Bounds
Illegal Motion
Full Coverage

Taking Chances

Twisted Up
Tangled Up

Opposites Attract

Completely Yours
Forever Mine

Single Titles

Hotblooded

Promise Harbor Wedding

Hitched

Tangled Up

ERIN NICHOLAS

Montlake
Romance

Published by Montlake Romance, Seattle

www.apub.com

Amazon, the Amazon logo, and Montlake Romance are trademarks of Amazon.com, Inc., or its affiliates.

ISBN-13: 9781503941366
ISBN-10: 1503941361

Cover design by Shasti O'Leary Soudant

Printed in the United States of America

To my family, as always.
To Mari and Kim for cheering me on, as always.
To everyone I blew off, canceled on, or was otherwise
a jerk to while trying to make this deadline (like the
customer-service rep at Verizon and the guy at Hy-Vee.
But not the woman at Orbitz . . . you totally
deserved it).
And to Lauren, who made this story shine.

CHAPTER ONE

"Damn, girl, you make me want to break all kinds of laws."

Bree McDermott—*Officer* McDermott—turned to him and raised her eyebrow. "You know I won't think twice about using my stun gun on you."

He did know that, as a matter of fact.

"You promise to be extra rough when you handcuff me?" Max asked her with a big grin.

Bree laughed and launched herself into his arms. "You're just hoping to get frisked."

He caught her, with his arms around her back instead of hands-on-ass as he was tempted to. "I'd frisk you right back. Just keep that in mind." He gave her a tight squeeze before dropping her back on her feet.

She looked up at him. "Where have you been? I thought you'd be here last night."

Max was in town, along with at least two dozen of their classmates, for their ten-year high school reunion. He'd meant to get home hours ago, but his job was unpredictable—to say the least. "Got caught up in some stuff in Oklahoma City and then had to stop by the farm."

He knew that Bree would know he was talking about Montgomery Farms, the huge operation that had been in his family for four generations. The three hundred and fifty acres included the best peach and apple trees in the state, sixty-five acres of pumpkins, and nationally renowned strawberries and watermelons. It was the biggest employer in Chance, Nebraska, and the heart of the town's economy.

The farm was now up for sale, and the family from Kansas that was interested in buying was coming to visit in two weeks. Everyone in town was pitching in to be sure the farm, and the town where these people would live and attend church and send their kids to school, was in top form.

"I had some lumber and supplies to drop off out there, and I got to talking to my dad," Max went on. "But I'm here for the next three days."

"You'd better be."

"So come on."

"What?"

"There's a storm brewing." He knew she heard the excitement in his voice.

That delight was reflected in her eyes as she processed his words.

"I knew there was a tornado watch in effect, but we thought only a thunderstorm was confirmed," she said, looking at the skies overhead.

When she met his eyes again, he gave her a wink. "I might know some things."

Her smile grew, and her eyes widened. "Yeah?"

"Yeah. Let's go."

She looked at her watch. "I've got fifteen minutes left on my shift."

Max looked around the square. Even on a busy day like today, with all the alums coming back for the big ten-year class-reunion party, Chance was as tranquil and safe as it got. Except for the weather.

Chance was a tornado magnet. It had the dubious honor of being the town hit most often by EF4- and 5-level tornadoes. They'd been hit nine times by the crazy-destructive storms since they'd been founded and had now been hit two years in a row. And it looked like something was coming again.

"Since you became a cop, Chance hasn't had a lot of crime to speak of, has it?" he teased.

It wasn't because she was a kick-ass cop, though she was. It was because she was no longer available to lead the hell-raising.

"I never did anything illegal," she protested as they started across the square.

"You never got *caught* doing anything illegal. Drinking before you're twenty-one, 'borrowing' Mrs. Gordon's barbecue grill for a party in the park, jimmying the lock on the rec center so you could play video games at one in the morning—all illegal."

"I didn't jimmy that lock," she said. "I just stuck a wad of gum over the latch when I was in there earlier that day."

Max laughed. "Oh, that makes it completely on the up-and-up, then."

She rolled her eyes but couldn't argue. She was very familiar with late-night mischief, reckless driving, and even public intoxication. If anyone knew how troublemakers thought, it was Bree.

"Come on. You can knock off a few minutes early," he said, noticing that they were approaching her squad car.

She looked around. "I guess if I was *patrolling* and happened to notice a change in the weather, that wouldn't be out of the line of duty," she said.

It cracked him up when Bree was overly concerned about rules and regulations. It was so different from the teenage Bree he'd known, loved, and worried about. "That's my girl."

"I mean, protecting and serving includes making sure that any severe weather is watched, right?" she said.

They were now at her car, and she'd already unbuckled her gun belt. She leaned in through the window and laid the belt and gun on the front seat. Only in Chance would the cop cars sit around the town square with their windows down and the keys in the ignition.

"Absolutely," Max agreed. "And text Avery and let her know I have my eye on something."

Avery Sparks was the town's fire chief and in charge of emergency management. She was also one of Bree's best friends.

"No problem. I'm watching for Jake for her, too," Bree said with a grin as she started unbuttoning her uniform shirt.

He wasn't sure what her plan was here, but far be it from him to *stop* a woman from unbuttoning her shirt in front of him.

She shrugged out of the short-sleeved navy-blue polyester shirt and tossed it in the backseat. That left her in only her white tank top.

Max swallowed hard and pulled his eyes from the toned, tan skin of her shoulders and arms and the swell of her breasts behind the soft cotton.

"Jake?" he asked, focusing on her words rather than her breasts.

"Avery wants us to warn her if we see him."

Jake Mitchell was one of Max's cousins, and he had a habit of getting the fire chief riled up whenever he blew into town. "You'll see him," Max told her. Jake would be here any time. His other cousin, Dillon, might already be in town.

The guys had all been born within two months of one another and had gone through every year of school, Little League, Boy Scouts, summer camp, and basic training together. They had now spread out for their work, but none of them missed a chance to come home, and the high school class reunion was a fantastic excuse.

"So what do you think's happening?" Bree leaned back against the side of her car and pulled a foot up to untie her shoe.

"Leave 'em on," he said of her heavy black work shoes.

She paused. "Really?"

"We might need to get out, go tramping around somewhere. Those shoes are perfect."

She set her foot down. "We might get out and go tramping around?"

He grinned at the clear enthusiasm on her face at the idea. Bree was, hands down, his favorite person to storm chase with. Hell, she was his favorite person to do most things with.

Storm chasing was an old passion for him, newer for her. She'd always loved storms—the wilder and louder the better, which fit her perfectly—but she hadn't gotten into their study the way Max had. He'd been storm chasing since he'd been a teen. Bree had started going along with him only a year ago. Now, whenever he was back in Chance, they had a standing date. Those were his favorite trips. He loved that he could say, "I'm heading out. You coming?" and she'd throw stuff into a duffel and be in his passenger seat in five minutes.

He was grateful this storm was rolling in, as if following him to town. This might be the last summer he and Bree chased together. For a while, anyway. Bree was taking a job as a skydiving instructor in Arizona. She was leaving in August. A little more than two months from now.

Of course, she'd probably be back by this time next year. As much as Bree job-hopped, town-hopped, hobby-hopped, she always ended up back in Chance. He'd been a resident of Oklahoma City for the past several years, but he still took whatever excuse he could to get back to Nebraska. This was home. His mom and dad and aunts and uncles and grandparents were here.

And so was Bree.

And now that he'd discovered how much more fun storm chasing was with her in his passenger seat, he was going to make the most of the time he had with her. It wasn't like he didn't have plenty of storms to chase where he lived. One thing Oklahoma City had plenty of was wild weather. But nothing in Oklahoma City spiked his adrenaline like chasing with Bree. She was a fast-and-furious type of girl. He could show up without notice, sweep her into his truck for a couple of days, and then drop her off on her doorstep before heading back to work. She was not only low maintenance enough to go without a blow dryer or hot water for a few days, but she loved spontaneity.

Keeping Bree McDermott on her toes was a tough job, but after knowing her for twenty-five years, Max had learned a thing or two. Surprises were key.

Max took a deep breath and squelched the familiar frustration he felt rising. He tried to keep things fun with Bree, light and exciting, because if he thought too much or dug too deep, her inability to settle down made him crazy. He knew where it came from. Her parents believed in making everything an event and an adventure. Bree thought that was how to really live life.

But it made wanting her very complicated.

He wanted to settle down with a woman who seemed allergic to the idea. A woman who was going to be a *skydiving instructor*, of all fucking things. Not a cop somewhere else. Not something normal. A skydiving instructor.

Max forced himself to focus on the moment. The wind. The impending rain. The brewing storm. But the coming tempest didn't do much to distract him. It was such a perfect metaphor. He'd been chasing Bree McDermott for years, and his feelings for her churned just like the clouds overhead.

"Those shoes are perfect for tramping around," he told her.

If Bree was the squealing type, he knew she would have let one loose.

Her smile shot straight through his chest, leaving a warm, prickly sensation behind. It wasn't unpleasant, exactly, but it was definitely noticeable.

He rubbed his chest and said again, "So, let's go."

She reached into the back of her squad car and grabbed the zippered hoodie on the backseat along with a beat-up ball cap.

Good girl. He'd taught her well. The main rule to storm chasing was to be ready for anything. Even in the sultry June air, you wanted to have something to cover as much exposed skin as possible. All kinds of things got stirred up in a storm, and it didn't take much to cause scratches, abrasions, or even worse.

"I have to take the car and my gun and stuff back to the station," she told him, pulling her curly blonde hair up into a mess on top of her head and sticking the cap on top of it.

"I'll follow you." Max spun his key ring around on his finger. "You eat recently?"

She rolled her eyes at him. "Yes, Dad. I had lunch."

"Just asking, 'cuz we might be out for a while."

She started around the front of her car to the driver's side. "What you're really asking is if there are cookies or anything up at the station, right?"

There were. He was sure of it. Max's aunt Heidi was married to Police Chief Mitchell and was one of the best bakers in Chance. Heidi made sure the station was always well stocked with homemade goodies.

He gave her a grin. "What I'm *really* asking is if you'll bring me some when you come back out."

Bree laughed at him. "I was already planning on it. They're peanut butter, and I thought of you as soon as I saw them."

There was that warm, prickly chest thing again. Max would have really thought he'd be used to it by now. And used to ignoring it. He'd been noticing little signs of affection from Bree for years—and had been brushing them off as nothing to get worked up over since he'd been seventeen.

Except for that one lapse in judgment two years ago.

He shook that off. "I'll see you up there," he told her, turning toward his truck.

He jogged across the square. A quick horn beep caught his attention, and he lifted his hand to wave at Jake. He felt his grin spread, knowing that Bree would be texting Avery.

Jake turned the corner that led up to the school, and Max glanced at his watch. It was early to show up for the reunion. He and Bree had easily an hour, probably more, before they needed to be there. And if they walked in a little late, it wouldn't be the end of the world. He was in a T-shirt and jeans and work boots, but he could quickly pull on his button-down shirt and tie in the truck and be dressed as formally as he ever got.

The darkening clouds overhead didn't care that the class reunion was going on, and that meant Max didn't care. Or, at least, didn't until the clouds moved on. Storm chasing wasn't just his passion; it was vital to public safety. Someone had to keep an eye on the weather, especially when the skies started rolling.

A few minutes later, he pulled into the parking lot of the Chance Police Department.

Bree was in and out in five minutes. That was just one more thing that made her the perfect woman—she didn't dillydally.

She was also carrying a plastic sack of peanut butter cookies.

No, *that* was his picture of perfection. A beautiful woman, ball cap on, ready to storm chase. With cookies.

She tossed the bag onto the middle of the seat and climbed up. Her hoodie was tied around her waist, and the cap was barely containing her wild curls.

"Okay, so what's going on?" she asked as he turned the truck onto Main Street and headed west.

"Tornado watch," he told her.

"But you think it's going to turn into more?" She was clearly excited by the idea.

He chuckled. He could never hang out with a girl who got scared by storms.

He could sleep with them—that he'd proven—but he couldn't spend real time with them.

The last time he'd had a woman with him during a bad thunderstorm had been the last time he'd seen her. He'd dropped her off after the storm blew through and lost her number. He'd stopped having women spend the night altogether through tornado season. Which meant no sleepovers from March through October.

"It's going to turn into more," he told Bree. "For sure."

"How do you know?" she asked, scanning the sky through the windshield. "Radar? Or something fancier?"

He could have used radar or even complicated calculations by hand. But instead, he was using something that was even more accurate. His gut.

"I just know."

"How?" She pivoted on her seat to look at him.

A lot of it was scientific, of course. Some of it they even taught in elementary classrooms during weather sections in science class. And, yes, with advances in technology, there were amazing things they could do with tracking weather patterns and seeing changes coming before they actually affected anything. But relying on his gut was much more elemental and, hell, fun. His instincts were typically spot-on, and he loved the thrill that came from plugging into what was going on around him and letting it talk to him. And being right.

It was sometimes like rolling the dice in Vegas. The bubble of adrenaline that rose up as he shook the dice in his hand, the moment of anticipation and "Come on, baby" just before spinning the little cubes out onto the table, and that sense of "Hell, yeah" that slammed into him when he won.

Of course, it wasn't completely appropriate to compare weather watching to Vegas. For one thing, he didn't—or at least shouldn't—get high on pending natural disasters.

He didn't *want* them to happen. But he did like knowing that he had the instinct for them. His instincts saved lives. When he knew a storm was coming, he could get people to cover.

But he couldn't deny that he loved the sense of anything-could-happen.

It sounded crazy. He didn't teach his true style of weather watching to his classes in the meteorology departments at the University of Oklahoma or the University of Kansas—two positions he held along with being the primary reconstruction specialist for Oklahoma, Kansas, and Nebraska. But Bree got it. In fact, she found it fascinating.

"I can feel it," he told her.

Her eyes sparkled with that addictive mix of excitement and wonder.

She was really beautiful.

That wasn't a new revelation. He'd always thought she was beautiful. Most men he knew thought she was beautiful. But it was really tough not to be attracted to his best friend when she looked that excited about something he loved.

"What do you feel?" she asked.

Loaded question, Bree. But she didn't really want to know. And they were talking about the weather, anyway.

"I'll show you."

He turned his truck south off the highway onto a gravel road. The clouds overhead were already tumbling over one another faster, and the glimpses of white were disappearing, but the storm was several miles away. Watching a storm develop required distance to take in the whole thing. The cloud that had caught his attention earlier as he came into town would have looked immense, but puffy and white to a casual observer. But Max wasn't a casual observer. He'd seen the clouds growing vertically and had seen the overshooting top as he'd pulled into Chance. Now there was a telltale anvil shape at the top of the formation. The rain would start soon.

"Do you have your radar and stuff here?" Bree asked, pivoting to look behind the seat and into the bed of the truck.

"I brought a couple things." He always had his laptop with him, after all. "But it's in the air."

Literally.

He could feel it coming.

Bree gave a little shiver that he knew was excitement, and he grinned.

They bumped over the gravel, faster than someone should travel on gravel generally, but Max had been driving trucks too fast over gravel and dirt roads all his life. Not to mention through ditches, fields, streams, and many other terrains. Bree just hung on, one hand gripping the handle over the door, the other braced on the dash.

Damn.

He knew that was an unusual thing to find sexy, but . . . a gorgeous blonde who took his crazy adventures in stride? Yeah. He had no hope of *not* noticing that.

Even sexier was that Bree had her own collection of crazy adventures. She was always on the go, always looking for something new, always willing to try anything.

Whenever Max was in town, they went out drinking and dancing, hiking, four-wheeling, road trips on their motorcycles, snowmobiling in the winter months—anything they could do where they could go hard and fast. Then five years ago they'd started taking a yearly trip together. Bree had put together a trip to the Grand Canyon, where they'd hiked to the bottom of the canyon and rafted on the river for seven days for Max's birthday. It had been the trip of a lifetime and something he'd told her he'd always wanted to do—two years prior. The fact that she'd remembered that, had gone to the trouble of planning the whole thing and then enthusiastically accompanied him had made it the best week of his life.

It had also planted the idea of a yearly trip to do some of the big, amazing things they'd both always wanted to try. Neither of them had a serious significant other or kids, they both had good jobs with paid time off and some disposable income, so they'd decided, *What the hell?*

The past five years of trips had been a definite mix of heaven and hell for Max, and he'd dreaded and anticipated each one. The trips had been to places he'd always wanted to go, to do things he'd always wanted to do. The only problem was that they were with a woman he'd always . . . wanted to do. He was totally attracted to Bree's wild spirit, and it was that spirit that meant they could never be more than friends.

He forced himself to focus on the clouds and the way the tall grass and trees were bending in the wind. He rolled his window down and took a deep breath.

Without a word, Bree followed suit. The air swirling through the truck was heavy with moisture and a touch of chill that hadn't been there before.

Max pulled over onto a short dirt drive that led into the cornfield to their right.

"Okay, come here." He got out of the truck and went around to the back and lowered the tailgate.

He pushed himself up onto the tailgate as Bree joined him. She hopped up beside him.

A strand of hair had escaped from her cap and was whipping back from her face.

Max grinned. That was another way to figure out the wind direction. He liked it.

"Okay, close your eyes," he told her.

She did. He took an extra moment to study her face—the smooth skin and the two dozen or so freckles on her nose that she never covered with makeup, the long blonde lashes that never had mascara on them, the lipstick-commercial-perfect lips that never wore lipstick. Loving the outdoors the way she did, she was faithful with sunscreen and lip balm, but otherwise she never wore makeup, claiming she had no time for "that stuff."

He loved the natural look.

Being an outdoorsy, low-maintenance guy himself, he supposed that made sense, but truly, in his mind, it was a chicken-or-the-egg question. He'd loved Bree all his life—first in a little-sister way, then as a cool tomboy friend, then as a girl he wanted to kiss, and now as . . . a very weird and confusing combination of all those things. So he knew his attraction to the natural girl-next-door type came from the fact that Bree had *been* the girl next door, literally, all his life.

"What am I doing now?" she asked, her eyes still shut, her face tipped up as if basking in the feel of the air.

He closed his eyes, too. "Just feel," he told her. "What's in the air?"

He heard her take a deep breath. "A lot of moisture."

"Right." It was definitely going to rain. That was a given. But Max could feel how much the clouds wanted to dump everything they had on them all at once. It was dumb, probably, to give the clouds and the air currents and the thunder human characteristics like desire and need and anger and relief, but that's how it worked out in his mind as a storm built, pounded the earth, then rolled out like a long, relieved breath.

"I can feel the air is a little cooler," Bree said.

Max nodded, even though she couldn't see him. "Right. Can you feel how it blows in and feels warm at first and then follows with the cold?"

"Yeah." She said it with a hint of excitement. "It is like that. I was trying to decide if it was just the breeze that was cool. It's like the warm air is sitting here against my skin, and then the cool rolls in, bumping some of the warm out of the way." She paused, then laughed. "That sounds dumb, doesn't it?"

"Not even a little," Max said, unable to keep his eyes shut. He glanced at her. Hers were still closed. "That's just what's happening. The cold front is moving in, taking over. The fronts are going to bump up against each other in a bigger way, but you're feeling the hints."

She took a deep breath. "I wish I were wearing shorts, but I'm glad I took off my shirt. I love feeling the air on my skin."

Max squeezed his eyes shut on that. Why was he teaching Bree about weather again? It was no surprise that she was absorbing all this and loving it. The rafting trip alone had proven to him that underneath the adrenaline junkie who needed to always go faster and harder, she also absorbed everything about the experience. She noticed the sounds, and the smells, even the *feel* of a place. She ran her hands and feet through the sand, dirt, gravel, snow, water—whatever was around them. And she wore as few clothes as possible.

It almost made their snowy ski vacation to Colorado his favorite of their trips because she'd been forced to be covered up.

Then again, it wasn't like he *minded* seeing as much of her skin as possible. It just made sitting comfortably a little more difficult.

"You don't know what might get to flying around out here," he said after clearing his throat. "It's better to be covered up."

Her eyes opened at that, and she looked over at him. "You think it's going to be a tornado?"

She had the typical look of anticipation in her eyes, but there was a bit of worry there, too. With reason. Chance had suffered through more than their share of trouble, thanks to twisters. They didn't really need any more.

He sighed. "I do."

"Damn," she muttered. She turned her attention back to the sky above.

"Do you feel it?" he asked for some reason. "Do you feel the pressure? The energy? Like something's coming?"

Part of him really wanted her to. There was such a strong connection between them already in their shared need for adrenaline. But he wanted more. More of a connection, more of an understanding. He'd gotten turned on watching this woman fill her hands with mud from the bottom of the Colorado River and spread it up her arms, for God's sake, and it hadn't been about the sensual slide of her hands over her skin. It was the unadulterated pleasure on her face as she did it. The joy. The way she threw herself into everything.

He really wanted her to be able to feel the power of the storm that was coming.

While part of him really wanted her to look at him like he was nuts. That would be so much easier.

Because if she *could* feel the weather like he did, he'd want her even more.

"I do feel it." She ran a hand up and down her arm. "It's like there's this . . . anticipation."

Dammit.

She looked over at him. "You know what it reminds me of? When you're coming up to your front door and for some reason you just *know* that everyone is hiding inside waiting to surprise you. Or when you're watching a horror movie and you *know* they shouldn't go down the basement stairs."

He laughed at that. "No one should ever go down the basement stairs in a horror movie at any time, for any reason."

She laughed, too, and in that moment he wished like hell that the horror flicks and roller coasters and other things that gave her the scared-but-thrilled rushes were enough. Roller coasters weren't hard on his knee, for one thing. And he'd love to cuddle up with her on the couch for a movie marathon.

Fuck, he sounded like an old man.

No. Old men didn't do roller coasters.

That was small consolation.

Keeping up with Bree was tough on him. He should be grateful it wasn't a 24-7 thing. She'd probably kill him.

For some stupid reason, he let his gaze drop to her mouth—something he really fought to not allow much when they were together—and all he could think was, *But what a way to go.*

◆ ◆ ◆

There was a storm coming. Bree could feel it, and that was *so cool.*

She'd never really tuned in to storms before she'd started talking with Max about them. Or rather, listening to Max talk about them.

He'd always been a storm-and-weather geek, and he'd talked about it as long as she could remember, but she could admit that she'd tuned out things like "atmospheric electricity" and "meteorological phenomena" back then.

She'd been into a million things, too, but they were different from Max's things. His were all good things, positive things, fun things. And so much of them had required brainpower. Hers . . . hadn't. Hers were more the sneak-out-of-school-early type things, while Max was tearing it up in science class. If she was on a motorcycle, it was with her arms and legs wrapped around a guy in leather. An older guy in leather. Who could buy beer. And who smoked weed.

She shook all that off.

They'd both changed. She'd eventually figured out that she got more of a thrill from riding the motorcycle herself, and climbing things and jumping off things gave her a high equivalent to beer and weed. In fact, she preferred downhill skiing and white-water rafting to weed. Weed made her mellow; the other things revved her up. She even preferred the more docile activities offered on the great plains of Nebraska—which was definitely lacking downhill skiing and white-water rafting—like dirt-bike racing and snowmobiling and flying small planes.

She liked being revved up. In fact, it seemed she was constantly seeking more and more ways to feel like that.

Which was why this weather thing was so interesting.

Max had mellowed as he'd grown older. He was still passionate about things, but it seemed that his enthusiasm had turned more intense. Or something. He could still talk nonstop about favorite subjects—that was something she could attest to personally. But now when he did talk, it was with a more focused . . . intensity. That really was the best word.

Or maybe it was his deeper, rougher voice.

She had to admit, her best friend had a sexy voice. Listening to him go on and on wasn't nearly as difficult now.

"You're gonna get wet," Max said. He had to raise his voice a bit now that the wind had kicked up.

"I'm okay with that," she told him with a grin. She loved rain and thunderstorms. She was less a fan of tornadoes—understandable, anyway, but particularly being from Chance, Nebraska, the tornado capital of the world.

"You sure?"

Bree felt the wind trying to lift her cap, and she put a hand flat on her head as she nodded. "Totally sure."

There was the definite feel of rain in the air rushing over her skin, and a moment later a fat drop hit her cheek.

"Here we go." Max looked like a little boy on Christmas morning sitting on the back of his truck, gripping the edge of the tailgate and watching the clouds roll toward them.

Bree felt the familiar affection fill her chest. He was such a great guy.

She and Max were friends. They'd grown up next door to each other. She'd known him since she was three. He'd taught her to climb a tree, to fish, to throw a spiral. They'd played hours of tag, they'd raced each other all over the fields between their houses, they'd challenged each other to every contest from spitting to arm wrestling to baseball stats. With Max she'd broken curfew, bones, and windows. She'd swiped and drunk her first beers with him, learned how to play poker, and learned what a hangover was—all in the same weekend.

It had seemed that whatever she wanted to try next, Max was right there with her. Whenever she got bored and wanted a new challenge, Max was up for it.

In fourth grade, she'd gotten a dirt bike. She remembered Max trying to talk her into doing some wind experiment with him one day, and she'd told him that was lame and had stubbornly headed for the field with her bike. Twenty minutes later, Max had been there beside her on his own dirt bike. Looking resigned. Max looked resigned around her a lot.

In high school, they'd tried dating. Logically, since they already spent a lot of their free time together, enjoyed every minute of it, and weren't dating anyone else, it should have worked perfectly.

It hadn't.

Max was a traditional guy in a lot of ways, and his idea of having a girlfriend was taking her to school dances and movies and holding hands at concerts in the park.

Bree had almost died of boredom. And disappointment. She'd wanted Max—poker-playing, joking, dirt-bike-riding Max—and some kissing.

She'd gotten the kissing. Which had been good. But she'd also gotten sweet, romantic, double-dating, let's-cuddle-on-the-couch Max.

And now . . . well, the kissing would probably still be good. Hell, if practice made perfect, then with the amount of practice she knew Max had gotten since high school, it would probably be phenomenal.

But he was still a traditional, romantic guy.

Bree didn't do traditional, and she wasn't that into romance.

So they were destined to be friends only.

Adventurous friends who shared a need for adrenaline. Which he clearly needed in smaller doses, less often than she did. He didn't date girls who liked to climb and race and get dirty. He dated nice girls who liked musical theater and art galleries and taking trips to places like Napa.

He saved his adrenaline rushes for his time with her.

"Okay, so walk me through the tornado thing again. How's it happen?" she asked him, focusing back on the moment as the raindrops began to fall more steadily.

His eyes lit up a little just at the question, and she smiled to herself. She didn't know if he was so easy to read because she knew him so well or because he just couldn't contain his passion for this stuff, but she liked seeing it either way.

"We don't know for *sure*, but we know the ingredients you have to have. We know you have to have a parent supercell. And then there has to be the right conditions to cause rotation. You start with the warm, humid air on the ground and strong south winds," he said, holding one hand in front of him palm down. "Then there's colder air with a west wind on top." His other hand moved over the first. "The different temperatures and moisture levels between the two cause instability. You add in some strong wind shear to the instability and an updraft to get things rotating, and you have a pretty good chance of a tornado forming." He moved his hands around each other and grinned at her.

Bree wondered for a moment if it was the information she was so intrigued by or if it was listening to Max. He got almost as enthusiastic talking about building stability and reconstruction. He'd even grab rocks and sticks to show her what he was describing, if needed.

"See the cloud formation?" He went back to studying the sky and pointing. "See the band of rain?"

She nodded.

"And then there's the rain-free base." He moved his hand.

She peered into the distance. She shook her head after a few seconds. "Where?"

He leaned in closer. "Up there," he said, adjusting his arm. "And there's the wall cloud."

"Nope, sorry," she said.

He pulled out his phone and took a picture of the scene in front of them, then pulled the photo up and pointed on the screen. "Rain-free base. RFB. Wall cloud. And then there's the Rear Flanking Downdraft, or RFD, and the Forward Flanking Downdraft, FFD."

"Wow, how can you tell all of that?" It looked like a bunch of clouds to her. She did see very slight variations where he was pointing, but without him guiding her, she'd have no idea what she was looking at.

"Practice," he said. "Lots of study. I have hundreds of amazing photos and videos. We can study them together."

Sounded good to her.

This was the most fun she'd had since the last margarita night with Avery and Kit.

She didn't need margaritas with Max.

The thought seemed to hit her out of nowhere. But it was true. And . . . it was a relief. She wasn't quite willing to admit it out loud to anyone else, but she'd been a little concerned by how often a good shot of tequila had been sounding lately. She'd always been a social drinker. She loved beer, loved most liquors, and could definitely handle her share. But it seemed lately that she wanted it more and more.

It was the rush it gave her. She knew that. And the fact that she was having trouble feeling that rush in other ways was something she should probably analyze.

Later.

Maybe.

"Great."

"So this is where the rotation is starting," he said, pointing to the photo and then up at the cloud formation again. "That will very likely produce a funnel cloud. We'll follow and see if it touches down."

Bree felt a little thrill go through her chest. Ah. She loved that feeling.

"Okay, let's go." Bree jumped off the tailgate and headed for the passenger side of the truck.

Just as she touched the truck door handle, the cloud overhead decided to dump some extra water. She jerked the door open and clambered inside, but not before she got soaked.

"A few seconds more warning would have been nice," she said with a grin, shaking water from her arms and running a hand over her face.

Max looked over. Then cocked an eyebrow at her. "If you're going to be storm chasing, you might want to invest in some tank tops in other colors."

She looked down. At her wet, white tank top. Right. She looked up at him. "Good thing it's just you and me, I guess."

He didn't smile as expected, but he turned his eyes back to the road. "Yep, good thing."

He pulled out of the small drive and headed west, into the storm.

"So now we're looking for a funnel cloud?" she asked, strapping on her seat belt.

"We're going to be looking for striations and a wall cloud," he told her. "The striations can indicate rotation. The wall cloud is usually behind the band of precipitation and sticks around fifteen minutes or so before a tornado. It can have some rotation to it, so let's check this one out."

Bree watched him as he drove, looking up out of the windshield and in the rearview mirror almost constantly.

"You already know, don't you?" she asked.

"What?" He glanced over.

"That it's going to turn into one." She didn't have to say *tornado* for him to know what she was talking about.

He didn't answer immediately but then gave her a simple, "Yeah."

"How?" She believed him, but she was curious. "You normally have your radar up and stuff, right?"

"I do," he said with a nod. "But I usually know anyway."

"How?"

He shrugged. "Not exactly sure. Just a feeling I get. In my gut. In my spine. I just . . . know."

"Wow." She focused back on the road. She couldn't remember a time that she *hadn't* had a good time with Max. Other than the Sweetheart Dance in high school, and the double date with Dillon and Abigail, and the time they'd tried to watch *Pride and Prejudice* together on the couch.

"Wow, what?" he asked.

"That's amazing."

He paused and then asked, "You believe me?"

She looked at him. "Why wouldn't I believe you?"

"It just . . . sounds kind of weird. That I can predict the weather. Doesn't it?"

"Maybe." She thought about that. "I guess I just know you too well to doubt you."

"What's that mean?"

"I don't think you've ever told me anything that wasn't true," she said. And she meant it. She couldn't think of a single time. Maybe when he said he was fine after a long hike or after he'd landed in the field after skydiving that first time. She knew his knee bothered him, and had ever since he'd injured it during the cleanup efforts in Louisiana after Hurricane Katrina hit, but they never talked about it. It was the one topic that seemed off-limits. And to Max, "fine" was being able to move himself from one point to another without assistance. So technically, he'd been fine.

Max didn't respond to that, and they both focused back on the clouds. The rain was coming harder as they drove closer, but Bree knew that behind the rain was the real threat.

"Okay . . . there." Max turned onto old Highway 36. It was a two-lane paved road with paved shoulders, unlike the gravel they'd been on before. But the new Highway 36 had been built ten years ago, leaving this one far less traveled.

"Is that the wall cloud?" she asked, peering out her window.

"Yeah. And see the beaver's tail?" he asked, referring to the tail of the cloud behind the area of precipitation. He slowed down so they could both watch.

"Yep."

"We'll head closer and see if we can spot anything coming down."

She nodded.

Bree could feel her heart pounding and her blood pumping through her veins. She felt like her body was humming and wasn't sure she was completely touching her seat. She could feel it. Maybe because Max had said it, and she believed anything Max told her, but she really thought she could feel the storm coming, the energy swirling around in those clouds, gathering power.

She hated tornadoes. Cerebrally. She knew they were destructive and unpredictable. But she loved this building anticipation. It was like riding up the incline on the roller coaster, knowing eventually you were going to tip over the top and go careening down the other side.

The tornado would be the careening part.

And honestly, she loved that part, too.

Within reason, of course.

"Hey." She looked around. She didn't drive out this way very often. "We're, what, about seven miles out of town?"

Max nodded. "That's probably about right."

"And we're west."

"Yep."

She looked over at him. "That means that if it does turn into a tornado, it's heading for Chance."

He gave her a grim look. "Right."

"Oh."

Why hadn't that occurred to her before? Holy crap. She hadn't really put it all together. With the excitement of the chase and the interest in what she was learning, she'd distanced the storm from the town, she supposed.

"Hey," Max said.

She looked at him again.

"That's why we're out here. That's why we do this."

She knew that. Of course. Storm spotters were vital to public safety. She, and everyone who had ever lived through a tornado, was grateful for the warnings and information that allowed them to get to shelter and be safe.

But . . .

"You *really* think this is going to turn into a twister?" she asked.

Instead of answering, Max said, "What do you feel?"

Dammit. She felt it. The power, the energy, churning and swirling up there. She nodded. "Yeah. I feel it."

Max just nodded.

"Dammit."

"It will—Sonofabitch." Max cranked the wheel and pulled over to an abrupt stop on the shoulder of the road.

She looked from him to the cloud. And saw what had caused his reaction a millisecond before he said simply, "Funnel."

He threw his door open and held up his phone. She knew he had better equipment, but this would do. He started filming as Bree fumbled for her phone. She needed to call Avery and Chief Mitchell, Bree's boss.

Bree dialed Avery's number, but it rang four times before going to voice mail.

"Dammit." She dialed the chief next and put him on speakerphone. He answered on the third ring. "Chief, I'm out with Max."

"There's a funnel forming five miles southwest. No touchdown yet, but we need to get people moving," Max reported.

"Got it. Thanks," Wes Mitchell said. "Where are you?"

"Seven miles out. West of town. We have a view of the storm from here, but we're going to get closer, try to see what's coming."

"Radar is showing some rotation," Wes said. "And we've got hail."

"Noted," Max replied.

"Thanks," Bree added.

"Be careful," Wes said. "I know both of you too well to think that you'll head for cover now. So watch your asses."

She smiled in spite of the reason for the warning. "But you also know us well enough to know we'll watch each other's asses."

"Keep your phone on," Wes ordered.

"Of course."

She disconnected as Max called, "Check it out!"

She opened her door and stood up on the running board. "Chief says there's hail," she called over the wind.

"Yeah. Check out the funnel."

She looked. It wasn't officially a tornado until it touched the ground, but there was enough debris swirling underneath it that it almost looked like one. There was only a small visible space to tell that it wasn't fully formed yet.

Max ducked back into the cab. As a well-trained, well-connected storm spotter, Max was a part of the Skywarn system that used volunteer spotters to track storms and call in reports. The National Weather Service's local offices could access the information as well as local law enforcement. He made his report, including location, time, and what he was seeing.

"Be advised this is a fast-moving storm, heading northeast. Touchdown seems imminent," he said.

Bree felt a shiver run through her. It was that familiar and beloved combination of excitement and dread.

She knew it was a little abnormal to love being worked up, even scared, so much. She knew she was wired differently than most people, including her two closest girlfriends. But the man sitting on the truck seat with her at that very moment reassured her that she wasn't completely crazy. Or at least wasn't alone in her insanity.

They were both lifelong adrenaline junkies. They knew they needed the rush, but they knew they had to be careful, too. They'd learned about scrapes and bumps and broken bones and sprained joints and concussions together as kids—jumping off things they shouldn't, climbing into things they shouldn't, flat-out trying things they shouldn't. But at least they'd learned caution, and first aid, before they were old enough to use things with motors and electricity and bigger consequences.

"We moving?" she asked as he put his hands back on the steering wheel.

He gave her a little grin. "Let's see what she's got."

Bree grabbed hold of the handle above the door, knowing the "she" was the storm bearing down on their hometown, families, and friends.

They were the only ones on the road, and Max stayed to the middle as he pushed the pedal and made the speedometer inch up. That kept him out of the ruts in the road and also meant he could keep most of his attention on the churning clouds without worrying about running off into a ditch.

"She's gaining," he said.

Bree nodded. The funnel was dipping lower now, and the width of the swirling debris had increased.

They kept going. The clouds seemed to be getting darker, and rain pelted the windshield. After another two miles, hail was pinging off the truck and growing in size.

"Dammit, I didn't want to have to replace another windshield," Max said.

Bree's throat was tight with . . . fear, she supposed . . . but she managed to laugh. "Your insurance company know that you chase tornadoes?"

"You should see my premiums."

A golf-ball-size piece hit right in the center of the windshield just then and did, indeed, make a mark.

"Dammit."

But he kept driving.

For another mile.

They were now within two miles of the storm.

"There!"

Suddenly Max pulled over and slammed the truck into park.

Bree didn't need to ask what he was talking about. She saw it. Her eyes grew wider, and her chest clenched to the point she couldn't make a sound.

The funnel had touched down.

Tornado.

Three miles from Chance.

Max made another report as he recorded for a few minutes. The storm seemed to be churning hungrily, sucking up the earth below it and then spitting it back out.

It was amazing to watch. Not amazing in the "Oh, wow, that's amazing!" way, but in the "in awe at the power of nature" way.

It was unbelievable. Even though she knew it was happening right in front of her, it felt surreal, like she was watching a movie.

Max shifted into drive.

"We're going closer?" she asked. She wondered if she sounded scared. Because she was getting to the top-of-the-basement-stairs-in-a-horror-movie point.

"It's moving away from us," he told her, pulling back onto the highway. "The one we need to watch for is the one behind us."

Bree pivoted on her seat so fast her seat belt pulled tight, trapping her. "Ugh!" She unhooked it and swung around to look out the back window. "Are you kid—"

But he wasn't. She saw the funnel directly behind them.

"Uh, Max . . ."

"Yeah, I know." He didn't sound happy. He kept looking into the rearview. "It just popped up. It doesn't have as much spin as that one," he said, pointing ahead of them. "But we need to watch it."

They drove another half mile.

"Do you know the odds of seeing two twisters touch down at once?" he asked.

If he'd meant the question to be reassuring, as in the chances were slim that the one behind them would actually turn into a tornado, the eagerness in his voice took away from it. Because Bree knew this man. He *wanted* two tornadoes to touch down at once.

"Maybe we should get inside somewhere," Bree suggested, her fingers digging into the seat.

"Yeah, probably. I don't really see anywhere, do you?" he said.

He was right. They were in between a bunch of cornfields; the nearest house was at least two miles from them.

"So we should—" Her eyes widened as the funnel behind them dipped a little lower.

"Fuck." He'd seen it, too. Max turned off onto the next gravel road, the back of the truck sliding slightly. "Ditch," he said simply.

It wasn't perfect, but it was better than being in a pickup on a highway.

Bree shoved open her door and jumped out as he stomped on the brake and turned off the ignition. A moment later, Max came around from the back, a huge blue tarp in hand.

"Put your sweatshirt on, for God's sake," he growled.

Right. Things were going to be flying around any minute. She grabbed it off the pickup seat. She took off her cap, tossing it into the truck, and started to pull on the hoodie, but Max grabbed her arm and pushed her toward the ditch.

"Move it."

"Okay!" she snapped.

He didn't let go of her as they ran for the ditch. Max flipped the tarp to spread it out so they weren't lying in the mud, but the wind whipped it up, threatening to take it away. Her hair flying around in front of her face, Bree grabbed for it and managed to snag a corner and keep it from blowing off. Dirt and grass spun around them. She felt the sting of something a little bigger than dirt, likely gravel from the road, against her cheeks. A tree branch went tumbling through the ditch only a foot or so from where they stood.

"Come on!" Max yelled over the whooshing of the wind.

They worked together to get the tarp down, then Max shoved her onto it as soon as it was spread out, and she landed on her knees.

"Okay already!" she yelled. He didn't have to be so bossy.

He started to yank on the tarp so they could flip it over them to protect as much as possible from more dirt, gravel, glass, and who-knew-what, but just then he looked to the side, swore, and dove at her.

He knocked her onto her back and landed on her.

CHAPTER TWO

Dizzy from the tumble and with her diaphragm not working for a moment with Max's weight on her, Bree froze. But then she became aware of him muttering something like, "Dammit fucking sonofabitch" and shifting off her.

He pushed up to kneel on the tarp. "What the hell—" He touched the back of his head and pulled his hand away, bloody.

"Max!" Bree was up on her knees and reaching for his head immediately.

He tried to push her back. "No, it's fine. Just get down."

"You got hit in the head!"

"I'm aware," he said drily.

"For fuck's sake, Max, what was that?"

"A tree branch. Coming straight for *your* pretty little head," he said with a scowl.

"Let me see it!" She pulled his hand away, but he arched back, not letting her get a good look.

"Get your ass down, woman!" he barked. "It's not over yet."

Bree frowned at him. Nobody called her "woman" like that. But he had sacrificed his skull for hers. She grabbed her sweatshirt, which she still hadn't managed to put on, and thrust it at him. "Put this against your head before you bleed to death."

"I'm not going to—"

Something in her face made him break off and nod.

"Fine. Now get the fuck *down*."

He pushed her, and she sprawled on her stomach. He lay down beside her and pulled the tarp over them both.

The rushing of the wind intensified, and Bree squeezed her eyes shut, linking her hands behind her neck as they'd been taught since kindergarten in tornado drills at school. Protecting the head, neck, and face was always priority one.

Which of course made her think of Max's head. And the fact that he'd saved hers.

She turned so she was facing him. It was dark under the tarp, but she could tell he was facing her, too.

"Thanks."

"Of course."

Of course. Two simple words. Nice words. Something anyone might have said. But this was Max, not just anyone. And he meant them. Not politely, not because he was a nice guy, but because it was her.

He made her feel safe.

It was a dumb thing to realize all at once, but Bree supposed that ducking for cover from a tornado in a ditch with him put things like safety and security and trust and comfort foremost in her mind.

But she also realized that she'd always trusted him to keep her safe and that Max was a big part of her being able to take risks. And enjoy it. She knew she'd be okay if he was around.

He hadn't been there every time she'd sped down the highway on her bike or every time she'd plowed through the drifts on her snowmobile or drunk too much or smoked some weed—okay, he'd never been there when she'd smoked weed—but he was *there*. A phone call away. Someone she could always count on. When he'd left for the Guard, it had been an adjustment. When he'd moved to Oklahoma, it had been worse. But she'd still known he'd be there. She could call, and if he couldn't make things better by talking to her, he would mobilize his resources on the ground in Chance.

He took care of her. And he made it seem like no big deal. So she'd always thought of it as no big deal.

But it was a big deal.

And if this was her last day on earth, she was . . . okay. She was okay as long as she was with Max.

"Max—" she started. But how did you thank someone you'd known your whole life—someone you'd taken for granted all your life—for all he'd done? How could she express what it meant that she could be herself, wild and crazy and you-only-live-once, because he got her and took care of her and was right there beside her—even when he wasn't?

"I think we're in the clear." He flipped the tarp back off them and looked up.

The wind had died down, and the hail and rain had stopped. She could tell the sun was even poking through the clouds, but his words took a second to sink in. In the clear? As in totally fine?

Another amazing thing about these storms was that they could disappear as quickly as they showed up.

Bree should look up. She should check it all out. But she couldn't stop looking at Max.

Maybe it was the near-death thing that was making her introspective. Though it hadn't been all that near, really. But she'd been scared. And *not* in the basement-stairs-in-a-horror-movie way, after all. Because the stuff in horror movies was fake. The tornado . . . and the could-have-been tornado . . . had been all too real.

"Max."

He was still studying the sky. "That one didn't amount to shit." His expression changed as he turned his eyes northward, toward Chance. He got up on his knees. The next "shit" was a muttered one.

Bree felt her heart flip in her chest. That wasn't good.

She didn't want to look for herself, and in that moment she decided to let Max protect her for a few more minutes and know something she didn't.

She got up on her knees, too, and reached for his hand. "Max."

At her touch, he focused on her. "You okay?"

She smiled. "Yeah. Someone kept me from getting knocked in the head or I might not be."

He grinned. "It's what us big strong heroes do."

He was obviously joking around, but Bree didn't feel lighthearted about it at all. "Yeah, I know," she said sincerely.

Max looked taken aback by her seriousness. "Hey, I'm fine."

"Yeah?" She picked up the sweatshirt she'd given him before and moved closer on her knees. She lifted the shirt to the back of his head. He winced when she pressed, and when she took the shirt away, there was fresh blood. Not a lot, but she showed it to him and said, "Oh, really?"

"I've had worse."

His voice was tight, and he was watching her with an unreadable expression.

She could always read his expressions. Though, in all fairness, Max was an open, happy guy for the most part. He was a passionate, intelligent, fun-loving do-gooder.

But for all that, Bree knew that Max had, indeed, had worse.

She lifted the shirt to his head again, more gently this time.

"It's still on the ground," Max said.

Vaguely she realized he was talking about the first tornado. She nodded.

His eyes were on hers, and she felt a strange sense of relief looking into those familiar brown depths. With the weather and adrenaline swirling around and through her, that feeling of comfort was welcome.

"Moving slower than I first thought."

She loved the rush of jumping out of a plane or ramping over a snowdrift, but she also appreciated the relief and satisfaction of the landing.

She nodded again, her mind *not* on the storm.

"It's sustaining longer than I suspected."

She registered *That's not good* but didn't get any further than that.

"Uh-huh."

"There could be a surge in the shear, or the updraft could be pulling—"

She leaned in and put her lips against his.

Bree didn't know which of them was more shocked by the kiss. She'd kissed his cheek about a million times in her life. They'd shared at least five New Year's Eve kisses—the quick, on-the-lips-but-not-a-*kiss* type of kiss. They'd boyfriend-girlfriend kissed in high school. Ten years ago.

This was nothing like any of those.

This was . . . holy-crap good.

Bree felt his strong arms wrap around her, pulling her even closer. She tipped her head to fit their mouths more fully together, and she felt a little rumble from Max's chest. That soft growl sent fire through her veins, and she wrapped her arms around his neck, her fingers dropping the sweatshirt so she could put her hands at the base of his head. She didn't touch the gash from the branch, but she wasn't sure either of them would have noticed something so minor as one of them bleeding from the head. Not when there was something as spectacular as this kiss going on.

Bree felt Max's hands grip the back of her shirt in both hands, and his reaction sent a thrill through her. And made her press even closer. Hard enough that he tipped over.

The hard abs that she hadn't spent nearly enough time in the past appreciating but that she was very much enjoying up against hers now flexed, and he slowed their descent. But he definitely didn't fight going to his back—and bringing her with him.

Bree was splayed over the top of him, the tarp crinkling under them, but she couldn't take her lips away from his, not even to breathe. Certainly not to rethink anything.

Especially when he cupped the back of her head in his hands and opened his mouth.

Holy . . .

Bree happily moaned when he slicked his tongue over her bottom lip. She let him in, and he stroked his tongue against hers.

It was like taking a shot of cinnamon schnapps *while* hitting the top of a big hill on a motorcycle and sailing down the other side. Except that drinking schnapps on a motorcycle was illegal. And dangerous. Which made this so much better.

Not only was this perfectly legal, but this was Max. She was completely safe. Max would never let something hurt her.

She moved her legs so that she was truly straddling him and pressed against the hard ridge of his fly.

There was another rush—feeling how into this he was. He was so hard already and—

Suddenly she found herself flipped onto her back.

Yes. Damn, she liked that.

Max leaned over her, one elbow on the ground beside her ear, his other hand still tangled in her hair. He tried to lift his head. "Bree—"

But she didn't want to talk. Not about the weather and storms, not about the fact that they were lying in a ditch on a plastic tarp, not about what they were doing on that plastic tarp. She tightened her arms around him. "More," she said simply.

She felt his hesitation. For about two seconds. Then he crushed his mouth to hers, fully, hungrily.

Yes. Just like the sweet heat of cinnamon schnapps.

Max ran his hand from her hair, down the back of her neck, over her shoulder, and down her side to her hip. He gripped her hip, pulling her up against him.

Better than cinnamon schnapps. Better than even *tequila.*

And thank God for that.

She wasn't going to become an alcoholic, after all. At least as long as Max was around.

And Max had always been around for her.

She arched against him, wanting to be closer, and she felt how he squeezed her hip harder when she pressed against his fly again.

He was so much bigger than she'd ever realized. And not just in the fly. All over. He was wide. And solid. And hot. So hot. She felt like she'd taken three shots, and it was warming her from her toes to her nose.

Her fingers and lips were tingling, too, just like when she downed that third one.

"Bree, Jesus," Max panted, lifting his head slightly.

She blinked up at him. She tried to make sense of what she was seeing—Max. Panting. On top of her.

He grinned at whatever he saw in her face. "You're welcome for saving your head already."

The giggle escaped before she even knew it was coming. "Maybe I'm kissing it to make it better."

"Kissing what?"

"Your head."

"I completely forgot I even have a head."

She started to laugh, but something in his eyes took her breath. Intense.

Max had never been this intense before he left Chance. That still threw her off at times.

"Then you kiss *me* and make it better," she said softly.

His eyes flared with . . . desire? Protectiveness? Something else? She wasn't sure.

"Do you need to be better, Bree?" he asked gruffly.

She took a deep breath. "Yeah."

"And you think I can do that?"

For sure. "Yeah."

But she really hoped he wouldn't ask why. Or what needed to be better. She wasn't sure. She just knew that things hadn't been *right* lately. She was restless, dissatisfied. But it made no sense. Her life was just what it had always been. Nothing bad or sad had happened; nothing had changed. So she didn't get it. But she knew it was driving her toward things that were clearly bad—drinking, too much and too often, for one. Looking for bad boys again because the good guys weren't doing it for her, for another.

But Max didn't ask her about all that.

He kissed her again instead.

It was like a switch had been turned on. She'd heard that expression before but wasn't sure she'd experienced a moment when everything suddenly seemed clearer and brighter and *on* compared to before.

Now it was definitely *on*.

Bree moved against him, her hands running to his back, her fingers pressing into the hard columns of muscle on either side of his spine. Then, because she couldn't help it, her hands continued down to the firm muscles of his ass.

She sighed.

Her best friend was built.

Obviously she'd always known he was strong and tough and solid. She'd seen him do amazingly physical things. He threw tools and equipment around like they were made of Styrofoam. She'd seen his arms and legs flex and work while running, climbing, and skiing.

But it had never occurred to her to *touch them*.

And now she wasn't sure she would ever stop.

Plus, there was a lot more that she couldn't reach at the moment.

Then Max's hands started wandering as well. The hand on her hip moved to *her* butt, and he held her cheek in one big palm, sliding over it several times. Then he moved down to grip the back of her thigh. He brought it up to his hip, and she gladly opened her legs and let him settle between them. His erection was unmistakable as he pressed against the middle seam of her pants.

Bree felt everything below her belly button heat and melt.

She had to free her mouth from his to take a huge gulp of oxygen. Wow, she hadn't felt *that* in a while. For a moment she let herself wonder if this was weird. This was *Max*, after all. Turning her on, making her moan, making her want stuff that she had made herself quit wanting when she quit the late nights and the hard liquor and the bad boys. Things that she generally took care of herself now.

But everything in her yelled at her not to cross this line with Max. And then yelled, *Get back in there, girl!*

She did. She squeezed Max's ass, lifting her pelvis against his, and kissed him greedily. She wanted more of all of it. More kissing, more hands, more pressing. Especially . . . right *there*.

Max moved so that he rocked against the sweet spot that wound her hot, melty insides into a knot of need.

"Yes," she whispered, not realizing she'd quit kissing him again.

Her neck was arched, and she was rubbing against Max with abandon.

It had to be the weather. The stirred-up air, the electricity that still seemed to pop on the current, the colliding fronts—something. Elemental and natural and unpredictable and, most of all, unstoppable.

She couldn't have pulled her body from Max's for anything.

"God, Bree." Max put a hand on her face, gripping her chin between his thumb and fingers, holding her still to look into her eyes, his breathing ragged.

She loved that.

"More," she said again.

Heat flared in his eyes, and he shook his head once. But it was in surprise, or wonder . . . yeah, she liked wonder better . . . rather than denial.

But just to be sure, Bree slid her hand down between them, creating space where she really didn't want any separation at all. But when her hand found the steel column behind denim, she didn't mind as much. And when Max gave a heartfelt, "Fuck," she happily pressed harder and stroked him.

"More," she repeated, while she had his attention. Or while she had his cock's attention, anyway.

Apparently he decided to follow her lead. His hot hand slid from her face, down her neck and chest, to her breast. He covered the mound, kneading gently but watching her face. Bree felt the need to squeeze her legs together in response, but she couldn't with the big, hard storm chaser between them. Instead, she tightened her thighs around him. Max moved his hand, rubbing her cotton bra and tank top over the tingly flesh of her breast and causing her nipple to tighten. That hadn't happened in a while, either. The last time she'd tried sex with a nice guy, versus her typical just-this-side-of-legal guy, his playing with her breasts had annoyed her. She'd moved things along quickly so he'd leave them alone.

With Max, he could stay there all day. Though she wouldn't mind if he got his mouth involved. The mouth that she'd had no idea could do what it did. With how good he was lip to lip, she'd love to feel those lips a few other places.

Max squeezed her nipple between his fingers, and Bree jerked as heat streaked through her.

She gasped and arched closer.

He did it again, and she opened her eyes, having not realized she'd closed them, to find him watching her with heat and a touch of what she could only call smugness.

Smugness.

Huh. But it was definitely that.

With his eyes on hers, he slid the bottom of her shirt up.

Yessss.

He gave another little growl, and Bree realized she'd said that out loud.

Instead of trying to cover that up, she decided to help *un*cover the part she wanted him attending to. She lifted her shirt so it bunched above her breasts.

Max's smug look disappeared.

Ha.

Without a second of thought, Max pulled down the cup of her bra, exposing her breast. He took in the sight. He brushed a thumb over the stiff tip, and Bree felt her clit pulse.

Damn. She'd missed this.

The want, the coiling desire, the sweet build of a pending orgasm.

She'd had some really good sex in the past. But the problem had been that it seemed she could only get really riled up when there was an edge of trouble to it all. Fortunately, she'd quickly realized that one-night stands with strangers or the sex in places where they could get caught were both really bad choices. So she'd resigned herself to so-so sex with nicer men, a great vibrator, and erotic romance.

But when Max put his mouth on her nipple and moved his hand over her belly and down to cup her through the navy-blue polyester uniform, she wanted to shout, "Hallelujah!"

If *Max* could get her going like this, this fast, in a *ditch*, then maybe she *could* have great sex that wouldn't get her badge pulled. Or give her rope burns. Yeah, that had happened once.

Bree gripped the back of Max's head, arching closer to his mouth and hand, urging him on. She stroked him firmly through the denim covering the part of him she was suddenly very interested in, and she found herself wanting to strip them both down. Here and now.

"Dammit, have to feel you," he muttered against her nipple. He switched sides, and she spiraled into the hot need, not noticing he'd moved his hand again until she felt him slide between the polyester and the cotton of her panties.

She knew he instantly felt how hot and wet she was, and if the primal rumble she heard and felt against her breast was any indication, he liked it.

He wasn't slowed a bit by her pants still being zipped. Even so, she sucked in her lower belly so he had more room. He took advantage. His fingers slipped under the top edge of her panties and up against her clit.

"Yes, Max. Damn," she gasped, arching her back.

"That's it," he urged. "Show me what you want."

What she wanted? His fingers moving faster, pressing harder, filling her up, making her come. She really thought that was pretty clear. Telling him all that out loud was going to take more breath than she had.

"I'm so close," she managed.

"Are you going to come for me, Bree?" he asked, his voice low and gravelly.

The huskiness sent desire skittering along her limbs.

"*Please.* Yes."

This is weird, a corner of her mind insisted. It should be weird, anyway. This was Max.

But her body, particularly the part Max was so masterfully stroking at the moment said, *Max has great hands, long fingers, and a magical mouth. Shut the hell up and enjoy this.*

A moment later, she didn't have a choice.

Max slid two thick fingers into her while sucking on her nipple at the same time, and she came apart ten seconds later.

And she *came apart.*

She felt the orgasm shatter inside of her, shards of pleasure flying out and covering everything. It wasn't just her girl parts that were happy, but her mind and even her heart felt the overwhelming combination of pleasure, joy, and relief.

She hadn't felt that combination since they'd gone zip-lining in the Appalachians last year.

Bree threw a forearm over her eyes and breathed in deeply and contentedly. She knew some people rolled over and went to sleep after sex. She was always revved up. After good sex, anyway.

She pulled her arm away as she felt Max shift beside her. She could tell he was getting up and off the tarp.

She'd had good *almost*-sex. She'd had an orgasm, and she was long overdue for one that wasn't self-inspired. But that hadn't been sex.

"Hey, what—"

"Radio," he said, not looking back.

Bree pulled her clothes back into place and scrambled to her feet as he headed for the truck. Radio?

Then she heard the squawking from the CB that must have caught his attention.

He leaned in through the passenger-side window, his jeans pulling across his ass and his shirt riding up.

Bree swallowed hard.

It was like that switch was still turned to *on* and the light was shining brightly.

Max, the most important person in her life, had just kissed the bejeezus out of her and given her an orgasm that was still making her nerve endings jump. And that wasn't all that was ricocheting through her body. Emotions—desire, amazement, happiness, and . . . fear— bounced around inside her head and heart. This was *Max* who had just touched her like that. That was awesome. And . . . now what?

He said something into the radio, and she had to force herself to pay attention as she climbed up the side of the ditch. She pulled the tarp along behind her. She was pretty sure the sex-in-the-ditch moment had passed.

But there were other moments to come. He was here for three days. And this was Max. She couldn't stop herself; she was already thinking about his next visit and the trip they were planning in the fall. Another trip. Bree's entire body got hot and happy at the idea of adding amazing sex three times a day to their vacation itinerary.

Maybe they should have done that a long time ago.

But they hadn't . . . because of *her*.

A couple of years ago, on their skiing trip, she'd taken a nasty spill on the mountain. She'd been shaken up, hurt, scared. Her neck had hurt, and she hadn't been able to move her arms or legs at first. Her arms and hands had tingled, and she'd had a hard time focusing her eyes for several minutes. She'd been positive that she was paralyzed and would spend her life in a wheelchair. Max was the first person to reach her—of course—and everything they'd done together, everything she'd *planned* to do with him, had raced through her mind, adding to her panic. Thankfully, it had turned out she'd only had a concussion and had been in shock. The moment the paramedics cleared her and she realized she could independently move all her limbs, she'd launched herself into Max's arms . . . and kissed him.

Later that night, Max had sprung a romantic night in his cabin on her.

And she'd panicked.

She'd chalked up her reaction on the slope to the adrenaline of the moment and had told him so. She'd told him that sleeping together would ruin their friendship and that trying a romance between them wasn't worth the risk. And she'd believed it. Max's friendship was the most important thing in her life. They could both get sex elsewhere, but they'd never find a friendship like theirs again.

Then she'd walked away. And gone out to the bars—partying, drinking, and singing karaoke all night long with a bunch of strangers.

Was that what was happening here? Was this just adrenaline and the relief after a near-death experience making her feel what she was feeling with Max?

Maybe. But she wasn't quite buying that this time for some reason.

When he turned away from the truck a moment later, his face held a completely different expression from what she'd been expecting.

"What is it?" she asked immediately, stepping close.

"Chance was hit."

Every bit of adrenaline that had been coursing pleasantly through her post-orgasm body suddenly seemed to reroute to her head and her heart. Instead of tingly arms, legs, and more intimate parts, her mind started to spin, and her heart began to pound.

"How bad?" she asked.

He leaned in and turned up the radio.

"We had some wind gusts up to one hundred and seventy," a crackly voice on the radio said.

Another answered, "We can confirm. We tracked the storm moving at forty to fifty miles per hour."

"Location?" someone asked.

"Highway eight, four miles north of town."

Bree mentally pictured exactly where the other trackers were. They'd been on the other side of the storm from where she and Max were.

The local weather service and law enforcement relied heavily on storm spotters, and she knew there were a few in the area, as well as more serious ones who'd noticed the radar and headed in this direction from some distance. This was Chance, after all. The odds of seeing something big were pretty good.

Storm chasers always wanted to see a big one and, while they also took their role in warning the public and helping with safety seriously, they also rejoiced when something like an EF4 formed.

Which was what had just hit Chance. The wind speeds alone categorized it at a four even without knowing what kind of damage it had left behind.

Her stomach dipped. Damage. In Chance.

"EF4," she said out loud.

Max gave a single nod.

He looked grim, and rightly so, but it was tough for a moment to reconcile this guy with the one who'd had his hands down her pants only a few minutes ago.

Bree brushed that off.

They had much bigger things to deal with at the moment. And for the next several foreseeable moments.

Their hometown had been hit by an EF4 tornado.

For the third time in a row.

But as Max took the tarp from her and stuffed it in the back of the truck, it felt like they were stuffing some other things away to be dealt with later, too.

They didn't talk as they bumped into town over the debris-strewn highway, each absorbed in thought. The closer they got to town, the slower it was. Max had to zigzag around a variety of unidentifiable obstacles—wood, plastic, metal. There were branches, some obvious shingles, fence posts, wood, and an overturned car.

She couldn't believe she'd gotten caught up in *sex* while a storm was ravaging her hometown. What had she been thinking? They'd been in a *ditch*. Not the sexiest location for a seduction; that was certain.

But that made the whole thing even more incredible. *Max* had made her forget things like a storm, the ditch, and Chance. There was definitely a niggle of guilt about that, but overall she was mostly just overcome by the fact that it had happened at all.

"Max, I—"

"Not now."

She pressed her lips together at his short retort.

"But—"

He sighed heavily. "I know you want to rehash the whole thing, but now is a really fucking terrible time for it."

It was true that Bree didn't bottle too many things up. If she was happy, pissed off, excited, worried, or stressed, pretty much everyone knew it.

"I just want to say . . ."

She trailed off as Max looked over at her. She had no idea what she wanted to say. *What the hell happened back there exactly? Thanks for the orgasm. Let's do it again soon.*

I don't want to lose you.

Those were all very real possibilities, but none really fit the churning emotions in her chest.

Max nodded. "Yeah, that's where I'm at, too."

Of course he knew that she was feeling a confusing mix of elation and fear.

Max pulled up next to another overturned car, and they both ran to be sure no one was trapped inside. It was thankfully empty.

As she made her way back to his truck, Bree acknowledged that they had a lot bigger things to concentrate on at the moment. Well, maybe not bigger, but more urgent, anyway.

But they would have to talk about what had happened. And if it was going to happen again. And what it meant. Her body tingled at the thought even as she felt a knot of unease in her gut.

She forced herself to focus on the moment and her job. They would have a chance to talk later after the immediate issues were taken care of. Max would be there for them all to lean on.

But her stomach twisted again. She *needed* Max to be there. Forever. Had they just ruined that?

They stopped and checked three more cars abandoned on the road. All empty, no one injured lying in the road or ditch.

Bree made a call to the office with the license plates so that they could work to track down the owners and be sure everyone was safe and accounted for.

"I need to go to the station," she told Max as she disconnected. "They're calling everyone in."

He nodded. "I assumed. I'll go with you and see what they know. I need to call Mom and Dad and then find Jake and Dillon. We'll do whatever we can."

Bree didn't miss the irony of having three of the most prominent men in Tornado Alley's emergency management all together in Chance for the third EF4 in a row.

Her mind went to her parents and friends as well. Her mom and dad were in Puerto Rico at the moment and wouldn't be home for a couple more weeks. Bree would let them know she was okay, but they probably wouldn't hear about the tornado until she told them. She really needed to talk to her friends Avery and Kit. Not only did she want to know they were okay, but she needed to talk to them professionally as well. Avery was the fire chief, and Kit was the town's psychiatrist. They would be knee-deep—maybe even armpit-deep—in the storm recovery as well.

They pulled up in front of the police station and took the steps two at a time together.

Chief Mitchell was there with the mayor, Frank Harvey.

"Max, thank God you're here," Frank greeted Max.

Wes Mitchell looked relieved to see him as well. He shook his nephew's hand. "It's rough. Have you seen much?"

"We just got back to town," Max said. "We were out spotting."

Wes nodded. "Bree called, and then I heard your report over the radio."

"Have you been out?" Max asked.

"Just heading there now. The reports so far say it's a big mess over in the trailer park, several other houses, too, but the school was worst hit."

Bree sucked in a breath. That's where Avery had been, helping set up for the alumni dinner tonight. That's where a lot of people had been.

"Everyone is accounted for except Avery and Jake," Wes said a moment later, as if he'd read Bree's mind.

Bree and Max exchanged a worried look.

"I thought Jake was at home with his mother," Wes said of his son. "But I just talked to her. He headed out a while ago. They reported from the school that Jake was up there before the touchdown," Wes said. "No one's seen him or Avery since."

"I saw him driving that way when I was picking Bree up," Max confirmed. "I'll head over there now. I haven't tried getting a hold of him."

"I tried his cell, but he didn't pick up," Wes said.

Bree wanted to say something but had no idea what it would be. Clearly her boss was concerned about his son, but he had to concentrate on the community as a whole as well.

"What can I do, Chief?" she asked.

"Go on patrol," he said. "We need to check homes and buildings, make sure we can account for everyone who is supposed to be in town tonight. If people are missing, we need to track them down." He sighed. "We have a lot of work to do. We might have to do some digging, too. The Methodist church was hit, but the three people inside have already been rescued."

Bree knew that at this point the digging would be through ruined buildings and homes to find people . . . or bodies. She nodded her understanding.

"I'll help with all of that," Max said. "But I need to find Jake first."

Wes nodded with a look of gratitude. "Thank you."

"I'll find him," Max said confidently. "Then we'll put his ass to work."

Wes grinned at that, and Bree felt a surge of . . . something . . . toward Max. He had an easy way about him. He was laid-back but confident. It was hard to get too worried or nervous or worked up around him.

Unless there was an EF4 twister bearing down.

Or he had his hand in her pants . . .

"Bree? Okay?" Max asked.

She shook her head and focused. "Um, sorry, what?"

"I'm going to head to the school," he said, clearly repeating himself. "Wes and Frank are going that way, too, but they're going to swing through the trailer park. You grab a couple other officers and start on the other side of town, okay?"

"I was hoping to talk to Avery."

Max glanced at Wes and Frank, but they were already discussing a new topic. "I'm going to find Jake," he told her.

She nodded. "I know, but—"

"Jake was up at the school. Avery was up at the school. I think it's safe to assume that when I find him, I'll find her."

Bree had to admit he had a point. Jake and Avery rubbed each other the wrong way, but they couldn't seem to stay away from each other. Bree knew they had some history that dated back to high school. She also suspected there was more to it than Avery had told her. But Avery was a tough nut. She didn't share personal thoughts and feeling easily.

"Okay," she agreed. "But call me when you know something."

"Promise."

She nodded her thanks.

He moved his hand as if he were about to lift it. But it dropped back to his side. "Be careful out there."

Had he been about to touch her?

He wanted her to be careful. It wasn't like he'd never said that to her before, but for some reason this time felt different.

The ditch? Had that changed things? And if it had, was it for the better . . . or not?

She nodded.

"Say it," he said softly. "Tell me you'll be careful."

Okay, that was definitely new. Him needing to hear it, him giving her a soft, firm order.

Her finding that kind of hot.

"I'll be careful," she promised.

He started to turn away, and she wanted to grab him. There was something there, almost like he was . . . frustrated? That couldn't be right. She wanted to know more about all the emotions behind his eyes. But they all had work to do.

Max found Jake and Avery. Together. With Avery in nothing but high heels, sweatpants with the high school's logo on them, and Jake's dress shirt.

There had always been something brewing between Jake and Avery. It looked like Jake had finally done something about it. Or lost his mind during a tornado.

Max knew a little about that.

Rather than curiosity or humor about Jake and Avery, he was hit by a strong wave of jealousy, and that did *not* amuse him.

Fuck.

He'd kissed Bree. In a ditch. During a tornado.

He wasn't sure which one of those things was the most dangerous of the three. The ditch had been dirty. The tornado could have killed them.

But yes, the kiss had been the most dangerous. For sure. And then there was what had followed the kiss.

What the fuck?

He lifted his bottle of water and took a few long swallows. He was now at the temporary shelter for workers at the Lutheran church with Jake and Dillon after several long hours of work. The three had been in different places around town all night. Jake had done what Max had—hit the streets, checking buildings and homes, making a record of who was where and what shape they were in and which buildings were of concern, and helping clear roads so emergency personnel could get through. Dillon had been at the hospital helping with medical cases.

The immediate stuff was done, and they were now taking a break, debriefing one another and trying to come down from the emotions of the night before trying to sleep.

The three of them had worked similar situations together in the past. Many times. They'd all three gone straight into the National Guard after graduation and had been at several disaster sites together. Bigger disasters than this, with casualties and years of rebuilding ahead.

But this one felt worse to him, and Max knew his cousins felt the same way. This was home. These were their neighbors, friends, and family.

In fact, their family's business had been directly impacted. Montgomery Farms was a mess. One metal storage building had been blown over, another had a tree sitting on half of it, and the main building had definite roof damage. The house, too, had lost shingles, some siding, and a couple of windows. About a third of the pumpkin patch had been tossed, there was a deep rut cut through the middle of the strawberries, and they were waiting until daylight to see how the orchard looked.

It was no exaggeration to say that the town's well-being hinged on the sale going through to the Kansas family, and their visit in two weeks would be their first in-person look at the farm and the town.

The farm and the town that was currently a bedraggled, stirred-up mess.

Max felt a tight knot in his gut, and his knee throbbed. It had been ever since the ditch and dive/fall on top of Bree. As usual. Whenever he was with Bree for more than a few hours, his knee felt it.

But the feeling that everything was a mess wasn't just because of the pumpkin patch or his leg.

He'd been feeling it since Bree had kissed him. When he should have been making plans and strategizing and prioritizing to get Chance dug out and fixed up, his brain wouldn't let him leave that ditch, or Bree, or the feel of her coming apart around his fingers . . .

"You and Avery in the shed, huh?" he said to Jake.

He needed to get his mind on something else. Something that would make him feel better. But he wasn't sure that the subject of Jake and Avery would do it. It simply reminded him that crazy stuff had happened during the tornado.

Jake glanced at Max with a mix of annoyance and resignation that said, *You just can't let it go, huh?*

Nope.

"Avery?" Dillon repeated. "You get your kiss already?"

Jake kissed Avery every time he came home to visit. Just a kiss. But enough to keep him on her mind once he left. Max could only assume the flirting and kissing that exasperated the pretty redhead was Jake's way of getting back at her for breaking his heart right after high school.

Max could relate to that. For years, he'd wanted Bree to regret her decision to dump him. Then, after she'd turned him down for a romantic night in front of the fire in Colorado two years ago, he'd realized that it wasn't him, it was her. But it had nagged at him until he'd truly accepted Bree for who she was. She wasn't wired for a relationship like the one he wanted. It wasn't her fault. It was just the way it was. And the only sucky thing in his life.

He was an *expert* at ignoring it now. She'd said romance between them would change their relationship. Of course it would. That was what he wanted. But it was definitely not what *she* wanted. So now he automatically tamped down *any* thought of changing things between them. Which meant that getting her off in the ditch had been a stupendously stupid thing to do.

That had, without question, changed how he'd look at her forever. He'd wanted her before. Now he was expecting some very dirty and inappropriate dreams. Forever.

Jake glanced over at the cot where Avery had fallen asleep. "We went out to get more streamers," he said with a shrug. "And . . . things happened."

"Things?" Dillon cocked an eyebrow.

"Things," Jake told him. "Like a tornado. For instance."

"You kissed her," Max said. "During a tornado. Again."

"She kissed me, actually," Jake said.

Max and Dillon both raised their brows at him. Avery usually avoided and ignored Jake as much as possible.

"Seriously. She initiated it."

What had been swirling around in that cloud that had made all the women go crazy?

"She walked out wearing only sweatpants and your shirt," Max added, making sure Dillon had all the details he had.

"That's a . . . long story," Jake said.

"Are you satisfied now that you got her naked again?" Dillon asked.

Max watched Jake with interest. Was he? Could he get Avery out of his system?

Because satisfied was really not what *Max* was feeling at the moment. In fact, if he had to label how he felt about *his* tornado tryst, it would be pissed off. Because what had happened in that ditch had been 10 percent about him . . . and 90 percent about that fucking tornado.

He knew Bree. He knew how she worked, what made her tick. *Adrenaline* got her going—fast and hard. And along with everything else swirling around in that ditch, there had been plenty of that.

It was just like Bree to get turned on by a tornado. He just happened to be the guy in the ditch next to her.

Maybe that was what had happened in the shed. Jake just happened to be there when Avery got all wound up.

"What do you mean?" Jake asked.

"This obsession with her," Dillon said. "Now that you've been able to seduce her again, are you over it?"

Jake frowned. "I'm not obsessed."

Dillon and Max laughed.

"I'm not."

"Dude, you romanced her at prom and took her virginity on graduation night and you thought that was something amazing and special. Then she told you she was sorry for the whole thing. That's been driving you crazy for years. Then last summer you kissed her again and you've spent the past year obsessed with proving to her that she's crazy about *you*," Dillon said.

"Come on. It's not an ego thing," Jake protested. "I like her. She's beautiful. Why wouldn't I want to sleep with her?"

The guys just grinned, and Max appreciated the conversation— even if it was at Jake's expense—that was lightening his mood.

Jake wanted to sleep with Avery because she didn't want to sleep with him. He was as addicted to a challenge, as Max and Dillon were. Along with a bit of DNA; an unmatched loyalty to, and love for, their hometown; and a desire to be big-shot heroes to the world at large, the three cousins also shared the habit of going crazy over the women who challenged them most.

Jake looked at them. "She is beautiful."

"She is," Dillon agreed. "She's also smart and no-nonsense and take-charge and kind of funny."

"What she is *not*, however, is crazy about you," Max added. "Which is why you're interested." Again, Max could have been talking about himself and Bree. He and Jake should probably just get T-shirts and start a club.

"You make me seem like an ass," Jake muttered.

"You're sure it's not *you* who's making you seem like an ass?" Dillon asked. "You're the one who's been kissing and teasing her for a year now."

"You've been thinking about that letter for ten," Max added.

The letter that had knocked Jake completely off his everything-is-now-good-and-right-in-the-world axis. Something else Max could relate to. Like when Bree had told him she didn't want to be his girl-friend because it was boring.

But Avery had written it down. That shit was forever. Over time Max would forget what Bree had said.

Like maybe in another fifty years or so. Because at the moment he could still recall it word for word. Twelve years later.

He focused on harassing Jake instead of wallowing in his own memories. "I think my favorite part of the letter was when she said she knowingly used alcohol and your hormones against you."

"Oh, *my* favorite part," Dillon said, "was when she apologized for taking her shirt off." He tipped his water bottle toward Jake in a sort-of salute. "I know you were pretty pissed about that."

"Time to shut up about the letter," Jake said.

"Fine," Max said agreeably. There were other ways to torture Jake. "How about we talk about you not kissing her anymore instead?"

Jake shifted on his chair. "She's never once told me to stop or pushed me away," he informed them. "Not once."

Max regarded him intently. Jake knew exactly what Max was talking about. Avery didn't push him away, but that didn't mean he wasn't doing something he shouldn't. Unless Jake wanted to step up and actually be what Avery needed, which was, for one, *here* in Chance full-time, then he needed to leave her alone.

Just like he needed to leave Bree alone now that the tornado had blown over. No matter how much he'd like to test that 90-percent-tornado/10-percent-Max theory he had going.

He and Bree weren't meant to be more than friends. Long-distance, see-each-other-once-a-month friends.

He couldn't train for the half marathons with her; he couldn't kickbox with her every night or hike and cross-country ski every weekend. His already aching knee throbbed at the thought.

That was one of the positive things about living hundreds of miles from her. He could come to Chance once a month and go hard for a weekend, then go back to his physical therapist in Oklahoma and bitch and moan through rehab after stressing his knee beyond its capabilities, without Bree ever knowing. His regular workouts were swimming and short runs and biking, and even those had their limits. Bree's favorite activities took a toll on him.

There were only two options for changing that. Surgery, which could improve his mobility but would potentially increase his pain and decrease his strength. Or Bree slowing down.

Part of him would love if she'd pull back a little, but he didn't want it to be because of him. If she could figure out for herself that taking things easier was okay, good even, he'd be thrilled. But he did *not* want to be the reason she gave up the things she loved.

He hated not being able to keep up with her, though.

When they'd been kids, she'd often been the instigator, the one saying, "Come on, Max!" But when he held back then, it was simply because he wanted to do other things—fish, swim, collect bugs, play baseball. She was the one always going at breakneck speeds and challenging the laws of physics. But he'd never hung back because he *couldn't* keep up. Now it was different. He loved being the one with her on her adventures. He hated that he was no longer at 100 percent. So he pushed it. Hard. The entire time they were together.

Which required at least a month of rehab after landing on it, twisting it, and pushing to the max of his range of motion and strength for a week.

But the surgery was no guarantee, and since his knee only bothered him when he was with Bree, and because he had the best therapist in Oklahoma working on him, keeping things exactly as they were seemed like the best decision.

Besides, it was very possible that there wasn't a single man on earth who could fully be everything Bree McDermott needed.

Max took at least some comfort in that.

"You going back to Kansas City on Monday?" Dillon asked Jake.

"I have meetings Tuesday," Jake said absently.

"Then maybe you need to leave Avery alone altogether," Dillon said.

Jake looked at him. "What do you mean?"

"You're leaving the day after tomorrow. You got a little sugar, now let it go. She's going to be swamped with stuff from the storm, anyway. There's no reason to get her all riled up or try to revisit your shed encounter, is there?"

Nope, there was no reason to revisit the ditch encounter with Bree, either.

But that little bit of sugar . . . it had been only a little, just a taste, just enough to wake up the addict in him.

Dillon leaned in, pinning Jake with a look. "So you're not trying to get her to fall in love with you now so you can get revenge for her *not* falling in love with you in high school and being the only single, straight female in Chance to not think you walk on water?"

Max didn't know about Jake, but Dillon's words were a direct hit for him. Damn. Dillon was good. He was a medical doctor, but he could give Kit Derby a run for her money. Which was funny because Dillon and Kit had been in constant competition since third grade.

But did part of Max want Bree to want him because she hadn't in high school or at the fucking ski lodge two years ago and his ego was still bruised?

Yep.

He'd felt damn good about himself when she was saying "More" in that ditch. Max grinned in spite of himself. Sure, it was torturous to think about the ditch, but that didn't mean he was going to stop. How hot and wet and sweet she'd been, how she'd wiggled and pressed against him, how easy it had been to make her come. He had a lot of experience to fall back on, and while he dished out his share of orgasms, a lot of them took some real dedication and time—dedication and time he was happy to give, of course—but not so with Bree. It had taken very little to start her up and finish it off.

Of course Bree would go hard and fast. That was her MO in everything else, so why not orgasms, too?

But remembering that orgasm had Max shifting uncomfortably on his chair.

Had her being so hot for him soothed his ego bruise a bit?

Hell yeah, it had.

Bree had been bored dating him in high school. Her words. But now, and over the past twelve years, he'd been the guy she most looked forward to seeing, the guy she dropped everything for when he showed up, the guy she'd spent the past five years having her greatest adventures with.

She definitely hadn't been thinking he was boring out on old Highway 36.

Max tuned back into the guys in time to hear Jake say, "You failed your psych rotation in med school, right?" to Dillon as he shoved his chair back and stood.

"I did very well on my psych rotation," Dillon informed him. Cocky and cool as ever.

"You must be rusty, 'cause you're way off. I don't *need* Avery to be in love with me. She doesn't even need to like me. But if she wants to keep kissing me, I'm not going to argue."

"You need everyone to love you," Max said to Jake to show he'd been listening. Kind of. "You've always gotten off on being 'such a great guy.'"

"The air quotes make you seem sarcastic," Jake said drily.

Max chuckled. "I don't want to *seem* sarcastic. I want it to be very clear that I'm being sarcastic."

"You'd think some of my greatness would start rubbing off on you guys eventually, wouldn't you?" Jake asked. "But no. I'm still the lone good guy in this bunch."

They just looked at him.

They didn't take insults from one another seriously, ever.

Jake finally sighed. "I'm satisfied. She was totally into me today. That's all I needed to know."

Bree had been totally into him, too. Totally. Like ignore-the-tornado-overhead into him.

"Good deal. No more sugar. We're both on a strict diet for the rest of our stay."

Dillon and Jake both froze.

"You're *both* on a diet?" Dillon asked.

"No *more* sugar?" Jake asked.

Max nodded. "Bree kissed me."

"*Bree?*" Dillon asked.

"*Kissed you?*" Jake added.

"She was out watching the twister with me. Got a little close for comfort, so I threw her in a ditch and got on top of her. Saved her pretty ass and got my head bashed in the process."

"You got your head bashed?" Dillon demanded, coming out of his chair.

"It was just a flying branch." Dillon grabbed Max's head in both hands and probed his scalp. "Ow! Fuck, Doc."

"You got stitches." Dillon let go of him.

He'd stopped at the clinic, but Dillon had been busy, so someone else had sewn him back together. That was probably what Dillon was pissed about. He loved being the hero as much as Max and Jake. He would have preferred to take care of every bump and scrape on every person today. It was a bitch to only have two hands sometimes. "Yep. No big deal."

"Your head is the hardest of any I know," Dillon said, scowling. "Stitches and possible concussions are not 'Oh, by the way' topics of conversation, though, got it?"

"Yes, sir."

"That's *Dr.* Sir to you," Dillon said. "Dumbass," he muttered under his breath.

Max rolled his eyes.

"Are you going to tell us more about you and Bree?" Jake asked.

"Was it good?" Dillon asked.

"Of course it was good." Max wondered if they could hear the mix of misery and want in his voice. Because, if nothing else, it had definitely been *good*. "Too good. It's so damned"—he sighed—"complicated."

"But it was good?" Jake asked. "That's something."

Well, *yeah*. His dream girl had thrown herself at him. He would have truly been the dumbass Dillon had accused him of being if he hadn't caught her. But he'd be an even bigger dumbass if he didn't realize what was behind it all. "It's not anything. It's just Bree being Bree. She's an adrenaline junkie. The storm got her all riled up, and she mistook that rush for other kinds of . . . excitement."

"You'd better be careful," Jake warned. "Tornadoes in Chance have a way of stirring up stuff you don't want stirred up. I kissed a girl during a tornado in Chance and look at how messed up I am."

"People do crazy, uncharacteristic things when they're in danger or feel threatened," Dillon said.

"Exactly," Max agreed with a nod. Or *characteristic* things in Bree's case. She jumped into things *because* of the danger and the thrill.

"What happened with you?" Jake asked Dillon.

Max focused on his cousin. Dillon did look a little . . . perturbed.

"Kit Derby," Dillon said sullenly.

Okay, *that* was worth pursuing. "Kit *happened* to you?" Max asked. "What's that mean?"

"Kit Derby, a storeroom at the hospital, and her damned body lotion happened to me."

"Whoa," Max commented. "Body lotion?"

"And?" Jake added.

"We kissed."

Max and Jake both watched Dillon, waiting. And got nothing.

"Jesus, Dillon, what the fuck *happened*?" Max demanded. Kit and Dillon couldn't be together for two minutes without snapping and snarking.

"She smelled good and we were in there alone and we . . . kissed." Dillon was clearly not happy about it.

"Just kissed?" Jake asked.

Dillon nodded.

Something had definitely caused everyone to go crazy during this tornado.

"She kissed you, too, though, right?" Max pointed out.

"Hell yeah, she did," Dillon said with a scowl.

"I don't know, guys." Jake stretched his arms over his head and linked his hands at the back of his neck. "This was one of the better tornadoes I've been in."

Max couldn't disagree. No one had died. All the damage could be cleaned up, repaired, or replaced. It was true the tornado had mixed up a lot more than buildings and houses and fields, but fortunately for Chance—and Bree, Avery, and Kit—Max and the guys were here. Max, Jake, and Dillon specialized in straightening things out after they got all messed up.

CHAPTER THREE

Bree stood to one side in the mayor's office waiting for the strategy meeting to start, chewing on her left thumbnail and waiting for Kit to show up. She'd heard Frank tell Robyn, his receptionist, that he was expecting Kit, Dillon, Avery, and Jake at the meeting this morning.

Max was already here.

He and Frank had been talking about the farm cleanup and if they needed to ask for some contractors and crews from neighboring towns to come help. Now he was filling Frank in on some of the notes he'd made about structural concerns around town. And Bree was dealing with finding all that bizarrely sexy.

This was a side of Max she knew existed on a cerebral level but that she didn't see often. When he was in Chance, they hung out, goofed around, acted like big kids. She loved that. In contrast, this was the serious, in-charge Max. And he was hot.

Bree really needed Kit to get here early.

She needed her shrink best friend to tell her that her dirty dreams about Max last night were normal after the ditch orgasm and that if she'd finally found a guy who got her going like jumping out of a plane did, she needed to hang on to him. Even if she had been hanging on to him in some form for most of her life.

What she really needed was for Kit to tell her that finding that amazing sexual rush with Max, of all people, was something special and she should go for it. Because that's what she wanted to do. She wanted to go for it. With Max.

Having a psychiatrist for a best friend could be really annoying at times. Because contrary to Kit's belief, Bree didn't like being analyzed while eating a Reuben or sorting her laundry or at commercial breaks during *Supernatural*. But now, getting Kit's educated perspective on things for free was going to be a well-earned perk of their friendship.

Kit walked in, and Bree made a beeline for her. She needed to hear the psychiatrist who knew *everything* about her—damned tequila, any-way—tell her that wanting to have hot against-the-wall sex with Max made perfect sense and that she should start *tonight*.

Kit saw her coming, held up a finger, and then pointed to the phone that she held to her ear under her long, dark hair.

She was on the phone? Now? Bree needed to talk. *Before* she talked to Max and said something stupid like, *Will you let me pour my favorite beer all over you and then lap it up with my tongue?* and ruined everything forever.

Max was someone she *needed* in her life. She could not mess this up for an orgasm or two.

But maybe—*maybe*—she was wrong to think it would ruin any-thing. Maybe she was denying herself something for no good reason.

If that was the case, she needed to know. Now.

She mouthed to Kit, *"It's urgent."*

Kit nodded. But kept talking.

Fortunately, Max and Frank had already been involved in their conversation when she'd approached the mayor's office door. Robyn had told her to go on in, so she'd slipped in, trying to go unnoticed.

She hadn't.

Max had looked over immediately and given her a smile that she'd seen four billion times—give or take—in her life. It was the smile that lit up his whole face and said he was happy to see her, and it always made her feel warm and happy.

Today it also brought back memories of her dream where Max stripped off her uniform pants and found her matching navy-blue lace thong—which was how she'd known it was a dream. She didn't do thongs. But she could be talked into them if Max would always tear them off with his teeth before putting his head between her legs and . . .

She felt the heat climbing through her body and was sure that her face looked like she'd just finished a three-mile run. Which she had earlier, trying to work off the jumpy feeling of electricity zipping through her body. But that had been hours ago, and she'd showered and gotten rid of some of the pulsing energy herself.

And it hadn't even come close to feeling the way Max's fingers had felt.

Bree gritted her teeth and gave Kit a hand gesture that meant *Hurry up.*

She glanced over her shoulder to make sure Max was still talking with Frank. He was, and Dillon had now joined them.

Dillon had come into the room and Bree hadn't even noticed? Great police skills there. She was that worked up.

Argh! She narrowed her eyes at Kit again and mouthed, *"Come on."*

Kit gave her a behave-yourself look that Bree had seen almost as many times as she'd seen the light-him-up smile that Max gave her.

No, that wasn't quite right. She hadn't been close to Kit that long. They'd gone to high school together and had known each other, of course. But they hadn't hung out. Kit had been running every committee and competing with Dillon for top spot in their class while Bree had been getting only high-enough grades that she could stay on the sports teams, and otherwise partying and doing stupid, risky things that she now busted kids for.

Bree studied her friend and admitted that they were still polar opposites. Kit was sophisticated and polished and put together. She was intelligent and cool under pressure and put off a vibe of "I'm way out of your league."

Bree, on the other hand, was down-to-earth, often a little rumpled, and never concerned with her appearance. Never. Which bugged the hell out of Kit. Where Kit was dark and sleek, Bree was blonde and curly. Where Kit had curves and looked great in heels, Bree was built more like a boy and would spend her life barefoot if she could. Kit was very routine oriented and didn't like change. Bree thrived on change. She loved trying new things. Kit did yoga and meditated and read biographies of amazing women. Bree ran and rode motorcycles and only read fiction. Bree loved to garden—that was about as peaceful as she got. Kit loved to get involved in political issues, especially women's issues—which was about as wound up as Kit got.

But they worked.

Kit was her best girlfriend. Kit balanced Bree, made her look at the world differently, and she appreciated their differences, and vice versa.

And Bree really needed to talk to her now.

She glanced at the door. Maybe Avery would get here soon. She could probably bounce this off Avery. Chance's fire chief was a newer addition to their friendship, and she was definitely tough to get close to. Kit understood the importance of close personal relationships and loved to delve into thoughts and feelings. Bree just couldn't keep a lid on most of her thoughts and feelings. She was an open book, for the most part. Avery was . . . not any of those things. She'd never had close girlfriends, so it was taking some time to get her to open up.

She'd come around.

But she wasn't even *here* yet.

Bree's girlfriends were definitely letting her down.

She looked over at Max again. She was behind him, so she could only see his back, but unlike in the past when she'd looked at him, today she was acutely aware of how wide his shoulders were and how tight his ass was, and that his hair was a shade darker than her favorite bock beer.

She was analyzing the color of his hair now? Really?

Bree whirled around on Kit and gave her friend her best cop look. "I need to talk to you *now*."

Kit's eyes got wide, and she nodded. "I will do that," she said into the phone. "Thanks so much."

She disconnected, and Bree grabbed her wrist and pulled her into the corner of the room farthest from Max.

"*What* is going on?" Kit asked.

"I had a sex dream about Max last night." Bree tried to say it in a whisper, but Bree wasn't really the whispering type.

They both glanced over at the men in the room to see if Bree had been overheard.

Thankfully, Max and Dillon and Frank seemed oblivious to their conversation.

"Tell me that's fine," Bree ordered.

"Well, of course it's fine," Kit said, recovering from her surprise. "Why wouldn't it be fine?"

"It's not crazy?"

Kit sighed. She hated when Bree referred to things as crazy. She said the term was tossed around too loosely. "Of course not. You and Max are close; you have a lot of feelings for him."

She did. And feeling like she'd do almost anything to get his fingers back where they'd been yesterday had now been added to the list.

"But it's *Max*," Bree said. "He's my best friend. We don't . . . do that." She hadn't even ever wanted to. Until now. Now she couldn't stop thinking about it.

"You were really happy he was coming home this weekend," Kit said. "You've been eager to see him, and then the tornado hit, and that brought a lot of unusual thoughts and emotions for all of us."

Bree hadn't seen Kit at all yesterday. They'd spoken briefly on the phone after the tornado touchdown, but they'd both been swamped and hadn't seen each other in person.

"Are you okay?" Bree asked.

Kit seemed to shake herself. "Of course. I'm fine. I'm just saying that when things happen like a tornado hitting town for the third year in a row, emotions get tangled up, and things can happen that wouldn't happen on a usual day. I wouldn't worry about it."

Bree was nodding as she listened. That all made sense. "It was the tornado."

"Probably."

She had felt a lot of things while they'd been out chasing and then hit the ditch. She'd been scared and excited. She'd felt her usual affection for Max and then something more when he'd gotten hurt protecting her. She'd also felt safe. And grateful. And then horny.

Huh.

"Is it possible to mistake one kind of adrenaline rush for another?" Bree asked.

Kit frowned slightly. "You mean to have adrenaline rushing from the storm, but to interpret it as being turned on sexually?"

"Yes. Yes, exactly."

"It definitely is." Kit had a strange look on her face.

Bree squinted at her. "Are you *sure* you're okay?"

"I'm fine. But yes, like I said, in a situation like that, where we're scared and confused and worried, it's easy to scramble a bunch of other emotions in there, too."

Bree looked over at Max. It had been the tornado.

She'd gotten horny because of a tornado.

Or she'd *thought* she was horny because of a tornado when really she'd just been excited and scared.

That was . . . not as much of a relief as she would have thought it would be.

She'd actually wanted to know that Max, the guy she trusted implicitly and liked more than any other she'd ever met, could also give her such a rush. She was always looking for more. More fun, more excitement, more thrills.

Hot, dirty, fun, amazing sex with the guy who'd been beside her for so many of the other big thrills in her life? Yeah, that had sounded pretty good.

But it was really just about the freaking tornado.

Anyone who'd been in that ditch with her could have taken advantage of her rushing adrenaline and made her feel the things Max had. It just made sense that it had been Max beside her. Max was always beside her for the big rushes now.

And apparently she was now projecting those feelings from the ditch onto the discussion he was having with Frank and Dillon. Because listening to him discussing the safe demolition of an old farmhouse about a mile outside town or the structural stability of the school was making her feel wiggly.

Thankfully, before she had time to further wallow in the unfairness of it all, Frank's office door opened, and his wife, Shelby, stepped through. Frank rose from behind his desk with a wide smile for his much-younger wife. Bree straightened as her friend Avery followed Shelby in with Jake Mitchell.

It was so . . . interesting . . . that Chance had been hit by another EF4 the same weekend Max, Jake, and their other cousin Dillon were in town. Yes, *interesting* was the word. *Unbelievable* was another.

All three men were ex–Army National Guard, and all had an interest in emergency management and disaster recovery. In fact, Jake and Max both actually made their livings with their specialties—recovery management and reconstruction after natural disasters, respectively—while Dr. Dillon was second in command in one of the busiest ERs in Fort Worth.

Avery shot Bree a questioning look as she came into the room, and Bree knew she was asking, *Why is everyone here?* Bree shrugged. She didn't know for sure what was going on, either. This was supposed to be a routine debriefing and strategy meeting. That meant the fire chief, police chief, mayor, and, okay, it made a little sense that Frank would want Max's and Jake's input considering their backgrounds. It probably also made sense to have one of the town doctors here to give an injury-and-recovery report, but Dillon was a visitor who happened to have a medical degree. He was hardly the town's medical leader. And Chief Mitchell should really be here instead of Bree representing the police efforts. Kit gave Avery a similar shrug.

So no one really knew why he or she was here.

Except for Frank.

"Thanks for coming in," Frank said as Shelby went to stand beside him. He put an arm around her waist, and she snuggled into him, beaming at all of them.

And Shelby. Shelby definitely knew what was up.

Shelby always knew what was up.

"We're going to burn the first bit of debris Wednesday night," Frank announced.

"You want the department to build and light the fire," Avery said.

Bree sighed. This was going to be a boring meeting. She knew it. No wonder Chief Mitchell had said she should come instead of him.

"Of course. We'll wait until right after dark. The city is providing hot dogs and marshmallows," Frank said.

Avery frowned. "Hot dogs and marshmallows?"

Frank nodded. "Jake suggested we make it a town bonfire. We'll get some music out there, have some food, make it a little party."

Avery turned to look at Jake. He was leaning against the bookshelf that ran the length of Frank's office. He gave her a smile.

"A bonfire?"

"It's a way of turning the negative into something positive," Jake said.

"You think people will enjoy watching their things burn?"

Bree gave Kit a look. Kit rolled her eyes. Avery and Jake could argue about what color the sky was.

Bree tuned out and worked on *not* looking at Max's butt.

"Is that right? I was getting my hands pretty dirty yesterday," Bree heard Jake say.

Bree straightened. Hold the phone. Was what this?

"That is not what I'm talking about, and you know it!" Avery exclaimed.

"If you're referring to the shed, then that's not what I'm talking about, either," he said, a smug smile in place. "After I got your pretty butt out of that shed, I was chainsawing and digging and working—"

The shed? Bree shot Max a look. He was grinning widely and gave her a wink.

Something was going on, and Max knew what it was. Maybe she shouldn't have been avoiding him.

Bree inched closer to Max as Jake and Avery continued to argue.

"What's going on?" Bree whispered.

Max laughed lightly and moved closer to her so he could answer without interrupting the Jake-and-Avery show. "The ditch on old thirty-six isn't the only place things got stirred up."

Bree worked on not reacting to the memories that bombarded her with the simple word *ditch*. Or to the low, gruff quality of Max's voice when he was whispering right by her ear.

It wasn't impossible to believe she'd gotten caught up in the electricity and chemistry of the moment yesterday, but she didn't think it was *all* about the storm. She'd had adrenaline-fueled sex before. She preferred adrenaline-fueled sex, as a matter of fact. But what had happened with Max felt different from anything she'd experienced before. "Oh yeah?"

"Well, you know how it goes—close quarters, nice breasts, possibly your last moments on earth."

She sucked in a quick breath and fought the urge to cross her arms over her chest. Max saying the word *breasts* made hers tingle, and if he glanced down, he might notice that her nipples were happy to see him again.

Bree cleared her throat, desperate to keep Max's eyes on her face.

She lifted a brow. "I'm with you. Though I'm not as into breasts."

"Just trust me on that, then," Max said with a chuckle. "Nice breasts make everything better."

And with that, she went ahead and crossed her arms. She really should have worn something other than fitted cotton.

But his chuckle made her narrow her eyes. He didn't seem overly affected by talking about breasts, or overcome with memories of what he'd done to *her* breasts yesterday. Had it all just been a crazy, swirling, what-the-hell moment for him, too?

"Really any breasts, though, right?" she asked.

"Any breasts?"

"No matter who Jake had been with in the shed, it would have been the same situation, right?" she said, even though she was definitely not talking about Jake and the shed. "It was really more about the storm than anything. Right?"

She wanted to know that what had happened out on the old highway had been inevitable. That she would have responded the same way no matter who she'd been with. That it had been some crazy *unusual* combination of natural forces that had turned on her I-want-Max switch, and because that exact set of circumstances would never repeat themselves, she didn't need to worry about that switch getting flipped ever again.

Except that she *actually* wanted to know that Max had laid awake in his bed last night replaying every second in the ditch and wound tight with lust and confusion like she had.

Max gave her a funny look. "No way. It's Jake and Avery. They have history. There are feelings there that have been brewing for a long time. Don't you think?"

Bree's gaze caught on Max's for a second longer than necessary. All that could have been applied to them as well. She glanced at Jake and Avery. "But still, in a situation like that, it's easy to confuse one kind of adrenaline for another."

Max didn't say anything. She looked back up at him. Again, she was struck by a detail that had been a fact for as long as she'd known him but that she'd never really thought about—he was about six inches taller than she was. She was five eight, so that put him at about six two.

And so what?

Just like his hair color, it was such a dumb thing to suddenly make a conscious note of. So why had she? And why was she now realizing that his brown eyes were a shade darker than his hair? More like the color of a good stout. An oatmeal stout, to be exact.

She loved oatmeal stout. And staring stupidly up into Max's eyes was no hardship. Stupid, yes. Hardship, no.

Bree pulled her gaze away from his and worked to get her shit together. She wasn't the type to stare into anyone's eyes; or notice eye color beyond brown, blue, or green; or to daydream in the middle of a professional meeting. Or to daydream at all, really.

She was falling apart. That had to be the answer.

"Why do I even talk to you?" Avery was asking Jake.

"Because you can't help it. For the same reason you can't help wanting to smack me."

Even Bree could see how smug Jake was about that fact.

Avery's eyes narrowed. "I should—"

A shrill whistle cut into their argument.

Everyone froze, then turned toward the sound.

It had, amazingly, come from Shelby. She was clearly upset. She had disentangled herself from her husband, and Frank had stepped back.

"Enough!" Shelby said.

"Shel—" Jake tried.

But Shelby cut him off. "No, I'm going to talk now."

The mayor's wife was very used to commanding the attention of a roomful of people—particularly the three men standing in front of her now. She was the only granddaughter on the Montgomery side of the family and had been doted on from day one. She was Max, Jake, and Dillon's first cousin, and the boys had been wrapped around her little finger since she'd been born.

Shelby put her hands on her hips. "This town *is* going to get back on its feet. Right now. We are going to clean it up, it's going to look *better* than it did before the storm, and *everyone* is going to do it with a damned smile on their faces."

Her three cousins looked like they were facing their drill sergeant. Bree was actually pretty impressed.

"Chance needs to rebuild, and we have to do it quickly," Shelby went on. "The Bronson family from Kansas will be here to see the farm and check out the town in two weeks."

No one in that room could, or would, argue with the fact that the farm and the Bronsons' visit had to be a priority. Bree put thoughts of amber eyes and nice butts and ditch orgasms out of her mind—or at least to the very back corner of her mind—and focused on Shelby.

She listened attentively as Shelby insisted that they all work together to rebuild Chance and ensure the farm sale went through.

And when she asked the guys to stay for a couple of weeks, they all readily agreed.

Bree frowned as the thoughts tumbled through her head. It *was* great. She loved spending time with Max. And there was no question that having him here would be a huge benefit to the town. But it had been a long time since he'd been around for two weeks straight. And after yesterday, it looked like she might be in for two weeks of naughty dreams and cold showers.

"You're going to be working together," Shelby said to Avery. "Jake is an expert in disaster recovery. You are *our* expert. It makes perfect sense that you would spend time together working on the recovery efforts. It will make the town feel completely secure and optimistic to know that you two are in charge."

Shelby then turned to Bree and Max. "Just like it makes sense for you two to work together. Chief Mitchell wants to put Bree in charge of more of the emergency-management efforts for the police department, and Max can teach you everything he knows. Max will be in charge of building inspections and rebuilding primarily, but, as the weather expert, we're also going to put you in charge of addressing questions about the storm itself."

Max and Bree both nodded their agreement. Because it did make sense. Bree wanted to learn from Max. She just needed to figure out a way to spend time with him and . . . keep her clothes on.

Shelby finally looked at Kit and Dillon. "Everyone knows that you're two of the smartest people to ever graduate from Chance. And you're both in health care. Knowing that you're teaming up for the physical and mental well-being of the people will make everyone feel completely at ease."

The mayor's wife smiled at them as if she was so very proud of them all. "Instead of talking about how they lost their special assortment of Christmas ornaments that they collected for almost thirty years or how they can't find their granddaughter's favorite doll or how their rocking chair was found in their neighbor's evergreen tree, they're going to be talking about all of you—how the guys have stayed to help their home-town recover and how amazing you women are, taking charge and leading the way, and how you've all teamed up to pull us through this. I am *sure* that you can find things to appreciate about one another." Her tone indicated that they *would* find things to appreciate about one another.

"Yeah, for, like, an hour at a time," Dillon said.

"More like fifteen minutes," Kit muttered.

"Really?" Dillon asked her. "That's how you remember it?"

She looked down at her nails. "I barely remember it at all."

Whoa. What was *that* about? Bree tried to catch Kit's eye, but her friend was stubbornly refusing to look anywhere but at Shelby.

"I'd rather have them speculating about you and Dillon in the hospital storeroom during the tornado than wondering if their insurance is going to cover," Shelby said to Kit.

Bree felt her eyebrows climb her forehead. She swung to look at Kit. "What happened with you and Dillon in the storeroom?"

"*Nothing,*" Kit insisted.

Dillon just ran his hand over his face. Max and Jake grinned widely.

Uh-huh. Bree *was* going to get this story later. If not from Kit, then from Max. Apparently the boys had been sharing more than the girls had about what had gone down during the storm.

Dillon and this storeroom story had to be why Kit seemed a little off today.

So it seemed that everyone had been knocked off-kilter by the storm.

Dillon started to speak again. "Shelby, I—"

Shelby turned to him. "Dillon, if I want you to dress up like a clown and juggle flaming batons in the town square to make Aunt Gigi smile, you will do it and *thank* me afterward for the opportunity."

Bree couldn't quite hide the smile that tugged on the corners of her mouth. Dr. Dillon Alexander was a big badass. Badass as in practicing medicine in the midst of jungles and civil wars and the aftermath of hurricanes and earthquakes. He'd done a lot and seen a lot. All the guys were pretty badass, really. But Jake was charming and Max was fun-loving while being badass. Dillon was the serious one. He could be charming, but she wasn't sure that he'd ever been fun-loving. At least not since the love of his life had died in a car accident when they were teenagers.

But Shelby Harvey was going toe to toe with him. And she was winning.

"I was just going to say that I'm happy to help," Dillon said mildly.

Shelby nodded. "I know." She pulled her purse strap up on her shoulder, kissed her husband on the cheek, then turned on her heel and left the office.

The door shut behind her with a resolute *thud* followed by a moment of silence.

"What just happened?" Kit finally asked.

There was a chuckle behind them. "You think an EF4 packs a wallop?" Frank asked. "You've been hit by a storm otherwise known as Shelby."

"We didn't stand a chance, did we?" Avery asked.

"Nope," Frank said cheerfully.

"Hi."

Max swung around from where he'd been studying the ceiling above, making notes and cussing about the fact that he couldn't climb up there and check things out for himself.

Bree stood in the doorway of the barn.

"Hey." He took in several details at once.

She was out of uniform—and in a black tank top and a pair of jeans that had obviously been a part of her wardrobe for some time, judging by how faded and fitted they were. She also had a tool belt around her hips, which, for a guy like Max, was just below lingerie on his list of turn-ons. But maybe most notable was the grin she wore.

"Where do you want me, boss?" she asked, propping her hands on her hips and looking around.

The ditch. Again. Up against the wall. Across Frank Harvey's desk. Max's bed. According to all the dirty thoughts he'd had since yesterday, there were several answers to that question.

None of which were appropriate.

"What do you mean?" he asked, turning to face her fully.

"I'm here to help." She focused on him again. "Chief Mitchell said you were looking for additional hands in doing the inspections. So you can have both of mine."

Max shook his head. So many problems there. Mostly that Bree mentioning him having her hands also sent several inappropriate thoughts tripping through his brain. Her hands. His. Where his had been the day before . . .

"You don't need to be using your hands somewhere else?" he asked. Then worked on not wincing, as that, also, sounded completely sexual.

He was starting to think that everything about Bree and this trip was going to sound sexual. And maybe not just this trip.

Dammit. It wasn't his fault. He'd given her an orgasm. That was kind of hard *not* to think about. Constantly. Especially when hands were mentioned.

Her smile faded, and her hands dropped from her hips. "No. I'm *so* bored."

Max lifted an eyebrow. "Bored?" God, he hated that fucking word from her, even if it wasn't being applied to him.

Besides, that was definitely not the word he would have chosen to describe the last twenty-four hours in Chance. Exhausting, depressing, crazy, worrisome—those were a few. And for those to occur to Max meant that those souls who were less optimistic and less prone to staying upbeat were probably really struggling. Max found the good in everything, looked on the bright side, all of that. But sometimes it was harder than others.

Cleaning up his hometown after an EF4 was one of those harder times.

Max had taken it upon himself to personally assess which buildings were safe and which needed repair or demolition. It was something he always took seriously. In his hometown, when the people going back inside those buildings were family and friends, it weighed on him even more than usual.

"Bored," Bree confirmed. "There's nothing for me to do. No one's looting, no one's fighting. Everyone's pulling together. There's no speeding—all the streets are blocked with debris or with vehicles working on cleaning up the debris. Everyone's too busy and too tired to get into any trouble."

Max shook his head, a small smile threatening in spite of himself. "You're disappointed that no one's getting into trouble?"

That shouldn't amuse him. It was exactly the reason she was heading to Arizona in two months to not only jump out of airplanes but to teach others to do it, too. Being a cop in Chance was *boring*, for fuck's sake.

Bree shook her head. "I just want something to do, some way to contribute. They don't need me in uniform, so I told the chief I wanted to do more. He said you needed more people helping with inspections, so here I am."

Max took in her appearance again. Her hair was tied back, and her jeans and boots were appropriate, but the tank was not. "You can't go climbing around inspecting buildings with all that skin showing."

She frowned. "It's interesting how often you're trying to get me covered up, you know that?" She turned on her heel and headed for the door.

Max watched her go. If only she knew how *un*covered up he'd like her to be.

Okay, that was a dumb thing to stomp out over, but he had to admit, he was going to breathe easier without her here.

He had work to do. A lot of it. And Bree was distracting him.

That pissed him off.

He could jump out of airplanes and downhill ski at breakneck speeds, drag race his beat-up old car around the dirt track at the fairgrounds, rock climb with her right by his side. They'd done a lot of risky things together, and he'd never had trouble keeping his concentration.

Then again, he hadn't known how greedy Bree became when her nipples were played with and sucked, and he hadn't known how sweet she looked and sounded when she came.

Heat pulsed through him, and he shifted to adjust for the increasing size of his cock at those thoughts.

It was definitely good that she'd left.

He was currently making notes on things he'd need someone else to inspect, and he needed to focus to be sure he got everything down. This all took longer than he liked. Taking careful notes so that whoever was helping him didn't miss anything, and then going over them with the other person, and then watching the other person do the actual inspection took three times the amount of time it would take if Max could just do it himself.

But he couldn't. His limited knee range of motion and strength kept him from safely climbing and balancing. With climbing gear on mountain sides, it was fine. Because of his climbing experience, he'd even helped out with some search-and-rescue in Colorado a year or so ago. But without the gear, he was taking a huge risk, and as much as it pissed him off right now, he wasn't going to do something stupid.

He'd accepted his restrictions and made the necessary modifications to his job. He had a ton of great guys working for him who could easily do the kneeling, climbing, kicking, pushing, and pulling that he couldn't. It was no big deal. Until he was here.

Now, here in Chance, he wanted to *personally* put his hands and feet all over the structures he was concerned about so when he passed them, he knew they truly passed. But he wasn't going to be able to do that. He was going to have to keep careful track and bring someone back with him and carefully instruct him or her in what he needed to do to feel good about passing a building, and none of the guys here were part of his regular crew. Some were just volunteers with little knowledge about construction. And that all worried him, too. If his regular guys were here, his explanations wouldn't have to be quite so detailed, and he wouldn't have to watch them quite as carefully.

He'd thought about calling Brad or Trent up here, but he couldn't wait even long enough for them to make the drive from Oklahoma City.

Part of him just wanted to tear down all the damaged buildings and start over with a sure, firm foundation, walls, and roofs. Of course, that was ridiculous. It would cost far too much money and time and really wasn't necessary.

But inspecting buildings where his family, friends, neighbors, past teachers, classmates, and multiple other people would be living and working was a heavier burden than he would have expected. He couldn't be completely objective here like he could everywhere else in the world.

So, he needed to pull his head out of the I-made-Bree-beg cloud he'd been in and do his job better than he'd ever done it.

Hell, he should be *grateful* for the work. If he wasn't busy with the cleanup and he and Bree were hanging out the way they usually did on his trips home, he would never be able to keep his hands to himself. And that would be a disaster on par with this tornado. Because Bree McDermott definitely had the ability to tear up his life. Or at least his heart.

The only thing that had let them remain friends after she'd rejected him in high school and then again two years ago was his own resolve to never again make the same mistake of trying to be sweet, romantic, and *boring* with Bree.

Max moved across the barn to the north side, shoving thoughts of Bree to the back of his mind where he'd been trying to keep them since the day before. They snuck out once in a while, but for the most part, it was working.

Until he actually saw her. Like in Frank's office that morning. He'd given her his usual smile, trying with everything he had to act normally, but seeing her for the first time since the ditch had nearly made his knees buckle.

Max pointed his high-powered flashlight at the ceiling, determined to focus.

Even this beam wasn't strong enough to quite reach the spot Max wanted to see more clearly. He really needed to get up there. *Dammit.*

The barn was the main building in the Montgomery Farms visitor's area. Everyone who visited the farm passed through here. They bought tickets and souvenirs and food here. They learned the history of the farm. They weighed their produce before taking it home. Some might believe this was the most important building to ensure was stable. Max disagreed. *Every* building where a single person would be was equally important.

But he'd started here because it was his family's business. Their good name was not only attached to the barn, it was literally painted on the side of it. It was the first place the Bronsons would likely visit. It was the heart of the farm. And it was the most severely damaged and would take the most time to repair. Max needed to get his inspection done so he could direct the repairs and make sure they were perfect. It would be tempting to rush through things, to patch it all up so it *looked* good for the Bronsons and then come back and actually fix it after their visit. That wasn't how Max rolled, and he was going to be sure this was all done right.

"Better?"

He pivoted at the sound of Bree's voice. She was back.

Well, fuck.

CHAPTER FOUR

Now she wore a light buttoned-up plaid shirt over her tank. Her arms and shoulders were covered. It was unbuttoned, but yeah, it was better. Not only was there less skin that could get scraped, cut, or bruised, but . . . there was less skin to be distracting him as he worked.

"You're still here."

She nodded. "Still here. I'm going to work with you."

"Bree, I—"

"I need to learn from you," she said, coming toward him. "I told you, Chief Mitchell wants me to learn more of the emergency-management stuff. I'm excited about it because, frankly, *all* of my job has been boring lately."

Max felt his jaw tighten. Boring. That fucking word. And of course she was bored. She'd been doing the job for three years now. That was the longest Bree had stayed at one thing in her life.

"Does the chief know you're leaving?" he asked.

She frowned. "I'm *thinking about* leaving."

Max felt his heart thump. "I thought you'd decided."

"I haven't given them an answer for sure."

He resisted rolling his eyes. He didn't want her to go to Arizona, but he was exasperated for the people there. He should have known that Bree wouldn't make a commitment two and a half months ahead of time.

She must have read his thoughts in his expression. "I only have to give thirty days' notice to the chief, and that's seventy-three days away."

She knew exactly how many days away it was. Max shook his head. She'd never had a job that required notice before this.

"You are thinking about it, though?"

He'd figured she was set on the job. It was skydiving. That would always be more exciting than law enforcement in a town where people stopped to let squirrels run across the street.

"Yes. But I have seventy-three days here still," she pointed out.

"And we definitely need to keep you entertained for those seventy-three days," he said tightly.

"What's wrong with you?" she asked. "You don't want me to know this stuff?"

There were actually several answers to the question about what was wrong with him. "Even in Chance, tornadoes don't happen every week."

"But there are other things," she said, either missing or ignoring the bitterness in his voice. "I would help with anything that went down— fires, blizzards, floods."

"You won't be here for blizzards," he said through gritted teeth.

"Well, the other stuff. A lot could happen between now and August. The more people who know how to handle those things, the better, right?"

"Fine. Let's teach you some stuff."

That time, she commented on his tone. "What's going on?"

"Nothing."

She frowned. "Clearly that's not true."

"You're a cop, Bree," he said, exasperated. "In a small town. Where you grew up. You knew it was going to be quiet. And cops, in general, should probably like when things are quiet, don't you think? Means things are good."

She frowned harder. "I did know it was going to be quiet."

"But did you think that through? Did you really ask yourself if you were choosing something that would stimulate you and make you happy? Or did you jump into it on a whim and because you got to carry a gun?"

He knew the answer. She'd already hopped jobs a couple of times before joining the force, and neither of those jobs had used the sociology degree she'd finally completed after changing her major three times. She'd seen Chief Mitchell take down a guy who'd stopped in at the convenience store off the highway and attempted to rob it while Wes was in there picking up milk and batteries.

She'd been so hyped up on adrenaline from first seeing the guy pull the gun and then seeing the chief drop him, unarm him, and cuff him that she'd immediately decided that's what she wanted to do.

She'd gone to the academy in the town thirty miles away and had actually enjoyed all her training. Then she'd come back to sleepy little Chance.

Max supposed he'd just been waiting for this "My job is boring" thing to come up. Now that he was thinking about it, Bree had lasted longer than he'd expected.

Bree looked angry now. "It's okay if I'm not enamored with my job every second of every day, Max."

"And let me guess, even before Arizona came up, you had been thinking about moving to another city because it would be a more dangerous job and 'exciting,'" Max said. He didn't want to push this. The idea had occurred to him, and he'd been ignoring it for months. He didn't want her to leave Chance. He didn't want her to go somewhere bigger and more dangerous. He didn't want her taking risks with things like bad guys with guns. Or a larger dating pool. Including guys who liked to jump out of airplanes.

It wasn't like he'd never thought about the fact that Bree could actually do what Max had so far failed to do—find someone else who wanted to go on her adventures with her. But in Chance the odds were smaller. Much smaller.

He'd assumed that he filled her need-for-thrills gaps like she did for him, and that she was getting whatever else she needed elsewhere. And he didn't spend a lot of time thinking about *that* at all.

Bree put her hands on her hips again and glared at him. "I have been thinking about that, yes."

He blew out a frustrated breath and shook his head. "Of course you have."

He loved her adventurous spirit. And he fucking hated her restlessness. It had always been there, but as she got older, instead of growing out of it, it seemed to be getting worse.

Why couldn't she just be *content*? Satisfied. Fulfilled. Happy.

That's where Max was. He loved his life, his work, the things he'd accomplished, his hobbies, his friends and family. He had seen so much loss and devastation that he was grateful for every damned thing he had. Yeah, his knee was messed up and gave him fits at times, but it was a badge of honor, dammit. He'd survived. He'd come back. It made him empathetic, and it helped others in crisis, physical and otherwise, know he could be trusted when he told them it would get better.

So yes, he was content.

Content was something Bree wasn't. Had never been.

And when he let himself think about it—he avoided thinking about a lot of things in regard to Bree—it made him absolutely crazy.

She had a great life, too. She had a job that was meaningful and that she was good at. She had family and friends who loved her. She got to travel and do amazing things. She had Avery and Kit. She had her motorcycle. Why, for the love of God, couldn't she look at what she *had* and be happy rather than always thinking about what she didn't have, what she hadn't tried, where she hadn't gone yet?

"What does 'Of course you have' mean?" she asked, now folding her arms.

Some men, maybe most men, would be intimidated by the look Bree was now giving him and the fact that she did own and know how to use a stun gun, but she was Bree. His Bree. The woman he'd known all his life. She couldn't scare him. At least not by looking mean.

"It means that you never *stay*."

"What are you talking about? I've lived in this town all my life. I went away to college, and I've moved a couple of times, but I've always come back."

He shouldn't be doing this right now. He had work to do. Important work.

But he couldn't stop now. Everything had been fine until she'd kissed him. Then, like a switch had been flipped, feelings and desires had spilled through him. Things he'd wanted but had been denying. Things he'd been pushing away and trying to ignore.

"And *why* do you keep coming back?" he asked.

Her brow wrinkled. "Because it's home. I've gone out, tried new things, lived in new places, experienced what that's like. But this is home."

He blew out a breath. He'd love to think she really wanted home, wanted to be in one place for good. "You know that a lot of people take jobs other places and stay *there*, right?" he asked.

She tipped her head, not quite rolling her eyes, but it was implied. "Yes. Like you. And Jake. And Dillon. Even Avery lived away for a while," she said. "I get it, Max. But the jobs I've had aren't like yours. They didn't require that kind of . . ."

She seemed to not be sure of the right word, and Max gritted his teeth as he waited to see if she'd come up with it.

"Commitment," she finally said.

Well, at least she knew the word. He sighed. She'd been a bartender in New Orleans for about seven months. She'd been a tour guide in San

Francisco for six months. She'd been a fitness instructor in San Antonio for nine months. But she'd always come home again. This was where she'd stayed for the long stretches. She'd been working as a receptionist in Kit's clinic before she'd joined the force.

"And why do you think you've never taken jobs that require you to settle someplace for a long period of time?" he asked.

She didn't want to be tied down. He knew that. But he wondered if *she* really knew it.

She looked puzzled. "Because I didn't want to be anywhere else for a long period of time."

He nodded. "Exactly."

But her frown deepened. "Because I was only taking those jobs to get a taste of living somewhere else for a little while," she went on. "I just wanted to see some places that were really different from here."

"Your heart has never *stayed* on anything for good, Bree. You're always looking for the next thing."

Her eyes were less angry now and more wary. And maybe a little confused.

"I don't know what you're talking about."

"You do know what I'm talking about," he told her, his voice quieter. He wouldn't look away from her. He had to see her eyes when he said this. "You've never fallen so in love with something that you stayed with it for any real amount of time. Not a hobby, not a job, not a place, not a . . . guy."

Her arms dropped to her sides, and she stared at him. It was several long seconds before she spoke. "So you think I'm waiting to fall in love with . . . something. Or someplace. Or someone," she said, her voice a little scratchy.

Max pulled in a breath. They'd always been honest with each other. That was the hallmark of a long-term friendship. But they'd never talked about this.

"No, I don't think you're waiting," he said. "I think you're living the life you think you're supposed to live, a life that keeps you jumping around and trying new things. And that means never settling . . . in a town or a job or a relationship."

She frowned, then took a breath, then wet her lips. Finally, she said, "Excuse me?"

"I think you know that you're not looking to fall in love with anything."

"Are we talking about hobbies or jobs right now?" she asked.

There was a slight wobble in her voice, and Max gritted his teeth. He didn't want to hurt her. But if her best friend couldn't help her see this, who could?

"I'm talking about all of it, Bree," he said. He realized he sounded tired as he said it.

Or maybe it was sad. Because he wanted her to be . . . not restless, not always looking for more, not discontented. He wanted her to be happy. She might love flying down a hill or falling through the air or climbing to a summit, but that wasn't doing it for her long term. If it were, she wouldn't keep looking for more things to fly down, jump off, or climb up.

"Are you saying that I don't want to fall in love?" she asked, actually looking slightly hurt.

"I think that if you wanted to, you would have done it by now," he told her, the words completely honest. "If you had fallen in love with flying, you would be flying every weekend instead of here and there in between other stuff. If you had fallen in love with the Grand Canyon, you'd be going back there every year instead of finding someplace new every time. If you'd actually fallen in love with Snickerdoodle Delight, you'd still be eating it instead of onto . . . whatever flavor you're onto now."

She blinked at him. "Snickerdoodle Delight?"

"Your *favorite* ice cream two months ago. The kind that you had three containers of in your freezer."

She frowned. "Yes, I'm aware of what it is, Max. I don't get your point. It's ice cream."

"That you said you loved."

"I did."

"And how much of it is in your freezer now?"

She took a breath. "None."

"What's in there now?"

She clearly didn't want to answer. "Cherry Chocolate Chunk."

"And you love it, right?"

She didn't answer that time.

Max sighed. "I'm not trying to make you feel bad. I'm explaining my 'Of course you have' comment. Got a little long-winded. Sorry."

"But you think I can't commit to things."

He *had* thought that, for a long time. Now he thought it was just that she wasn't made to stick with one thing for long.

Or something.

It was frustrating as hell, and he wished it were different sometimes, but at the same time—how could he really say that? It was who she was. Like her green eyes or blonde hair or that she thought Amy Schumer was funny—it was just a part of her, how she was put together.

This was Bree. She was his best friend. In spite of the fact that she changed her mind often and was easily bored. She was still the best time he'd ever had.

"I think instead of settling down on one thing or one place or one person . . ." That one always hurt a little. It wasn't just ice cream flavors she didn't want long term. "You're meant to have lots of adventures and do a lot of interesting things and keep the rest of us on our toes," he finally said.

She gave him a look that said, *You're totally full of shit.*

"Not everyone is wired for long term," he said.

The look intensified.

"Come on, Bree. It's just . . . who you are. I didn't mean to hurt your feelings."

"I'm not *wired* for long term?" she said, her feelings obviously hurt, anyway.

How was this *his* fault? Like him stating the sky was blue, it wasn't his *fault* the sky was blue. He was just pointing out a fact.

"Well, how do you explain it?" he asked. "You used to hate bacon on your burgers, now you love it. You used to love Melissa McCarthy, now you don't. You used to—"

"Hey!" she said, putting her finger nearly in his nose. "I still love Melissa McCarthy. It was *one* movie."

Max looked down at her finger, then back up to her eyes.

"You used to love Sweet Cream Dream. You haven't eaten it in more than a year."

She let her finger drop. "What is it with you and my ice cream choices?"

"Sweet Cream Dream is the best ice cream ever made," Max said. "If you can get over that, you can get over anything."

"And so I must not be *wired* for long term?" she asked, glowering at him again. "Because I don't eat the same ice cream over and over and over?"

"What do you think 'long term' means?" he asked. "It means the same thing over and over and over."

It was an analogy, but it was easier on both of them than talking about her not being willing to settle down and do the every-day-over-and-over thing with *him*.

She chewed on her bottom lip thoughtfully and nodded. "Got it. I totally see what you mean. Ice cream's easy, right? It's always good, never argues, always understands. And I can't even be happy with the same ice cream all the time. So . . . there's no hope for anything else lasting."

Yeah, well, that wasn't exactly what he'd said, but he suddenly really wanted out of this conversation.

"I'll talk you through some of this stuff if you want to learn, but we need to get to work," he said, turning away and focusing back on the job at hand.

Why had all that come pouring out now? None of those thoughts were really new for him. He'd been keeping it all to himself for years. Why did he feel the need to dump it all out there now?

Was it her use—her *overuse*—of the word *bored*?

Maybe.

Was it because he was tired and stressed and pissed off about this job?

Probably.

Was it because he'd now had a taste of something he'd thought he'd stopped wanting?

Yes.

He'd told himself at age seventeen that he and Bree weren't going to be anything more than adrenaline-junkie friends. He'd repeated that to himself at age twenty-seven when she chose going out for shots and karaoke with strangers over making love in front of the fireplace with him. He'd convinced himself that she was giving him what she could and that it was enough. He'd told himself he was happy, fucking *content*, with how things were between them.

But that had all been a hell of a lot easier before he'd kissed her, seen her naked breast, sucked on her nipple, and felt her come on his fingers.

Fuck.

And *she'd* kissed *him*, by the fucking way.

He stomped to the spot below the most concerning area of roof and looked up, making himself focus on the overhead beams, the discolored portion, the . . . Dammit, what was he looking at?

"You're wrong."

He sighed.

So much for being done with the conversation.

That might be nice, actually. To be wrong about *any* of the stuff he'd said. To think that Bree had at least *a little* long term in her, to think that she was at least *a little* satisfied.

"About what?" he asked, making notes on his clipboard without really thinking about what he was writing. Just noting the discoloration on the ceiling wasn't as helpful as getting up there and describing the spot more fully. It was likely water, but he'd rather be right up there . . .

"You."

He glanced over at her with a frown. "Me?"

"You're something I've loved for a long time. I've never found another you. Never even looked."

Max couldn't have named the emotion that knifed through him beyond *Ouch*.

He knew what she meant. She loved him as a friend, her best one. But he also knew what she *didn't* mean. And it took his heart a second to catch up with what his brain was already painfully aware of.

Bree had moved closer while he went through the usual "Don't be a dumbass" stuff.

"I've had a long-term relationship with you, Max," she said. "I always love to see you."

That was enough of *that*. "I know you do, Bree." Max shoved a hand through his hair. "I have a lot of work to do. You helping or not?"

She was still studying him, and Max worked on not shifting uncomfortably or telling her to knock it the fuck off.

"Bree?"

"Yeah, I'm helping," she said with a nod. "Don't I look ready for anything?" She spread her arms wide.

Max gritted his teeth, working to keep his gaze above her collarbone. He'd had plenty of opportunities to appreciate Bree's body in the past. And he *had* appreciated it. Best friend or not, Bree McDermott was a gorgeous woman. But that had been before he'd touched her. At least before he'd *really* touched her. Right now every single detail from the day before was hitting him like bullets to the chest. How her mouth tasted, how her hands felt gliding over his back, how she felt squirming underneath him, how hot and wet and—

He breathed out and turned away. "Fine." His voice sounded choked even to him.

"You don't think I know how to use this thing?"

He glanced back. She had her thumbs hooked in the top of her tool belt, her hip jutting to one side, one eyebrow up, looking completely cocky. Bree had been a tomboy growing up, and she was tough and resourceful. She could do anything athletic, didn't scare easily, and could use almost any weapon. But she barely knew which end of a hammer to hold on to.

In spite of everything, he laughed lightly. "No, I don't think you know how to use that thing."

"I'll have you know, I can use every single thing in this belt."

"Somebody been giving you lessons when I'm not around?"

Hell *no*. Not only did he not like the idea of her learning things from someone else, period, these were *tools*. This was Max's domain. No one knew construction better than he did. If anyone was going to teach Bree how to screw something . . .

He lost his train of thought there.

And then it further derailed when she pulled a juice box out of one of the pockets in the belt.

He felt his lips twitch. Now *this* . . . yeah, this made sense. He knew one of those pockets had gummy bears in it. He didn't know if she enjoyed high-energy activities in part so she could get away with eating all the crap she loved, or if she was just lucky that she liked to burn all the calories she took in. The woman was trim and toned, and she ate like a fourteen-year-old boy.

"So, gummy bears and licorice, too, right?" he asked, feeling the tight band of want and regret around his chest loosen slightly.

"Hey, and raisins. It's not all junk."

"You were worried about being stuck out here for days without being able to get to food or water?" he asked. "You had to stock up just in case?"

Bree frowned. "What are you talking about? These are bare minimums to get through an eight-hour workday. If I were afraid of actual meals for *days*, I'd be pulling my rolling cooler along behind me."

He couldn't fight the grin that time.

Damn. How could he not love her?

He *couldn't* help it. He'd known that since he was seventeen. But he sure as hell could hide it and deny it and ignore it.

Practice made perfect.

"Eight-hour workday? Girl, you're saying you want to hang with *me*. We're talking twelve or fourteen. We have a timeline, remember?"

She grabbed a handful of what looked like M&M's from a pocket and tossed them all in her mouth. "I can go fourteen hours without blinking."

He knew she could. Even without chocolate. She was tough, and she was in better shape than any of the guys he had working on his crews—here or in Oklahoma.

"Okay. But no whining," he told her.

She flipped him off.

He grinned unabashedly at that.

He moved under the spot in the roof he was concerned about again and looked up. "See that spot up there? The ring? It's probably water damage, and it could be old—there might be shingle issues or something up there—but we need to know for sure. And get it fixed. Need some measurements. And we'll have someone check out up on top, too, of course."

"Up on top? The roof?" she asked, studying the spot.

"Right."

"Who are you going to have check it out?"

"One of the guys. Whoever I hear from first." He made a note on the clipboard.

"Why one of the guys? Why don't you do it?" she asked. "You need a ladder or something?"

She looked around the interior of the barn.

"I've got what I need. Someone else will come check it. I'm just here making notes on things of concern."

"But how do you know it's a concern unless you get up there?"

Max rolled his neck. "We need to repair it either way."

"And you need to know about the integrity of the wood and shingles, don't you?" she asked. "To see how much needs replacing and stuff?"

"Yes." And if she was going to nag and question everything, this mentorship was going to be short.

"You suddenly afraid of heights or something?" she asked.

His knee never bothered him until he was around Bree. Whether it was landing after a jump or storm chasing or crawling around in barns, it bugged the shit out of him that he was being held back. So he pushed. Often way too hard.

The barn had never been an actual livestock- or hay-type barn, but it had been built to look as authentic as possible, and that meant there were beams everywhere, crossing the ceiling, running along the walls. There were plenty of hand- and footholds—at least for someone used to climbing and who was able to stretch and who had some decent core strength.

If it wasn't for his damned knee, he'd climb up into the loft, get up on the first crosswise beam, reach overhead, pull himself up onto the beam along the top of the wall where the roof started, and then swing up onto the closest beam that ran across the room. It was narrow, so he would belly crawl out to the spot right below the damaged area of the roof. Then he'd stand, grab the beam above, and take photos of the damage with his phone. He could upload those and do measurements from there.

"No," he said calmly. "You have to be flexible and sure on your feet to get up that high safely."

She met his gaze and hesitated for a moment. Then her gaze dropped to his knee, and he knew she'd put it all together.

He knew that she knew about his injury. It had made the paper, not just in Chance but in the *Omaha World Herald*. He was a local guy who'd been injured helping with rescue-and-recovery after Katrina. It had been a feel-good, local-hero-type story. He'd been in the Army National Guard. He'd fallen from a roof, and then a metal beam had fallen on him. There had been broken bones, torn muscles, multiple surgeries, and pins and plates. He'd been in the hospital for a week, then rehab for months.

But he and Bree never talked about it. She'd never asked him about it and never asked if he was sure he could handle any of the things they went to do. He'd always appreciated that.

"Lucky for you, I'm sure on my feet and *very* flexible," she told him.

She unbuckled her tool belt and let it drop to the floor with a *thunk*.

"No fucking way," he said. Still calmly but with a firmness he knew she wouldn't miss.

She gave him a grin and headed for the wooden ladder that led to the hayloft, anyway. There was no hay stored there, of course, but the loft had been added for the sake of authenticity and to give them more storage space.

"Come on. Hands-on is the best way to do things," Bree told him.

Flexible. Hands-on. Yep, it all still sounded sexual.

"You're not climbing up there, Bree," Max said with a sigh. "Let one of the guys do it."

She was two-thirds of the way up the ladder when she looked down and asked, "Why?"

"Because they're . . ." *Do not say "men." Do not say "stronger than you." Do not say "Because I don't care as much if one of them breaks his neck."* He did, of course. But they were highly trained and experienced. They wouldn't fall. "They're highly trained and experienced."

"And how did they get that way?" she asked as she reached the loft and headed directly for the wooden beam he'd identified as the best one to climb up on.

No matter how highly trained or experienced you were, you always took the shortest, easiest path.

Unless, of course, you were mountain climbing with Bree McDermott.

But that was another situation entirely.

Or was it? Max felt his heart thumping as he watched her scale the barn wall and swing herself up onto the first crossbeam.

She had always been smart even when taking risks. She used the best equipment, always wore protective gear, did double checks on everything, and took things slowly and easily when needed.

Max watched her reach for and climb onto the beam that ran across the room. His mouth got dry as she held the beam with her hands and legs and scooted carefully along.

She didn't have equipment or protective gear this time. She was going slowly and easily, but she could easily slip and plummet to the floor. The fall might not kill her, but she'd break something. More than one something, probably. And if she landed just right on her head or neck, she really could . . .

Max made himself suck air in through his nose and shut down those thoughts.

She was doing exactly what any of the guys who worked for him would have been doing to get to the spot, and he wouldn't have been standing there hyperventilating watching them do it, either. She was lighter than he or any of the guys were. She was an experienced climber and an intelligent woman.

And as oxygen started flowing to his brain again, he couldn't help but notice how sexy she looked.

Her body was toned from all kinds of physical activity, and he couldn't help but think about how those thighs would feel gripping his waist. She was, as she'd promised, very flexible, which led to many other very nice images. Her blue jeans seemed to love her ass, which made his jeans fit a little tighter in the front. And, most of all, she was clearly having a great time. Even from where he stood on the floor below, he could see her concentration, her excitement—that heady mix of fun and fear that was so familiar to him as well—and then her feeling of achievement when she got to the point under the damaged part of the roof.

She grinned down at him. "Piece of cake."

"Well, it's clear that the cake and gummy bears haven't attached themselves to your ass. And from this angle, I would notice." Joke about it. Keep it light. Not only would it hide that he'd been nervous about the climb, but it would hide his attraction. As usual. If he joked about it, she wouldn't take it seriously. It had worked for years.

Bree pushed herself up so she was sitting on the beam, straddling it. "Is that right?"

"Why do you think I always let you climb up in front of me?" he asked. "Mountains, ladders, steps into airplanes?"

"You like my ass, huh?" she asked. "And here I thought it was my breasts."

Max's grin faltered. So she remembered his comment in the mayor's office that morning. He'd tossed that out like he did all innuendos, but there had been something in her eyes that time—like she was thinking about it and wondering about it.

Her comment now was the most direct either of them had been about what had happened in the ditch. And that brought to mind just how much he'd liked her breasts. Seeing them. Feeling them. Tasting them.

He cleared his throat. The ditch had been a fluke. A tornado-induced fluke. "I've never had a problem with your front or your back," he said easily. Or he made it sound like it was easy.

"Well, thank you very much. I like your front and back, too."

As he was blinking at that—because there had never been a hint between them that she was physically attracted to him—she shifted so she could get her feet under her and stretched to standing on the beam.

Max's heart rate accelerated so fast he felt a little dizzy. Her feet were positioned as if she were standing on a balance beam in a gymnastics competition, and she quickly grabbed onto the metal bracket above her head, but there had been a tick of time where she'd been simply balancing on a foot-wide piece of wood sixty feet off the ground. Where she could have plunged to the ground. Where she could have—

Max worked on reeling it in. Jesus. He did this stuff all the time, and he never worried about his guys. Was he a chauvinist? Maybe. Or maybe it was just that this was Bree.

You've seen her throw herself out of an airplane. Calm down.

Yeah, with a parachute!

And now he was arguing with himself. Great.

But he was right. If she had a parachute up there, he wouldn't be worried. Bree was a great jumper. Better than he was. She stuck the landing every time.

Now, though . . . well, he wasn't sure what to think of her shimmying up the wall and walking out over the hardwood floor sixty feet below with no equipment, having never done it before, having never watched someone else do it before.

This woman—she twisted up his guts, his brain, his heart. No matter what she was doing.

"Get the photos and then get down here," he ordered as he worked to not overreact to her balancing precariously completely out of reach.

"Just photos of the damaged spot?" she asked, letting go of the metal support to reach into her back pocket for her phone.

Max breathed in and out, nice and steady, twice before saying, "Yep. A couple snaps. We can upload them and go from there." *Down here on the floor. The solid, flat, unrisky floor.*

"Okay." She held up the phone, swiping over the screen with her thumb. Then she moved the hand holding the phone toward her other hand, which was gripping the bracket.

"What are you doing?"

"Zooming. Can't do that one-handed."

Max scowled as she used both hands on the phone. Sure, she was technically still hanging on to the metal piece, but not as tightly. She wasn't concentrating. She was too worried about the phone and the photos.

"Don't need the fucking thing zoomed," he said loudly. "We can enlarge it on the computer."

"It might be blurry."

"I need simple dimensions. Quit messing around!"

"I'm not messing—"

Max saw the phone slip from her fingers and the instinctive jerk of her hand to try to catch it. He also reacted instinctively, taking two steps and then diving with his arm outstretched.

The phone fell into his palm and then bounced out onto the floor. But he'd cushioned the blow. The phone was in one piece.

He looked up. Bree had grabbed the bracket with both hands and was staring down with wide eyes.

"Get your *ass* down here *now!*" he ordered.

He pushed himself to his feet, wincing as a pain shot through his knee. He'd probably torn some scar tissue landing on it like that. That had happened before. Not a big deal. In fact, sometimes people had manipulations done on their joints for that very purpose. So no damage done. But it hurt like a mother.

He looked up to see Bree on her butt on the beam, inching backward the way she'd come. He glared at the phone and then stooped to pick it up.

He'd saved the phone.

If that had been Bree falling, he wouldn't have been able to save her.

Fuck, this working-together thing was a really horrible idea. She was a smart woman who could do a lot of this job. But he wasn't sure he could let her.

Let her.

Ha.

As if he had any say in what Bree did or didn't do.

That was the problem, really. He had no say. He was her friend, his opinion mattered to her, but he had no right to hold her back from things she wanted to do.

And it had never been an issue before. Before she'd kissed him.

That kiss had made him actually acknowledge that he didn't just care, didn't just love her as a friend, didn't just want adventures with her. He wanted it all.

Fucking sonofabitch.

He'd been okay until she'd kissed him.

By the time Bree was back on the floor of the barn, Max was worked up and pissed off. He stomped over to her and thrust her phone out. "Don't you ever—"

"Oh my God, that was fun," she gushed, her cheeks pink and glowing, her eyes bright.

She was gorgeous like this, and for a moment, all the air was sucked out of Max's lungs.

He'd seen this look so many times. At the bottom of a snowy hill, at the finish line of a racetrack, in the middle of a grassy field with a parachute billowing behind her.

In the ditch off old Highway 36 as the ripples of her orgasm faded and the clouds roiled above.

Max tore his eyes from her face and dragged air in. *Dammit.* Adrenaline.

That's what it was. That's what it always was. Her addiction to it fueled his. Because, while he loved the rush, too, he loved seeing her like this even more.

Even at age nine, he'd recognized how much he wanted to be with her when she looked that happy.

He'd been happy fishing and four-wheeling and swimming in the pond and doing science experiments and looking through his telescope. But Bree had started wanting more excitement. She'd gotten a dirt bike, had told him telescopes were boring—his first taste of hating that damned word—and had gone riding off.

So he'd asked his parents for a dirt bike. And had gotten Bree's attention and time back.

He knew even then that he would happily spend every day of his life putting that joyful look on her face.

But that was the problem. She didn't like things that happened every day. She didn't even eat leftovers.

"That was risky, and we're not doing that again," he said firmly. "There's nothing else that high to check." Or if there was, it was going on someone else's list, or he'd check it out when Bree wasn't with him.

"Oh, come on! That was great!" She opened her phone's photo gallery and turned the screen to face him. "And see, great pictures. You needed these."

They were good pictures. They'd be very helpful. "Thank you," he conceded. "Those will work. But no more of that. Jesus, you could have broken your neck."

"What if I wear my helmet next time?" she asked with a grin.

He scowled at her, wanting her to take this seriously. "No."

A frown quickly replaced the smile, and she put a hand on her hip. "You're supposed to be my fun friend. Kit is the one who's supposed to worry and tell me to be careful."

He was the fun one. Or had been, anyway. He'd always loved knowing that he was the person in her life she had the best time with. *Dammit.* Everything had been ruined by that kiss.

"Yeah, well, storm cleanup isn't fun."

"It can be." She gestured to the rafters overhead.

"*No*, it can't be. This isn't a playground or some crazy obstacle course. If we're going to be working together, I have to know you're safe. When we climb and ride and dive, I can be right there beside you. But this stuff—"

Bree stepped forward, put a hand at the back of his neck, and pressed her lips to his.

And just like yesterday, his entire body instantly went up in flames. *Dammit.*

But his ire was short-lived. Her hand moved up into his hair, she tipped her head to the side, and opened her mouth against his.

Trivial things like common sense ceased to matter, and he cupped the back of her head and stroked his tongue in along hers. She arched into him, lifting higher onto her toes and wrapping both arms around his neck.

He backed her up against the tall center post in the room and pressed into her. God, she felt good. Like she was meant to fit against him. Max slid his hand from her hair and down to her ass. He lifted her more firmly against him, and she moaned against his mouth, and fire licked through his veins.

She wanted him.

She wanted a ditch repeat. Maybe more than that.

But she didn't want what he wanted.

Max took hold of her upper arms and somehow managed to push himself away from her, holding her at arm's length. Literally.

She was breathing fast, her cheeks flushed, her eyes sparkling. Beautiful.

Just like when she'd climbed down from the rafters.

Fuck.

"Stop," he said firmly.

She licked her lips, and Max's body tightened.

"Stop?" she asked. *"Stop?"* she repeated as if it had just sunk in.

"I'm not a fucking dirt bike, Bree."

She looked more worried than angry at that. "What's that mean?"

"I'm not here to just give you a hard, fast ride for the weekend."

Her eyes widened. He was as stunned as she was by his words. But it was true.

"That's not what . . . I-I didn't mean . . ."

It was rare that Bree McDermott stuttered.

"That is what you meant. You're looking for a new rush. You think I'm it."

And he could be. Definitely. They could burn things up for a few days. He could give her a rush like she'd never had. He could become her new addiction. That wasn't the problem.

The problem was that her "addictions" lasted, at most, a couple of months. That would never be enough for him.

He never jumped without a reliable parachute, and there was no protecting him from the landing that would result after this particular jump.

She licked her lips again. Max had yet to let go of her, and he sensed her leaning toward him as he held her. "I do think you could be it," she agreed. "And I want that. I want *you.*"

"Because of an orgasm in a ditch?" he asked. "Really, Bree? You're smarter than that. You know what that was. That was all about the tornado."

"I wasn't thinking about the tornado at all when you put your fingers—"

"Stop it." He pushed her back. "Jesus, Bree."

"It's true."

"This is Breckenridge all over again. Remember that? You took a fall, and you jumped right into my arms afterward. But it was all fear and adrenaline. You told me so yourself."

Her expression changed. She looked surprised—maybe that he would bring it up—and regretful.

"It's not like I kiss you every time I get an adrenaline rush," she said. "How many times have we jumped out of airplanes without kissing?"

Twelve. Not that he was keeping track.

"No, it's only when you almost break your neck."

"No, Max—"

"The other day in the ditch, you were facing the idea you might not walk away from it. So when you did, you were overcome. I know how that feels, what it's like to have all the energy bouncing around inside after something like that happens. And that it just needs to get *out* before you explode. A hard, fast orgasm is *one* possible way to release that energy. Screaming, crying, running, throwing up—those are other ways. I happened to be there, so you went with door number one." He turned away and sucked in air. He *really* needed to remember all of this himself later when he was in bed and replaying the ditch. As he had last night. Over and over.

She didn't say anything, and he finally turned around. She had her arms wrapped around her body, and she was chewing her bottom lip, watching him.

"Kit said the same thing," she said. "That I was confusing the adrenaline from the storm for desire."

Oh, she had, huh? Even though Max knew it was true, it irked him a bit that Kit had already come up with that theory. Was it *that* difficult to believe that Bree might actually be turned on by him?

"And she doesn't even know about Breckenridge."

Bree hadn't told Kit about Colorado. Interesting.

"There you go," he managed to say.

"But I think you're both wrong," Bree said. "Again."

He should ignore all of this. Bree never thought he was wrong. She never thought Kit was wrong. No one ever thought Kit was wrong. Even Dillon had to admit that girl knew what she was talking about.

Still, he wanted to hear what Bree was thinking. "What makes you say that?" he asked. Because he'd never been able to *ignore* Bree in his life. His voice was gruff. He told himself it was irritation, not desire.

"I didn't kiss you because of the tornado or because of the fall down the mountain; I kissed you because I realized that in serious, potentially life-changing situations, I want to be with you."

Her words hit him right in the chest.

God, he wanted to believe that. And maybe it was true. But if she needed to be facing serious injury or death to want him, a long-term, day-to-day relationship was doomed. Especially when he wanted to do things like cook dinner together and watch *Game of Thrones* together and just sit on the couch and read together. The opposite of dangerous and life-threatening. He would end up being her Snickerdoodle Delight . . . replaced by Cherry Chocolate Chunk next month. Or like being a cop, replaced by skydiving. Or like backyard campouts with a telescope, replaced by dirt bikes.

"And kissing you is safer," she said with a small smile.

The fuck if it is. That was his immediate thought.

Kissing him wasn't safe at all. If Bree had even an inkling of how much Max wanted from her . . .

Maybe he should tell her that he wanted *everything*. Forever. Hell, maybe he should tell her that he was thinking about moving back to Chance.

That would freak her out. That would keep her lips off his.

Bree didn't want anything every day. That's what kept him in Oklahoma City. That's what made him leave even after an amazing weekend or an awesome trip together. Bree needed a chance to miss him. That was how he'd stayed in her life. He gave her just enough of something she loved, enough to keep her coming back for more, enough that she couldn't wait until next time, but never *enough* that she'd get her fill and then get over it.

"Bad idea, Bree. No more risking your neck. And no more kissing."

She wanted to argue; he could see it. He could practically hear the wheels turning in her brain. Her imagination was running, and he wasn't so sure that was a good thing.

"Let's get these pictures on the computer and start checking things out." He could distract her with work. Maybe.

He had graphs and formulas. He could get her on the website for building materials. He could show her his power saw and get her cutting boards if she needed noise and something to do with her hands. Hell, he'd even take her over to the smaller barn and get her up on the roof if he needed to. Sure, they'd be off the ground, but with a much wider surface and far greater odds of *not* falling off. Climbing around on roofs was a much different thing than the tightrope-walking shit she'd done earlier.

And he did realize, where tales often grew taller with repeated tellings, the width of that beam shrank every time he thought of it.

"Fine. Let's get to work," she suddenly agreed.

He looked at her quickly and opened his mouth. Fortunately, he thought better of it before he asked her what was going through her head. Her easy acquiescence made him skeptical, but he decided to take advantage.

He was an expert at roofing. He was an expert at ignoring his feelings for Bree.

So, he decided to focus on those two things. Feeling like he was in control of things for a while would be nice.

CHAPTER FIVE

"Come on, guys, everyone's tired and stressed," Bree said to the two big men squaring off in the middle of the street. She stood between them, a hand up to each, hoping to hold them back from each other. "Let's just take a deep breath. Maybe we should exchange the beer for bacon. It's seven a.m., after all."

She was in uniform for a couple more hours and had been the one to respond to the call from the guys who worked with these two men. Randy Grees was the local electrician, and he and his crew had been working all night on the hardest-hit parts of town. Gary Grant was an electrician from Ashford who had come up to help out with some of the smaller jobs around town.

Apparently Randy was feeling territorial.

"He's cutting corners," Randy said, pointing at Gary. "That shit's not happening in my town."

"Fuck you," Gary told him. "I'm doing my job."

"There's no way. You've done five houses in two days. If you're doing it right, you wouldn't be going so damned fast."

"I'm fast because I'm good."

She knew both Gary and Randy had been working through the night. Everyone in town understood that time and days ceased to matter in the midst of a project like the tornado cleanup. The job had to be done, and everyone worked as long and as hard as they could, stopping only when they simply couldn't go on. Like now. The guys had decided that everyone needed a break, and they'd all gathered around the coolers for a bit before heading home for showers and sleep. But they hadn't reached for water bottles. Now they were exhausted and tipsy. Not a great combination. Apparently as they'd talked about what they'd been working on, Randy had gotten more and more irritated with Gary, a guy who was usually his competition. It was tough doing cleanup like this. Going through people's homes and belongings, looking at the destruction up close, was difficult emotionally. If Randy was going to let off some steam, Gary was probably a logical target.

"Hey, *I'll* buy the bacon," Bree said. "And *coffee*."

"You're fucking with my friends, my neighbors," Randy said to Gary, his voice rising. He completely ignored Bree. "I'm not going to let you do that."

Yeah, Randy was feeling protective. Which was nice. But misplaced. Gary was a good guy, and Bree was sure he was doing a good job.

"Randy, I'll buy you pancakes, too," she said. "Let's just all relax, take a deep breath, and come at this after everyone has a chance to rest."

"You're not going to *let* me?" Gary said, advancing a step toward Randy. Also completely ignoring Bree. "Who the hell do you think you are?"

Bree felt her heart rate accelerate as the adrenaline kicked in. She braced her feet and curled one of her fists. She could pull her gun and remind everyone who was in charge, but she'd never actually shoot either of them.

She would deck one of them, though. Or both, if needed.

"I'm from here, you asshole," Randy said. "Who the hell do *you* think *you* are?"

"I'm the guy who is going to help you get the lights back on in this town. You're a crew of six guys. You can't do all these jobs!" Gary exclaimed.

Randy took a step forward, too. Bree moved more directly between them. She put a hand on Randy's chest. "Randy, don't."

"These are my people, Bree," Randy said, not looking down at her.

"Don't make me handcuff you," she warned him. Randy was a big guy. He outweighed her by at least a hundred and fifty pounds and towered over her. But he was tired and sore and a little drunk. If she caught him off guard, she could flip him. Or she could Taser him.

Both options made her heart pound, and she had to fight the urge to grin. That would be completely inappropriate.

She felt Gary move in behind her. She'd Taser his butt, too.

She turned and put a hand on his chest as well. "Gar—" she started.

"I get it," Gary said to Randy. "You want to be fixing all of it. You want to do all the work. I get it. I'll switch with you if you want. We can work on the school; you can do the homes."

Randy strained against Bree's hand. Another pump of adrenaline hit her bloodstream. If he swung, she was definitely in the way. She primed her nerves to react quickly when Randy started the motion. "Randy," she said warningly, "back down."

But Randy's eyes were on Gary. "No," he finally said.

Bree frowned. "I don't want to lock you up. We need you," she told him. At the same time, she pushed on Gary. He finally took a step back.

"It's your call," Gary told him. "But you can't do it all. If you want the houses—"

"No," Randy said again, interrupting. "I can't."

Bree felt the tension drain out of him all at once. He stepped back, and his shoulders slumped forward. Her hand dropped to her side, but she kept her eyes on him. "Randy?"

He finally focused on her. "I can't do the houses, Bree," he said. "I want to. I feel like shit about *not* doing them. But I'm glad Gary is here doing it because I can't."

Bree moved to face him completely. "I know. I get that. But they're not all that bad. Some are—"

"My house. It's bad."

Bree nodded. She'd been by his house. It was bad. She knew Randy and his wife and daughter were living with his mom at the moment. "I know. I'm sorry."

"And part of me wants to get back over there and rebuild it. And another part of me can't handle that, and all I want to do is throw myself into other stuff. More neutral stuff. Like the school and the buildings on Main. Which is great, because those things need done first. We have a place to stay. We're fine. We're safe. The businesses need fixed before the Bronsons come to town. But then another part of me resents that all that is more important than my house and family."

Bree pressed her lips together. *Dammit.* This wasn't beer or fatigue or being territorial.

"What's your address?" Gary asked.

"Three twenty West Starling."

Bree glanced at Gary.

The other man nodded. "Oh. Fuck."

Bree looked back at Randy. He blew out a long breath.

"Randy?"

"Gary was at my house today," he told her.

"Did he mess something up?" she asked.

He shook his head. "No."

Bree looked at Gary again. "What am I missing?"

Gary looked pained. He ran a hand over the back of his neck.

"What am I missing?" Bree asked again.

"The house is a loss. There's no use doing electrical work," Randy said. "Gary had to tell me."

"I didn't know it was yours," Gary said, his voice tight.

"I know. Doesn't matter," Randy said. He sounded tired.

"It does matter," Gary said. "And I'm sorry."

Bree looked back and forth between the men.

Gary looked apologetic, and Randy looked sad. But neither looked like they were ready to beat the crap out of the other anymore.

"Tell you what," Gary said. "*I'll* buy the bacon and pancakes."

Oh, so they *had* heard her.

"Then I'll get the coffee," Randy said.

"Sounds good."

The two men turned toward the diner and headed inside together.

Bree watched them go, then looked around. The other guys were gathering their things and heading for their trucks or following Randy and Gary in to breakfast. She puffed out a breath. Well, that was anticlimactic.

She headed back for her car. Her shift was over, and she should head to bed, too, but she was too worked up.

The juice was still coursing through her system, and there had been no flipping and handcuffing to expel any of it.

She needed another outlet.

Max.

Her first thought was of the man who had been on her mind almost constantly since he'd rolled back into town and brought a hell of a storm with him. No matter what he and Kit said, Bree was becoming more and more sure that her new feelings for Max were not just a product of the storm.

Yes, she'd told him that was why she'd kissed him in Colorado. She'd believed that was the reason when she'd said it. Or she'd believed that was a really good excuse, at least. Kissing him on that snowy slope had taken her by surprise as well. It had been spontaneous and, yes, had followed on the heels of the fear that she'd seriously injured herself, maybe permanently.

In those scary moments, she'd wanted Max. Not because she needed an outlet for the adrenaline, but because he was . . . Max. The person who made her feel safe and loved and *good* no matter what was happening.

And wanting him so much, realizing that she wanted him in the scary, bad moments as well as in all the good, fun moments, had freaked her out more than the idea of spending the rest of her life in a wheelchair.

She'd been taught to live life fully, boldly, loud and large. She'd known, always, that being with Max would mean a different kind of life. How could she choose that? How could she choose a quiet, easy life when the whole reason she was alive was because her brother wasn't?

Her adventure-loving, curious, and brave brother had died at age eleven from a rare form of leukemia. She'd come along ten months later. She was the replacement child for her parents, the thing that kept them going, the thing they poured all their love and passion and purpose into.

But she couldn't keep chalking up her feelings to adrenaline when it came to Max. It was hurting him. That was obvious. And it was hurting her not being with him.

That was the thing that made her the most certain her feelings were for real. She didn't want to go out for a ride or a run or storm chasing with him. She just wanted to *see* him.

And, okay, kiss him some more.

But in the absence of storm clouds and barn rafters, that had to mean something.

Which was exactly what she was going to prove to Max.

The idea of convincing Max that she really did want him made her feel . . . wiggly. Or itchy. Or something.

And she loved it.

Bree knew that was probably a strange reaction. But she'd never fallen in love before. She'd heard about it, though. That had to be what this was. She wasn't sleeping well. She hardly had an appetite—except for gummy bears, of course. She couldn't concentrate because she was thinking of him. She felt energized, like she was waiting for something exciting to happen, as if the next day was her birthday or Christmas. Or as if it was the night before a big trip with Max. The night before they took off together on their adventures was better than Christmas Eve.

He'd said no more kissing. He'd said that he didn't want to mess around and just be her newest thrill. But something had changed for both of them in that ditch. She didn't care what he said. Yesterday, when he'd looked at her in the barn, when he'd been barking orders at her and acting all protective and worried, he hadn't been the same guy she was used to hanging out and goofing around with. This Max was . . . more.

She was grinning as she headed to the station and changed out of her uniform. She'd get to bed soon. But maybe not alone.

She was still putting her hair up as she jogged down the steps of the police station. Max wasn't answering his phone, but this was Chance. It would take her fifteen minutes to find him. Tops. Ten if she started at the coffee shop and asked Ruth if she'd seen him. The fifty-something shop owner had always had a soft spot for Max. Bree knew that Max would have stopped in for coffee and that Ruth would have given Max the third degree—how things were going, if he was eating enough, if he had a girlfriend, and what his schedule was like for the day. The last was the only thing Bree didn't know the answer to.

Eight minutes later, Bree was making a beeline for Max across the square. He was at the gazebo, sipping the French roast with cream that Ruth had made for him and flipping through pages on a clipboard.

Bree slowed, taking it all in. He was in a pale-blue button-down shirt, the sleeves pushed up on his forearms and the front open to reveal a soft gray T-shirt. His faded jeans showed off the powerful thighs and tight ass she had somehow been missing over the past few years, and his work boots had clearly seen a lot of time on work sites. He somehow looked relaxed, yet ready to take charge of whatever came up at the same time.

He looked like he always did. But today her heart stuttered. Bree's attention went from his wide shoulders to his ass and finally settled on his hands gripping the clipboard.

Those hands.

They'd picked her up. Literally and figuratively. They'd clapped for her. They'd caught her. And now they had made her feel unmatched pleasure.

She knew it didn't make her a good person, but she wasn't sure whether she cared if he had a girlfriend.

"Morning," she said brightly as she came up beside him.

He looked up. "Morning." His low, gruff voice made a hot shiver trip down her spine.

The gruffness might have been because it was early, or a lack of caffeine. But it also might be that he was feeling a little bit of what she was feeling. Of course, if he was feeling even a little of that, he'd already be taking her clothes off.

"Thought you worked through the night. Shouldn't you be in bed?" he asked.

His gaze ran over her from head to toe, almost as if he didn't mean it to but couldn't help it. She liked his eyes on her. Even if he was trying to fight the urge.

"I'm on my way there now," she said with a nod.

He went completely still.

She moved closer and touched his arm. "When were you last in bed?" She stroked her hand over the corded muscles. The hair on his arms made her palm tingle, and his skin was so hot.

His arm tensed under her touch, but he didn't say or do anything.

She ran her hand up over his biceps, appreciating for a moment how thick it was, then up to his shoulder. His solid, hard shoulder.

Bree registered the muscle jumping in his jaw one second before he dropped the clipboard, grabbed both of her wrists, and pushed her up against the side of the gazebo.

Max pressed close, his whole body against hers, hard and hot and strong. This was good. This was very good.

He stared down at her, and Bree took a long, deep breath.

"I told you no more of this," he practically growled.

"I decided not to listen to you."

He paused a heartbeat, then shook his head. "Dammit."

She swallowed hard, trying to calm her breathing so it didn't look like she was panting over him.

But she was.

He looked pained.

"What?" she asked softly.

"You like this."

"Having you up against me? Yes, very much."

His hands squeezed her wrists. "You don't mind my holding you like this?"

Bree arched closer. "Max?"

"Yeah?" His voice was even gruffer.

"If I *didn't* like it, you'd be on the ground right now."

The corner of his mouth twitched, but he narrowed his eyes. "You're going to bed alone, Bree. And you're going to stop talking about your bed with me."

She shook her head slowly, as if she truly regretted what she had to tell him. "I don't think that's going to happen."

"The alone part? It fucking better," he said roughly.

He was *not* immune. She knew it. Bree felt a little shot of triumph. He couldn't feel jealous and protective *and* not want to take her to bed himself. "The stopping," she told him. "Any of this." And she didn't mean just the conversation. *This* was everything that had clearly been there, in her subconscious, for a long time—maybe even before Colorado—but had gotten stirred up in the storm. *This* was a whole bunch of emotions she couldn't shut off now that they were on. She suspected it was the same for him. But she wanted to know for sure.

A couple more seconds passed before Max responded. But finally he huffed out a soft breath that could have meant he was exasperated or that he was fighting a flood of emotions here, too.

She felt his grip loosen on her wrists, and she felt panic flutter in her chest. She didn't want him to *let go*.

"Tell you what," he said, shifting his weight back, definitely *away* from her. "When you're ready to stay in bed for an entire twenty-four hours with nothing on your body but my hands and mouth, let me know."

The panic was only slightly sharper than the shot of lust that went through her. "Let's do that," she said quickly.

He moved back farther, putting space between his abs and hers. She immediately missed the pressure.

He didn't look shocked by her sudden enthusiasm; he didn't look frustrated or even turned on, really. He looked skeptical.

"There will be no dirty books, no whipped cream, no handcuffs," he said. "Just you and me, naked for twenty-four uninterrupted hours."

He was watching her carefully, so Bree fought the urge to wrinkle her nose. Not that being naked with Max would be a hardship. It might take her twenty-four hours to memorize, and lick, every groove and plane and scar on his body. Something she really wanted to do.

But she wasn't good at just straightforward, unembellished, her-him-and-a-bed sex. Especially for twenty-four hours. He hadn't been *completely* wrong in the barn when he said she had a hard time sticking with things for long periods. But she wasn't sure she liked that her best friend was the one pointing out her flaws. Or what he thought were her flaws, anyway. But if a best friend couldn't do that, who could?

Bree had to admit she'd been thinking about, and trying to avoid thinking about, his comments about her not being wired for long term. And that it was obvious he was disappointed in her for that.

Max had never been disappointed in her. He'd been frustrated. Even angry a couple of times. But disappointed felt different. She didn't like it at all.

Still, sex wasn't the same thing as watching TV or reading a book or chatting. But, yeah, okay, she'd probably run out of positions in about six hours.

If he wanted to keep her in the bedroom for twenty-four hours, she was going to need the whipped cream at least.

"That's what I thought," he said as he fully released her and stepped back.

"Hey." She frowned. "I didn't say no."

He chuckled, though it didn't sound completely amused. "I just offered you twenty-four hours of sex. That's not something you should have to think about."

"I was just—"

"You're not a twenty-four-hour-straight kind of girl, Bree."

She hated that. Except that she didn't. She'd never seen that as a fault. And she thought Max liked that about her—that she was always up for something new and fun.

And why did it have to be all or nothing with him? She had to have sex with him for twenty-four hours straight or not at all? That was stupid.

Maybe *this* was why he didn't have a serious girlfriend. The guy was intense. Maybe it was good that she only saw him for a few days at a time. And that when it was for a solid week, they had hiking and skiing and stuff to do.

Bree opened her mouth to tell him all that—because damn if her ego wasn't stinging—but suddenly another voice gave them an even brighter "Morning!" than Bree had.

They both turned to face the young woman who'd approached while they'd been . . . doing whatever they'd been doing just now.

"Morning," Max said with a smile.

Bree tried to analyze the level of gruffness in his voice compared to when he'd greeted her. She thought she could tell a difference. But her blood was still humming, with desire and frustration in equal parts, and she was still thinking about how long twenty-four hours really was, so she couldn't be sure.

"You're Mr. Grady, right?" the woman, a beautiful blonde who couldn't have been more than twenty, asked.

Bree actually snorted at that. She had never in her life heard Max called Mr. Grady.

"Yes, I'm Max," he said, ignoring Bree and sticking out his hand to the other woman.

The hand that had just been holding Bree's wrists together behind her back. The hand that had been down her pants in the ditch. The hand that—

Bree's thoughts cut off as the other woman took that hand and shook it.

"I'm Ashley," the girl said, blushing slightly.

Blushing?

Bree looked back to Max's face. He was smiling widely.

"We spoke on the phone," he said.

Ashley nodded. "It was so nice of you to agree to this."

"It's no problem," he said graciously.

What had he agreed to? Suddenly Bree wasn't as eager to get to her bed. Especially now that she knew she was going by herself.

"I know I'm early," Ashley said. "I just couldn't wait."

Ashley was really pretty. And young. And she clearly thought Max walked on water.

"Hi, I'm Bree," Bree inserted, holding out her hand as well.

"Oh, hi. Ashley Swanson." Ashley took Bree's hand.

"Welcome to Chance," Bree said. The girl was tiny, too. She couldn't have been more than five foot two. She had long blonde hair, big blue eyes, and, of course, big boobs. Bree was pretty sure she could snap her into two pieces. She could, for sure, flip Ashley over her shoulder.

"Ashley is part of a student research group from the University of Nebraska," Max said. "I spoke to their program two months ago about the weather phenomenon, or lack thereof, actually, here in Chance. When their professor heard about the EF4, he called and asked if some of the students could come out and study the readings and graphs and hear my firsthand account of the storm."

Ashley nodded. "We've been studying storms in Nebraska over the past fifty years looking for patterns or predictors," she said. "We're charting everything from temperature to wind speeds to land formations in the area. But, as you can imagine, Chance is an area of intense interest and study." She gave Max a bright smile, as if Max had personally made Chance so incredibly interesting.

Bree fought the urge to roll her eyes. There was some big-time hero worship going on here.

"Over the past year, I've been part of the group specifically studying Chance and Mr. Grady's firsthand accounts and video and photographs, comparing the Chance tornadoes to dozens of others in other places."

Max gave Ashley a huge grin. "Call me Max." He glanced at Bree. "I've told her that there are no obvious differences between Chance and everywhere else. There's nothing in the topography or geology to explain why Chance is different. But I'm happy to help however I can."

Bree saw something else in Ashley's eyes besides the clear adoration for Max. Intelligence. The woman was clearly fully into everything Max said, and although Bree wasn't stupid enough to not notice the attraction, Ashley clearly shared his weather passion.

She was shocked, completely, by the emotion that flooded through her. Not because she didn't know what it was. She just wasn't used to feeling it.

Jealousy. Pure, unadulterated jealousy.

"There must be a hundred people interested in all this," Bree said. "I didn't know you were giving personal interviews to everyone."

Max finally looked away from Ashley to Bree. "There are a lot of people interested," he agreed. "But these are students at the university in the state where it keeps happening. And they don't just want to do a story. They're trying to figure out how to improve our warnings, and see if there's anything we can do to reduce the impact of the storms."

"Oklahoma and Kansas both have him on their faculty," Ashley said. "We just can't believe you're willing to work with *us*."

Yes, Bree knew that Max was on faculty at the universities in Oklahoma and Kansas.

She'd just never really thought of that as heroic. Or hot.

But she was suddenly looking at Max through Ashley's eyes and thinking . . . there was something kind of sexy about it. In a hot-nerd-college-professor kind of way.

Hot nerd. That, surprisingly, fit Max better than she'd realized. He'd always been active and athletic, but he'd loved reading and studying and experimenting, too. He'd been one of the top students in their class. If it hadn't been for Kit and Dillon, Max might have been the valedictorian.

Yeah, that was kind of sexy.

As was the way his face lit up when talking about the group of students coming to town to study weather with him.

"This is your state," Max said to Ashley. "And you all showed the most enthusiasm."

"So you're not Ashley's professor?" Bree clarified.

He smiled. "No, but she and her team will get credit for the work they're going to do here. I often host students in fieldwork. I'm a resource to the departments and to projects like the one Ashley and her team are doing. The University of Nebraska agreed to make me an adjunct professor for this particular study."

"He's amazing," Ashley said. Then she blushed as if she hadn't meant to say that. "His blog is—"

"I've read his blog," Bree interrupted.

"You have?" Max asked, clearly surprised.

She nodded. "Yeah, I have. I even understood the big words," she added drily.

Okay, she had needed to Google a couple of the words. He didn't need to know that. She'd understood and even been impressed with his articles. However, she wasn't going to admit that reading through his posts and articles had been okay, but that she much preferred storm chasing *with* him and having him explain things to her in person. She could practically see his head growing already from Ashley's clear admiration.

So Bree had a hard time sitting still and paying attention for long periods of time. So what? That didn't make her unintelligent. In fact, her mom had had her tested for ADHD, and the results had come back normal, with above-average intelligence. The school psychologist had explained that gifted kids sometimes had a hard time staying engaged in the regular classroom environment because the pacing was too slow for them, and Bree was simply looking for more stimulation. So there.

And so what if Ashley hung on every word Max said and thought he was the greatest thing since the invention of Nutella? Bree thought Max was great, too. She wanted to take him home and do all kinds of dirty things to him.

Maybe not for twenty-four hours straight, but . . .

Ashley laughed at something Max said that Bree had tuned out, and she thought, *Okay, I could totally do twenty-four hours.*

"How old are you, Ashley?" Bree asked. She shot a look at Max. Ashley was too young for him. He shouldn't be flirting with her.

"Twenty-four."

Bree blinked at the other woman. "You're twenty-*four*?"

Ashley nodded.

Okay, so she wasn't that young. Max would be twenty-nine next month.

"And you're still in college?" Bree asked. Max had been annoyed by how many times Bree had changed her mind in college. Looked like Ashley had done the same.

"Well, I'm in my master's program," Ashley said.

Master's program. Right. A master's program in something that Max loved even more than he loved . . . anything.

Bree sighed. "That's great," she told Ashley. She couldn't personally imagine studying something for five or six years, but she got that a lot of people did it. "What's the plan for the day, then?" she asked.

Ruth hadn't said anything about Max teaching a bunch of students today. Then again, Ruth had said, "He was heading to the square to meet up with Jake," and Bree had taken off out of the coffee shop.

"We're spending the next twenty-four hours with Mr. Grady—I mean, Max," Ashley said with a smile up at him. "He's going to teach us everything he knows about Chance and the storms."

Twenty-four hours.

So Max had gotten a woman to agree to do something with him for twenty-four hours straight, after all.

Bree was sure that wasn't ever a problem for him. Except with *her*.

She felt a tightness pull across her chest and into her throat. Why *couldn't* she just chill out and concentrate on something? Why couldn't she just do twenty-four hours of something because it was something Max liked? Would that really kill her? Especially if they were naked?

"Well, I happen to know that Max is free for the next twenty-four hours," Bree said, her eyes on his.

He just lifted an eyebrow. "What I have in mind might actually take longer than that, now that I think about it," he said.

Bree didn't know if he was talking about the plans with the students or if he was talking to her about the no-kinky-sex thing, but it didn't matter. Bottom line was that he was making the point that he needed more, whether it was from her or from Ashley, than Bree gave.

She gave him a nod to show that she got it. "I might hang out for a while. Maybe I can learn something," she said. "But you know I can't last twenty-four hours."

Something flickered in his eyes, but he nodded to that. "Yeah, I know."

For some reason, that made the tightness in her chest pull hard. Damn. They were acknowledging something that they both knew. It wasn't a big revelation that Bree liked lots of variety and activity. But at that moment it felt like she'd failed a really big test.

"Hey, Ashley," Bree said. "Have you ever been skydiving?"

Ashley's eyes got huge and round. "Um, no. Why?"

"Just wondering if that was a meteorology thing or something, because Max loves it."

"Really?" Ashley looked up at Max. "I'd be petrified. I'd need someone with me the whole time. Holding my hand."

But Max was looking at Bree.

Bree gave him a tight smile. Maybe Ashley could talk about weather for twenty-four hours straight, maybe she'd even do the naked-all-day thing with Max for twenty-some hours—that thought made Bree's chest ache even more—but Max liked the adrenaline-rich craziness, too. *She* would always be the one who got that side of him best. She would always be the one he'd first seen the Grand Canyon with. She would always be the one who'd talked him into going a little higher and ending up on the mountain peak with the most breathtaking view either of them had ever seen. She would always be the one who'd talked him into going another hundred miles on their first motorcycle ride and introduced him to the best waffles of his life at a hole-in-the-wall diner they stumbled upon.

She would always be the one who pushed him to go farther, faster, and harder with the big payoffs.

He should know by now that he was missing out by not going along with how Bree wanted to do things. Like handcuffs and whipped cream for, like, six hours straight.

It was his loss. It really was.

But she really did feel like *she* was missing something.

Five more students from the university showed up just then, pulling Max and Bree out of the sudden staring contest they seemed to be having.

Introductions went around, all the students taking their chance to tell Max how much they admired his work and how excited they were to be in Chance with him.

"And this is Bree McDermott," Max said to the group. "She's a police officer here in town and an integral part of the emergency-management and recovery effort here. She was with me when the storm hit," he said. "You can ask her questions, too. What it's like to organize rescue efforts, the role of the police department, what it was like out there when the tornado touched down, anything."

Bree straightened. She couldn't help that her thoughts went to inappropriately dirty places thinking about what it had been like out there with him during the tornado, but she couldn't help being surprised by the way he'd introduced her. Not just at him using the word *integral* to describe her role, or him insinuating she had knowledge and experience the students would find interesting, but at the note of pride she thought she heard in his voice.

The students looked at her with intrigue, and over the next thirty minutes, she answered three questions about how the police force prepared when they knew the storm was coming. She couldn't deny that she felt a little thrill talking about it, and at the interest from the students. She was proud of the job she did and the people she did it with, and it was fun to talk about it.

When the talk and questions turned to cloud formations and the track of the storm, Bree knew she should head home to bed, but she wasn't quite willing to leave.

A lot of what Max was telling them was stuff she'd heard over and over—there was nothing unusual about the topography, geology, or atmosphere around Chance; the tornadoes here had all formed like any other; the fact that Chance had been hit so hard and so often was a true mystery.

But today, something kept her there perched on the railing of the gazebo, listening. And it wasn't the cute Ashley with stars in her eyes.

It was Max.

This was the Max who went out storm chasing and sat on the tailgate and watched the clouds with a building excitement that was palpable in the air around him. This was the Max who grinned at her before strapping on his goggles and pushing off the most challenging run in Breckenridge. This was the Max who whooped a loud "Hell yeah!" after landing from a jump.

This—teaching, talking about the weather, answering eager questions from students who shared his passion—was clearly as thrilling for him as any of the high-adrenaline activities he did.

And watching him like this made all the earlier itchy, wiggly energy return. Like someone had turned on a burner underneath her, Bree felt the heat building as she listened to him and, more specifically, watched him.

Max Grady was hot, no matter what he was doing or talking about. *Dammit.* When had that happened? And how had she missed it?

"Hey, boss, uh, I think we need you."

Max turned away from talking with Dave Atkins, the plumber who'd been looking at the damage at the school. There was a leak in the kitchen, and it had taken far too long to find where it was coming from. They were going to have to redo some pipe work, and that meant tearing up part of the floor. This was not good news.

"What's the problem?" he asked Bill, one of the contractors who'd come in from Kingston to help out.

"Said her name is Bree."

Max bit the inside of his cheek to keep from swearing. Bree. Of course it was.

"What's she doing?"

"Climbing around in the ceiling and taking videos," Bill said. "She's come upon a bunch of live wires and wants to know what to do about them. Thought maybe you should take this. I don't know what the wires are for, but from how it looks to me, could be a fire hazard. Not sure if you want to kill all the power to find out what's going on or what?"

Bree was up in the ceiling with live wires that could be a fire hazard.

"Why is she the one up there?" Max asked, striving to keep his voice calm as he started for the hallway where Bill and a couple of others—apparently, including Bree—had been working.

"Well," Bill said slowly.

"What?"

"She climbed up faster than anyone else. Overheard us talking about getting up there to see what's going on. Shimmied up the ladder before I could assign anyone."

Max could tell the other man was frustrated.

Max was well beyond frustrated.

"Where is she?"

"Hundred yards that way," Bill said, pointing down a hallway to his right.

Max stomped in that direction. She wasn't even supposed to be here. She should have been out hauling branches or directing traffic or helping serve sandwiches at the shelter. Something safe and easy.

She was here because of Max. But sonofabitch. If she wanted to learn about what he did, she needed to stick by him. If he wanted to keep her out of trouble, apparently he needed to keep her right by his side. But the last place he wanted her was within arm's reach.

It was like there was an electrical current running between them. If he looked at her directly, touched her hand, brushed against her, shocks of awareness zipped between them. If he grabbed her wrists and pinned her against the side of a gazebo, it was like he was holding on to an electric fence.

He needed a day off from her. At least. Instead, he'd had about six hours off while she'd gone home to sleep. Not nearly enough.

"Bree!" he yelled when he was at the bottom of the ladder she'd used to climb up.

"Max!"

He located her voice about four feet farther down. "Get your ass down here! Come down the way you went up!"

"Did you see the photos?" she called back. "Are those wires a concern?"

"Of course they are! Get down here!" Max barked. *"Now."*

He didn't have to see her face or hear her to know that she'd just sighed heavily and rolled her eyes. "If you cut the power, it won't be a problem. I can get the rest of this done."

He grabbed the ladder and climbed up. He got his head above the ceiling tiles and shone his high-powered flashlight around the area above the ceiling. She was a few feet to his right. She had her tool belt on, which, in spite of himself, made him almost smile. Too bad gummy bears wouldn't keep her from getting fried from touching a live wire or burned up if the ceiling caught on fire.

"Get your ass over here, now!"

She narrowed her eyes at him. "No."

"What?"

"Someone has to do this inspection, Max. I'm taking photos and video for you and the guys to look at later. You can talk me through what you're looking for."

"I'm not in the mood for this," Max managed through gritted teeth. He was clamping his jaw so tightly his temples were beginning to throb.

Just one day off from her. Just one day off from her being everywhere he turned, tempting him, driving him nuts. It was one thing for him to spend a week with her on a vacation where their relationship was clearly defined and agreed upon on both sides. They were friends. They'd been friends for twelve years. No matter how attractive he'd found her, no matter how much he might have wanted her deep down, it had worked because he'd never seen her naked breast, never had his finger pressed deep inside of her, never let her know, in no uncertain terms, what she did to him.

But even all that would have been okay—in that he would have eventually gotten over it, probably—but now she was asking him for more. She wanted him now, too. And was reminding him of that every second she got.

And he was stuck here now. He couldn't escape at the end of the weekend or use the excuse that he had to get back to Oklahoma. He was committed to being here until the cleanup was done. Worse, he was supposed to be working with her, side by side.

This was his own personal hell. No question about it.

He was a good guy. Basically. He didn't deserve this.

"If I come down now, someone else will have to get up here," Bree said reasonably. "I just have to go a little farther."

She wasn't wrong, and that pissed Max off, too. Someone had to check this out, and she was already up there.

He shone his light around and located the bundle of wires she was referring to.

As he looked around, his gut tightened even further. There was a lot of damage up here. Tiles to the ceiling under her were missing, parts of the roof overhead were gone, ducts were hanging loose, and some of the support beams were torn away.

He swallowed hard, his emotions quickly shifting to annoyance because she wasn't listening to him. "Bree, this is a mess. Come down. We'll tear out the ceiling so we can really see what's going on."

"I'm already here. Just tell me what to do about the wires, Max." Exasperation was clear in her voice.

"Don't do anything about the wires," he said. Squinting at them from where he was, he couldn't tell what was what.

She sighed heavily. "If they're a hazard, we need to cut the power or cover them or something, right?"

They needed to cut the power. But to do that without cutting the whole building required a closer inspection to determine which wires they were.

Dammit.

"Don't make me come up there and get you, Bree," Max warned.

She turned toward him more fully and lifted an eyebrow. "There's no way you can climb up here and throw me over your shoulder."

Distracted by the idea of that, he asked, "You don't think I can?"

"I think your knee will make that pretty damned difficult even if *I* don't flip you over *my* shoulder, put my perfectly functioning knee in your back, and handcuff you."

He stared at her. Had she just blatantly pointed out that his knee put him at a disadvantage? They never talked about his knee. Or that it might not allow him to do something she could do. And had she just threatened to handcuff him?

He knew she'd done a lot of self-defense training. But she couldn't actually throw him. Could she?

"You think you could flip me?"

"No question about it. Especially knowing your weakness."

Whoa. There it was again. They were going to just put his knee out there like that?

"Not cool, Bree."

"And you insisting I get down from here *is* cool?" she asked. "I'm an intelligent woman, Max. I get that there is some risk up here, but someone has to do it, and I want to learn. Since I knew you would say no if I asked, I decided not to ask first."

And wasn't that just exactly like her. "Dammit, I—"

"And," she went on, "you can't climb up here and do it. Your knee won't let you. I get that, and it doesn't matter. I know that you're not totally comfortable with these other guys here today. You don't know them; they're not from here. But I am. I care about all these job sites as much as you do, and you *do* know me. You can boss me around and second-guess me because we know each other and I won't take offense. I can be your eyes and hands up here. You can guide me through it, and I'll follow your directions to the letter, I promise. But you have to admit that you need help and that I can be the best one to give it."

Max let oxygen pump in and out of his chest a few times before answering. She was right . . . again. He couldn't get up there, but it drove him nuts to have someone else do it. The other contractors would not appreciate him questioning everything they did, and they wouldn't be taking pictures and videos so he could get eyes on the problem. They also wouldn't be taking every one of his suggestions. In fact, if he pissed them off, they might slap something together just to get it done or walk off the job completely.

He'd been balancing on a narrow edge with them since the tornado had hit. He wanted to do it all himself. Since that wasn't an option, he wanted to control every piece of what *they* were doing. It was making him pissy and wasn't winning him any friends.

Bree really might be the answer to those problems.

If he could get past the fear that seemed permanently jammed in his throat.

"Fine," he conceded shortly. "I'll walk you through it."

Her whole body seemed to relax as she sighed. "Okay. Let's start with these damned wires. Tell me what to do."

"Get closer. Don't touch them, and keep your feet on the wooden beams," he told her. "I need you to get photos of the wires and send them to me so I can tell what's what. If we can figure out what they are, we can maybe cut just a portion of the power."

She walked carefully forward, getting within inches of the wires. She leaned in and started snapping photos.

Max's phone dinged as she sent them over as texts. He opened them and somehow pulled his eyes from her to study what was in front of her.

"Can you get a better shot of the other side?" he asked.

She stepped wide, putting a foot on another beam, and leaned in.

Yeah, his knee would not have let him do that.

And he knew it was inappropriate, but he couldn't deny that her ass looked fantastic in her jeans when she leaned over like that.

"Max?"

He jerked himself back to the moment. Bree was watching him with an expression that meant she'd already asked or told him something he hadn't heard.

"Yeah?"

"Now what?"

He looked down at his phone again. The photo clearly showed which wire was which. This was good.

"Okay, follow the black one up with your flashlight. Can you find the box it came from?" he asked.

Bree shone her flashlight on the wire and traced it up. She had to take a step forward to see behind the rafter overhead.

"Careful," he told her. "Step back to the right, and go forward from there."

He would not survive watching her bump up against a live wire and electrocuting herself.

She did exactly as he'd coached. "I think I see it," she told him, peering into the shadows above her and way out of his line of sight.

"We need to get to the box and check the labels. Then we can shut down the breaker," he told her.

She looked over at him. "How do you want me to go up?"

Max stared at her for a moment. She was actually asking him for input rather than just using the first thing she saw as a makeshift ladder.

He looked around. It was a good question, too.

"See those pieces of wood?" he asked, pointing with his flashlight to two long pieces. They had obviously collapsed in from the roof. There was a hole right above them, which, despite the problems it caused, was allowing in more light than they would have had otherwise.

"Yep."

"Can you prop one against the wall and walk up?"

He would have never suggested that to anyone else. It was certainly not the safest method ever. But it looked like the only option at the moment, and it would work. Bree would have no trouble balancing on the board. It was wide enough for a good foothold and, well, it was Bree.

She looked startled that he'd suggested it but quickly started in that direction. It was probably just as surprising as what he'd felt when she'd waited for his coaching.

Maybe they could make this work, after all.

He trusted her as much as he trusted Jake and Dillon. If either of them had been here, he would have had them do the same thing Bree was doing now.

But, while he loved his cousins and would do anything he could to protect them from harm, he didn't feel *protective* of them like he did Bree.

With Bree it was much more a gut-deep, instinctual *need* to make sure she was safe.

Max forced himself to concentrate on what was happening in front of him instead of all the emotions that had been swirling through him since the storm.

Bree made her way to the longest of the wooden planks. "Give me some light," she called as she tucked her flashlight into her tool belt so she could grab the piece of wood with both hands.

Max illuminated the area for her as she dragged the wooden plank into position. She propped one end against the wall, making an incline that would allow her to get high enough to check the electrical box.

"Okay, nice and easy," he told her. "It should support your weight, but go slow."

"Hey, it'll support my weight," she told him, mounting the board and beginning to inch up.

"I'm just saying that gummy bears can catch up with you after a while," he quipped. Making light of things was his coping method for stress—with the people around him and for himself.

Bree concentrated on her footing, but that didn't keep her from saying, "Thought you said my ass looks good."

Her ass looked *really* good.

So did her legs, her waist—encircled with a tool belt—her breasts, her hair, her face . . . she looked in her element, and he couldn't deny that it was beautiful. He also had to admit that her getting that look while working with him on a project like this made him feel a crazy new level of attraction. She was enjoying this, and as stupid as it sounded, getting her excited over a construction-and-restoration project was better than her excitement while parasailing or skiing. Anyone would get a little excited about those activities. Not everyone found this stuff interesting.

"Your ass looks good." He managed to keep his tone light. "But you could put on fifty pounds and I'd still think that."

She stopped climbing and wobbled slightly on the beam. She looked over at him. "Really?"

Well . . . yeah. He shrugged. "Of course."

She straightened slightly. "That's really sweet."

Shit. That had been the wrong thing to say, obviously. This wasn't lighthearted teasing now. "Keep climbing, Bree." He gestured with his flashlight.

"Yeah, okay." She seemed to focus back on where she was and what she was doing. But she didn't start moving again immediately. "I'm still just getting used to the idea that you have a thing for my ass."

"A thing?" he asked, though he knew he shouldn't.

She started moving up the board again. For her to reach high enough, the incline was steeper than was ideal, so she had to concentrate on her foot placement, and as she moved another few inches, she finally had to squat and hold with her hands, too. "It's okay. I have a thing for your hands."

"My *hands*?"

"Oh yeah. I mean, I knew they were big and obviously strong. I love that you work with your hands, get dirty, always have a few scrapes on the knuckles, and have a few scars. But ever since the ditch, I've had a new appreciation for them."

"Jesus, Bree," Max muttered. They were going to talk about this *now*? Or at all? He was really pretty good with the ignore-and-deny thing he'd perfected since Colorado.

Max knew she was talking to distract herself from the fact that if she fell off the beam, she wouldn't stop falling until she hit the tile floor in the hallway of Chance High School. But *this* had to be the topic?

"It's almost enough to make me think that naked-for-twenty-four-hours thing is doable."

Max gripped his flashlight tighter as want throbbed through him.

But she didn't mean it. Bree had been in this uncharacteristically flirty mood ever since he'd taken that branch to his head. Or maybe all of this was some crazy dream. Maybe he was unconscious in that ditch.

That would make more sense.

But he couldn't be so lucky. This was all totally real.

But he wasn't doing that with her. No way. He'd said that this morning to make a point. Before he'd finished his coffee. Any sex with Bree would ruin him. Hot, naked-for-an-entire-weekend, multiple-orgasms, give-me-everything-you've-got sex would forever take away any chance of being happy with someone else.

"I might even put up with one of your sappy, romantic dates if it ended naked," she said, nearing the top of the wooden beam.

Max gripped the flashlight harder again. *Naked.* Yeah, that was not a word he needed to hear from Bree. Ever.

He should be concentrating on her climb, but he had to admit that not focusing on what could happen if she fell was good. His heart pounded harder just eyeing the ceiling tiles below, which would do nothing to stop a fall.

And, damn, the idea of taking her on a romantic date was really tempting.

Not because *he* liked the romance, but because *Bree* had never been romanced before.

Bree was fun. No doubt about it. No guy would say no to drinking and dancing at A Bar or going to a concert or four-wheeling or heading to the shooting range or any of the other things Bree loved to do on the weekends. But no one insisted he just wanted to *be* with her. None of those guys would be content to just talk to her, or cook for her, or take her to a beer tasting, or make love to her in front of the fireplace, making sure the foreplay lasted at least an hour.

He didn't spend a lot of time thinking about Bree and her dating life, but he knew her, and he knew any sex she had was hard and fast, and the guy definitely didn't spend the night. If they even made it inside her house in the first place.

"I don't go on sappy romantic dates," he told her, ignoring how much he loved the idea of romancing her. He *wasn't* going there.

She made it to the top of the plank just as she snorted. "Of course you do. You love the sap."

"I love the romance. But it's not sappy."

She braced herself with a hand on an overhead beam and looked down at him. "What's the difference?"

He sighed. Not the right time for this conversation. With Bree, there would probably never be a right time for this conversation. Still, he said, "Romance is showing the other person you care, that you're there with her in the moment, that you want her to be happy, that you're happy just being there with her, no matter what you're doing."

"What's sap?" she asked.

"Depends on the woman," he said. "It's the stuff that seems romantic but doesn't really mean anything."

"How does it depend?"

"If you bring a woman roses because the first time you met her was when you ran into her—literally—in the grocery store and she dropped the vase of roses she'd just picked up for her mom and the vase shattered and the roses went everywhere, then it's romantic. Because the roses mean something. If you send a woman roses after one dinner without knowing if she likes roses or without any special meaning, then it can be sappy."

Bree was watching him with a strange look on her face.

"What?" he asked.

"Did that happen to you? The roses-in-the-grocery-store thing?"

He nodded. "Yeah."

She frowned slightly, then turned to look at the electrical box.

Had that been a flash of jealousy? From Bree? About another woman in his life?

Well, that was new.

And he liked it.

She balanced on the beam and pointed her flashlight at the electrical box. She pulled out her phone and snapped a few pictures.

Max's phone dinged, and he checked the photos. "Perfect," he told her. He sent the pictures to Bill with a message: Cut the power to that section.

Bree pocketed her flashlight and phone, then made her way back down the plank with Max's light guiding her way. She came down faster than she'd gone up. She returned to where Max was positioned on top of the ladder.

"I'd bring you polliwogs," she said when she was standing in front of him.

From his vantage point, he was eye level with her knees.

He looked up. "What?"

She squatted down in front of him. "I'd bring you a mason jar with polliwogs in it. That was the first thing you ever gave me. I was five, and we'd gone looking for them at the pond but hadn't found any. I was so disappointed. The next day you showed up on my porch with a jar with four polliwogs in it."

He stared at her. He wanted to kiss her more than he'd ever wanted to do anything.

"That would be romantic, right?" she asked.

He cleared his throat. "Um, yeah. It would."

She gave him a satisfied smile and stretched to her feet. "Bet none of your other girls would think so, though."

Max tried to think of even one woman he'd dated, ever, who would consider larval frogs romantic. And, not surprisingly, came up blank.

"What else do you need?"

Max looked up at her. "What?"

"While we're up here," Bree said. "What else do you need to look at?"

He forced his attention back on where they were and what they were doing and away from picturing the fully grown, gorgeous woman in front of him wading into the pond to collect polliwogs. Because she would, even now. And he would find that incredibly hot.

"Can you get over to the east wall?"

He coached her through several other checks. She sent photos and gave him verbal feedback on everything he needed, and Max had to admit this had turned out well.

With her up in the ceiling and him on the ladder, she was out of reach, so smelling her hair and keeping his hands to himself wasn't a problem. And it felt like something had shifted today. They'd acknowledged that they needed each other—he needed her to do the actual physical, hands-on stuff, but she needed him to tell her what she was looking at, what it meant, and what it should look like.

They were a good team.

"Okay, think we're done," he said.

She headed back for him as she dug into a pocket in her tool belt. She pulled out two pieces of licorice and handed him one. She also gave him a huge grin just before she bit off the top half of her piece.

"That was fun."

The look on her face was a total turn-on. "Yeah?" he asked with his own grin.

"I learned a ton, and we got a lot done, and you were completely reasonable about all of it."

He bit off some of his licorice and shook his head. "I've never been unreasonable about anything."

She laughed at that.

"Let's get down and see what else we need to take care of today," he said. He took two steps down the ladder but froze when he heard a loud crack. "Bree—"

But his mind didn't process the sound or location fast enough.

The next thing he saw was a piece of the roof crashing through the ceiling tiles a few feet in front of him, and then Bree dangling through the new opening from the waist down.

CHAPTER SIX

"Bree!" He scrambled back up the ladder and was already reaching for her before he even got a clear view.

He grabbed her wrists, pulling with all the strength in his upper body, but his position was precarious on top of the ladder. He couldn't get a good foothold himself, and the ladder wasn't fully stable.

"Max, hang on!"

"I've got you!"

It was immediately clear what had happened. A large section of the roof, right next to the hole that was already present, had come loose and fallen. It had punched through the ceiling tiles and metal beams beneath it, taking the beam Bree had been standing on with it.

Thank God it hadn't hit her directly.

Max tried to climb up a step on the ladder to give him more leverage to pull Bree back up, but he couldn't get his bad knee up on the next step.

"Bill! Somebody!" Max hollered. "Bree, hold tight!"

"I'm not going anywhere," she promised with a shaky voice.

He could tell she was trying to hold on to him and pull herself back up at the same time, but with nothing to push off with her legs, she was just wiggling.

"Stop, I've got you," he said, the muscles in his arms and upper back screaming.

The sounds of running footsteps came a second later.

"Shit!" someone said.

"Max, you okay?" Bill asked.

"Yeah, somebody get Bree down."

"I've got her," another voice said. "Put your feet on my shoulders," he said to Bree.

She must have done it, because a moment later her upper body moved up.

"Can you get your elbows under you?" Max asked.

"Yeah. Think so."

"One at a time."

Max let go of one of her wrists so she could brace herself, but the moment she pushed, the metal piece under her shifted.

"Dammit," Max cursed. He grabbed her again. "You gotta go down instead of up," he said.

She looked at him and nodded. "'Kay."

"You guys got her?" he called down to the man below.

"Yeah, we've got her."

"You ready?" Max asked.

Bree took a breath. "Yep."

Of course she was. Later, she'd think this was the most fun part of the day. "That's my girl."

She looked up at him quickly, and there was something in her eyes that made his heart thump, though he wasn't sure why. She gave him a quick grin, "See you down there."

He didn't want to let go of her.

Even if she dropped from this height, the worst that would happen would be a sprained ankle—*maybe* something broken if she didn't land right. This wasn't any more treacherous than a hundred things they'd done together over the years. But this felt different.

He had his hands on her. He had a hold of her. He was keeping her from falling. But he couldn't pull her back up; he couldn't climb up to where he could be any real help. The realization sent a hot shaft of regret through him.

Dammit, that seemed way too symbolic.

"Letting go," he said, his voice rough.

She nodded. "Not for long, 'kay?"

Oh yeah. He let go of her wrists, and she slid away.

He ducked down quickly to watch as the tallest of the guys took Bree's weight on his shoulders, then slowly squatted to the point where two other guys could grab her and lower her to the floor. As he descended the ladder, Max couldn't help but note that he would have never been able to squat like that.

Bree's feet hit the floor about the time Max's did, and he took the three steps to where she stood, wrapping his arms around her. She curled into him, her arms going around his neck and burying her face against his chest.

Okay, this was not so new. This was a lot like Breckenridge, and he didn't care. He needed to hold her. Just like he had then.

He ran his hand up and down her back. "Hey, now, you're okay."

She nodded.

He held her for another long minute.

"You hurt, Bree?" Bill asked.

She shook her head. Because the guys probably couldn't see that, Max said, "I'll be sure she's okay."

"'Kay, we're gonna head back down the other hallway," Bill said. "Holler if you need us."

"Thanks."

Max continued to hold Bree, not sure what else to do. This wasn't a first, but it was unusual. She'd taken falls before. She'd had plenty of almost-falls, too. But she always popped back up with a big grin.

"Bree?"

"Hmm?" Her response was muffled against his shirt. She took a big breath and seemed to snuggle even closer.

He tugged on her ponytail, tipping her head back.

She was still curled against him, which meant her lips were right *there*. As close as they'd ever been other than when they'd been kissing.

"You okay?" he asked gruffly. "You hurt?"

"I'll have a couple bruises, but I'm fine."

"Then what's with the clingy thing?" he asked gently.

"The damsel-in-distress thing has some perks," she said with a tilt to her lips. "I never realized knights smelled so good."

He lifted his eyebrows. What the hell was she doing? "You haven't been a damsel one minute in your life."

"Not true—remember the time we were sledding, and I went down the wrong side and almost slid out into the street? You dove after me and grabbed the sled before I hit the pavement."

He did remember. They'd been seven. His heart had almost burst out of his chest when he'd seen her heading down the steepest side of the hill and toward the street. In retrospect, the danger had been more that she would have hit the pavement and gone flying off the sled onto the cement. Traffic on that street was extremely light. Still, he remembered the feelings of panic and the surge of adrenaline that had allowed him to catch her.

The panic and adrenaline were the same today. But he hadn't been able to help her this time.

"We were seven," he said, trying to keep the emotion out of his voice.

"I guess some good guys start early."

What *was* this? And why did he like it so much? Okay, some of it was the feel of her plastered against him. But he knew Bree thought he was a good guy. He knew she appreciated him. He knew she admired him, even. But there was something in her eyes and her voice right now that made this feel different. Feel like *more*. Of something.

"So you're fine? You're not freaking out or hurt?"

She looked up at the ceiling. "I was freaking out for a minute. But then you grabbed me, and I knew I'd be okay."

The regret was just as sharp now as it had been earlier. He set her back from him, needing a little space. "Maybe your knight is the tall guy with Bill. He's the one who got you down."

"You had a hold of me."

"And that's it. I couldn't do more than that." He couldn't believe how much that pissed him off.

Only with Bree. His knee only fucking mattered with Bree.

"Well, maybe being a knight isn't always *doing* everything but just being the hands that make me feel safe."

He stared at her. He loved that. For one second. Then reality crashed in. "Stop it."

"What?"

"The sap."

She frowned. "That was sappy? How is that not romantic?"

"Because you're saying stuff you think I want to hear. But it's not you. Romance comes from who *you* are, too."

She tipped her head back. "I'm not a romantic, I admit that. I've never gone after a guy. But now that you're staying, maybe I need to learn."

Staying.

Yeah, he was thinking about that. Maybe more than thinking about it. But how did she know that?

Fucking small town.

"Roger *just* talked to me about that a couple of days ago," he said with a frown.

"Roger?" she asked with a frown. "I meant you were staying for another week, at least."

Okay, maybe she didn't know. If she did, she'd know that Roger was Roger Swanson, the owner of the biggest and best construction company in the area, and that he'd asked Max to buy him out and stay in Chance.

Roger had actually asked him the same thing about a year ago, but Max had put him off with a "Let's talk down the road."

Apparently now was "down the road" enough for Roger. He wanted to retire, and if it wasn't Max, he'd sell to someone else. Max had to make a decision in the next week or so.

He hadn't had a chance to think about what that would mean for Bree and him.

At least not more than twenty-seven times in the past twenty-four hours.

He'd stayed away from Chance in part because it made his relationship with Bree work. He could have as much as she could give, and he wasn't seeing her, talking with her, every day and wanting more.

But he wanted to come home. He wanted to be around his family, he wanted to be in his hometown, he was very excited about owning his own business, and . . . as for Bree . . . well, he didn't fucking know. She was the one thing keeping him from saying yes to all of it. If he came home, he'd want her even more. He couldn't imagine living in Chance and not having Bree. Bree and Chance went hand in hand for him. But she didn't want what he wanted. He couldn't just be her friend. He couldn't watch her with other men. He wouldn't be interested in any other women. It would be a miserable existence.

Unless she went to Arizona.

Then she could be the one coming home to visit, having the go-hard weekends, before she headed out again.

He could have his business; he could be home.

But it wouldn't really be home without her.

If they were still doing weekend visits and weeklong vacations, nothing would really change. And he wasn't sure how much longer he could keep all of this up. Then, of course, there was a 99 percent chance that she would come back to Chance to stay eventually. Then things would be a lot like the past few days had been.

So it would be hell.

What he was sure of was that he was not ready to talk with her about this now.

Rather than elaborating on Roger and his request, Max lifted both eyebrows. "So because I'm going to be here for another week, you want to . . . what?"

"Have about fifty more orgasms," she said. Then her voice softened. "And to see what it's like. I've never been romantic with anyone else."

Jesus, even hearing her say the word *orgasm* slammed into him with a heat that stole his breath.

"So you want to try it with me?" he asked, a myriad of emotions welling up. Annoyance was definitely one of them. He didn't want her to be romantic. It would be so sweet to have her trying, to be the first guy Bree McDermott actually went after, to have her navigate all of this with him, for him.

And then he'd never recover when it was over.

That might be worse than having amazing soul-shaking sex with her.

No, it *would be* worse.

He'd had some damned good sex in his life; he'd had some really good romance, too, and yet he'd never fallen in love with any of the women.

He was already mostly in love with Bree. Add in soul-shaking sex and he'd be in big trouble. Add in romance where it might seem like she was feeling the same things, and yeah, he'd be single for the rest of his life.

He didn't want to be single for the rest of his life. He really didn't. He wanted the family, the kids and wife, and everything that went with that.

"We've already tried that once," he said. "If you remember."

She met his eyes again. "Of course I remember. And I know it didn't work. But that was a long time ago. I was just a kid."

The annoyance grew. "Dammit, Bree."

"What?" she asked.

"Only you would get horny almost falling through a ceiling."

She looked up, then back at him. "That didn't make me *horny*."

"You're not horny right now?"

"No."

"You're not feeling the same way you did in the ditch and in Colorado and after climbing around in the barn? Don't you think it's interesting that the only times you want to get close to me are following a big scare like that?"

"That is *not* what I'm saying," she said, her brows pulling together. "I want *more* than what we have now. I want more than sex. With you. I want to try all this romantic stuff that you want."

"Bullshit."

That startled her. *"Bullshit?"*

"You're wound up because of the job you did up there, then the fall. The adrenaline is coursing again, and I just happen to be the guy standing next to you when you need an outlet for it."

"That is *not* what this is," she insisted. "This is about you catching me. And the fifty-pounds thing. And the polliwogs. And the fact that you trusted me today, and we worked together. *That's* what's making me want to kiss you, not the fall."

Nope. He wasn't going to let his heart believe any of this.

He grabbed her wrist and pulled her down the hallway.

"You're limping."

He gritted his teeth. He was. He never limped. Until the morning after a day with Bree. Considering the way the last week had gone, he was surprised he could move at all.

He stopped at the first door—the boys' locker room.

He yanked the door open and pushed her inside. He stepped through and turned the lock that only the janitor and coach's keys would open. Neither of them was here today.

Then he backed her up against the wall.

"What are you doing?" She was breathless, and her eyes were wide—with excitement.

God, he knew her so well.

"Proving that you *are* horny right now. This isn't about romance, Bree. This is all about hormones and adrenaline, and you're a junkie on a high saying things you don't mean."

"I am *not*—"

He slid his hand under the edge of her T-shirt and then slid it up and over her head, leaving her in a plain white bra.

Her nipples were hard, poking against the white cotton, and he could already feel the firmness on his tongue. He met her gaze as he reached behind her and flicked open the tiny hooks. She sucked in a quick breath as he dragged the bra down her arms and dropped it beside them.

"You're telling me your nipples got hard from thinking about polliwogs?" he asked.

She wet her lips. "Max—"

Before she could finish whatever that was going to be, he pulled open the button at the top of her jeans, lowered the zipper, and pushed the denim to the floor.

She gasped again as he ran a hand over the front of her white cotton panties with the black polka dots.

"And you're telling me that you're *not* wet right now? That if I slid my fingers inside your panties, I wouldn't find you hot and sweet and dripping?"

Bree let her head fall back against the wall behind her. "Well, *now* I am."

"This isn't about me or any romantic feelings, Bree," he said, moving in to put his mouth against hers. "This is your body's reaction to excitement—no matter the cause."

"No."

She tried to shake her head, but Max had gone too far to stop. He captured her lips in a searing kiss that he felt vibrate through his body. She *was* hot and wet, right under his fingers, only a thin layer of cotton between him and her sweetness, and at the moment he didn't care why she was wound up, only that she was.

Her tongue met his stroke for stroke, and her hands went up to cup the back of his head, holding him close.

Max slipped his thumbs into the top of her panties and slid them to her ankles, letting them bunch at the top of her jeans. Her work boots would be too much trouble to remove. But he didn't need them completely off.

He ran his hand up the side of her thigh, then around to her bare mound. Hot. She practically burned his hand as she arched into his palm. He wasted no time sliding his middle finger into her slick heat and absorbing the part gasp, part moan that elicited.

Bree's fingers dug into his scalp as he brushed his thumb over her clit, feeling the point pulsing against him.

He tore his mouth away, leaning back to look at her face as he slid his finger in and out.

"Max."

The soft whimper almost undid him.

"I can help you get rid of all this pent-up energy, Bree," he told her gruffly. "But no more thinking it's anything more than your sweet little body bottling up all the rushing adrenaline and excitement, okay? No more talking about romance, or you and me doing anything more than this."

Max acknowledged—to himself only, of course—that touching her like this was not purely altruistic. He had some pent-up emotions of his own that he needed to let loose somehow. And he was pretty damned close to mistaking *his* wound-up feelings of desire and worry and affection for Bree as something more as well.

This would help them both get perspective.

As soon as he helped her out here with an orgasm, she'd settle down and stop talking about romance. As soon as he let off some steam, he'd stop thinking that orgasms had changed anything between them.

"No, Max, it's—"

He pressed over her clit again, and her eyes closed as she gave a long moan.

"You're turned on by all the excitement of the day, not by me," he told her. He hated that more than a little, but it was important they *both* realize the truth.

Her head rolled back and forth against the wall, but her eyes didn't open, and she wasn't able to form words.

He did like that.

The adrenaline might have turned her on, but right now it was *his* hand making her feel this way.

He reached up and cupped a breast, rubbing a thumb over the tip as he did the same to her clit with the other hand.

She arched closer. "Max."

He loved hearing his name from her lips like that.

"I want you. I want more," she said huskily.

He looked from his hand on her body to her face. He knew she wanted him. In this moment, in this exact situation. Her body was craving something he could easily give her.

He held her gaze as he went to his knees. "Whatever you say, Bree." Then he put his mouth against her.

Her fingers tangled in his hair as he leaned in, and when he swiped his tongue over her, she gripped his hair hard. He smiled before he licked again. He'd known she'd be incredibly responsive. She was probably going to get really loud, too. Bree was the type of woman to tell him exactly what she wanted, where, how hard. He loved that. He hadn't let himself think about Bree this way, but if he had, he would have pegged her as a woman who was a full, equal participant in every way. She'd tell him what she liked, and she'd give as good as she got.

She couldn't spread her legs very far with her jeans around her ankles, but he did move her feet a little farther apart. Then he returned his tongue to her clit and slid a finger inside her, pumping deep.

"Oh my God," she whispered above him.

"Let it out, Bree. Tell me what you want, what you're feeling." The acoustics in here, with the cement floor and walls, would be amazing when she shouted his name nice and loud.

"I just . . . more," she said softly.

He paused and looked up. Her eyes were closed, her mouth slightly open, and she looked completely overcome.

Not exactly what he'd been expecting.

"What do you like?" he asked. "Faster? Harder?"

"Yes. I don't know. Anything."

He nipped the soft skin on her inner thigh, causing her to gasp, then he dragged his tongue up her thigh and licked over her clit. He felt her fingers tighten in his hair. He sucked on the sweet nub, and her knees wobbled.

"Talk to me, Bree." She was a talker. Always. He never had to wonder what she was thinking or feeling. There were lots of shouts and *Hell yeah*s and whooping that went on when they climbed and jumped and raced. He wanted some of those now. He wanted to know that he could make her feel like falling out of a plane did.

"I just can't," she said, her voice completely breathless. "Keep going."

He licked and sucked again and waited, but when he stopped, she was still leaning against the wall as if it were all that was holding her up, and apparently turning it all over to Max.

With a frown, he rose. He took her chin between his thumb and finger. "Bree, look at me."

Her eyes fluttered open.

"Tell me what you want."

She said nothing for several seconds, then she shook her head. "I can't."

His frown deepened. "Why not?"

"Because you might stop. I want this your way."

"Might stop? My way? What are you talking about?"

"All I know is I'll die if you stop, so do it your way."

Heat, need, frustration, and affection all slammed into him at once. This woman completely tangled him up.

"My way?"

"The whole slow, romantic way."

He couldn't help it—he chuckled. "I've got your pants around your ankles in the boys' locker room, Bree. Not sure this qualifies as romantic."

She gave him a sweet smile. "But it's *you*."

God, he wanted her. He shouldn't. It was a horrible idea. He'd regret it. But he wanted her, and he was only so strong.

At least he could keep from completely losing his mind. He wouldn't make this sweet or intimate. He wanted her legs around his waist, her eyes locked on his. He wanted to tell her all the things he loved about her. He wanted to coax her to talk, to tell him what she was feeling. He wanted to take her up and over the edge with his mouth and then his fingers before he ever sank deep.

So those were all the things he could *not* do.

"Turn around," he told her firmly. His voice was scratchy, but she still seemed to respond to the commanding tone. He couldn't help but make note of that.

She swallowed hard.

"Bree. Now."

She did, turning to face the white brick wall.

"Hands on the wall. Don't move them." He ran a hand appreciatively over the curve of her bare ass—the ass that had, indeed, been driving him wild ever since he'd let himself really notice it.

He wanted to give her a little smack and see what happened. But she'd probably like it. And then he'd have to live with that idea in his head going forward.

He'd apparently paused for too long because she started to turn to face him. He gripped her hips and didn't let her move. "Hands on the wall. Don't move them," he repeated. "And don't make me repeat myself again."

Her head dropped forward as goose bumps broke out on her skin.

Max grinned in spite of himself. She liked being bossed around a little. Good to know.

No, that *wasn't* good to know. *Dammit.* He couldn't do things that would take his fantasies to a new level. Not that he didn't want her to like what he was about to do, but for him, pushing things beyond good old everybody-does-it sex started to get to that intimate place he wanted too much with Bree.

But he couldn't help running his hand over the curve of her ass a couple of times before he made himself move his hands. He unzipped his own jeans, fishing a condom out of his wallet before shoving them and his boxers down his legs. He was achingly hard, and if this was really the way he wanted it to be, he'd have Bree's hot little hands wrapped around his length. And her mouth. For sure. He'd have her on her knees for at least a few minutes. But wanting it so badly was all the more reason to keep this to sex for release only.

He moved his hand between her legs, stroking over her clit and slick folds before easing two fingers into her again. "You ready for me?"

"So ready," she breathed.

He had to agree when he felt the wet heat waiting for him. He moved in, positioning himself at her entrance. For just a millisecond he hated that this was the way it was going to be the first time. The only time. He wanted to see her face; he *wanted* to tell her all the things she made him feel. But this was sex. Only sex. If she needed a release, he'd give her that release. And afterward, when she realized *that* was really all she'd wanted, she'd stop all this talk about romance and anything long term.

He gripped her hips, banishing the regrets from his mind and heart, and thrust forward, burying himself in her.

She did cry out then, and Max had to grit his teeth to keep from pounding on ahead without letting her adjust.

"Oh my God, you're amazing," she gasped, her fingers gripping the bricks in front of her.

Amazing. Yeah. He fucking was.

He pulled out, then surged forward again, stroking deep and relishing the feel of her tight, hot body around him. It was so damned good. Even just this much. Even without everything else.

He'd been right to stay away from everything else.

Max reached around for a breast, rolling the nipple between his thumb and finger, and moved his hips, stroking in and out again.

Bree pressed back against him, locking her elbows and seemingly pulling him even deeper into her body as she flexed her inner muscles.

Max gritted his teeth, willing himself to last, but this was going to be hard and fast. Just the way she liked things.

"Max," she moaned. "Harder."

Yep. Exactly the way she liked things. He tugged on her nipple as he picked up the pace and felt the response around his cock.

"You feel so fucking good," he told her roughly, unable to keep completely quiet.

"You, too." She pressed back again. "So good."

"I want to feel you come, Bree," he told her, leaning in and kissing her neck, then sucking slightly.

Again, he felt her response around him. He loved this woman's body. Everything was connected to her pleasure. She was so physical in everything she did. Always had been. He was sure that she did, indeed, have an orgasmic-type reaction to her skydiving jumps and crossing the finish line in races. He'd love to know how worked up he could get her with simple touches in places other than the obvious erogenous zones. He'd love to see how responsive she was to dirty talk, to the building anticipation, to various sensations like ice cubes or feathers.

He never had experienced such a strong desire to challenge his partner.

But he knew Bree. She could take it. She'd revel in it. He wanted to push every one of her boundaries.

He wanted to wring her out.

No man had ever done that. That he did know.

No man had jumped out of an airplane with her or hiked the Grand Canyon with her, either.

Except for him. If anyone could help Bree find her sexual peak, it was him.

He reached for her clit and circled it as he picked up his rhythm. She had to come first. That was nonnegotiable.

"Bree, let go. Give it to me."

She gave a soft whimper, and he felt her muscles contract.

"That's it. That's it," he praised softly. "Let it go."

He circled faster and thrust harder, and within minutes he felt her tightening around him. She cried out, and Max let himself go. He pumped deep only three times before his release grabbed him, and he muffled his shout against her neck.

They stood, breathing hard for almost a minute after. But Max made himself pull out and turn away. He dealt with the condom, zipped up, and washed his hands, all without looking at her. Even that would be too much right now.

He heard the rustling of her clothes and was thankful that she'd be dressed when he did finally face her. But when he did meet her eyes, he realized it wasn't her naked breasts that would send him to his knees.

Those eyes. That smile.

He wanted her again.

In that moment, everything in him wanted her. Still. Even more than he had before.

He wanted to start all over again, and this time tell her everything he loved about her as he touched every inch of her body, worshipped her from head to toe.

He was sure she could see everything he was feeling on his face.

Her smile softened, and she took a step toward him.

One step. And everything in him felt like he'd been shot with electricity.

This was *Bree*. How had he thought for even a second that he could do this and walk away unchanged? Max opened his mouth to say . . . *something*. Just as her phone rang.

Still watching him, she answered it. "This is Bree."

She ran a hand through her hair, giving Max a strange surge of satisfaction for being the one who'd messed it up.

"Hey, Avery," Bree said.

Max frowned. Typically a call from one of her girlfriends wouldn't be a concern, but this friend was in charge of the emergency-management efforts at the moment.

"Yep, I can come right over," Bree said in response to whatever Avery had told her. She paused again, listening. "No, it's fine. You stay there. I've got Mags."

She disconnected and licked her lips while smoothing her hands over her shirt. "Do I look okay?" She moved to check herself in the mirror over the sink.

She looked like she'd just been fucked hard against a wall.

To him she looked amazing.

And like the biggest heartbreak of his life.

"Some of Avery's crew stopped over at Maggie Norman's house to burn the rest of the debris, but they found Maggie there, and she won't leave."

Maggie lived on the south edge of town, her place visible to everyone coming into town on Highway 7. There was very little of her house left. "Maggie is *there*?" Max asked.

Bree nodded and turned to face him with a grin. "She told the guys that if they made her leave, she was going to tell all their mothers on them."

Max smiled. He was certain Maggie meant it, too. "Want me to come along?" He didn't really want to. He needed some space from Bree. He needed to review all the reasons he should not press her up against the wall again right now and kiss her until her knees buckled.

But *damn*, he liked being able to make her knees buckle.

The image of her sagging against the wall to hold herself up as he tasted her flashed through his mind. Bree McDermott had done a lot of amazing things over the years that had made that gorgeous body of hers feel good. Knowing that he could take control and give her pleasure that made her weak and forget where she was for a little bit felt damned good. Too good.

He was a smart guy. In spite of that, he lifted a hand and ran his thumb over her bottom lip. Her breath caught, and he loved that, too. She lifted on tiptoe and pressed her lips against his.

"I don't want to go, you know," she said.

But he needed her to go, because even that tiny lip-lock made him want a million more—over coffee in the morning, on their way out the door to work, when he walked in the door at night, when they said good night. Every damned time anything good, or bad, happened in his life.

"But I've got this," she said, settling back onto her feet. Her lips were still a little puffy, her shirt was wrinkled, and damn if she didn't have a slight glow about her. None of those things had been there before.

She definitely looked like she'd been fucked well.

And then she was gone, the door bumping shut behind her.

He sighed. He should have been relieved, but instead, he thought it was appropriate that *he* felt like the one who was totally fucked.

The house had been completely leveled. As was the bizarre way of tornadoes, the roof and every wall was gone, but the fireplace still stood. So did the two recliners and the small end table and lamp that had sat between them for four decades.

"Hey, Mags," Bree said, stepping over several pieces of wood and drywall onto the pale-blue carpet that Maggie had likely vacuumed the morning of the tornado.

"Hi, Bree." Maggie sat in her dusty, overstuffed rose-colored recliner. Knitting. "I'd offer you some coffee, but I'm out. Oh, and my kitchen is gone."

Bree dropped into the navy-blue recliner that Maggie's husband, Gene, had sat in every night until he'd passed away last year. "Well, good thing I had an extra-large this morning," Bree told her.

Maggie chuckled lightly at that.

Bree leaned back and pulled the lever to recline the chair, propping up her feet. She linked her hands on her stomach. "Mags?"

"Yeah?"

"Whatcha doing here? We thought you were staying with your daughter in Sapphire Falls."

"I'm finishing this baby blanket."

Bree looked over. "Your knitting stuff was all still here?"

Maggie nodded and continued knitting.

Bree shook her head. "Tornadoes are crazy."

They sat quietly for a few minutes, Maggie's needles clicking together as a soft breeze ruffled Bree's hair and birds chirped. It was actually pretty relaxing.

Bree's thoughts started to wander to Max and what had happened just before Avery's call, but she shut them down. When she thought about it again, she wanted to really be able to replay every detail in full Technicolor. Finally, Bree said, "You can't stay here, Maggie. You'll get really wet the next time it rains."

Maggie nodded. "I won't be here when it rains again."

Bree looked over quickly. "You mean you won't be *here* in the house, right?"

Maggie laughed again. "Right. There's going to be too many mosquitoes with all of my window screens missing."

Bree gave a little snort. The missing screens would definitely be a problem. Not to mention all the windows. And the *walls*.

"So you're here now to . . ." Bree trailed off for Maggie to fill in.

"Finish this blanket. Look at my fireplace one more time. Sit in my chair in front of the fireplace one more time."

Bree sighed. She hated that so many of the people she knew were going through this same stuff. Tornadoes sucked. "I'm sorry, Maggie. I'll definitely get some of the guys to take your chairs and table and stuff to your daughter's."

Maggie shook her head. "I don't want to sit in this chair anywhere else."

"But—"

"I'll get a new chair. And I'll make great memories in that chair, too—reading new books, knitting new blankets, watching new TV shows, holding my grandkids. I just needed to do all of this one more time, knowing it was the last time."

Bree traced her finger along the seam on the arm of Gene's old chair. "Why is it important to know it's the last time?" she asked gently. Kit would have been proud.

"Because I didn't know it was the last time I made Gene breakfast," Maggie said.

Bree put the foot of the chair down and turned slightly on her seat. "What do you mean?"

"The day he had his heart attack, I made him scrambled eggs. If I'd known it was the last breakfast, I would have made caramel French toast. His favorite."

Bree felt her heart clench. "Oh, Mags."

"I know. It's silly. It doesn't matter. But that's been bugging me for a year. Now this . . . I knew I'd need to downsize eventually. I knew this house was too big for me. But dammit, *I* wanted to decide when it would be the last time I knitted in this chair in this room." Maggie clenched her hands, bunching the yarn in her fists.

Bree wished Kit were here now. "I don't know what to say," she told the other woman honestly. "I get it. I really do. This all really sucks."

Maggie looked over, making eye contact for the first time. She gave Bree a smile. "Yeah, it does suck."

"I wish I could make it better."

"Well, sweetie, you can." Maggie's hands relaxed.

"I can?" Bree really wanted that to be true. "How?"

"I decided that I was going to come back and finish this blanket in this chair in front of this fireplace before the house was completely gone. And you're not going to drag me out of here before I'm done."

Bree felt relief go through her. Something she could do. Thank God. Bree leaned back and pulled the recliner lever again. "Knit slowly. I could use a break."

Maggie picked up her needles and started again.

After a few minutes of gentle clicking, Bree said, "I always really liked your house. How long did you live here?"

"We moved in the day before our tenth wedding anniversary," Maggie said. "So, forty-two years."

"You were married to Gene for fifty-two years?" Bree asked.

"Yep. And I would have taken another fifty-two."

Bree watched Maggie knit for a few moments, the yellow stripe getting wider as she went. Maggie had been happily married to the same guy for *fifty-two* years.

Obviously some people *were* wired for long term. And Bree could see where Max might get the idea that she wasn't one of them. But she just wasn't so sure he was right about that.

Bree rolled to her side in the recliner, putting a hand under her cheek. "Hey, Mags, can I ask you something about you and Gene?"

"Sure, honey," Maggie said, still concentrating on her stitches. But a sweet, almost-subconscious smile curved her lips, and Bree could tell that Maggie was still very much in love with her husband.

"How'd you keep things exciting for so long?"

Maggie laughed at that. "Exciting? Oh, Lord, sweetie, thank goodness it wasn't exciting that whole time."

Bree felt her eyebrows raise. "What? It wasn't fun?"

"I didn't say it wasn't fun. But it wasn't exciting."

"I don't understand." Bree pushed herself up to a sitting position.

Maggie put down her knitting and looked over at her. "You know how you go on a trip and you have the best time and you feel great and you try new things and feel thrilled the whole time?"

Bree nodded. "Yes. Of course. I love that."

Maggie smiled. "My favorite trip was an Alaskan cruise."

Cruising wasn't really Bree's style, but she said, "I love doing new things."

"So you know how you get home after the trip, and the first thing you do is take a great big breath and then you get into your own bed and lay down on your pillow and you just . . ." Maggie gave a big sigh. "You just feel wonderful? The trip was great, but there's nothing like coming home."

Bree found herself nodding along to that. "Yeah, I'm with you." She always took that big, satisfied breath after a landing or a race or at the bottom of the snowy hill. She loved the exhilaration, but she also loved the sense of contentment that came after.

"Gene was that big, deep breath for me," Maggie said, her smile growing. "He was what I always came back to. He was home . . . the place I always wanted to be no matter where else I could be."

Bree felt like Maggie had just sucked the oxygen from her lungs.

He was what I always came back to.

The place I always wanted to be. No matter where else I could be.

That was Max.

But . . . was that . . . did that . . . Bree felt her mind spinning and her lungs fighting to expand and wondered if she was having a panic attack.

Bree put the footrest down on the recliner and stood swiftly. She paced to the fireplace, running her fingers through her hair.

"You okay, honey?" Maggie asked.

"After you fell in love and settled down, did you ever miss the exciting times?" Bree asked, turning to her. "Didn't you miss the things that made your heart race? The things that made you get all . . . tingly?"

Maggie didn't laugh at her. Instead, she considered the question. "I guess my heart never stopped racing," she said after a moment.

Bree felt her eyes widen. "What do you mean?"

"I mean, my heart raced every time he walked into a room. It still does, even now, when I think of him," Maggie said. "It raced for fifty-two years. Each time I told him I was pregnant, every time I saw him holding one of our children or laughing with them or pushing them on the swings, the first time he made me an anniversary gift because we didn't have enough money to buy one. My heart flipped when he got his first promotion, and then when he told me he was going to start his own business. It fluttered whenever he fixed something around the house or worked on the car or made dinner—anytime he was taking care of us. It was a regular thing, honey."

Bree was fascinated by all that. "Really?" She tried to think of something Maggie might have done in her younger years. "That was equivalent to sneaking out after curfew and going skinny-dipping in the pond?"

Maggie laughed at that. "Oh, no. It was a . . . softer excitement. But so much deeper. It lingered. If that makes sense."

Bree had to admit that it did. The high from racing or jumping seemed to fade faster than the warmth she'd been feeling since she'd started noticing things about Max.

Bree took a deep breath. So babies and new businesses and him making dinner. Would those things excite her? As much as jumping out of airplanes?

"What about the trips? Learning new things?" Bree asked. "You didn't miss those?"

"I didn't give up any of that," Maggie said. "The trips became family trips, and I never stopped learning new things. I learned to knit when I was forty."

"I'm not really the knitting type, Mags."

Maggie just shook her head. "And I'll tell you what's even better—the thrill of learning something new or going somewhere new multiplies as you have people you love with you. Seeing them light up is even better than being excited yourself."

Bree stopped pacing at that and looked at the older woman.

She realized she knew exactly what Maggie meant. Seeing Max at the end of a ski run or on the ground after a jump, or watching him when he was storm chasing or when he was talking about weather was just as good as doing something *she* loved.

"So things with Gene *were* exciting," Bree said.

Maggie's smile softened. "They were. And Gene was my anchor through it all. He was the reason I could be neck-deep in everything, enjoying the swim, but not be swept away by it."

Bree could suddenly take a deep breath again.

She got it.

Max could let her push and try new things and take risks, and he was always there—smiling at her on the way down, grinning at the end, making her feel safe the entire time.

Bree crossed to the chair and sat down again.

"You okay?" Maggie asked.

Bree took another deep breath, then admitted to them both, "Yes. I actually think I am."

"Good." Maggie gave her an affectionate look, then picked up her knitting again. "Girls like us, who love to take those big leaps, need to be sure to have a reliable parachute, you know."

Bree smiled. "I thought those of us who like to dive into the deep waters needed a good anchor. Was Gene your anchor or your parachute?"

Maggie nodded. "Yes."

Bree laughed and leaned the recliner back again. "Okay, tell me about some of your big leaps and deep waters over the years."

So Maggie did. For nearly an hour. And when she was done, she had a beautiful blanket for her first granddaughter, who was due to arrive in October.

CHAPTER SEVEN

"Gentlemen." Max greeted Jake and Wes in the town square. He hadn't seen Bree in almost two hours, and those hours hadn't been nearly as restful as he would have liked.

"How far did you get?" Wes asked.

Max knew his uncle was asking about how far along he'd gotten on the building inspections and repairs at the school, but he couldn't help that his mind immediately went to how far he'd gotten with Bree. Damn. "Not as far as we wanted," Max told him. He meant that in multiple ways. He wanted a lot more than he'd gotten from Bree—mutual orgasms or not.

"I can give you a couple of my guys tomorrow," Wes told him.

"We'll take them."

"How are things going with Bree?" Wes asked.

Max's spine went ramrod straight. "What do you mean?"

He didn't miss the look that passed between Jake and Wes. They definitely seemed amused.

But Wes said, "She was excited to learn more about building inspection and repair from you. Has she been helpful?"

Wes was Bree's boss and had been supportive of Bree learning more so she could take over the majority of the emergency-management tasks. Of course he would want to know how she was doing.

Which meant Max had overreacted—and given himself away. He cleared his throat. "Fine. It's all . . . fine."

Fine was definitely not the right word, but Max was not going to hash this out with his cousin and uncle at the moment.

Wes chuckled. "With anyone else, I'd warn him that Bree can be a handful, but I don't have to tell you that." He clapped Max on the shoulder.

That was for sure. No one knew Bree better than Max, and calling her a handful was accurate. But the term made his thoughts skitter off in inappropriate directions this time.

"Yeah, thank—"

"Chief Mitchell, you have to help us!"

Max, Jake, and Wes all swung toward the young voice at once.

Wes stepped toward the little boy who'd come running up. "What's going on?" he asked the kid.

There was another little boy slightly behind him, and Max realized they were Tim Hubert's sons. They looked just like their dad.

"Chief."

That voice Max knew very well. He turned to find Bree approaching from across the square.

God, she looked beautiful. She was in uniform now, but he knew that there would be a slight whisker burn on her collarbone and possibly a small love bite on her inner thigh. His body hardened as their eyes met briefly. In that flash, he knew she was recalling everything from a couple of hours ago as well.

"What's up, Bree?" Wes asked, his hand still on the little boy's shoulder.

"Altercation on Main," she said, pulling her attention to Wes. "A tow-truck driver got into it with some guys who are doing the tree removal."

"Okay, I'll be right there." Wes looked back down at the little boy. "Brody, what do you need?"

"Kayley won't come out of our house."

Wes frowned. "What do you mean?"

"She thinks our dog is still in there."

Max remembered that Tim had two sons and a daughter. He guessed Kayley was Brody's little sister.

"We can help Brody out," Jake said, pointing between himself and Max.

Wes nodded. "Brody, this is my son, Jake, and his friend Max. They went to high school with your mom and dad. They're soldiers. They're going to help you and Kayley."

The kid looked impressed with the soldier thing, and Max grinned. They were in.

"Thanks, son." Wes started toward Main with Bree.

"No problem." Jake turned just in time to see Max watching Bree go. Max couldn't quite regret it, though. The view was spectacular.

Thankfully, Jake didn't have time to rib Max about anything. They had an assignment.

"Let's go," Jake said. He looked at Brody. "I'm going to grab my bag from my truck, then we're right behind you."

Max ran to his truck to grab his supplies as well. There was no telling what they were going to run into. Max did remember reading a report that the Hubert house had sustained a lot of damage.

As they headed across the yards and between houses toward the Huberts' place, Brody explained that his parents were busy with cleanup activities elsewhere and that Brody had been put in charge of babysitting his younger siblings.

"Kayley snuck out?" Max asked him.

"Yeah. But I know where she went. She won't stop talking about Cooper. We couldn't find him after the storm. She thinks he's stuck somewhere in the house."

So Cooper was the dog.

"How old is Kayley?" Jake asked.

"Six."

Well, dammit.

They arrived in front of the big two-story house four blocks from the square. The front looked fine, but even a few inches of shift could make the house a disaster waiting to happen.

"Nobody goes in but me," Max said as he pulled a high-beam flashlight from his bag.

"I'm going with you. It'll be faster," Jake said. He also pulled out a flashlight and some rope.

"Just give me a minute," Max told him.

"If that little girl's in there, it's not gonna matter if you think the place is unstable," Jake said. "I'm going in there to get her."

God save him from his heroic cousins. Max sighed. "Fine."

"Stay here," Jake told the boys. They nodded, eyes wide.

Jake and Max headed for the front door. Max scanned the structure, looking for obvious signs of problems. The front door seemed to be level and shut tightly. There were no cracks or obvious shifts on the porch, doorway, or the windows on this side of the house.

"So far, so good," Max commented. He checked the door, but it was locked.

He glanced back at the boys. "How'd she get in?"

"From the back," Brody said.

Max and Jake exchanged a look, then headed for the other side of the house.

They rounded the corner and instantly realized that things were not as they seemed. "I'd like to edit my assessment of the situation," Max said.

"Glad we have your expertise here," Jake said wryly. "Otherwise, how would we know when a house is structurally unstable?"

While the front of the house had looked untouched, it was the only part of the structure where that was true. The back and one side of walls were gone. The roof had been lifted off, and the remaining inner walls of the house slanted precariously. Windows were broken; furniture, clothing, and belongings were scattered; and most of the second floor was resting on the first.

"Dammit." Max started forward.

Jake was right behind him.

Thirty minutes later, Max and Jake escorted all three kids back to the church, where they were supposed to be playing until their parents came to pick them up. Kristin and Tim were already there when the kids went running in through the front doors. Tim grabbed up all three of them at once in a huge bear hug, holding them tightly, his eyes squeezed shut.

Max felt as if something had punched him in the chest. His ribs ached, and his lungs wouldn't expand. He rubbed a hand over the tightness, working on not actually tearing up over a man hugging his kids. Max had seen this stuff before. Every disaster he'd ever worked had moments like this. This was the good stuff. The stuff that made the hard work and heartache worth it—when things worked out, when things were good, when hope and happiness prevailed.

But damn if today it wasn't hitting him a hell of a lot harder than usual. He'd seen families reunited. He'd seen people pulled from wreckage alive and well who should never have survived. He'd seen people find personal items that had been scattered more than six miles away. Heck, he would never forget the scene of an old man reunited with his dog after almost a month. But today was different. Today his heart actually hurt with how much he wanted a family and a home and personal belongings and a dog that meant this much to him.

Maybe because it was Chance. Maybe because he was getting older and losing his edge.

Or maybe it was Bree.

Maybe it was because he now knew he could have everything from the woman he loved *except* a home and family.

A few minutes later, Jake and Max were making their way back to the square, ready for whatever was next.

"You okay?" Jake asked as they crossed Main Street.

"Why do you ask?"

"You're limping."

Max swore. "Shut up."

"I notice that you don't really limp. Unless you're in Chance."

"Jake?"

"Yeah?"

"Shut the fuck up."

Jake chuckled.

They walked another block before Jake said, "You looked like you were having some trouble back there. And I don't mean your knee."

Max sighed.

There were four people in the world who would have noticed that—Jake, Dillon, his mother, and Bree.

"Just got to me," he said. "Seeing Tim with the kids. It was a weird moment."

"It was a good moment," Jake said.

Max nodded. "Yeah." Of course it was.

They walked another half block, and finally Max asked, "You want to have kids, right?"

"Sure," Jake said. "Eventually."

There. It wasn't strange for Max to want that.

"But it's weird to think about having them anyplace but here," Jake said after another moment. "I can't imagine them not growing up with your kids and Dillon's kids."

Max thought about that. Jake was right. That did seem weird. "I guess it's weird for me to imagine anyplace else being home long term for me."

"But we've all already been gone for ten years," Jake said. He stopped by his truck, parked along the curb on the east side of the square. He tossed his bag onto the passenger seat. "Time's getting away."

Max felt a jolt of awareness go through him. Jake was right. Of course he was right. It wasn't as if Max didn't know that it had been ten years since they'd lived in Chance. But hearing Jake say it like that made Max really think about how fast that time had gone. He'd been wrapped up in work. He'd been busy. He'd been living a life that he could easily enjoy for another ten years. But really, he'd been killing time. Until it was time to come home.

It wasn't as if he didn't like his life. He was proud of the things he'd accomplished, was rewarded by his work, and played as hard as he worked. But deep down he knew that he'd always thought of Oklahoma as temporary.

He'd been killing time until he could get over Bree and handle living in the same town, full-time, without it hurting too much. Or until she left Chance.

Max felt irritation course through him. Why did he have to be so hung up on her? Why did she want a sexy, hot affair *now*? Five years ago, he would have taken her up on every single bit of that. They could have been sharing sleeping bags and fucking like bunnies in Steamboat and the Florida Keys.

Dammit.

Now she wanted that, while he wanted to settle down, have kids, and get a dog.

He stomped to his own truck and threw his bag in the back. "Fuck."

"You need a beer," Jake observed.

Max tipped his head back and stared up at the sky. The cloudless, clear sky. Where had *this* sky been on Saturday when everything in his world was about to get turned upside down? "Actually, the last thing I need is something to take away my inhibitions."

Jake cocked an eyebrow. "Is that right? What would happen without your inhibitions?"

"Bree would find out that the locker room earlier was just a warm-up."

Jake whistled. "Thought you weren't going to have any more sugar?"

"Thought you were going to leave Avery alone."

"Touché." Jake sighed. "I don't think leaving her alone is an option."

"Yeah." Max knew exactly what he meant.

"Coffee instead?" Jake asked.

"I gotta try to sleep tonight," Max told him. Though he was pretty sure that wasn't going to happen.

"So I'll just pray for you, then." Jake gave him a grin.

"You're a prince," Max told him, lifting his middle finger.

Jake laughed and headed back for his truck. Max got behind his wheel and started for his mom's house.

But at the corner of Vine and Fifth, he had to fight not to turn down the street and roll into Bree's driveway.

He deserved more. Even if she felt like everything he wanted.

Two days later, Bree approached the door to A Bar, as eager to see Kit as she was to sit, relax, and have a drink. A Bar was the only bar in Chance and was actually named Sorry Mom, We Bought a Bar, the name the twin-sister owners had decided on when they told their mother their dream, and she said, "Can't you do something more important with your life?"

It was also where the people of Chance came to get out of their beat-up houses and away from the mess for a while. The sassy sisters had invented a couple of new drinks, too—the Storm Warning, which was spiked lemonade, and Liquid Lightning, the ingredients of which were a secret. Instead of ignoring the tornado, they were facing it head-on and trying to poke some fun at it.

Bree knew that Kit had been here all day in the back party room, with the kids whose parents were busy with cleanup. It was essentially a makeshift day care, but Kit had decided to get involved and turn it into a sort-of therapy session as well. The kids got to talk about the tornado, ask questions, and have some fun, rather than watching their parents and the workers go through their personal belongings and tell them that no, they hadn't found their favorite book or toy. They were doing tornado-themed crafts, eating tornado-themed snacks, watching *The Wizard of Oz*, and playing games around a huge tornado made of chicken wire, tissue paper, and twinkle lights.

It was great for the parents and great for the kids.

It was exhausting for Kit.

If anyone needed a drink, it was the town shrink.

Bree pulled the door open and stepped inside. She smiled, and greeted the people just inside the door. There was quite a crowd already, and Bree had to push her way to the bar.

She scanned the room and saw Kit sitting at their usual round table. Bree waved, and Kit pointed at her empty glass. Bree grinned and nodded.

"Two of the Liquid Lightnings," she told Becky, one of the sister-owners who was tending bar tonight.

"Kit's was a martini," Becky said, filling a shaker.

"She needs something more than that, don't you think?" Bree asked.

Becky laughed and served up the specialty drink in, of course, hurricane glasses with twisty straws.

With a drink in each hand, Bree made her way to where Kit was sitting.

"I don't—" Kit started.

"You drink one of 'em or I'm drinking both," Bree told her before she even got out her full protest.

Kit eyed the glasses as Bree sat down. Bree took a drink from one of the straws. "Good stuff."

"I just—"

Bree took a drink from the other straw. "Really good stuff."

Kit sighed and reached for one. Because she knew Bree would absolutely down them both, given the chance.

Kit hadn't started lecturing Bree on her increased liquor intake lately, but Bree was sure it wasn't far away if she didn't let up a little.

Her mind immediately went to Max. He was the only thing she could imagine being better than liquor at making her feel good.

Maybe she should tell him that. He needed to have sex with her to save her liver.

She chuckled lightly. He'd probably do it, then. Max was always taking care of her.

"What's funny?" Kit asked.

Bree focused on her best friend. Oops. She knew better than to let on that she was thinking about something interesting that she didn't want Kit to know about. Her friend was like a bloodhound when it came to emotional turmoil.

But why wouldn't she want Kit to know about this? She was a professional—in mental health and all things Bree.

Bree picked up her glass and took a long draw on the straw. "You need to fix me."

Kit took a tiny sip of her drink. "Fix you? What do you need fixed?"

"I am incredibly attracted to Max, we're best friends, we're working together, and now we've had a major breakthrough. He let me do more at the work site, and it was awesome. We finally talked about his knee, kind of. And we had really hot sex in the boys' locker room at the school right before I went over to Maggie's." She drank again as she watched Kit process all of that.

It had now been two days since all that had happened, and Max had been avoiding her, assigning her to work on one of the farm buildings yesterday and today with a crew from Kingston rather than with him.

But Bree thought she'd let Kit start with the other stuff first.

Kit's eyes said it all—she went from pleased to confused to concerned to surprised.

"You were talking about his knee?"

Bree swallowed and grinned. "That's where we're starting?"

"Well, I do think that's pretty big."

Bree felt her heart flip. "You do?" She wanted to think so, too, but she was a novice at this emotional-relationship stuff with guys. At least when it came to emotions other than the basic happy or bored.

She knew there were other emotions, of course, and she knew it was probably a red flag that those two were the only ones she ever really thought about with the men she dated. But she didn't need to go any deeper with guys. Either she had a good time with them and was happy, or she didn't and wasn't. That was as deep as it needed to get.

Until Max.

"I do," Kit said. "He's opening up about something he's been really stoic about until now."

"In all fairness, we didn't talk about it so much as I said there was no way he could climb up into the school ceiling and actually *make* me come down because of his knee. He basically acknowledged that was true."

Kit looked at her thoughtfully. "So you were willing to stir that up. You weren't sure how he'd react, but you still went there."

Bree shrugged. "It's bugged me for a long time that he hasn't wanted to talk to me about it. For a while I didn't really want to hear about it. But I thought we'd eventually talk it out. Like every time he jumps out of a plane or hikes up a mountain and it bothers him."

"You're both pretty happy with the status quo. Him in Oklahoma, home every once in a while, tons of action while he's here, then gone again."

There was something in her tone that made Bree frown. "So? Status quo is bad?"

Kit shook her head. "Not necessarily. Status quo is easy and comfortable."

Bree nodded. "That's Max for me. Easy and comfortable."

"And *that* is what's interesting."

Bree narrowed her eyes. "Interesting how?"

"You don't really go for easy and comfortable. You like challenging and new."

"Well, yeah, but . . ." She really didn't know how to finish that. Because Kit was right.

"Even with me. I think that we got close as adults in part because I challenge you. I make you think about things differently."

"I got close to Avery, and she's super easy."

It was true. Avery didn't have a lot of experience with close personal relationships, so she didn't expect or demand much.

"You let Avery get close because you've got a big heart and she needed us. And because I told you to," Kit said. "But Max doesn't exactly *need* you. He's very well adjusted and has a lot of relationships. But he has always been that steady, easy guy for you," Kit pointed out. "Clearly that works for you. For you both."

"He challenges me," Bree tried to protest. "You think jumping out of planes is *easy*?"

"I think Max jumps out of planes because you do, not the other way around," Kit said with an eye roll.

It was true. Max was easy. Max did whatever Bree wanted to do.

"You think I'm changing things with Max?"

"Aren't you? You're working with him, not just playing. He *is* challenging you in that. And you're spending a lot of time with him, more than usual when he's home. And he's been here longer than usual. On top of that, you're pushing him on the knee thing. Oh, and let's not forget the making out and sex."

The sex.

Yeah, there was definitely no forgetting that.

"I'd say you're changing everything," Kit said. She sipped her drink again. "But the question really is, *why*? Things have worked for so long."

Bree thought about that. "It probably is because he's been here longer this time. I don't like anything for too long." Just like Max said. "Travel, activities, guys . . . ice cream."

"Why do you think that is?"

That was the kind-of-annoying stuff that Kit always did—asked her a question instead of giving her an answer.

Bree sighed. They'd talked about this before, though. "Because I was a replacement child for my parents, and after Brice died, they wanted to embrace life fully and experience everything fully, and so they've always pushed me to do all kinds of amazing, fun, exhilarating things."

Bree's father, Denny, had been over the moon about having a second chance to be a father and had gone overboard in everything. He'd taken Bree everywhere with him, had taught her everything he knew, had bought her every piece of sporting equipment and every age-appropriate motorized machine there was—and even a few that hadn't been age-appropriate. Molly, her mother, had worked past her instinct to be overprotective in therapy. As a part of overcoming her own fear about how suddenly life could change, she had encouraged Bree to be a risk taker and to try everything and do anything she wanted to. The result was a tomboy who'd been fearless as a child, reckless as a teen, and adventurous as an adult.

It was all really good in many ways. Her parents had always encouraged her natural curiosity and her love for high-adrenaline activities. Rather than sinking into a depression after their son's death, they had grabbed ahold of life, for themselves and for their daughter. They were outgoing, active, happy people.

But to Bree, they also seemed restless. As she got older and became more self-aware—in no small part thanks to the woman across the table from her now—Bree realized that her parents seemed to be trying so hard not to sit still or think too hard or deep about things. Maybe that was the only way to keep the sadness at bay. Bree knew it was no coincidence that her parents had been kayaking in Puerto Rico on Brice's birthday last week.

Kit took another dainty sip of her drink. "You have projected those things that worked for you and your dad onto the other most important man in your life. Max. Because Max always liked you and enjoyed being with you when you were doing things like playing ball or messing with snakes and stuff. But just because that's where you started doesn't mean that's all you can ever have."

Bree swallowed hard and leaned in. It was time for the all-out honesty. "Max thinks I'm not wired to fall in love. He thinks that's why I keep getting bored with things—and guys. He thinks that's just who I am."

"Do you agree with that?"

She took a deep breath. "I do change my mind a lot."

"You think so?"

Bree frowned at her. "Don't you? Have you seen me eat the same ice cream for more than two months straight?"

Kit smiled gently. "Bree, you are the most steady thing in my life."

Bree straightened. "What?"

"You are you. You are the most *you* person I know. You never change. I always know what to expect. You're the same person today that you have always been. You don't let other people influence you. You don't really care what others think. You like to try new things, you've had a few jobs, you don't date anyone long term, and you like lots of kinds of ice cream. But *you* are you. Always. Funny, smart, loyal, unfiltered, unapologetic, adventurous, interesting."

Bree stared at her for several ticks.

"What?" Kit asked.

Bree's stomach felt like she'd just gone over the top of the roller coaster. She couldn't describe the way Kit had just made her feel. Startled, yes. But also warm. Flattered. Happy.

"You are *really* good at this," she finally told her friend.

Kit laughed. "This was an easy one."

Loved.

Bree realized that was how she felt. Loved. Accepted. Appreciated.

"I *can* fall in love. I love lots of flavors of ice cream, but ice cream is still my very favorite of all foods in the world—and *always* has been. And you can love a lot of different kinds of ice cream and a lot of different people, but it's still love, right? Like you would be lemon sorbet, and Avery is Pistachio Pizzazz, and my dad is"—she laughed lightly—"Rocky Road, probably."

Kit looked intrigued. "Why am I lemon sorbet and Avery is Pistachio Pizzazz?"

"You're sophisticated and a little tart while being sweet underneath," Bree told her with a grin. "Pistachio is green with nuts in it—doesn't look like something you want to really dive into, but when you do, it's amazingly wonderful."

Kit's smile was wide. "Yeah, Max is full of shit. You definitely know how to love people."

Bree nodded as a feeling of rightness went through her. "Yeah, he is."

"So, what kind of ice cream is Max?"

Bree sat back in her chair. "Sweet Cream Dream."

"Not Peanut Butter Passion or Sinful Cinnamon or something like that?" Kit teased.

Bree shook her head. "Sweet Cream Dream. I don't eat it all the time, but it's always the one I know will be awesome if I get it. He's the one that I always go back to. The one I want after indulging in the other ones." He was like Chance to her—home. No matter where she went or what she did, this was where she came back to.

Kit's eyebrow rose, no longer laughing or teasing. "Okay. Well, then, I think you need to tell him that."

"Okay. How? Just like that?"

Kit narrowed her eyes, thinking. "Max thinks your feelings for him come from the adrenaline of whatever is going on around you. You need to show him that you don't need danger and drama to want to kiss him."

"Okay. How?" She wasn't going to let Kit get away with not answering this one, or answering with a question.

"Do stuff with him that's not dangerous or dramatic and see how you feel."

Bree thought about that. That seemed too easy.

"And what if I actually don't want to kiss him then?" she asked, voicing the fear that was nagging at the back of her mind.

"Then you definitely need to *not* kiss him anymore."

Bree let that really sink in. She couldn't imagine not wanting to kiss Max, but she did owe it to him—to both of them—to prove that it wasn't about adrenaline. At least not falling-out-of-a-ceiling adrenaline. The idea of showing up on his porch with ice cream and leaving her helmet and parachute and tool belt and everything else at home sent an unmistakable thrill through her, though.

"I need to get home," Kit said a few minutes later. "I'm beat."

"But you haven't told me anything about Dillon yet," Bree protested. "You got all my dirt, and I got nothing from you."

Typical. Kit was a magician when it came to getting people to spill their guts, but she only shared *her* guts when she was good and ready.

"There's nothing to tell." But Kit wasn't meeting Bree's eyes.

"At lunch on Sunday, Avery told us she and Jake got busy in the shed, and you said you kissed Dillon in the storeroom at the hospital. You're saying nothing else has happened?"

"Of course not," Kit said. "I told you, it was a heat-of-the-moment thing. It didn't mean anything."

Bree narrowed her eyes. "You remember I'm a cop, right?"

Kit tipped her head. "And?"

"I'm trained to know when people are lying."

"I'm not."

"You do this thing where you play with your earring when you're lying," Bree said.

Kit gave her a shocked look, and her hand flew to her ear. "I do?"

Bree started laughing. "No. But you just confirmed that you *have* *been* lying to me."

Kit pushed her chair back and stood. "Not cool."

Bree couldn't stop grinning. Kit hated when Bree figured her out. "You're holding out on me."

Suddenly Kit's shoulders slumped, and she looked every bit as exhausted as she claimed to be. "It's complicated. And I really am too tired to go over it right now."

Bree stood, too, and pulled Kit into a hug. "Okay," she said soothingly, rubbing her friend's back. "That's fine." Then she said quietly in Kit's ear, "But I'll bet all this prim-and-proper buttoned-up stuff is driving Dillon crazy, and he's fantasizing about taking you back into that storeroom and ripping your power suit right off you."

Kit pulled back with a frown. But her cheeks were also flushed. "Stop it. Dillon's not fantasizing about me at all."

"Mmm-hmm," Bree said. "Whatever you say. But I'd put good money down on that man being downright dominant in the bedroom."

Kit's face got even redder, and she grabbed her purse and smoothed a hand over her suit jacket.

And now Bree would put money down on Kit *wanting* Dillon to be dominant in the bedroom. With her.

How interesting.

Bree took a drink, not at all bothered by how flustered her best friend seemed. Truthfully, Bree thought Kit needed to be flustered a little more often. And by a guy who would boss her around a little bit.

Dillon Alexander would be perfect.

"I'll talk to you tomorrow," Kit said, stepping around the table.

"You bet. Sweet dreams," Bree said with a grin.

Kit looked around, and when she saw no one was watching, she lifted her middle finger. Then she blew Bree a kiss and left the bar.

Bree laughed. Kit was very careful to cultivate her smooth, calm, professional facade, but Bree had seen her raving angry, puking drunk, and can't-stop-giggling silly. She really did wish more people could see those other sides, too.

Her straw sucked up nothing but air on her next pull, and Bree realized she was empty. She headed for the bar.

She should go home, too. She could use the sleep. She definitely didn't need the alcohol.

But the idea of her cold bed, where she'd no doubt lie awake for at least an hour like she had ever since Max had come back, wasn't a bit appealing. Not even with her favorite vibrating buddy there to help her through. After their rendezvous in the locker room, her purple plastic friend hadn't been quite satisfying.

"Another?" Becky asked, indicating Bree's empty glass.

"A beer and a shot," Bree said.

"You got it."

A moment later, Becky set a bottle of beer in front of her and then slid a shot glass of red liquor across the bar to her. Cinnamon schnapps. Her go-to. The sweet fire of the shot always made her feel better. She loved that it was sweet but also burned a bit. It was like a lot of things she loved—the rush on the way down was nice, but the end always stung a little. And just like it was a bad idea to have shot after shot after shot, it was impossible to go up again and jump, then up again and jump, then up again and jump.

But sometimes it felt like that was all that would really make her happy.

"Hey."

She felt the solid heat of him against her shoulder as his voice made goose bumps trip down her arm. She felt her stomach flip a little, and it startled her. She wasn't sure her stomach had ever flipped while she was sitting down and having a beer.

Bree pivoted toward Max as Joey Conner vacated his stool to let Max slide up beside her. Max shook Joey's hand and then held a finger up to Becky, who set a beer in front of him, too.

Max lifted the bottle as he turned to her. "How are you?"

"Good." And she realized she was better now that he was here. That was always true, actually. Yep, she could definitely count on Max to make her happy—a lot like Sweet Cream Dream.

But damn, that first bite of the Caramel Cashew Cache last night had been moan-worthy.

"How are you?"

He gave her a half smile. "Tired."

She studied him as she took another draw on her beer. Did she really have to choose between something that would always make her happy and something that would make her moan?

She immediately flashed back to the ditch and then the locker room and the fact that Max—her Sweet Cream guy—*had* made her moan.

In fact, she felt heat spread through her belly . . . and lower . . . as if she'd just taken the shot of schnapps. Sweet and hot. That definitely described how things had been with Max.

She knew from experience that things that made her moan were awesome. And short-lived. She'd moaned with pleasure over more than ice cream. She'd had that same reaction to her first jump, her first dirt-bike ramp, her first dive, and so many more experiences.

But the high faded. The happiness—that was much more consistent and long lasting.

She studied Max as she drank again.

Happy *and* moaning. That's what she wanted.

She'd been getting it from a combo of Max and their adventures, but the moans had been harder to come by lately.

Until that ditch where *this*—whatever it was—had started.

"I missed you today," she told him. One thing she and Max had always had was full honesty.

She watched Max swallow his mouthful of beer hard and cough slightly. Then he looked at her.

"You saw me this morning."

"When you started me on a job with Kevin and then disappeared while I had my hands in drywall paste," she couldn't help but point out. Not flirtatious, but she was a little annoyed by it and couldn't totally let it go.

He shrugged and studied his beer bottle. "Something came up."

She turned more fully on her stool. "Really? What was that?" She tipped her bottle again.

"I had to deal with Jake."

Bree arched a brow. "Deal with Jake?"

Nobody *dealt* with Jake Mitchell. Except maybe Avery. And Bree was sure Max wasn't taking care of Jake the same way Avery did. Jake was typically the dealer. He took charge wherever he was, and one of the beautiful things about having Max and Jake both home at the same time was that they could get twice as much taking-charge done. Jake would go one way and Max would go the other, and they would take care of everything together. Add Dillon into the mix, and it was the trifecta of get 'er done.

"We had a disagreement about the roof on the barn you and I inspected the other day."

Ah, the barn. It had been fun scaling the wall and getting out on that beam. She knew it was dangerous—that was part of the thrill. But she wouldn't have done it if she thought she couldn't handle it.

And she'd wanted to handle it. For Max.

He wasn't getting up there because of his knee. She knew it. He didn't have to admit it. The comment about strength and flexibility had been as close as he'd ever gotten to confessing that it held him back sometimes. But she got it. Without climbing gear, getting up in those rafters was riskier. If he wasn't 100 percent sure of his footing and balance, it would have been a dumb move. But she *was* sure of her footing and balance.

She didn't like that he'd doubted her, and she hadn't gotten the reaction she'd wanted after she'd proved it, either. She'd wanted to see admiration in his eyes, maybe even pride. A "Wow, Bree, that was awesome" would have been perfect.

Instead he'd griped at her.

Then the last couple of days, she hadn't even had the chance to impress him. He'd dumped her off at a site and hightailed it out of there.

She suspected that he was afraid she might try to kiss him again.

He was right.

She *had* to know if Max could be a source of that hot, sweet thrill over and over.

If not, well, things would be the way they'd always been. They'd be friends, they'd have adventures, he'd be her Sweet Cream Dream.

But if he could be that *and* a Cookie Dough Frenzy once in a while . . . wouldn't *that* be the perfect world? She wouldn't have to keep thinking up new ways to take on gravity and physics. Instead, she could be buying lingerie and browsing sex-toy sites on the Internet.

Now *that* would be a new adventure.

Heck, they could even come up with some new ways to enjoy Cookie Dough Frenzy.

Her heart kicked as she thought about those possibilities, and her gaze dropped to Max's lips as he took another drink of beer. The warmth she'd felt in her stomach dipped lower between her legs, and she pulled in a short breath.

"What was the disagreement about?" she asked.

"He doesn't think we should take the time to reshingle the entire roof."

She was distracted from thoughts of licking ice cream off Max's washboard abs for a moment. "You think you should reshingle the entire roof?"

He nodded. "Best way to be sure it's all fixed and solid."

"That will take days," she said. "Patching the one spot will be only a few hours."

He frowned. "Thought you wanted to learn from me."

"I do."

"Then lesson number one is you don't half-ass things."

"Jake doesn't do half-ass things," she said.

Max frowned at that. "Apparently he does," Max told her. "The water damage is old. That means the shingle issue is old."

"In that one spot."

"If there's one spot, there's a good possibility that there are others we're just not seeing yet."

"But that will take time—"

"I have a crew coming up from Grand Island just for that job," he said, cutting her off. "It won't take any manpower away from anything else. And Jake has the National Guard here to give us more hands and feet." He frowned at her. "You wanna go follow Jake around and learn how he does things instead?"

Was that a twinge of jealousy from Max? And why did that make her pulse trip? She didn't like jealous guys.

She could tease him more about this, but instead she decided to let Max know exactly what she was thinking and feeling. She'd never seduced someone before. She'd never even really flirted. She might not be great at this, but she already liked the sense of excitement that went with the anticipation of it.

She reached out and covered his hand with hers. "I don't want to follow Jake around, Max. I want to be with *you*."

His gaze dropped to her hand. He took a deep breath. Then he pulled his hand away from hers, wrapped it around his bottle, and lifted it.

"Tomorrow. I want to be with you onsite tomorrow," she insisted.

"Yeah. Okay." He didn't sound thrilled, by any means.

She wanted him to be thrilled. Max liked being with her. He came home regularly, in part to see her. She knew that. She wanted him to look at working together like he looked at going zip-lining together— with anticipation and that grin that always got to her.

She hadn't realized it until right then, when she *wasn't* seeing it, but she loved that grin. The grin that said he was happy and excited and totally into the moment with her. Partly *because* of her.

She was tuned in to him. That idea sent a buzz through her. She knew he was tuned in to her as well. Max knew her better than anyone, and suddenly, that was . . . exciting. To be close, to really appreciate and enjoy him, to let go with him all sounded so tempting. Which was crazy. She'd been close to him and had enjoyed him and let go with him a number of times. Or so it seemed. She'd known him forever, always loved spending time with him, had done some wild things with him.

Now, in this moment, for some reason, it didn't seem like *enough*. She wanted more closeness, more letting go.

It seemed to her that meant a couple of orgasms. But that might just be her hormones talking.

"I was on your website last night and read a bunch of your articles. I'd love if you'd show me an example of a concrete foundation that needs replacing versus one that could just be repaired," she said.

He looked at her quickly. "You were on my website last night?"

She nodded.

"Why?"

She ran her hand up his arm and squeezed the impressive biceps bunching under the soft cotton of his Henley. She assumed that touching him like this was flirtatious, but that quickly became a secondary concern as she felt the heat against her hand and appreciated the solid contour of the muscles. She didn't need any other reason to touch him besides liking it. A lot.

"Because I didn't work with you all day, and I wanted to somehow get into your head."

She felt his muscles tense under her hand, but she wasn't sure if it was because of her words or her touch.

"You wanted to get into my head?"

She nodded. "I want a lot of things from you."

"Bree—"

"No, listen." She leaned in closer. "I know you said no more climbing or kissing, but I spent the whole day with my feet on the ground and not seeing you, and it was completely—"

"If you say 'boring,' I swear to God I'll throw you over my shoulder, take you outside, and paddle your ass."

Bree felt her quickly sucked-in breath lodge in her lungs, then blossom and heat, spreading through her chest and up the back of her neck, making her tingle from her nipples to her scalp.

Holy *crap*.

Not only had the idea of having her ass paddled *never* turned her on, but she would have never in a million years imagined hearing those words—or that sexy, firm tone—from Max. In fact, she wasn't sure she would have believed that Max would ever snap like that. Not at her. When she pictured him at work, it was with the same humor and smiles that he always displayed. Of course, she'd assumed that there were times he had to be commanding and firm. But he had never been that way with her. Ever. Max was the most accommodating person in her life.

The other day when he'd told her to get down from the rafters, he'd had a little of that command in his voice, but since she'd been up in the ceiling at the school, he had definitely been dictatorial. And the tingles were still not fading.

"Hi, Bree."

Little shocks of awareness still dancing through her body, Bree turned toward the sweet voice.

It was Ashley. Bree noticed that the rest of the university students had filed into the bar behind her.

"Uh, hi, Ashley," Bree said.

Ashley gave Max a little smile, but her attention came right back to Bree. Shockingly.

"I was wondering," Ashley started. "I just thought—I was really interested in talking to you some more."

"Me?" Bree asked. She glanced at Max. He was smiling, but his eyes were on the TV behind the bar.

"Yeah. I think you being a cop is really cool, and after Max told us all the things you've been involved in with the emergency management around here, well, I'd love to talk to you about it. And maybe do some shadowing while I'm here?" Ashley almost acted shy as she asked.

Bree stared at her. "Seriously? You want to follow *me* around?"

Ashley nodded, her smile bright. "What you do is really great."

"But the weather stuff is all Max," Bree said. What had Max said about her exactly? Clearly Ashley had gotten the wrong impression.

"Oh, I know. And he's awesome," Ashley said, smiling at Max. "But I've been trying to figure out what I want to do with my degree, and emergency management is really exciting to me."

"You're getting a master's degree in—" Bree wasn't even sure. But it wasn't criminal justice. "Why would you want to go to the police academy?"

Ashley shrugged. "I don't know about the academy, but I'd love to do what you do with the emergency-management piece—the storm chasing, the recovery and construction—all of it. You're just really a"—Ashley blushed—"a great role model for a strong, independent woman."

Bree had no idea what to say to that. She had *never* been a role model to anyone before. But she could tell Ashley meant it, and the rush that gave her amazed her. It was like what she'd felt the other day when the students had been asking her questions, but amped up by a factor of ten. Or a hundred.

As to how Ashley even knew these things about her—Max had been talking about her. And, well, maybe he *was* proud of her.

She wasn't sure *why* he was talking about her to his students. But apparently he was saying very nice things.

"That's all really flattering," she told Ashley.

Ashley's face brightened. "So would it be okay if I followed you around for a day while I'm here?"

"Yeah, I guess," Bree said. "I don't know how exciting it will be. I'm helping with some of the rebuilding and repairs."

"That's fine. I like to get my hands dirty, too," Ashley said quickly.

For a split second, Bree wondered if this was a ploy for Ashley to impress Max. But then Ashley said, "But would you be able to go over what you and the department do to prepare for emergencies—all kinds—and how you personally combine it with the storm chasing and everything?"

Bree's mind started spinning through all the things that happened before, during, and after a storm, then she jumped to the big grass fire that had happened last fall a mile from town. The flood that had happened two summers ago. Then the blizzard two winters ago. It seemed like Chance was the unluckiest place on earth, but truthfully, all those things were just part of life in Nebraska.

Okay, maybe not the constant, crazy tornadoes.

But Bree found herself smiling. All these things made her love her job—and it wasn't the excitement of it. It was the protecting and taking care of this town.

"Yes, I'd love to do that," Bree told her. "How long are you here?"

"Another couple of weeks at least," Ashley said. "The summer session is six weeks long, and we have permission to stay here for as much of it as we need to."

"Great," Bree said, feeling her heart flutter as she thought about the things she could tell Ashley. "Give me a couple of days to finish some stuff, and I'll put some things together for you."

There were a lot of things she could talk about when it came to preparedness and recovery. Max, Jake, and Dillon were the three pros, but Bree had the small-town experience. Two years ago, her cross-country skiing and snowmobiling experience had been hugely helpful when the blizzard hit. She'd been able to get out to a couple of houses to check on people and bring them supplies, and she'd been able to get two older women to safety in town. Her hiking and camping and canoeing experience had helped when two kids had gone missing along the river last summer. And her climbing experience had been very helpful during this cleanup and recovery—Max would have to admit that.

She wondered if Ashley would be interested in learning those kinds of skills as well. Basic climbing, hiking, and water safety could be helpful.

Places like Chance relied on volunteers for almost everything. They got training, but not the intensive teaching that full-time professional emergency-management teams did. They didn't have the high-tech help or high-level equipment, either. They had to depend on the intelligence, dedication, and resourcefulness of the volunteers. The more training that could be provided, the better.

"I'm really looking forward to it." Ashley beamed at her, much as she had at Max the other day. "You're awesome to do this."

"It's great. I'm looking forward to it, too," Bree said, surprised by how true that was. "Call me."

Ashley leaned in and gave Bree a quick, spontaneous hug, then turned and disappeared into the crowd to find her friends.

Bree turned back to the bar, still feeling a little stunned.

Then she looked at Max.

He definitely looked smug.

"I stole your biggest fan."

His grin grew. "Yep."

"What was that all about?"

He shrugged as if it were no big deal. "I was telling them about the storm and what we were doing—"

"Oh, really?"

He gave her a look. "I left out a few details."

She grinned. "I wouldn't have minded you telling them all the dirty details."

His smile faded, and heat replaced the teasing glint in his eyes. "I wasn't sure that was what I wanted them to learn about storm chasing."

Bree took a casual drink of her beer, even as her entire body felt like it was vibrating. From adrenaline—flirting with Max, thinking about mentoring Ashley, remembering all the things she'd been a part of in Chance.

"Anyway," Max went on, "I kept talking about you, and Ashley wanted to know more, and now . . . I guess she thinks you're awesome."

Bree tried not to look giddy at that. But, yeah, Ashley thought she was awesome. That felt—weird. And great.

"You built me up," she said, turning her stool toward Max so her knees bumped his.

"Just told the truth."

Bree was overcome by emotions at that. She knew Max cared about her, liked her, wanted her. But now she saw that he actually respected her, too. That was . . . surprisingly attractive.

A shiver danced down her spine. A shiver that felt a bit like the one that went through her when she first climbed into the cockpit of the small plane she'd learned to fly solo.

She loved that shiver.

"Jesus, man, I heard you about lost your asses out there!" Ted Miller exclaimed as he bellied up to the bar. "I knew you were a crazy sonofabitch chasing those storms, but damn, man."

Max nodded, casting a quick glance at Bree. "It got close."

The storm wasn't the only thing that had been close on old Highway 36.

"Well, nobody else has been that close to that ass in a really long time," Ted said, his eyes dropping to Bree's butt.

Bree jerked her elbow back, connecting with Ted's ribs. But he was too drunk to really feel it. *They're drunk. They're just kidding around. No need to punch anyone in the face.*

"Yeah, hunkering down in a ditch is as dirty as Bree's gotten with anyone around here," Adam Franklin said before laughing loudly at his own joke.

She looked at Max. "Well, I do like things dirty." She saw Max's fingers tighten on his bottle.

"I can get you dirty, babe," Adam said. "My duck blind can be downright cozy. You just say the word."

That was never gonna happen.

Even if Adam were her type—and he wasn't—that wasn't gonna happen. Hunting wasn't her thing. Thankfully, her dad hadn't been into that stuff, either, or there was no doubt she would have killed her first animal at a tender young age. Just like she'd learned to throw, hit, and kick a ball; handle bugs and small critters; get muddy; and consider scrapes and bruises tiny trophies for playing hard.

And she was pretty sure that if Adam were standing in the open door of an airplane at twelve thousand feet with only a piece of nylon on his back, he would cry.

They would definitely not be giving her the huge grin and a wink before bailing out that Max did.

Bree looked at Max. He looked pissed. Finally, something other than mildly interested and amused. He was clenching his jaw and his beer bottle. The smiles were gone. He was usually the optimist, the life of the party, the fun guy. Now he was growly and bossy and moody.

It was intriguing.

She didn't totally get it, either. Was it just the stress and fatigue from the storm cleanup making him grumpy? Or did he really not like the other guys teasing her?

She also didn't understand this urge to push him even further to see what happened.

Okay, that wasn't entirely true. She always pushed. When there was something exciting, even something she thought *might* be exciting, she pushed.

Like now.

"Thing is," Bree said, her eyes still on Max, whose eyes were on his beer bottle, "ducks are kind of . . . boring."

Max's head swiveled slowly to look at her. She met his gaze with an eyebrow up.

He shook his head and sighed. "Okay, let's go."

Bree's stomach flipped, and even her bones felt warmer now.

She reached into her pocket for money to cover her tab, but Max tossed enough bills onto the bar to cover his drink and hers, as well as Ted's and Adam's.

"You guys out already?" Ted asked.

Max wrapped a hand around Bree's upper arm. "Yep."

CHAPTER EIGHT

One-syllable words? That wasn't Max, either. Bree knew she shouldn't feel like grinning, but this was new.

She loved new. New was exciting.

As Max tugged her off the bar stool and escorted her, gently but firmly, to the door, Bree felt like she was standing on the platform, waiting to launch herself off over the woods in the Appalachian Mountains on a zip line.

Oh yeah, this was what she wanted.

It took a little bit to make it to the door. People kept stopping them, wanting to chat. But eventually they were outside. Alone.

Max didn't stop until they were standing beside his truck, in between it and another F-150. He dropped his hold on her and turned to face her.

It was dark, but the tall lights that circled the parking area allowed them to see each other's faces clearly.

She clasped her hands together and watched him, anticipation building.

She was trying not to look *eager*.

Max shook his head. "Don't."

"Don't what?"

"Don't look like someone's about to serve you a combo pizza with extra cheese."

Apparently she looked eager anyway.

She grinned. "Sorry."

"The thing is, you're not. You're pushing me."

"Maybe a little," she admitted.

"Why?"

"I like this new side of you."

"New side?" he asked.

"This dominant, ass-paddling side." She knew her grin was big again.

Max narrowed his eyes and looked at her, saying nothing for several ticks. "It's not new," he finally told her.

She laughed at that. "Um, I'm pretty sure I would have remembered you promising to smack my ass, Max."

His jaw ticked. "Just because I never said it out loud doesn't mean it's new."

Dang. Was it the dark or the Liquid Lightning or the fact that she was already a little revved up or what? His voice was gruffer now, and his words sent heat spiraling through her.

"You've thought about it before?" she asked.

He looked at her directly, and she could feel the heat in his gaze. "Many times."

She swallowed hard. "So you're saying that this sexy, bossy side of you isn't new? It's just new to *me*."

Max took a step forward, the six-inch difference in their heights all the more obvious as he towered over her. Because he'd never done *that* before, either. He'd never been aggressive or dominant or even the least bit bossy.

"Guess so."

Her mouth dropped open. "You *guess so*? Have you or have you not been hiding a man I want to lick from head to toe?"

She heard the low rumble that sounded almost like a growl. Then he said simply, "That's enough." He turned away.

Away. When all she could think about was how close they could get out here in the dark before anyone came out. And, of course, the idea that they could mess around and possibly get caught also sent a spiral of desire through her.

She grabbed his arm. "Hey, you can't walk away."

He pulled out of her grasp. "The fuck if I can't."

She grabbed him again. "Max, stop. I want to talk about this. Why have you been hiding this from me? Especially if you knew I'd like it? And just how *not* sweet and nice and romantic are you?"

He swung around at that. "That's the thing, Bree. I *am* sweet and nice and romantic."

"But you've got this other side. A side that *totally* works for me," she said.

Max shut his eyes and rubbed the back of his neck. And swore again.

"Max, think about it. Best friends, who love all the same things, who have all this chemistry. Now you know I'm into the stuff you like in the bedroom, too. This is perfect."

He opened his eyes and shook his head. "That's just it, Bree. You're *not* into the stuff I like."

"I *love* things hard and fast and *dirty*, you know that."

"That is not what I'm talking about." His voice was low and even a little menacing.

Bree couldn't quite suppress the shiver of delight at that. "Tell me what you're talking about."

She didn't think he was going to for a moment. But then he stepped forward, backing her up against the truck behind her. He leaned in and braced a hand on the truck, beside her shoulder. She swallowed hard.

"I don't think you'll be able to get there with the way I like things."

"Are you kidding? I got there in the ditch the other day with just your fingers."

His eyes narrowed. "Not what I meant."

"Then what?"

"You won't go for the intimacy that has to come first."

"I'm pretty sure that there are plenty of women getting tied to beds and fuc—"

"Stop it," he bit off. Max pushed back away from her and the truck. "That's exactly it. I don't want to fuck you, Bree."

Well, *ouch*. "You were pretty into it the other day in the locker room."

He nodded. "I was. And that's how I know I don't want to do that again."

Definitely *ouch*. "Hey." Okay, Max didn't know everything she'd realized about her feelings for him. Kit thought she needed to tell him. Fine. She'd never done this before, but she could. She took a deep breath and grabbed the front of his shirt in both hands. "I'm in, here, Max. In. For all of it. Whatever you want."

He shook his head and pulled her hands from his shirt. "You're not. You forget how well I know you. If I thought there was any chance you *would* be in, I would . . ." He shook his head, clearly frustrated. "But I do know you," he said without finishing the first thought.

"What do you think you know so well?" she asked.

"That this all sounds exciting only because it's something new and different for us, and you're always up for new and different. And I know you could be into some really fun stuff that would take a long time to get tired of," he said.

She opened her mouth to reply, but he wasn't done.

"But even that high will fade, Bree."

"So you'll keep helping me find it again," she said. "Just like our trips. You and me and the best sex-toy catalogs in the world."

For just a second, Max's eyes flared with heat.

But then he said, "I won't survive when you move on after all of that."

"How do you know I'll move on?"

"You always move on."

"But if it's amazing with you, if it's everything I need—"

"That *if* is not a risk I'm willing to take," Max said.

It wasn't a risk. This was Max. Her and Max. "It's not—"

"Do you know why I live in Oklahoma City?" he asked suddenly.

She stopped. "What do you mean?"

"It's because I know you. I know what makes you tick, what stays on your mind, what makes you love something."

She felt a combination of confused and curious. "What does that have to do with Oklahoma City?"

He clenched his jaw, then crossed his arms, feet apart as if bracing for a fight, and met her eyes directly. "I only see you for a week at a time—at most—because that works best with you. I come to town, we do something fun and exciting, give you your adrenaline fix, and then I leave before you decide I'm your Sweet Cream Dream."

He *was* her Sweet Cream Dream. But Bree knew he didn't understand that the way she did. "You live in Oklahoma City and only come to Chance for short visits because you think that's what keeps me interested in our friendship? In *you*?"

"It keeps you from getting bored."

Bored. He thought she got bored with Sweet Cream Dream. And everything else that she only stuck with for a little bit at a time.

"Bored with *you*?" she asked.

"And the time we spend together."

This was crazy. Bree's heart was suddenly pounding as her head swirled with what he was telling her. "You live in Oklahoma City because of *me*?"

He shrugged. "And my job."

"But you live away from Chance because of me?"

"More or less."

"But Max . . . we're . . . friends." She felt hurt. Or something.

"We're friends." He nodded. "On my terms."

She felt her eyes widen at that. "I don't understand."

"I come visit no more than once a month because that's how long it takes for you to get antsy to go and do something big. I'm never in town more than thirty minutes before I have you out on your bike or on a dirt bike or a snowmobile. I make sure when we're together, we're doing stuff you love. And then I leave while it's still fun and you haven't come down from the high yet."

She stared at him. "You have it down to the minute like that?"

"I've known you for a long time, Bree. And I've been paying attention."

She had no idea what to say to all this. The hurt feeling intensified even though he was telling her that he was doing it because he knew her well and cared about her being happy. "I can't believe you do all of that for me."

"I do all of that for *me*," he said firmly.

She shook her head and started to reply—with what, she wasn't sure.

"I started riding dirt bikes because you were bored with the telescope and swimming. But then you wanted to learn how to water ski. Then you wanted to learn how to rock climb. Then you wanted—"

"Okay." She cut him off. "Point taken. But you loved—still love—all that stuff, too."

"Yeah, but I never got tired of the old stuff."

A long, long moment passed.

Max thought she'd get bored if they spent more time together, if he was here more often and longer at a time. She really didn't want that to be true. But they'd never tested it. He'd been away from Chance for ten years.

"I know I can give you what you want," he said after the silence between them had stretched several seconds. "But *you* can't give *me* what I want."

A shot of irritation streaked through her. Really? She couldn't, didn't, give him *anything* that he wanted? Anyone could warm his bed, but she was the only one who would spend a week in the Grand Canyon with him. She was willing to sacrifice showering and going without gummy bears for a week for this guy. Could the other women say that?

"How many women have you taken skydiving?" she asked, braced to feel intensely jealous if he said even one. She'd always thought that was all theirs, something that was special.

And that's when it hit her that, while she loved the adrenaline—a lot—it wouldn't have been as good without Max. She looked forward to the skydiving because he was going to be there with her. The jumping was fun. But she wasn't so sure she would have done as much of it if he hadn't been there with her every time.

He pulled air in through his nose and let it out through his mouth. "I don't meet women who want to jump out of airplanes very often," he admitted.

"You meet women who want candlelit dinners and cuddling on the couch," she said.

"I do."

"Because you also like those things."

"I do."

God, if he ever found a woman who wanted candlelight and cuddling *and* jumping out of planes . . . Bree could lose him. A sudden panic made her heart flutter. She'd been assuming that she'd always have him, would always have *them*. But that was ridiculous. She'd never thought about it—which was crazy—but someday, surely, Max would meet a woman who would take Bree's place. Because Max was a romantic. He wanted a long-term, committed relationship. He wanted to get married.

It hit her like someone had slapped her in the face. Max wanted to get married. Or he would. Someday. Surely. And Bree would lose him.

Finally, she lifted her chin, working hard on not letting the tears in her eyes show. "Okay, got it."

He frowned slightly, studying her face. This was Max. She couldn't hide what she was thinking or feeling.

"What have you got?"

"What you said about me not giving you what you need." Bree pushed away from the truck and started in the direction of her car.

Max caught her by the arm. "I didn't . . ." But he trailed off.

She prayed for a second that he would say something that would make it all okay. That he would ease the huge fist that seemed to be trying to crumple her heart.

Instead, he stared into her eyes, then let go of her arm. "Five years ago, I would have taken you up on all of this. Even two years ago. I do want you. God." He shoved a hand through his hair. "More than I've ever physically wanted a woman ever. Most of the time I'm convinced you're the reason I can't get serious about anyone else."

Even as she knew there was a "but" coming, Bree felt warmth spread through her body. "But now? What do you want that you're not taking me up on this now?"

"I want . . . it all. I want to settle down. Get married. Have kids. I've wanted it for a while now."

She pressed her lips together and nodded. She'd been right.

"And I want to come home."

Bree felt like that same fist was now squeezing her lungs. "Oh."

He nodded.

She frowned. "And you can't come home because of me. Because you're afraid I'd get bored with you."

"I guess . . ." He clearly didn't want to go on.

"Come on, Max," she said. "I think we need to have this *whole* conversation."

She could point out that she could leave at the end of August. If he wanted to be home and she was keeping him away, she could go. But suddenly, that didn't seem pertinent. Because they both knew she'd end up back in Chance eventually? Because since talking to Ashley she'd remembered the things she liked about her job here? And that she was good at it.

Or maybe because the things Max wanted didn't sound so bad.

"I didn't know if it would . . . work," he said, clearly frustrated. "How it would feel being with another woman, seeing you with other men. If I lived here full-time, we would have to deal with that. And they would have to deal with us spending time together and the trips . . . I just didn't . . ."

"The time together and trips would have been over," she said, filling in what he wasn't willing to say. He was right. But she'd never thought about any of this. Because he wasn't here. And her boyfriends didn't stick around long enough to care about her excess time and trips with Max.

"Yeah," he agreed quietly.

Looking into a face she knew as well as her own, her heart ached. She wanted him. But he didn't want her the way she was. He wanted a version of her that she wasn't even sure existed. She had never been romantic.

She needed some ice cream.

She needed *a lot* of ice cream.

"I'll see you at the site tomorrow?" she asked, starting for her car again.

He didn't stop her this time or balk at the change of topic. "At the update meeting, probably."

Right, the morning strategy meeting in the mayor's office.

"Right. I'll be there."

"After that I'm starting at the school," Max said. "Then probably heading back to the farm. I need to check on the Wilson place, too."

"I'm up for it," she said. "Whatever. But I don't want you to dump me on someone else."

She might not be able to give him what he needed in the relationship department, but *he* would give her what she needed in her emergency-management training. *Dammit.*

"I'm not dumping you, Bree."

There was something in his voice that made her feel like crying again, but she wasn't going to analyze that. Didn't matter.

Nothing had changed. They were still them. Still friends. Still fellow adventurers. She still did, by God, give him things no one else did.

And if she was suddenly noticing a bunch of really tempting things about him, well, that was tough. She and Max were perfect together in almost every way.

Almost was going to have to be good enough.

It didn't matter that *almost* was one of her least favorite words.

Almost making it to the top, almost nailing the landing, almost making the curve—those didn't work in her world.

But maybe she was going to have to get used to being *almost* the perfect woman for Max.

Friday morning started off the same way Thursday morning had. They were in Frank's office where everyone gathered for updates on how things were going. Max and Bree were acting like friends who were also professional colleagues and not like two people who had screwed their brains out in the boys' locker room at the school.

"Morning, everyone."

Bree turned in her chair in front of Frank's desk to watch as Jake strode in with a huge smile.

"Morning, Sunshine," Max said drily from where he was leaning against the wall.

"How are things around town?" Jake asked Avery as he handed her a folder.

"Um, great," she said. "But you know that."

"How's the mental health of our fair city, Doc?" Jake asked Kit.

Kit looked from Avery to Jake. "Fine. For the most part."

"Great, good job." Jake handed Dillon a folder. "And the physical health?"

"Improving." Dillon lifted an eyebrow at Jake but took the folder.

"How about the public safety?" Jake asked Bree.

"Everyone's safe and sound, Sergeant Major." Bree gave him a little salute, and she got a grin, and a folder, in return.

She was glad someone could be upbeat.

"Mr. Mayor, our fearless leader." Jake handed Frank a folder. "How are things looking from your perspective?"

"Couldn't be better, Jake," Frank said happily. He clapped Jake on the shoulder. "You've all done a hell of a job so far."

Jake stepped in front of Shelby. "And my beautiful, sweet, caring, impetuous cousin. Are you happy?"

She gave him a funny look. "You're acting weird. What's going on?"

"I'm here to tell Frank the idea he and I were kicking around the other day is going to go."

"The idea?" Shelby looked at her husband.

Frank's head came up quickly. "Really?"

Jake nodded. "I've been thinking about it a lot, and I think we should do it."

"When was this?" Shelby asked.

"We were talking about it Tuesday morning," Frank said. "I was with the reporters, answering a million questions about how it felt to get hit for the third time in a row, what I thought about this area getting hit ten times total, all those stupid-ass questions, when one of the reporters asked me what advice I would give to other communities."

"It occurred to us that our tornado epidemic has made us the experts in preparing and recovering from them," Jake said.

"A training center?" Max and Dillon asked at the same time, looking up from their folders.

Bree quickly flipped hers open as well.

Sure enough, Jake had just handed them all an outline for an emergency-management training center in Chance.

"It's perfect timing," Frank said to Max and Dillon. "We can get your input on everything."

"What do you mean?" Dillon asked.

"Everything from our warning systems to our posttrauma care has been tested over and over," Frank said. "And, if I do say so myself, we're damned good at all of it. We can use our knowledge and experience to train other communities. Take the negativity of our repeated hits and turn it all into something good."

Bree looked up, her heart knocking against her sternum. Holy . . .

Jake continued the commentary. "Small communities like Chance, and ones smaller, don't have the resources bigger cities do. And preparation and recovery in a rural area is different than in a metropolitan area anyway. Small towns are, as you all know, dependent on volunteers mostly. This resource-and-training center will focus on those areas and people. We'll give them specific hands-on training they can take home and implement immediately."

Bree's gaze flew to Max. He was looking at Jake, but as if he felt her eyes on him, he looked over. His expression was hard to read.

Had he known about this? Did this have anything to do with him talking her up to Ashley? But he couldn't have known Ashley would come to Bree. Ashley had been pretty obviously enamored with Max. And he definitely couldn't have known all the thoughts that had gone through Bree's mind with Ashley's request for mentorship. He couldn't have known that the idea of training and teaching would excite her. *She* hadn't even known that.

Of course the idea of instructing skydiving students had given her a little thrill. Sharing her passion and knowledge with people who were drawn to something she loved would be fun. Exciting, even. Had Max known that about her? He clearly felt that way himself.

But she knew he would want to be a big part of this. Max loved teaching and training. It was a lot of what he did now in Oklahoma. But the training center would make it possible for him to do it here.

He'd said the other night that he wanted to come home.

Was the training center enough to give him a full-time position?

Bree forced herself to breathe. She could not hyperventilate in the middle of a meeting in Frank's office.

"We want the city departments involved," Jake said, and Bree realized the rushing in her ears had made her tune out a lot of what he'd been saying.

"It's one thing to go in as an outsider to a community that's been affected; it's another to be from the community," Jake went on. "You can all offer a fantastic perspective on what it takes to rebuild from the inside and to work as a team. Typically we pull in specialists from all over to lead a summit or training session. This will be unique in that people will be learning from a team that works together all the time. Our students would be coming here. They will see up close and in person what it's like in a community that's been rebuilt, how the town prepares, the immediate action plan, the long-term efforts, everything."

The word *team* made Bree look around the room. She would get to work on this with Avery and Kit, and Jake and Max. Maybe even Dillon. They really did represent a hell of a team for this. And a surge of excitement managed to make it past the panic.

She loved working with all of them, and the last few days working with Max had been awesome. Yesterday had been a little awkward, but once they'd gotten to work, it had been good. She'd found herself impressed with him again, and intent on learning what she could from him.

This training center could be an exciting step in her career, too. If the idea of working with Ashley had seemed fun, this was a thousand times more so.

Bree felt a little flutter in her stomach at that as well. Chief Mitchell wanted her doing more. Had he known about this plan? Teaching other cops how to handle emergencies in their hometowns based on her experience in Chance?

"Yes, yes, we'll want all of you involved," Frank agreed.

"We're going to share everything we know," Jake said. "From the off-season education and preparations to what happens on the day of a storm to what's happening the next day, the next week, the next month. And we won't need a specific building. We can set up the headquarters here at city hall and use the conference rooms. But we'll take our students all over town—to the police station and the fire station to witness some reenactments of what the day of a storm might look like, to some of the businesses and even homes that have been hit and rebuilt. The whole town will be like a living, working resource center."

"Avery and Bree, we would want you to walk other departments through the various stages of preparing and recovery," Frank said enthusiastically. "You can cover what your departments need to know, your roles before, during, and after the storm. All of that. Jake will be happy to help you, I'm sure."

Bree liked the sound of all this. It would be a new challenge for her.

"We've done this before, without Jake," Avery said.

"I'm sure Avery and Bree will do a great job," Jake said. "Though if you'd like some input, all you have to do is ask."

Bree couldn't help but look at Max again. She needed to step up her training with him over the next few days. She wanted to know *everything* she needed to know. If she was going to be teaching others, she had to be fully prepared.

"I'd be happy to consult on emergency medical preparedness," Dillon offered. "We could run some drills. Maybe have some past injury victims talk about their experiences."

"Good idea," Frank agreed. "That would be good for those survivors, too, to focus on the positives."

Kit nodded. "I like that idea."

Bree glanced at her friend. Wow, Kit was saying Dillon had come up with something good? Things really had shifted in Chance.

"This is so great," Shelby suddenly gushed.

Everyone looked at the bubbly blonde. She was practically bouncing up and down.

"All of this is part of the overall message we want to send—to the people outside Chance and to the people who live here," Shelby said. "We want everyone who lives here to stay and feel safe, and we want people to not be afraid to visit or consider moving here. So we'll focus on expecting the unexpected."

"Expecting the unexpected?" Bree asked.

Shelby nodded. "Tornadoes aren't unexpected here. Neither is the damage or the cleanup needed afterward. That's our message. We know the storms will come, but that doesn't change our happiness. We live our lives fully in spite of knowing the rain will come again. We plant flowers in spite of the certainty of hail. We rebuild our churches and schools even though we know they could get knocked down. We appreciate the sunny, warm days more because we know not every day is like that."

The room was quiet for several long moments. That was all really nice. And true. Bree felt a swell of pride for her hometown.

No, it wasn't exciting all the time. At least not in the sense that jumping out of a plane was exciting. But she felt a definite thrill at the idea of working with her best friends, people she admired, on something that would show off their town and help other communities. It was a different kind of excitement. It was like what Maggie had said the other day about life with her husband and kids. It was a deeper kind of excitement. More of a steady buzz rather than an acute rush.

It was a good feeling that could be sustained. The only way to keep getting the rush from a skydive was to keep jumping.

This felt more . . . satisfying.

"We pull together," Shelby went on. "The storms remind us what's important and *who* is important." She gave them each a beatific smile.

"Nicely said," Jake finally responded.

"And June will be our big month," Frank said. "We'll train all year, but we can invite people to Chance in June to see us in action."

All year.

Yes, this could definitely be complicated. But this could be good for both of their careers, and Max wanted to come home. How could she be okay knowing she was the reason he wasn't in Chance where he wanted to be?

They went on for a little while about their ideas for the center, a museum about Chance and their tornado history, various drills they could run, and how to involve multiple city departments.

"It's *perfect*," Shelby gushed. "This is our opportunity to put a positive spin on everything. Pun intended."

"Hey, we could do a camp for the kids," Max said. "The kids could spend time learning about meteorology and storm tracking, how tornadoes form—"

"They could make their own tornado in a bottle," Shelby said. "Have you seen that? It's like a science experiment where you have water and food coloring and you tape the two plastic bottles together?"

Bree couldn't help but grin at the way Max's eyes lit up at the thought of making tornadoes in plastic bottles.

"We could go over tornado drills and stuff with them, too," Jake added. "Each kid can leave at the end of the week with a supply kit and safety plan for his or her family."

Bree was impressed, she had to admit. Avery even offered an idea for using some of the storm debris to build a sledding hill for the winter.

Bree looked at Max again as they wrapped up the meeting with promises for more brainstorming soon. Her heart thumped at the look of pleasure on his face. He wanted to be a part of this. He *should be* a part of this. For his sake and for everyone else's—the team here in this room, Chance, the people who would come for training. She couldn't handle the idea that he might not do this because of her. Because he didn't think they could live in the same town full-time.

And she wanted to be a part of this. A part of something great for her hometown, working side by side with these people who she liked and admired, and above all else, working with Max on something he was this happy about.

Chasing storms put that look on his face, too. That was one of the reasons she liked going out with him. Skydiving, white-water rafting, zip-lining—all of the things they did together—were fun for her in part because they made Max look like *that*.

Kissing her in the ditch had put a similar look on his face.

She wanted to be a part of anything that made him look like that. That made him *feel* like that.

Even if it meant changing everything she'd thought she knew about Max. And herself.

"Kit." She grabbed her friend's arm as Kit started past her as the meeting broke up.

"Hey." Kit gave her a big smile that faded quickly into a frown. "You okay?"

Bree lowered her voice. Max was still lingering with Jake and Frank. Dillon had already left, and Shelby had linked her arm with Avery's and was leading the fire chief out. Avery rolled her eyes at Bree as they went past.

"I think so. I've decided to go after Max."

Kit didn't look shocked. "Good."

"Good? That's it?" Where was her brilliantly insightful friend when she needed her? Bree frowned. "How about some advice?"

Kit laughed. "You don't need advice, Bree. Just go for it."

"No. I told you last night about how Max thinks I'm not the right girl for him. The whole can't-settle-down thing." She'd called Kit as soon as she'd gotten home from A Bar. Well, as soon as she'd swung by the store, picked up some ice cream—Sweet Cream Dream, thank you very much—and was in her pj's on the couch with a spoon.

Kit put a hand on her arm and looked her directly in the eye. "Bree, stop letting Max tell you who you are. Yes, he knows you and has for a long time. But *his* feelings are in the way of him seeing everything about you. *You* tell *him* who you are for a change."

Kit let that sink in for a minute, then she gave Bree a gentle smile, hugged her quickly, and said they'd talk soon.

Bree nodded, her eyes on Max. She needed to tell him who she was.

She felt her heart flip. Excitement. Anticipation. Nerves. She recognized this feeling well. She'd felt it dozens of times with that guy right by her side.

But this time it was all about Max. There were no mountains, no special equipment here. No parachute—literally or figuratively.

And maybe that was how it should be.

CHAPTER NINE

Max opened his parents' front door Friday night to find Bree on the porch.

"Hey," he greeted, gripping the door frame as everything in him strained to pull her into the house and press her up against his mother's living-room wall.

The last two days of work with her had been hell on earth.

At the same time, they'd been some of the most satisfying and fun he'd had in a long time. Bree was an enthusiastic student, and she was smart and never shied away from a challenge.

And she looked damned good in her jeans and tool belt. The tool belt that now had a hammer hanging beside the pockets full of candy.

"Hey."

She gave him a smile that grabbed him right in the heart. He'd seen it before. It was the one that said she was happy and excited and there was no place she'd rather be. Of course she was usually standing on the top of a mountain or about to punch the gas.

Now she was giving it to him from his mother's front porch.

"What's up?"

"I brought you something," she said, holding up a gift bag.

"You got me a present?"

"Not exactly."

He waited for her to go on.

"Aren't you going to invite me in?" she asked.

"I'm not sure it's a good idea."

"Don't worry about getting naked with me in your mom and dad's house. I'm not taking my clothes off tonight," Bree said.

Part of him wanted to tell her that he could definitely get her out of her clothes if he wanted to, but he bit his tongue on that. Instead he said, "So you won't be staying long?"

There was a flicker of something, maybe hurt, in her eyes at that, but she lifted her chin a moment later and said, "Oh, I'm staying. I know your mom is out at Gigi's with her sisters putting some stuff together for the Bronsons' visit, and your dad is helping get the orchard cleaned up."

Max nodded. The Bronson family would be staying at the farm, in the guest rooms at the main house, during their visit. Several women were doing some meal preparation as well as cleaning and assembling welcome packs. Max and his crews were putting the buildings on the farm back together, but the farm itself—the pumpkin patch and the strawberry fields and the orchard—needed work, too. It was a good thing the sun stayed up until past nine this time of year. They needed all the daylight they could get.

"I'm glad you're not out there with them," Bree said. "You've been working your ass off and deserve some downtime."

"Not exactly downtime," he said. He wasn't dirty and sweating and doing manual labor, but he was working. "I'm catching up on some stuff from Oklahoma City. E-mails, reports, that kind of stuff."

She smiled at that. "Great. I'll keep you company."

She stepped past him without invitation, but Max could hardly barricade the door. For one thing, it was his mother's house, and she loved Bree. Jodi would never keep Bree from coming into her house, and if Jodi found out Max had, she'd yell. And no one could yell like Jodi Montgomery Grady. Avoiding that was always a good idea. For another, he didn't want to keep Bree out. He wasn't sure he wanted to let her in, either, but saying no to her was an impossibility. He'd learned that a long time ago.

Of course, any hope of getting his work done was gone now. He wouldn't be able to concentrate on e-mails with Bree around. She was the best kind of distraction. He loved to talk to her. She was witty and intelligent and interesting, and the way she said whatever she was thinking was one of his favorite things about her.

But now he was toast.

Not because of the locker room or the bar parking lot the other night, but because of the way she'd lit up when Jake told them about the training center. Max had seen the way she'd responded to Ashley's interest in her mentoring. The look of wonder and excitement had made him want her even more than her tight jeans and white tank tops did.

But that was only a spark compared to the blaze he'd seen lighting her up in Frank's office.

Damn.

If he'd been kind of in love with her all this time, that meeting had pushed him over the edge.

There was no way he'd be able to concentrate on anything but Bree and all the complicated, intense, amazing, painful things she made him feel.

Out on work sites, it had been okay. They'd had work to concentrate on and other people milling about. But here, now, it was just them.

It was a good thing this was his mother's house. He'd already have her naked if they were at his place. Or hers.

She didn't live that far away, in fact. They could . . .

He shut that down immediately.

She headed for the living room where Max had his laptop set up on the coffee table, files spread out, his report for Hays, Kansas, pulled up on the screen.

Bree plopped onto the couch in front of his computer. She grinned at him. "Come open your present."

So it was a present. That was . . . weird.

It wasn't weird that she'd gotten him something. They exchanged gifts on birthdays and at Christmas. Always had. When they'd been seven, she'd given him potato chips. Not even a full bag. The last half bag of her favorite potato chips. With a bow on it. Even as a seven-year-old boy he'd understood the significance of her sharing half of her favorite chips with him. It was funny how twenty-some years later, when he saw those chips in the store or a gas station, he thought of her. And smiled.

But this was weirder than the chips, because there was no occasion. And the bag was nowhere big enough to hold the new climbing boots he'd been not-so-subtly hinting about wanting.

He took a seat beside her but made sure there was some space between them. He took the bag and set it on the floor between his feet.

"Why a present?" he asked.

"I've actually had it for a while. This seemed like a good time to finally give it to you."

"Why is that?"

"Just open it."

She looked excited, and maybe a little nervous. That was sweet. And curious. Bree very rarely got nervous.

Max pulled the wad of tissue paper out of the top of the bag. "You had a gift bag and tissue paper?" he asked. That, too, was weird. Bree wasn't big on presentation or frills. If she'd gotten him the boots, she would have handed them to him in their original box, no wrapping.

She laughed. "Kit had them."

Ah, that made sense. No doubt Bree had told Kit about this, and Kit had correctly guessed that Bree wouldn't wrap it if Kit didn't give her the supplies. Max had to grin at that. Bree was . . . Bree. You knew what to expect and got what you saw.

He hesitated over that thought. Bree was the most . . . unwavering person he knew.

"Come on," she urged.

He pulled the black rectangle from the bag. It was a picture frame. He turned it over and, for a second, couldn't breathe.

The photo in the frame was a bright, beautiful flash of lightning in a dark night sky. Over Chance.

He looked at her. "Wow. This is amazing. Where did you get it?"

Her grin was huge, her eyes sparking, and Max almost forgot what they were talking about.

"I took it."

"You *took* this photo?" He looked back down at the photo. It looked professional. It was gorgeous.

She was practically bouncing on the couch cushion. "Yes. Late last summer. You would not believe how long I had to lie there and wait to get that shot. I got a lot of other ones, too, but this is the best, for sure."

He shook his head. "Wow, I'll bet. And you did it." Being still and waiting wasn't something Bree did well. She even had a rule that she wouldn't wait more than thirty minutes for a table in a restaurant.

"I did it," she echoed, her smile proud.

"Why?"

Her smile faded, and she turned on the cushion, tucking one foot underneath her. She just looked at him for a long moment. Then she said quietly, "For you."

"What do you mean?"

"I took it for you, for your birthday. That shot was *on* your birthday. Remember how last year you weren't here for your birthday because you had that seminar to teach?"

He did remember that. Of course. But that was almost a year ago. "Yeah, I remember."

"Everywhere we've gone, I've taken pictures, but just with my phone's camera. And they're great, for looking back and remembering. But I was getting frustrated because the photos were just not capturing the beauty and the awesomeness of it all. So I decided to invest in a good camera, and I took a class at the community college in Grand Island, and I learned to take pictures. I've even done some of the developing myself."

Max watched her face, aware of the way his chest tightened at the tone in her voice. She was excited about this and proud of it, he could tell. But she was also nervous telling him about it for some reason.

"Why didn't you tell me?" he asked.

"I wasn't very good at first. I wanted to practice before I showed you anything."

He frowned slightly and turned on the cushion to face her. "You don't have to be good at stuff before you tell me about it, Bree."

She pressed her lips together for a moment, as if contemplating what she was about to say. "I know that, actually. Or I think I do," she finally said. "But I'm not good at . . . not being good at stuff. That comes from growing up always wanting to impress my dad. He would teach me new things, and I'd go through them with him the first time, but then I'd go practice before the next time. It's why I always bugged you and Dillon and Jake to play ball with me or ride dirt bikes and snowmobiles and stuff with me. I practiced with you guys before I was out with my dad the next time. Then he was always really impressed by how great I was doing so quickly." She stopped and swallowed, her gaze on the photo Max still held instead of on his face. "It's carried over with you as we've gotten older and not seen each other as much, I guess. I didn't really realize it, but you're right. I don't let you see me not do something well. I always want you to be impressed."

Max's heart thudded in his chest, and he had to clear his throat before responding. "I've always been impressed by you, Bree. And that doesn't come from the things that you *do.* It's who you are. I think you're amazing. You can . . . let me in."

She looked up. "Okay."

The thudding turned to pounding. "Okay?"

"I'll let you see me less than amazing."

He couldn't stop the smile. "Not possible."

She gestured to the photo. "I thought, at first, that was why I didn't give you the photo last year. I thought it wasn't as good as it could be, so I was going to try again. But that's not why I held on to it."

Something inside of Max tightened. It felt like anticipation, times a thousand. "Then why?" he asked, his throat tight.

"Because it's romantic."

The tightness intensified.

She gave him a small yet nervous smile. "It's exactly what you said the other day—it's a gift that means something special to the person you're giving it to and says something about you, too. That photo is something I planned to get especially for you. After you taught me about lightning and thunder and clouds that summer, I knew that a photo like this, over Chance, would be the perfect gift. I wanted to take it myself. And I had to sit out there for hours to get it right. You know I don't sit still very well, and waiting is hard for me. But it was worth it." She stopped and took a big breath. "But then, after I'd done it and had it framed and everything, I realized it was . . . big. Too big. That wasn't just a friendly birthday gift. And I chickened out. I didn't really know why, or how to explain it, until you said that stuff about romance." She wet her lips and looked up at him. "I couldn't give it to you before now because it was romantic, and I wasn't sure either of us was ready for that. Even if it was mostly subconscious for me."

Max tried to swallow and couldn't quite get it done.

He tried to breathe. That wasn't working either.

"Be right back," he choked out as he lurched to his feet and headed for the kitchen.

Please don't let her follow.

He needed a second. Or five hundred seconds.

She got it. Kind of. She'd heard him when he talked about romance, and she'd understood it, and . . .

Dammit, that photo was *romantic.*

Max braced his hands on the edge of the sink and let his head drop. How was he supposed to resist her? He wanted her. He'd had her and he wanted more. So much more. And now she was giving him the most thoughtful gift anyone had ever given him *and* realizing it was big. Really big.

He was a goner. He was screwed. He was in way too deep.

He lifted his head and stared out the window over the sink.

He wasn't sure he'd ever wanted anything more in his entire life.

Okay, so he could do this. He was going to go out there, finally throw her over his shoulder, take her to her house where they could be uninterrupted for the rest of the night—and maybe most of tomorrow—and do everything he'd been denying he wanted for the past twelve years.

Max pulled in a final deep breath and pushed away from the counter.

But when he went back into the living room, he found her curled up in the corner of his mom's couch, her shoes kicked off, knees pulled up, the throw blanket over her feet. She had a notebook open and balanced on her knees.

She didn't look ready to be thrown over his shoulder.

She glanced up. "You okay?"

"Not sure." He crossed to the couch and sank down slowly. "What's the plan here?"

"We hang out."

"Hang out?"

"Yeah. You said you had work to do. I do, too. So we'll work together."

"You have work to do?"

She smiled. "It's my plan for the day Ashley's going to shadow me. The things I want to cover and how."

He turned on the couch, draping an arm over the back and narrowing his eyes. "Just a quiet night at home?"

"Yeah."

"Why?"

She closed the notebook with her finger marking her spot. "Really?"

"Yeah."

"I want to see if I still want to kiss you when there's no danger or drama."

Max felt his heart bang against his ribs. That was big, too. And she got it.

Yeah, he'd really like to know that, too. He also really loved that she wanted to know that.

He'd worry about what it meant later if she *did* want to kiss him without danger or drama. Or if she didn't.

He gave her a nod. "Okay."

"Yeah?"

"Yeah."

She smiled and opened her notebook, and Max turned to his computer.

Over the next thirty minutes, Max was very aware of her. He was used to being at home in the evenings alone, and it was amazing how another person, just being there, changed the feel of the room. The air seemed to smell sweeter and was warmer than usual in this case.

He noticed her breathing and was aware that her toes periodically slid on the cushion and up against the side of his thigh before she tucked her knees up again. But he was, surprisingly, able to concentrate. He got his Hays report done even while wondering about what she was planning, and noting that, according to the page-turning rate, she was a fast writer. He smiled to himself at that. Of course she was fast. Writing was a relatively quiet activity, but it still engaged her mind and emotions, and she would do whatever part of it she could . . . fast.

Her toes bumped against his leg again, and he took hold of her feet and settled them in his lap.

He glanced over and found her smiling at him.

"This is nice," she commented.

He didn't know about her, but *he* definitely wanted to kiss *her*.

"It is," he agreed.

But it made him nervous anyway. Because at age seventeen, sitting on the couch like this—on *this* couch like this—had bored her.

"What are you working on?" she asked.

"Just some plans for the training center."

She put down her notebook. "Already? That just came up."

"Jake and I have talked about it before," Max said. "And I've had some of these ideas for even longer."

"Did you know he was going to bring it up at the meeting?" she asked.

"No. But I wasn't surprised. Jake wants to move back."

Bree's eyes widened. "Really?"

"Yeah. Really." He was jealous of his cousin. Of both of them. They both had offers that would make it easy for them to move back and call Chance home again.

He had an offer, too. But nothing about it would be easy.

"So the center had nothing to do with you gushing to Ashley about me?" Bree asked.

Ah. She thought he'd set that up. Maybe to keep her in Chance. The idea that this could keep her here had occurred to him after the meeting. But he'd been a lot more focused on what that could mean for *her*—contentment, a rewarding job, a chance to feel needed and admired. In fact, her staying in Chance made his decision to move back more difficult for all the reasons he'd outlined the other night at A Bar.

"I didn't even realize how much I was talking about you to the university group until Ashley commented on how awesome you sounded," he said honestly. "It was all sincere, but unintentional gushing, I promise."

She considered that, then gave him a nod. "Okay. So what ideas do you have so far?"

He looked from her to the computer. "Just plans. For shelters and stuff. Boring stuff."

She leaned in, resting her elbows on her now-outstretched knees. "What is it with you and that word?"

He looked at her. "What word?" He knew exactly what word she was talking about.

"Bored. Boring. You got mad at me using it the other night. Now you're saying this would bore me. What's up with that?"

Well, she'd been honest about coming over here to see if she'd still want to kiss him. He could be honest about what he was thinking.

"Just remembering sitting on this couch with you one time when you told me you didn't want to date me because you were bored."

That surprised her. He could feel the increased tension. She tried to pull her feet out of his lap, but he hung on.

She stopped pulling and looked at him. She seemed to be considering what she was about to say. Finally, she wet her lips and said, "I was seventeen."

"And you were bored with me."

"With dating you, yes," she said honestly.

He nodded. "So you can see why this time I'm a little gun-shy."

"I was *seventeen*, Max," she said again. "I thought bad boys were exciting and that I was going to backpack across Europe by myself and then become a CIA agent."

"You're still the same person," he said, absently rubbing his thumb over the arch of her foot.

She moaned softly, and his body tightened. *Dammit.* She was *too* responsive. And he was too responsive to her responses.

She cleared her throat. "I am the same person."

"Which means you'll still be bored with this quiet on-the-couch stuff."

"I probably would be. If it was the same quiet on-the-couch stuff," she agreed.

"Like this."

She shook her head. "*Not* like this. You wanted to hold hands and watch romantic comedies and go to dances and pool parties. *You* were the one who changed when we tried dating, Max. I was the same girl. If you had wanted to go hiking or skiing or you'd wanted to watch horror movies or play poker with our friends or dance at a club or skinny-dip after sneaking into the pool after hours, I would have been all in. If you had wanted to keep doing the things we'd done before we became an 'official couple,' it would have been great."

"You always needed the thrill." He sighed. "I wanted to be the thing that thrilled you. Not what we were doing."

"What we were doing was partly thrilling for me because you were there."

"You don't have to—"

"Yes, it was," she insisted over the top of his words. "When I was six, I first climbed that huge tree down by the river. I climbed it because you were already at the top. The climb was exciting, the view at the top was awesome, but what I can *still* remember, twenty-three years later, was you encouraging me, and then the huge grin you gave me when I got to the top."

"Bree, I—"

"And when I was eight and got on that dirt bike the first time, do you know what I remember? Crashing and scraping up my leg, and you running over, grinning and telling me that I'd taken the fall like a pro."

"But I—"

"I was a freshman when I got the starting spot on the varsity volleyball team. I was trying to hold back and not make the other girls hate me, but you walked behind me while I was at the serving line in our first game and you said, 'Play ball, for fuck's sake.' Do you remember that?"

He nodded. She clearly was building up to a point.

"There are probably a thousand other examples over the years," Bree said.

"Examples of what?"

"You pushing me to go harder and faster and do more and . . . be myself. Do the things I loved full-out."

He nodded. "Of course. I always loved all of that about you."

She sat back. "Exactly. At least, that's what I thought. But then we started dating and you wanted to do all of this stuff that wasn't me. All I could think was that you liked me as a friend when I was myself, but to be your girlfriend, I had to be something else. Something softer and quieter."

Max's heart squeezed hard in his chest. He stared at her.

Fuck.

She *did* have a point.

He swallowed. "So you thought *I* was the one who didn't want you?"

"I just thought we were obviously happier as friends doing all the stuff we'd always done."

He pressed his thumb into her arch again, dragging it along the curve.

"Oh my God," she moaned, her notebook falling onto the cushion.

He stroked along her foot again, getting another moan and having to shift her feet away from his fly or give away how much he was enjoying those sounds.

"You paint your toenails?" he asked, noticing for the first time the deep-purple color.

Because of course it wouldn't be pink or red. She also had rings around her middle toes and pinkies.

She nodded. "Kit."

Of course. "Kit talked you into more girlie stuff?" he asked, wondering how Kit felt about lingerie, and then pushing that thought away.

"No, she made me fall in love with sandals, and then told me she wouldn't let me wear them unless I painted my toes."

Bree was more of a barefoot girl, but she'd spent plenty of time in tennis shoes and various types of boots. She was all about function and safety, and considering her hobbies, she understood good footwear was important.

He continued to rub her feet and grow even harder at the way she responded.

"Should have done more of *this* in high school," he said.

Her head had tipped back and her eyes had slid shut. "*This* would have made it really tough to dump you for sure."

His mouth quirked. He couldn't believe he was actually smiling about her calling him boring in high school, but now, he had to admit that he probably had been.

And he finally let the realization really sink in—Bree was the same girl she'd always been. The woman sitting with him now was not that different from the girl who had sat here with him easily a hundred times in his life.

She had always liked action and thrills and junk food. She'd always gone hard and fast. She'd always given her all to everything. And she'd always been hard to keep up with.

That thought made him pause.

Bree had just said that he'd pushed her to give her all to things. She was right. He had always encouraged her to be *her*. So why had he changed things up when they'd started dating in high school? Was it because he wanted the quiet nights at home and romance?

Or was it because he'd been intimidated by the idea of being compared to her older, more exciting boyfriends?

Yep. Definitely that.

So he'd gone the other way. Romance. Sweetness. Tradition.

He'd made up his mind that he wanted all that and that *she* didn't want him if she didn't want those things, too. When really, he'd just been afraid of not being enough for her.

His telescope hadn't been enough for her. Even getting and riding dirt bikes with her hadn't been enough—she'd always moved on to something else.

But she'd always wanted him there with her.

"I'm guessing you've gotten better at this since we were in high school, though," she said.

He pulled his thoughts back to the moment and looked over at her. "You think so?"

"I'm guessing you've had a lot of practice in the past twelve years."

He gentled his strokes and ran his hand up to her ankle, then her calf, before coming back to her foot.

"I've maybe done this a few times."

"So maybe it's a good thing that we're doing this now rather than back then," she said.

He thought about that. He couldn't imagine regretting having her in his bed, in his life more fully, over the past twelve years, but . . . she'd already had a few good points tonight. "Maybe."

"The past twelve years haven't been so bad, have they?" she asked.

Max shook his head. "Of course not."

She smiled, looking almost relieved. "You've gone off and done your thing in the big wide world, and now you won't be wondering 'What if' about all of that."

"You think I would have wondered?"

She laughed. "Max, you do amazing work that you love and are proud of. If you'd stayed here and gone into construction from the beginning, you would have missed out on all of that."

"I'd have a knee that worked right."

"Your knee makes you even more amazing."

He felt the grip on his heart again. "Yeah?"

"Of course. The things you do in spite of your knee. The things you were doing that led to the injury. Those are all amazing. Those are all such a part of you. They've made you an even better version of the guy I've always known."

They had never talked about his knee. Her comment at the school had startled him. But now, this seemed right. They weren't being flippant about it, but they weren't delving into all the gritty details, either. The details didn't matter anymore. Just the here and now. "It's kind of sexy, too, right?" he asked her. "The whole wounded-hero thing?"

She gave him a smile that lit up her whole face. "It's absolutely sexy."

He matched her smile. But he had to ask the next question. "Do you have any what-ifs?"

She hadn't been here permanently, but she hadn't really left, either. Not really. That thought struck him hard, too. She hadn't *really* ever left. Not in her heart. And not for good.

Consistent. Steady. In spite of her jumping around, seemingly changing her mind.

She shook her head. "Nah. The things I've always wanted to do, I've been doing. The Grand Canyon, my pilot's license, that stuff." She sighed and dropped her gaze to her toes. "I guess my goals and dreams were always about me, weren't they? Yours were about changing the world and helping other people. Mine were about doing stuff I liked that gave me a thrill."

He wasn't sure what to say to that. "A lot of yours were about your brother."

She took a deep breath. "Yeah. But really, I've just been trying not to sit still. I mean, I have no idea if Brice would have liked San Antonio or would have liked snorkeling. I've just been doing . . . everything I can. Trying to cover the bases."

Her words grabbed Max's heart and squeezed. She'd been jumping around, restless, because she didn't *really* know where to go or what to do. Just that she needed to *do* something.

"You're a cop," he said. "You keep people safe. You've jumped into this cleanup. You're trying to learn everything you can so that you can do the emergency-management stuff in the future. That's about helping other people."

"But it's all really fun, too."

He chuckled as he stroked over the top of her foot. "You know you can like it *and* help other people, right?"

"Well, I want to work on that." She looked up at him. "You make me want to be a better person."

If his heart kept squeezing like this, he might be in some cardiac trouble. "I do?"

"Yes. So tell me about your ideas for the training center."

"You really want to hear it?" He really wanted to tell her.

"Of course." She pulled her feet off his lap and swung them to the floor, facing his computer.

Well, there was only one way to find out if she was really interested in all this.

Max pulled up his various plans and sketches. He had a lot of them. He really had been thinking about a lot of this for a long time.

"Wow, you really love this stuff," she said after thirty minutes.

He gave her a sheepish smile. "I do."

She leaned in and put her hand on his leg. "It's sexy."

He snorted. "Uh-huh."

"It is. I love the look on your face when you talk about this stuff."

He looked down at her. "Oh, really?"

"Definitely. I love when you get into stuff. It's how you look when you're storm chasing, too. That's what made me want to learn more about it. That's what made me lie still for hours to get that photo for you."

Max couldn't resist then. He needed her. Just a taste. Or two.

He leaned in—just as the front door banged open.

"We're back!" Jodi Grady called, coming through the door.

"Max, come grab a box, son," Sam added, following his wife into the house.

Max sighed. "Of course." He gave Bree a smile. She winked at him.

He *almost* kissed her anyway. But he got to his feet and went to help his parents.

"What is all of this?" he asked as he grabbed a box from the porch.

"I'm making chicken and noodles," Jodi said, with more enthusiasm than chicken and noodles really warranted. Though hers was the best in the world.

"You're making chicken and noodles for the entire town?" Max asked, looking into the box he was carrying. There were cans and cans of chicken broth.

"Fifteen pans."

"Fifteen?" Max asked.

"Bree!" Jodi had just noticed her on the couch.

"Hi, Jodi."

"Girlie, it's so good to see you," Jodi said, clearly struggling with the fact that with her arms full she couldn't grab Bree and hug her.

"You, too. Need help with the chicken and noodles?"

"I would love that, honey. We can set up an assembly line."

Jodi continued on to the kitchen, and Bree got up off the couch and headed for the porch for another box.

Max felt a crazy sense of satisfaction watching his mom and Bree interact. Jodi and Bree had known each other all of Bree's life. Bree had been a regular feature in his house, in his family. They were completely comfortable together, and for some reason, today it felt so much better, and more important, than it ever had before.

He followed his mom into the kitchen and set the box on the table.

"Bree's here," Jodi said, pulling bags of chicken breasts from the box she'd put on the counter.

"Great," Sam said. He turned to his son from where he was unloading bags and bags of noodles. "So there is something going on with you two?"

"What do you mean?" Max asked, trepidation creeping up the back of his neck.

"Adam Franklin said something to Dave, who said something to Bob, who told me."

Adam Franklin had been at A Bar. Along with the rest of the town. The very small town that *loved* nothing better than juicy gossip.

"There is definitely something going on," Bree said, coming into the room. She gave Max a look that made his gut, and lower, tighten. "We just didn't expect everyone to figure it out before we did."

"Well, we're pretty bright. And have been right here watching for a long time," Jodi said.

Max's heart thumped hard, almost painfully. His mom and dad would love to have Bree in his life as more than his best friend. They'd love to have her in *their* lives. This was so dangerous. Anything he and Bree messed around with affected everyone they cared about.

Bree seemed oblivious to that fact as she laughed. "Oh, really?"

Sam grinned. "Looks like Max is the bright one, if you ask me," he said.

Bree gave him a sweet smile that made Max's heart thump again, but softer this time. She looked so genuinely happy. But a different happy than he was used to seeing. She was certainly happy white-water rafting and going full speed on her snowmobile. But this was a different look, a different kind of happiness. It almost seemed to come from someplace deeper. And it was because of the idea of being with *him*.

Max felt almost humbled by that.

"Well, thank you very much," Bree said to Sam.

"Us Grady men have amazing taste in women." Sam leaned over and kissed Jodi's temple.

"And amazingly big egos," Jodi added with a wink at Bree.

Max felt a warmth spread through his chest, and he took the chance to pull Bree up against his side and kiss her temple as well. "Can't argue. With either of those things," he said.

Bree leaned into him and wrapped an arm around his waist.

His parents smiled and went back to unpacking.

This felt good.

Probably too good.

Could this be real? Could this turn into something? No, not just *something* but *everything*?

Right on the heels of the warmth and softness he felt was a shiver of unease.

It all seemed wonderful and perfect. Bree here with him, happy to have a quiet evening together, then time with his parents who clearly loved Bree. And vice versa.

Perfect.

He was really skeptical of perfect.

Not because he didn't think perfect was attainable or because he didn't think he deserved it. He wasn't that guy.

It was because perfect was impossible to maintain.

Hell, that was why he'd stayed away from a full-time life in Chance for the past ten years. Because the perfection he attained with Bree on his trips home couldn't be maintained.

Or could it?

Had he been staying away because of Bree's restlessness, or because of *his* fears about not measuring up?

But now, tonight, he had to wonder if all that was just bullshit he'd told himself to make it easier to handle Bree not wanting to settle down with *him*.

He could maintain what was going on here. Sharing their work, spending time with friends and family. Hot sex in random places.

This wasn't like the women he dated in Oklahoma. If he broke up with them, no one in Max's life was affected. His parents hadn't met any of his girlfriends. He hadn't met any of their families. They rarely had friends in common. Max kept it all very private. He thought about that for a moment as his hand seemed to settle naturally on the curve of Bree's hip. He hadn't realized that before, but it was true. His relationships were about him and the woman he was involved with at the time. It wasn't an "It takes a village" kind of thing.

A real relationship was, though. The forever kind, anyway. It was a blending of families and friends. It was sharing everything, not just bodies and time.

Okay, so he'd done the intimacy thing one-on-one, but maybe true relationship intimacy meant bringing the woman into his *whole* life.

And that's where things were easy with Bree. And complicated.

The hard part should have been bringing a woman into his life. Incorporating her into the family, making sure his friends liked her, finding someone who supported his work.

The sex was easy.

With Bree it was the other way around.

Bree was already a huge part of his life. She was involved with his family and friends and hometown and memories and was supportive and interested in his work, even to the point of getting involved in it herself.

"Okay, so we've got three Crock-Pots, and then we can do some of it in the oven. Max, you're in charge of chicken. Bree, you do noodles. Sam, you're on broth. Ready?"

"Sure," Max said. "But why are you making enough chicken and noodles to feed a small country?"

Jodi laughed. "There are thirty families in town who have extra people living with them because their homes aren't livable. The rest of us are helping with meals and supplies. Having a whole other family move in with you means going through food and laundry detergent and toilet paper at double the rate."

Max nodded and felt a surge of pride for these two people he called his parents. They were good people. People he sincerely liked as well as loved.

"I'm totally ready to do noodles," Bree said, clapping her hands together. "As soon as you tell me what I'm supposed to do with them."

Jodi laughed and grabbed Bree's hand, pulling her up beside her. "Right here, honey. I'll show you."

Bree was someone he liked as well as loved, too.

Max felt such a sense of *rightness* watching the scene in front of him that he almost couldn't breathe.

"I know what you're thinking," Sam said to him quietly.

"You do?" Max asked. Somehow he believed that his dad knew how much Max wanted what was right in front of him.

"There is something very sexy about a woman and chicken and noodles."

Max rolled his eyes and laughed. He didn't want to talk to his dad about what was sexy or what wasn't. But Sam was right. "Let's just leave it at that."

Sam chuckled and clapped him on the shoulder. "We love Bree, Max. This is great."

Yeah, it was. It was really great.

And he needed to get her in his bed as soon as possible.

Not in a ditch, not against a wall in a locker room. His *bed*. Or better yet, *her* bed. So that every time she got between the sheets, she thought of him, and so that when he made love to her for the first time and truly made her give him *everything*, it was in the most intimate place in her life.

Max shook that off for the time being and got ready to help his mother feed half the town. He and his parents and the woman he loved would pull together to help their town, and their friends and neighbors, because that's who they all were.

And *then* he was going to show Bree McDermott that she was going to give him the rest of who she was.

◆　◆　◆

Two hours later, Bree washed her hands, dried them on Jodi Grady's dish towel, and looked out the kitchen window.

And had a hard time taking a deep breath.

She'd washed her hands, gotten drinks of water, rinsed plates, and cleaned bloody scrapes in that sink. The plastic stool in the cupboard under the sink that she'd used to reach the faucet when she was little was still there.

She felt completely at home in this kitchen. She knew the glasses were in the cupboard above the countertop where they piled their mail. She knew the silverware was in the drawer next to the refrigerator. She knew the peanut butter was in the corner cabinet above the coffeepot. But the coffee grounds were in the cupboard above the stove—for some reason.

Moving around the kitchen, cooking and talking and laughing with Max's family, felt very comfortable. And it made her heart race in a new way. In a way she thought Maggie Norman would appreciate. Like the times her beloved husband had made her heart thump just by playing with their kids or fixing the leaky bathroom sink. Being a part of tonight with Max and his parents had felt like a comfortable old pillow she would always want to come home to.

She could absolutely see herself here helping with food for holidays and birthday celebrations, Sunday dinners and football Saturdays.

She could see herself making coffee and sitting at the table with Jodi as they frosted Christmas cookies. She could see herself convincing Sam he wanted one more piece of pie. She could see herself pulling out that plastic stool and helping little kids up on it to wash their hands and fill glasses of water.

That was the part that made it especially hard to breathe.

Those kids wouldn't be Max's nieces and nephews. He didn't have any siblings.

If there were little kids in this kitchen, they would be his.

If she were helping with them, they would also be—

"Bree?"

She spun away from the sink, sucking in a deep breath. "Hey."

Max had been in the living room having coffee with his parents a minute ago. Bree had come into the kitchen to refill her cup.

He gave her a funny look. "You okay?"

"Yes, of course. Definitely. No problem at all."

He was clearly suspicious of that. "You sure?"

"Yes. I'm completely fine."

She really was. What was *wrong* with thinking about family dinners and Christmas cookies? Nothing. It was all nice stuff. Fine stuff.

Of course there was the small issue of the kids and the plastic stool.

Kids were really long term. Marriage and family—that was big stuff. That was not stuff that she could get bored with and move on from.

"I was hoping I could take you home."

Oh boy. His words sent a shiver down her spine. There was promise in his eyes. *Promise.* Not lust, not heat, not desire.

A lot more than that.

And the shiver was part want and part worry.

"I'm good. I'm fine," she said, waving her hand in a no-big-deal gesture. "I'm going to head out now. Big day tomorrow."

She started to skirt around him, but Max grabbed her arm before she got past him.

"Bree."

She took a deep breath and risked looking up into his eyes. "Tonight was so great."

"It was," he agreed. "I want it to be even better."

She swallowed. This was Max. She had to be honest. "I know you do. And I'm not sure I can do that. Tonight. Right now."

"You're feeling it, too."

"What?"

He gave her a look. "You're feeling it, too."

Finally, she nodded. "Yeah. I am." She was feeling every bit of how *right* this was, how much hope and happiness was in the air, how *big* this was, how . . . permanent.

She wanted Max. She wanted the mind-blowing physical stuff, the rush he gave her, and the amazing friendship she'd always had plus all the new things—the working together, the quiet nights on the couch, the way her heart flipped when he walked into a room. But tonight she'd finally understood that to have it all, she had to *give* it all.

"Okay, I'm going to let you go home and feel it by yourself tonight. But I'm not going to keep letting you go. You need to know that."

The shiver that followed was a lot more want than worry.

She nodded. "Thanks."

"I will see you tomorrow." There was a lot of promise in that, too.

He leaned in, kissed her temple, and let her go.

Bree escaped before he changed his mind. There was still the throw-you-over-my-shoulder thing he'd threatened . . . that she kind of wanted to see.

She said good night to Jodi and Sam and made it to her house and into her bathtub with a bottle of beer before she let herself think anymore.

But once she'd sunk into the warm, bubbly water—one of her very rare feminine-pampering-girlie indulgences—she couldn't *stop* thinking.

Max.

Max's family. Max's family home. *Their* hometown.

God, it had felt so *good* over there tonight.

It had been dangerous going over there. Bree had known that. She'd known spending a quiet night, a normal night, with Max would very likely result in deepening their relationship, moving it on to whatever was next.

But whether it was the addition of his parents or the noodles or just him—as in "It would have happened anyway"—this had turned out a lot more dangerous than she'd expected.

She sank down deeper in the bubbles.

And the most dangerous part was yet to come.

Max wanted the intimacy. Sure, part of that was sitting on the couch together and making dinner together and talking about their work. All of that had been surprisingly easy to give him.

The next part she wasn't so sure about.

He wanted sexual intimacy. He might pull out the silk ties and the blindfold—her heart sped up slightly at that thought—but she knew it would be a lot more than sexy or exciting or hot. It would be . . . the end of their relationship as they knew it.

Was she ready for that?

Max had always been there. He was, as she'd told Kit, comfortable and easy for her. But as her thoughts spun, she had to admit there was a lot more steady and comfortable in her life than she usually realized. Her parents had lived in the same house all her life. She'd been filling up her gas tank and buying gummy bears and licorice at the same convenience store. The grocery store specifically stocked her brand of ice cream because she bought so much of it and had for so long. She ordered the same thing at the diner every time she went in. She listened to the same radio station in her patrol car every day.

She was a lot more stable and set than she gave herself credit for.

Than Max gave her credit for.

Bree sat up quickly in the tub, water sloshing up against the side.

Max was wrong.

He was wrong about her not being able to decide what she wanted, and he was definitely wrong about her not being able to fall in love.

She stood up swiftly, water and bubbles sluicing down her body, and grabbed for her towel. Then she noticed the still-full beer bottle next to the sink.

She didn't need it. She knew it wouldn't help her restlessness. It wouldn't—couldn't—give her the rush she was seeking. The rush she'd been looking for since even before the tornado. But just like the tornado that had taken Dorothy to Oz, Bree had landed in a new world after the one that had hit Chance. A new world where she'd figured out that what she'd always wanted had been right in front of her the whole time.

Bree took the bottle and turned it over in the sink, watching the amber liquid foam and swirl as it ran down the drain.

CHAPTER TEN

Ten minutes later, Bree was climbing up the tall oak outside Max's childhood bedroom window.

She'd done this about two million times in her life as well.

It was almost midnight, and the house was dark. Bree had dressed for the climb in jeans and T-shirt and her best tennis shoes. She knew exactly which branches to put her weight on and which ones to avoid.

She'd fallen out of this tree only once in her life.

She climbed out onto the roof outside his window and crawled up the slight incline. She knocked softly. His bed used to be right inside the window, so she didn't have to knock hard.

The window slid up a moment later.

"Really?" he asked, his voice gruff from being awakened.

He didn't sound irritated, though. He sounded really sexy.

The tree blocked some of the light from the streetlight at the curb, but it was very clear that he was wearing only boxers.

She smiled. "I forgot to tell you something."

"And you had to climb on my roof to tell me?"

She nodded. "Yep. Needed to tell you in person."

"You could have called me to come over to your house," he said, his voice dropping a little lower. "I would have been there in two minutes."

"We have history in this house, at this window," she told him. "I was really overcome by that tonight. I guess it felt right to tell you this here instead of at my place where we have a lot fewer memories."

Max braced his hands on the windowsill, his triceps bunching and making her tingle. "Okay, what did you have to tell me?"

"That I definitely *did* still want to kiss you tonight. Even with no drama or danger around."

He just watched her, his eyes roaming over her face.

She smiled softly. "Just sitting with you and planning, talking about the training center, cooking and laughing with your parents—that all made me want to kiss you even more than any of the other times." She swallowed when he still didn't say anything. "And I thought you should know."

He didn't respond right away. He looked at her for a long moment. Then, hands still on the windowsill, he leaned closer. "Show me."

Her heart thumped in her chest, and the heat and tingles that had shown up the moment he opened the window intensified.

She shifted to her knees, took his face in her hands, and kissed him.

Max kissed her back, his lips moving against hers, his tongue meeting her strokes, but otherwise his hands and body stayed still.

Bree felt like everything inside of her was lighting up. She was turned on and happy and relieved and hopeful. If she could have a fun day working with Max, followed by a quiet, easy night, and end it with a kiss like this, then she was right where she needed to be. Maybe they could even throw in some hot, hard sex in a random place in the middle of the day once in a while.

She pulled back after several minutes, her lips tingling. She smiled at him. "How was that?"

"It was a good start."

"What do you—"

A moment later, his big hands grabbed her around the waist and pulled her through the window.

It turned out that his bed was still right by the window.

He tumbled her onto it and followed her down, bracing himself on his elbows on either side of her shoulders.

"I'm guessing we're going to do this your way now?" she asked breathlessly from her back.

"Damn right we are."

He kissed her again. The pure *need* in it made her entire body go hot and melty.

He lifted his head and said gruffly, "Tell me you didn't climb that tree and sneak in my window to have sex with me while my parents are just down the hall because it's a bigger thrill than inviting me over to your place."

She shook her head. "I didn't come over here for sex at all." But she made no move to get up or push him back. "I realized I hadn't kissed you good night, and I really wanted you to know that I wanted to." She put her hand against his face. "You were the one who pulled me through the window."

"It was what you said about our history in this house."

"Yeah?"

"I thought I wanted to make love to you for the first time in your bed, so you'd think of me every night, but I realized that making love to you *here*, where I've dreamed about you so often, is even better."

Her heart swelled. "You've dreamed about me?"

He leaned in and kissed her. A soft, sweet kiss unlike any of the others. "So often."

"Like naughty dreams when you were a teenager?" she asked, arching up against him and feeling clearly that he was as turned on as she was. And they weren't even naked yet or talking dirty or touching other than his body stretched out over hers.

"Yes," he admitted with a half smile. "And plenty of them as an adult, too."

"Really?" She liked that. Until she'd kissed him in the ditch, she hadn't thought of him that way, but she could admit now it was probably because she hadn't let herself. She'd known it would complicate things.

Which it would. It was.

But she was ready for the complications now.

And maybe the tornado was a part of that. Maybe putting things back together, turning things right side up again, was making her realize the things she liked the way they'd always been and the things she could change and rearrange.

"Really," Max said. "And I've had some nice dreams, too."

"Daydreams or actual night dreams?" she asked.

"Both."

"What were the dreams?" She wanted to know this. Badly. She was quite sure that no man had ever *dreamed* about her before. The guys she dated were just . . . guys she dated. And she was just a girl they dated. They did the stuff people did when they were dating, but now, in this moment with Max, Bree thought it was very possible that few of them thought about her much when she wasn't with them.

And dreams were a whole other level.

"Us traveling—sometimes trips we'd already taken, sometimes ones we haven't yet. Us doing things like tonight with my mom and dad."

"Really?" That was hard to grasp. That she'd seeped into his subconscious like that. And she liked the "ones we haven't yet." That sounded very present, and very much like that was going to be a part of her future.

Even thinking about the word *future* made her shiver with pleasure.

"I would love to make some of those dreams come true," she said, not even sure where those words had come from. That was so not a typical thing for her to say.

Max's eyes flickered with emotions. "Oh, you're going to," he said huskily. "*We're* going to."

Damn, another delicious shiver. The type that usually happened because of a touch or a dirty suggestion, not from something so sweet.

She wrapped her arms around his neck, wanting to absorb it all. She loved these rushes of pleasure she got from the nice things like watching him with his mom, or hearing that note in his voice when he talked about his work, or the way he smiled at her that seemed different from the way he looked at and smiled at everyone else in the world. Even the people he loved. He talked to his parents and Jake and Dillon differently, with an affection that was clear. But he had a special look for her.

And it had always been there.

That wasn't new. That wasn't just since the tornado.

A thought occurred to her, and it sent a definite thrill through her—Max loved her.

Not loved her like a friend or even like the men he was like a brother to, but *loved* her. The love that was unlike any other, the one-and-only kind.

The thrill of that realization was stronger than the one she'd felt when she was at the top of a ramp about to fly down on her dirt bike, stronger than the one she'd felt going up and over the waves the one time she'd tried to surf.

And maybe the best part? She could keep on feeling this. This rush wouldn't go away after the weekend ski trip was over or after the storm passed. This rush would come every time he smiled at her, every time he called, every time she listened to him get impassioned about his work or laugh with his dad.

She could have this every single day, always.

"Kiss me," she said to him. "Please, kiss me."

"Once I start, I'm not stopping for a very, very long time."

She felt her heart flip over at that. "Good."

So he did. He kissed her; he pressed his body against hers; he stroked her tongue with his; he ran a hand along her side, squeezing her hip and then taking her thigh and lifting it so her leg was wrapped around him and he could press against the soft, sweet spot that was aching for him.

He lifted his head after several long minutes of simple making out.

"This is going to be different from the locker room," he said.

She knew that. She already felt it. Nodding, she said, "I know."

"And tomorrow is going to be different because of it."

She smiled and nodded again. "I know."

He held her gaze for a moment. Then he said, "No holding back."

She wasn't sure what that meant, but if he meant he wanted her to beg and whimper and let go when her orgasm threatened . . . she was all in on that. "Okay."

He pushed back and got up onto his knees. "Need to see you. All of you."

He reached over and turned on the lamp on the bedside table.

Oh, lights on. Okay. Well, this was already new. She liked sex in the dark.

But as her eyes settled on Max's body, still clad in only boxer shorts that did little to hide his huge erection, she had to admit that lights-on had its advantages.

"Take your clothes off, Bree," he said, settling back on his heels. "Slowly."

A striptease. Okay. New, but not bad.

She reached for the bottom of her shirt, her heart suddenly pounding. She knew that Max would demand the intimacy he'd been so clear about the other night. She'd known this would be different from how it was with other guys.

But she was still nervous.

Bree pulled her shirt up and over her head, tossing it to the side.

She looked at Max watching her.

The heat in his eyes was enough to make her bones melt, but there was something else—that affection or pride or whatever she saw so often.

That was enough to make her *heart* melt. Yes, this was going to be different, maybe a little scary, maybe even difficult, but this man had been beside her on every snowy hilltop, rushing river, and airplane doorway. This was Max. He might be the one pushing her, but he'd also be the one making sure she was safe.

"God, you're beautiful," he said, a roughness to his voice that sent goose bumps skittering everywhere.

"You've seen this much of my skin before, in swimsuits and stuff," she said.

"This is different," he said. "You've never been spread out on my bed, mine to touch and kiss and lick."

The goose bumps got goose bumps.

He ran his hand over her stomach, almost reverently. Then he slid it up between her breasts, over one shoulder, and down her arm. He cupped one breast, his thumb rubbing over her nipple through the silk.

Goose bumps and then some.

"Take it off," he said.

"You could take it off me."

"Yes, I could." He lifted his gaze to hers again. "But I want *you* baring yourself to me. Deliberately. Aware of me the entire time you're taking it off."

Bree wet her lips. This already felt so much more intense than any sex before. That had been mostly stripping quickly in the dark, doing it hard and fast. Then pulling things back on shortly after it was over.

She had a feeling she was going to be *very* bare with Max. Because there was definitely more to stripping down than taking off clothes.

She reached behind her for the clasp and unhooked it, sliding her bra down her arms slowly. Her nerve endings jumped with electricity just from the very purposeful removal, and she marveled that Max knew all of this.

"You're good at this." Her voice was breathless.

"Am I?"

"You know you are."

"What do you mean?" he asked, running his big, hot hand back and forth over her stomach.

"You've had a lot of practice."

He shook his head. "Not like this, Bree. Never like this."

She really wanted that to be true.

She laughed lightly and knew it sounded nervous. "You don't even have the blindfold out yet."

"Don't want that with you. Not this time." He slid a hand up and cupped her breast again, this time without any barrier.

Without any barrier. That was a pretty good description for all of this.

"Why not?" she asked, just before sucking in a quick breath as he thumbed her nipple, making her entire body clench.

"Just having you here, willingly climbing in my window and taking off your clothes, that's all I need."

"What do you usually need?" she asked, sensing something underneath his words.

"To prove myself," he said. "That *I* can do it all for them."

She rolled her head on the pillow. "Never mind, I don't want to talk about this." Max and the other women he'd bedded? Yeah, not her favorite topic.

"*I* want to talk about this." His hand slid down to her hip, and he just held her, waiting for her to look at him.

She sighed. The talking. That was also new. The guys she was used to didn't stay perfectly silent, but there definitely wasn't talk about intense feelings. "Oh, baby, that's so good" was about as involved as it got.

"Fine."

He gave her a smile that said he knew she was uncomfortable. There was a challenge to it. Like the time she'd almost chickened out at eighteen thousand feet on their highest skydiving jump.

"You need to know this," he said. "I *liked* them. We had some emotional connection. The intimacy beforehand made the physical better—but mostly for them. I couldn't get as emotionally connected as they could."

"You wanted them to all fall in love with you," she said.

He didn't deny it right away. And then he gave a slight nod. "Maybe a little."

"And you didn't want to fall in love with them."

He sighed. "Actually, I'd been hoping one of them would really get to me and make me fall head over heels," he said. "But it hasn't happened."

Her eyes widened. "So essentially, you've been going around being this romantic, amazing guy, getting these women emotionally connected to you, not because you fall for them but because your ego needs *them* to all fall for *you*?"

"*A little,*" he reiterated.

She rolled her eyes now. "So maybe they don't want to have your babies and spend their lives with you, but they're pretty hung up on you."

He gave a slight grimace. "Maybe a little."

"Max!" She swatted at his hand. "Why do you do that to them?"

He looked directly at her and sighed again. "Because of you."

"Me?"

"Because I wasn't able to get you to fall in love with me. I had to prove that I could make someone fall."

"Oh, for God's sake!" she exclaimed. "We were teenagers. That was forever ago."

"We weren't teenagers in Breckenridge, Bree."

She stopped. Then slowly nodded. "I know."

"That was—not a great trip for me."

"I panicked."

"I know."

"I shouldn't have."

He shook his head. "You weren't ready. But that was worse for me, because we'd been seeing each other all that time, and you hadn't fallen for me."

She wet her lips, reluctant to say what first came to mind. Then she did anyway. "You're sure about that?"

"I'm sure things are changing," he said without blinking.

"So the emotional stuff is pretty one-sided with them."

"I *like* them. I don't take every woman I meet to bed. I don't take a different woman to bed every week. I date these women and like them and enjoy them."

"Max, are you trying to get me to fall in love with you so that you can get some kind of revenge for me *not* falling in high school?"

"Or for the past twelve years," he reminded her.

"Right. For all of that. Is that what all of this has been? You showing me I was wrong?"

"That would make sense," he said, as if he hadn't thought of that.

Her heart twinged a little. "It would, I guess."

"But no, that's not it."

She blew out a breath.

"Because this isn't about me only doing things for you," he said. "It's about me *getting* some things, too."

"Are we talking about blow jobs here?" she asked, hopeful and trying to lighten the moment.

He didn't even smile. "That's not what I'm talking about."

Of course not. She was sure he got plenty of those anyway.

"So these women don't give you what you need?" Beyond the obvious blow jobs, of course.

"No."

"But you think I can?"

"I think you're the only one who can."

That made her toes curl. She was absolutely sure that had never happened before.

"So what do you want from me?" she asked softly.

"Everything."

She'd been afraid he was going to say that.

"You know I'm not very good at that."

He cocked an eyebrow. "At giving everything you've got to something? No, Bree, I don't know that. I know that you go all in, that when you're in a moment, that's all that exists. *That's* what I want—to be that moment where you're fully there and there's nothing else that matters."

She swallowed hard. Damn, this intense side of Max was still rattling her.

"You didn't want that from any of them?"

"Oh, I got that from them."

Cocky. She'd known he had that side, but she'd never seen it in regard to women. It was kind of hot.

"But it didn't matter enough?"

"It *couldn't* matter enough."

"Why?" she asked softly.

"Because they're not you."

Her heart slammed against her ribs, and she stared at him. "Seriously?" Her voice was suddenly scratchy.

"Seriously."

They stared at each other for five hard thumps of her heart.

"Toss your bra," he finally said.

The command was soft but firm.

So she did. It landed on the opposite side of the bed from her shirt.

He ran his hands all over her again, taking extra time on her nipples with his fingers and tongue, until she was writhing.

"Keep going," he said huskily after a few minutes. He sat back to watch.

Breathing hard, her hands shaking, Bree wiggled out of her jeans.

He caressed her from head to toe, kissing several spots in between as well, before telling her to toss the panties, too.

She did.

His hands returned, this time turning her into a quivering mass of jelly. Except she was hot jelly. Sweet and sticky and . . . yeah. Hot jelly. That was a good analogy.

But he wouldn't use his mouth and tongue.

"Max," she begged softly. "Please, more."

"Show me," he said gruffly.

"Show you what?"

He leaned back. "Show me what you want."

She pointed. "Your mouth right there."

His mouth curved up into a sexy smile that made her want those lips on her body even more.

"*Show* me."

"I don't—"

He put one of her hands on her breast and the other between her legs.

"You know what I want, Bree."

Yeah, she did.

Intimate. *Dang.* He kept using that word, and it was *really* accurate right now. She had never touched herself like this in front of another human being. And certainly not spread out with the lights on and him with a front-row-and-center view of it all.

"Show me the most personal thing you do. Show me this moment when you truly, fully let go."

She wasn't real big on being this personal and vulnerable. In fact, she hated it. But then there was the gravelly tone in his voice and the heat in his eyes, and she thought that maybe, just maybe, she didn't *hate* it, hate it. The way he was looking at her, what he was asking, made her feel shaky, like she couldn't catch her breath. But it also made her feel energized and tingly, like she was about to go over a waterfall in a tiny raft. She felt a bit of fear, a bit of "I can't do this," along with a lot bigger surge of "I can't *not* do this."

She wanted an adrenaline rush.

She just hadn't realized she could get the mother lode with Max and a mattress. And not a parachute in sight.

So she did what he asked. She touched herself. She let herself fall into the sensations that were heightened by his soft, sexy coaching, the look in his eyes, the way his body seemed to vibrate with the same energy she was feeling.

Bree went up and over the peak faster than she ever had by herself, and before she'd come all the way down, Max said, "My turn."

And he took it. He sent her flying within minutes of putting his hands and his mouth—finally—on her.

Then he rolled her onto her stomach and proceeded to kiss and caress every inch of her on that side as well.

When he turned her over again, she was completely relaxed and pliant. But when she looked up into his eyes, her heart and stomach and *soul* flipped. There had never been an adrenaline rush equal to what she felt right then.

He definitely loved her. She could see it in his eyes. And considering she'd never seen that in a man's eyes before, it was pretty remarkable she understood what she was looking at now.

But she did.

"Now?" she asked with a smile that she hoped conveyed even half of what she was feeling.

"Now." He eased into her, his eyes locked on hers.

Somewhere along the way, he'd taken off his boxers and had put on a condom. Probably while she'd been floating in the I-never-knew-it-could-be-like-this fog. Then again, she was still floating in that fog.

Max began a slow, easy motion, and Bree arched her neck, letting her eyes slide shut. She didn't usually like it slow and easy. She wasn't patient; she didn't like taking her time or waiting. But this . . . rushing *this* would be a crime. She didn't want to speed past any of it for fear of missing a second of goodness.

Bree wrapped her arms and legs around him, holding him close, breathing deep, downright wallowing in the whole thing.

Until he said, "Open your eyes, Bree."

She did.

He was looking at her with love and desire, but also with a confidence that made her heart pound. Max was looking at her as if this was exactly where he'd always wanted to be.

Max had loved her for a long time. She realized that now. He'd known how he'd felt about her since he was seventeen. Maybe before that. She had only realized it a few days ago. It felt good and right . . . so right. But it was new.

She had never been in love before.

She didn't know how to do it, if she was good at it, if she'd still feel this way a year from now.

"Hey, stay with me," he told her, his voice low and sexy as he stroked in and out of her body. "Eyes on me."

She did what he asked, keeping her eyes on his, losing herself in the sensations, the way he filled her and made her nerve endings sing and dance. She concentrated on everything physical—the weight of him, the bunching of his back muscles under her hands, the heat and scent of his skin. But the emotional stuff kept sneaking in. The way he'd always been there for her. The way he laughed. The way he gave his cousins shit but would beat someone else who did the same. The way he made her feel funny and brave and interesting.

The way he went all in with her. For her.

Max would have never jumped out of a plane if it wasn't for her. But when that was what she wanted to do, he'd been right beside her, giving her that grin.

He was all in here, too, she could sense it. From this moment, it was all about forever for Max.

What if she'd just asked him to take the one jump that could really hurt him?

She squeezed her eyes shut.

"Oh, no. Come on, Bree. You and me."

Her eyes opened, and he picked up his rhythm, thrusting harder, and in spite of the jumble of emotions in her chest, the rest of her body responded.

God, he felt good. He moved just right. He *was* just right.

She wanted to be good for him. The best for him.

She moved against him, running her hands over his back, grasping his ass, lifting her hips for his thrusts.

Soon she felt her inner muscles tightening, and she heard Max's answering groan. She arched, her fingers digging into his back, and just as he thrust a final time, her third orgasm of the night rolled over her. This one slower and deeper and longer.

The ripples hadn't even fully faded when Max took a huge shuddering breath and rolled to his side.

He stretched out his bad knee with a little groan.

Her chest tightened. "Are you okay?"

He turned his head and grinned. "Totally worth it."

Yeah. Worth it. Worth the little bit of panic there. Worth having to work hard to figure out this love thing. Because she wanted it. She wanted him. She wanted to be what he wanted.

For a flicker of a moment, she again remembered him saying that she couldn't be what he wanted. But he'd said it was because she couldn't do the intimacy thing. Well, she had just proven she could. To both of them.

In a contented, sleepy voice, one that Bree wanted to hear over and over and over, Max said, "Stay."

She looked over at him. She wanted to. "Yeah?"

He nodded and draped an arm over her stomach. "Yeah. Mom said something about cinnamon rolls in the morning."

Bree laughed. "I'm not having cinnamon rolls with your parents in the morning."

"Why not?"

She gave him a *Seriously?* look. "That's more or less announcing our engagement, isn't it? My coming downstairs in the morning for breakfast with your parents after spending the night in your childhood bedroom? We might as well go pick out china."

"We just took everything to the next level," he said, clearly undeterred by her words or her sarcasm. "What did you think would happen?"

She wanted to protest. She wanted to say he was pushing, he was moving too fast, he was jumping to conclusions. But she liked things fast. So she took a deep breath, tipped her head back, and admitted, "This."

"Exactly."

It was just like Max to be completely sure of her. Even before *she* was sure of her.

"Now go to sleep," he said softly, spreading his fingers out wide on her stomach, hot and heavy. And perfect.

She lay staring at the ceiling, debating slipping out after he'd fallen asleep.

But she kind of wanted to have cinnamon rolls in the morning with Jodi and Sam.

That was a risk. A big one. It was one thing to move forward with Max. It was another to bring everyone they cared about along with them.

Still, bottom line, she was a risk taker.

And in the morning, when she protested again and tried to slip out the window, Max carried through on one of his threats—he threw her over his shoulder and carried her downstairs to breakfast.

CHAPTER ELEVEN

Max Grady was a tough guy. He worked hard, he played hard, he demanded a lot from himself and the people he worked with, and he could drink and swear like a trucker. He had calluses on his hands, he could build anything, could use any tool there was. And, yeah, he liked to be in charge in the bedroom.

But apparently, when he was in love, he glowed.

Or so his smart-ass cousins informed him with glee every time they saw him in the week following Bree sneaking into his bedroom window.

And he didn't care a bit. He was *wallowing* in it. That glow was because Bree was fully his now. She was beside him at work every day, her gummy bears and laughter and eagerness to learn making this easily his favorite job ever. Not to mention that he could now not only ogle her sweet ass in her jeans, but he could now touch it whenever he wanted.

Life was good. She was with him at the dinner table, whether hers, his mother's, or the diner's, every evening. And she was in his bed every night.

"Hey, watch it! I need both of my thumbs!" Dillon groused as Max ran the power saw a little close to one of Dillon's hands.

"Relax, Doc," Max said. "I'm not going to risk Kit's wrath."

Dillon didn't rise to the bait. He simply turned the board he was holding for Jake to nail into place.

"You know, because if you lost fingers, she'd be annoyed with me," Max pressed. "Because she *likes* your fingers. Because of what you *do* with them."

Dillon said nothing.

Jake laughed. "Aw, leave poor Dillon alone. You know what it's like to be sexually frustrated."

Max pretended to think about that. "No. Can't say that I recall what that's like."

"You've been with Bree for, like, three days," Dillon finally snapped.

"Seven. But she's ruined me for all other women," Max said smugly. "Jake knows what I mean, don't you?"

Jake nodded sagely. "I most definitely do. Give in to the inevitable, D," he told Dillon. "Look what it's done for Max and me."

"No sense fighting destiny," Max agreed. He certainly wasn't the only one glowing. Jake was quite happy having his hands full with Avery. Literally.

"If Kit Derby is my destiny, I'm going to—"

Max cut off Dillon with the loud whining of the saw. He sliced through the piece of plywood smoothly, then shut the saw off again.

"Don't say things you don't mean," he told Dillon. "Because Jake and I *will* remember them and *will* repeat them at some inappropriate time when she's around."

Dillon glared at him. But didn't say anything else. Which Max and Jake both thought was hilarious.

Looking at Jake and recognizing the happiness in his cousin's eyes, the more relaxed set of his shoulders, the smile that came a little easier, warmed Max. Jake was a great guy, and he deserved a woman who made him look like that.

They nailed the last board into place and stood back to admire the eight makeshift benches they'd made to surround the fire pit in the town square.

"How many more?" Jake asked.

"People can take turns if that's not enough," Dillon said.

"What's wrong, Doc?" Max asked. "You got a blister?"

Dillon flipped him off with a finger that didn't seem injured in any way.

Max just laughed. "We have enough wood and stuff for four more." The benches would hold three or four people each as they roasted their marshmallows for the s'mores that were being provided later that night.

It was one more party in a week of parties that had started three nights ago when Boy Scouts from several towns in the county had arrived and asked if they could help out. The scout troops set up tents in the square and planned to stay for the duration of the cleanup. Other volunteers had joined them, and Max, Dillon, and Jake had gone door-to-door gathering burgers, hot dogs, buns, chips, and other supplies to provide them with dinner. The food, laughter, and light-hearted air had drawn more people, and the impromptu barbecue had turned into a relaxing, fun social time that the people of Chance truly needed.

So, the next night, Dillon had come up with the idea of projecting a movie on the side of city hall and serving popcorn. The party had grown from the night before, with several more volunteers and Chance natives joining them in the square.

Last night, a couple of local teens had volunteered to play DJ while the grocery and convenience stores got together to donate ice cream and root beer for floats, and the party had grown even more.

Tonight they were having s'mores, and someone had brought over a karaoke machine. Max, Jake, and Dillon were happy to pitch in however they could. They'd enjoyed the burgers, root beer floats, and, most important, the feeling of goodwill the parties were inspiring. Things were going well, and they were no longer concerned about the Bronson-family visit on Saturday. Everyone deserved to celebrate how much they'd accomplished and to have a chance to blow off some steam.

But Max and Jake *did* find it interesting that Dillon was heading up these party efforts. Jovial socializing in large groups wasn't really Dillon's thing, and Max and Jake had speculated that Kit's influence might be behind Dillon's concern for the mental health of the people involved with the cleanup efforts.

And if making some quick wooden benches helped get his cousin laid by the prim and proper Dr. Derby, Max was all for helping out. Dillon was an intensely intelligent guy who had never let a rule stand in his way of doing what needed to be done, and Max figured he could be as good for the calm, cool good girl as she could be for him.

"Hey, guys."

At the greeting, every nerve ending in Max's body sat up and started wriggling like a puppy whose favorite person had just come home. He turned to face Bree. "Hey, babe."

Her grin grew, and Max realized he was relieved she wasn't reacting negatively to the "babe." When was he going to stop wondering if he was pushing too hard and too fast? This was what he wanted. She knew that. She knew where he was coming from. And she was still in his bed, in his life, every day. This was happening. He had to trust it.

Besides, he'd decided he was going to go for what he wanted. He wanted to come home; he wanted to settle down. If this was too fast or too much for Bree, then he needed to know sooner rather than later.

But some of that was just tough talk. He wanted to come home and settle down. But mostly he wanted *Bree*.

"Kit said there would be s'mores tonight," Bree said.

Max angled a glance at Dillon. So Kit *was* behind some of this. Or at least Dillon was keeping her in the know. Interesting. Was badass Dillon trying to impress a girl? Or was he her muscle, carrying out her wishes and whims? Either way, it was definitely interesting.

"And karaoke," Max affirmed.

"Dang. Was hoping for more charades," Bree said. "I kick ass at charades." Which she had, indeed, proven last night. She linked her arm through his and grinned up at him. "I guess we could go to my house and play dirty charades, just the two of us. I kick even more ass at that."

Max felt hot blood rush south even as his heart swelled at her flirtation in front of Jake and Dillon. The last three nights she'd been right beside him, whispering in his ear, running her hand up and down his arm, linking her fingers with his, all as if they'd been doing it for years. He'd loved every second.

"There's always dirty karaoke," Jake said with a chuckle.

Bree laughed. "That would go over so well in the middle of the town square with the Boy Scout troops all over." She squeezed Max's biceps. "But I would definitely rock dirty karaoke."

Max's body tightened.

He wasn't an idiot—dirty charades and dirty karaoke, especially a private show of both, sounded like a hell of a good time.

But there was a bit of trepidation that wiggled through his gut. It was stupid, but part of him just couldn't let go of the idea that Bree doing regular things like a regular couple meant more than her playing dirty charades. Bree was definitely a dirty-charades kind of girl. No doubt. She was not really a regular-charades girl. So the night before, playing charades with their friends, had meant a lot to him. It had been exactly what he'd been looking for all the times he'd tried the romantic, typical-couple thing with other women. Except that this time it was *right*. It had never been right before. Because it had never been with Bree.

But how did a sane, heterosexual man who got turned on just *thinking* about her say no to her offer? Especially in front of the two men who wouldn't hesitate to harass him relentlessly for turning her down?

"I was thinking—"

"Max!" A booming voice interrupted, and Max sighed with relief.

Relief that was short-lived when Max realized it was Roger Swanson coming toward him.

"Hey, Roger," Max greeted as his pulse began to hammer. Yesterday, he and Roger had outlined the details of a deal for Max to buy Roger's construction business. Roger had wanted to run it past his lawyer and talk to the bank.

"It's a go," Roger said enthusiastically. "Everyone's thrilled."

Max's heart flipped even as he felt Bree shift to look up at him.

"What's a go?" she asked.

"Max!"

Max turned to find his parents heading toward him now. "Hi, Mom. Dad."

"Roger just told us."

Jodi grabbed him and pulled him into a hug, and Max felt Bree slip away from him.

"I'm so excited, honey," Jodi said, pulling back and smiling widely, her eyes sparkling with tears. "I know you probably wanted to tell us, but I couldn't be happier."

"Such great news," Sam agreed, thumping Max on the back. "Good move, son. Good move."

"What's going on?" Jake asked, looking from one person to another.

Max searched for Bree and found her standing behind Roger, looking confused. No, not confused. Worried.

The sliver of unease grew in his gut.

"Max bought the business from me," Roger said with a wide grin. "Well, we haven't signed the papers, but everything is a go. I'm retiring the first of the month, and Max will move up here and take over."

"Awesome." Jake pulled Max into a one-armed hug. "Happy for you, man."

Max hadn't taken his eyes off Bree. She was biting her bottom lip and watching everything unfold, detached from the group and, Max feared, detached from the excitement of the news.

But she'd known he was thinking about buying the business. She'd heard Jake's proposal for the training center. She'd heard Max himself say how much he wanted to come home. She couldn't be shocked.

And no, he had to admit she didn't look shocked. She just looked concerned.

That pissed him off.

So they'd only started sleeping together and admitting they had feelings that went beyond their longtime friendship a few days ago. This was still nothing to be *concerned* about. Bree McDermott could do anything she set her mind to. Challenges fired her up, fed her soul. This was not a concern; it was a challenge. And she would rise to it.

But it also bugged him that *he* was a little concerned.

"It's going to be great to be home," Dillon said, also pulling Max into a brief hug.

It was. It was going to be *great*.

"We need to celebrate!" Jodi exclaimed. "Dinner at our house? Roger, you and Sue need to come. And Jake and Dillon—I want you to invite your parents. Does tonight work? Or should we do this weekend?"

Max moved through the little crowd, letting them work on the plans for dinner. He took Bree's arm and steered her away from the group.

Once they were at the gazebo, he turned her so her back was against the wooden slats and moved so she was boxed in. "What's going on?"

"Really?" she asked, eyes wide.

"I was going to tell you. Things weren't finalized, and I had no idea Roger would get everything done today."

"I'm just . . ." She trailed off and lifted her shoulder. "It's really real. Just letting that sink in."

"That we can have what we've had for the past week all the time now?" he asked, unable to help the frown he felt pulling his brows together.

It would be okay. It had to be okay.

The past week had been exactly what he wanted. Forever. Her in his life. Seeing her during the day, spending time together with friends and family, curling up on the couch together to watch *The Late Show* while sharing a bowl of Sweet Cream Dream, then going to bed to make love until they fell asleep wrapped around each other. A normal, happy life.

She nodded. "You'll be here all the time now. For real."

Max leaned in, bracing a hand on the wooden railing just above her head. "Don't freak out on me. You can do this."

Bree pulled her bottom lip between her teeth and nodded again.

"You can, Bree. I know long term is new for you, but I need you to face this the way you've faced every other challenge—straight on. You just need to dive in and know I'm here beside you."

"You're not scared?" she asked him softly.

He considered that as he looked into the blue eyes he wanted to be gazing into on his hundredth birthday.

Was he scared? Definitely. In part because he was putting everything on the line and trusting that Bree would still want what they'd had for the past week fifty years from now.

But there was more. Something bigger.

The past week had been comfortable and easy. Things had been his way. Everything had been his way since he'd pulled her through his bedroom window.

Because he was afraid to do things her way.

It was like high school all over again, and that irritated the ever-living hell out of him. He'd never been truly afraid. Not in basic training, not during Katrina, not during rehab, not in the path of an EF4 tornado.

But this woman, and what she could do to him, scared him.

"Yes," he admitted. "Sometimes the stuff we've done together has hurt. But," he added before she could respond, "I bailed out of that first airplane because of the look on *your* face. Because I love being a part of that thrill and that happiness for you. And believe it or not," he said, cupping her face in his hand and brushing his thumb over her bottom lip, "you've had that same look this past week."

This might be pushing. But he didn't care. He'd been clinging to this. And he needed her to acknowledge it.

She swallowed hard. Then said, "I know."

"Do you? You know that you've looked as happy this week as I've ever seen you? As happy as when you're flying down a mountain or flying through the air?" Doing things his way.

Bree didn't even blink. "Yeah, I do know that."

"And do you have any idea what that does to me?" he asked her, his voice suddenly gruff. Seeing her happy, knowing *he* was the reason, had made this the best week of his life. Better than the Grand Canyon week. Hands down.

She put her hand against his cheek and rubbed over the day's worth of stubble. "I know what it does to you, because seeing you that way does the same thing to me."

Max's heart turned over. "So you know this is going to be the greatest adventure we've been on together?"

Her lips finally curved up into a small smile. "Yeah, I know that, too."

The knot in his gut eased. He leaned in and kissed her. When he lifted his head, he said, "Dinner with everyone tonight to celebrate?"

Her gaze jumped to the group over his shoulder. "Any way we could celebrate just us tonight?" she asked. "Big dinner tomorrow?"

"Yes," he said without hesitation. "Just us tonight." Bree to himself, doing the couple thing, would always be his pick.

"Okay. I'll see you at my place later? When you're done with everything?"

"Definitely."

She gave him another quick kiss on the lips and then ducked under his arm.

He caught her wrist and pulled her back to face him. "How about dirty charades?" Maybe they could celebrate Bree-style this time.

She gave him a smile that went straight to his heart. "Something better."

Max watched her go, love and hope filling his chest. But he couldn't shake the damned sense of worry. And guilt.

She was letting him do this all his way, too. But her words from the other night, about him wanting to change her, nagged at him. Had he really wanted that? Maybe. But how could he want it now? Bree was . . . Bree. The only woman he'd ever loved. He had to let her be her.

There was no parachute here.

He never jumped without a parachute. No wonder he was twitchy.

He blew out a breath. *Fuck.*

"Let's go, lover boy!" Dillon yelled. "I'll put you on graham-cracker duty tonight if you don't get over here and help finish these benches."

Max turned. His parents and Roger had dispersed, and Jake and Dillon were starting on the last four benches. Max strode toward them, more than ready to be finished now. He was almost afraid to give Bree too much time alone to think about the huge life change coming her way. She was more a seat-of-her-pants kind of girl. Which had been part of the reason he'd been waiting to tell her until everything was finalized. Hell, he'd considered saving the news until he had all his furniture in the back of a moving truck sitting in her driveway. Spontaneous. That was the way to go. She was planning on celebrating together later on, but he thought showing up unexpectedly early was definitely a better idea. Surprise was a good thing with Bree.

"You're just jealous that I got some time with my girl," he told Dillon, shaking off the feeling that reminded him a lot of how his gut felt when a storm was pending.

Dillon scowled. "I don't have a girl."

"Even more reason for you to be a grumpy pain in the ass." Max got back to work, sawing and hammering more quickly than he had before.

Forty-five minutes later, all the benches were done. Max had his tools packed up and was headed for his truck.

"Hey, where are you going?" Jake called.

Max glanced back. "Bree's."

"Great, let's go." Dillon started toward him.

"You're not coming," Max told him.

"You're going to bring everything back? I figured you'd want to stay once you got there." Dillon looked very put-upon as he said it.

Max frowned. "I am going to stay. What is everything?"

Dillon looked irritated. "Kit texted me and said that all the supplies for the s'mores are at Bree's. Evidently, Bree called and told her she wasn't going to make it to the party tonight." Dillon gave Max a "This is your fault" look. "So she asked if I could go grab the stuff."

"And you're going to do it?" Max asked, amused by Dillon jumping at Kit's command.

"What's the point of irritating her?"

It seemed to Max that there had been *years* where Dillon hadn't minded irritating Kit a bit. In fact, he'd seemed to thrive on it.

"Fine. Let's go." Max tossed his toolbox into the back of his truck. "But bring your truck. I'm not leaving for a while."

"Yeah, yeah, life is perfect, you're in love, whatever," Dillon muttered as he rounded the front of Max's truck and walked to his, which was parked right behind Max's.

Jake came jogging over. "I'll help."

"Help with what?" Max asked.

"Whatever you guys are going to do," Jake said with a grin.

Max pointed a thumb at Dillon's truck. "You're with him."

Bree only lived three blocks from the square. Dillon pulled into the driveway behind Max a few minutes later.

Max strode toward the front door. "You're in and you're out," he told them as Jake and Dillon got out of the truck and followed him up the path.

"We don't want to be rude," Jake said. "If she invites us in—"

"You say no." Max ground his teeth. He was already worried about Bree's state of mind. Or maybe it was *his* state of mind that had him concerned. And now he had these two jackasses with him.

Jake seemed completely unfazed.

Max rang the doorbell.

And that irritated him, too.

He wanted to be able to just walk into her house.

Hell, he wanted it to be *his* house, too.

"It's open!" Max heard Bree call through the door.

He turned the knob and pushed the door open.

"Hi! I was hoping you'd—" Bree stopped midsentence, her eyes widening as she looked at Jake and Dillon.

Max was positive Jake and Dillon had no idea what her eyes were doing, however.

Bree stood just inside the door in cutoff denim shorts, holding two bowls of ice cream in front of her breasts. Which was fortunate, considering they were bare.

If she'd been a cup size bigger, the bowls wouldn't have kept her decent.

Hell, if she'd used less whipped cream on the top of the sundaes, she wouldn't have been decent.

She shook her head and carefully kept the bowls exactly where they were. "I just got everything ready and was going to text you," she said, as if she weren't half-naked. "I'm glad you came over early." She wet her lips and crossed one bare foot over the other.

"Yep, I could go for some ice cream," Jake said.

Max didn't even have to look at him to know he was grinning widely.

"Definitely," Dillon agreed.

"Leave," Max growled.

"But that is *a lot* of . . . ice cream for just one guy," Jake teased.

He was on edge, his woman was half-naked in front of his cousins, and he was done messing around. Max leaned in from the porch, grabbed the door, and shut it with a slam, blocking their view of Bree.

"Son of a bitch." He pushed a hand through his hair.

"Oh, relax. We didn't really see anything," Jake said.

"We've seen her in bikinis before," Dillon added. "That's kind of the same thing as what we just saw."

"It's not that." Max knew every bit of his irritation was showing.

"Still need the marshmallows and stuff," Dillon said, not at all apologetic about what had just happened.

"I'll get them. Just give me a fucking minute," Max said, pacing to the railing and blowing out a breath. He was torn right down the middle—he wanted to head straight inside and throw Bree over his shoulder and not stop till he got to her bedroom. He also wanted to walk down the porch steps, get in his truck, and drive his ass right back to Oklahoma.

"What is your problem?" Dillon asked.

When Max glanced at him, Dillon didn't look worried. He looked suspicious.

"The hot fudge and whipped cream," Max said. He was aware he was about to sound like an idiot. But if he could make Dillon and Jake understand what he was thinking and feeling, there was a chance that it made some sense.

"You're mad that she had ice cream sundaes ready for you?" Dillon asked with an expression that clearly said that was the stupidest thing he'd ever heard.

Max shook his head and turned slowly to face Dillon and Jake. He settled his butt against the porch railing and crossed his arms. "She's bored. Already."

Jake's expression went from confused to concerned. "What do you mean?"

"We've been having ice cream every night together for the past week. Just ice cream. Sweet Cream Dream. Our favorite."

Dillon spread his feet apart and crossed his arms. "And?"

"I've loved it. It's been enough. It's been perfect. But now she wants whipped cream and hot fudge."

"Okay," Dillon said, clearly not getting it.

"I'm Sweet Cream Dream to her," Max said. "Not hot fudge. I don't know if I can really be hot fudge. Or if I want to be."

Dillon's forehead creased. "What the hell are you talking about?"

"People have high expectations for hot fudge. People expect hot fudge to be amazing. Every time."

"Max," Dillon said calmly, "you sound like an idiot."

Yeah, he knew that.

"It's hot fudge," Dillon went on. "That's it."

But it wasn't.

"It's an analogy," Max said, shifting on the railing because he was uncomfortable with how pathetic he was about to sound.

"Go on," Jake encouraged.

"When I first told her why I didn't want to get involved, I used her ice cream habit as the example as to why. She can't eat the same kind over and over. And a long-term relationship is just like that—the same thing over and over."

Dillon gave him a nod that made Max think maybe he didn't sound completely nuts.

"So we've been eating the same ice cream together every night since we decided we're more than friends."

"And she knows that this is somehow acting as proof of her commitment to you?" Dillon asked.

Max nodded, ignoring Dillon's clear skepticism. "I'm sure she does."

The carton of Sweet Cream Dream on her countertop that first night when *she* had offered him ice cream while they watched TV had been significant.

"And now that she came to the door with ice cream to celebrate you staying . . . how is this a bad thing?" Jake asked.

"Hot fudge," Max said simply. "And whipped cream, nuts, cherries. God knows what else."

"Yeah, she might even have *sprinkles* in there," Dillon said drily. "What a bitch."

Max scowled at him. "It's an *analogy*."

"Right." Dillon didn't roll his eyes, but it was definitely implied.

"She's bored with the same old thing already. She's adding extra stuff now that she knows I'm staying and she'll be getting the same thing over and over forever."

Max felt a coldness in his chest that had nothing to do with ice cream.

"Come on, Max," Jake said. "You're overthinking *ice cream*. If you're afraid of boring her, the solution is pretty simple. Don't be boring."

Max frowned at him. "Thanks, Dr. Phil."

Jake shook his head. "Seriously, man. If she wants hot fudge, give her hot fudge. Hell, throw in some caramel sauce once in a while. Or go really wild and get *chocolate* sprinkles."

"It's a fucking *analogy*!" Max bellowed.

"I know," Jake said, undeterred by Max's annoyance. "So was mine. What I'm *saying* is, she clearly wants to do the things she does with *you*. So do them the way she likes them. If you think she might need to mix things up, take her on a new trip or buy her a new bike or get her a herd of alpacas."

Max's eyebrows went up.

"Alpacas?" Dillon asked.

"It would change things up," Jake pointed out.

"That it would," Dillon agreed. "So, alpacas hang out in herds? Are you sure they aren't flocks? Like sheep?"

"I don't know. We should Google that—" Jake reached for his phone.

"*Okay*," Max interrupted. "I've got it."

Jake leveled him with a look. "Do you?"

Max continued to frown at them both. But, yeah, he couldn't quite blow off what Jake had said.

"She hangs out between your visits, just waiting for you to come back," Jake said. "She never skydives or flies or skis or dives with anyone else. And she's never been serious about another guy. *You're* her guy, the one who matters, the one she wants to be with."

"When she's jumping out of an airplane, maybe," Max argued.

"For Bree, that's the biggest, most important, most exciting and fun thing she does," Dillon said. "And she only wants to do it with *you*."

Max shook his head slowly, but he couldn't deny there was a little piece of his mind—or maybe it was his heart—that had to admit they had a point.

"She was—*is*—fuck, I don't know—*was* planning to go to Arizona to teach skydiving," he said. "Then she'd be skydiving with lots of people other than me."

Dillon frowned. "Well, she hasn't left yet. She's here, Max. In my experience, Bree goes when she wants to go."

"She can't. She finally has a job where she has to give notice, and the new job doesn't start for a while."

"Yeah, well, she doesn't act like a woman who wants to teach skydiving in Arizona," Dillon said.

No. She was acting like a woman who was getting bored with her relationship in Chance. "I can't leave her alone, but I can't *make* her want what I want," Max said. "And I don't know for sure that I can be what she wants—"

"You're right. The ice cream *is* an analogy."

The guys all swung toward where Bree was once again framed in the doorway. She'd set down the ice cream and pulled on a shirt, though.

Max's heart felt like it hit the floor at her words. He'd known it. She wanted to change things up. Now that she knew he'd be here for good, she needed to.

Bree stepped onto the porch in her bare feet, carrying a cardboard box. "Here's the stuff for Kit," she said to Dillon, handing over the box of graham crackers, marshmallows, and chocolate bars.

"Thanks," Dillon said.

"Now, if you guys will excuse us, Max and I need to talk."

And suddenly he didn't want Jake and Dillon to go. Max started to tell them that, but they were already down the porch steps and across the grass.

Dammit.

He turned to face her and drew a long breath. God, she was beautiful.

At the moment, she also looked vulnerable. Something he'd noticed more and more since he'd been home this time. He kind of hated that. It was a softer side of her, and he would have thought that he'd like that. But it wasn't *her*. Bree was confident and kick-ass and sure of herself.

And right now she looked very *un*sure. Of him.

That hit him hard. Of all the things he'd seen on this woman's face, that had *never* been one of them. She trusted him. She knew he loved her and was there for her. Feeling unsure and vulnerable because of him was not acceptable.

That was all it took for him to realize what had to happen.

As Dillon's truck doors slammed, Bree turned on her heel and headed into the house. Max followed reluctantly. He kicked the door shut behind him as Bree stopped next to the couch and faced him.

"You're wrong about me, Max."

"Am I?"

She crossed her arms. "Yes."

"I'm wrong that you've realized that Sweet Cream Dream isn't what you want every single night?" he asked. He tucked his hands in his pockets. He wanted to reach for her, but if he did, he wasn't letting go. And they needed to work some things out before he held on to her forever.

"I've realized that I've always been that way." She similarly tucked her hands into the back pockets of her shorts. "And that you've loved me anyway. All along."

Max had a hard time swallowing for a moment. "Yes, I have," he finally admitted.

"So, this—" She gestured to include the coffee table where the bowls of ice cream, hot fudge, whipped cream, nuts, and cherries sat. "This is who I am."

"I know," he said, his heart thundering. "You just can't do it entirely without the hot fudge," he added. He knew she would know *it* wasn't ice cream. But *hot fudge* wasn't really hot fudge, either.

"Sometimes plain is going to be just fine," she said. "But yeah, sometimes I want hot fudge."

"Okay."

She dropped her arms, evidently surprised he wasn't arguing with her. "So—"

"I'm going back to Oklahoma."

Bree stopped, her mouth open.

He nodded at the question he saw in her eyes. "I want everything you can give, Bree," he said, his voice suddenly gravelly. "And I've realized that you *have* been giving me that. Everything you're able. More than to any other guy. And that matters to me. I get it. If it's once a month for a few days at a time for the rest of my life, that's better than not at all. And it's better than being here every day and watching you try to change to be what I want. You deserve to have this your way, too. I want you just the way you are. And the best way for us to be together is how we always have been together. That's been working for more than a decade."

Bree was staring at him. "Are you *serious*?"

He nodded.

"You would go back to Oklahoma. Give up the business and your family and friends and hometown to keep things status quo between us?"

Max spread his arms. He hated it, but yeah, he would keep the status quo. Because the status quo meant he wouldn't have to give her up—or have her give him up. "I'll be your Sweet Cream Dream when you want that. And when you're in the mood for Cappuccino Crusade or whatever the hell, I'll . . ."

She took a step forward, frowning as he trailed off. "You'll what?"

Max ran a hand over his face. "Probably get rip-roaring drunk."

He focused on her again and she frowned. "What are you talking about?"

"When you're ready to have pizza in front of a Netflix marathon of *Chuck* or you need a New Year's Eve date or you want to play charades with our friends, I'll be there."

"I'm guessing you're talking about regular charades, not dirty?"

"Yeah. Regular charades."

"And who will I be playing dirty charades with?" she asked, studying his face.

That was something he didn't want to think about. "I guess whoever is your . . . Peppermint Passion."

Her face hardened slightly. "So whoever is my flavor of the week?"

He gave her a nod. "Guess so."

"That's what you think is happening? That I pulled out the hot fudge because I'm tired of Sweet Cream Dream?"

"Isn't it?"

Her eyes narrowed. "What if it is? Your pretty little wife and the mother of your fourteen children and your three dogs and four cats isn't going to like you hanging with me for *Chuck* and New Year's Eve."

Max's stomach tightened. There was no way in hell he was going to have a wife or a mother of his children if it wasn't the woman standing in front of him right now. The reality of that sank in fast. "Guess my bachelorhood is pretty confirmed, isn't it?"

Suddenly her mouth dropped open, and she pulled her hands from her pockets. "You would give up all of that? No white picket fence or babies or dogs?"

"Of course I would." Fuck, how did she not know this?

But *he* hadn't really known it—or at least, hadn't admitted it to himself—until he'd stepped into that room and realized that he wanted Bree, in any way, in any amount he could have her.

She stared at him. "Are you *kidding me* right now?"

He frowned. "What?"

"You can't give all of that up, Max!" she exclaimed.

"Look," he said firmly, "I'm in love with you. I'm not going to marry someone else just so I can have kids and dogs. Hell, I can get a dog anyway. But I want *you*, and if it's once a month like it's always been, then it's once a month."

"That's not fair. You deserve to be happy and have everything you want," she argued. "You're amazing. You make so many lives better; you deserve to have the life *you* want, too."

He took the three steps that separated them and put his hand against her face. "You," he said simply. "*You* are what I want."

"But—"

"You're a force of nature, Bree McDermott. I've always known that. And I should have realized this sooner—storms that stir things up as much as you do, maybe they're only meant to be chased, not caught." He brushed his thumb over her jaw. "And God knows I do love the chase."

She sucked in a quick breath, and her eyes filled. "Max—"

Suddenly a piercing beeping split the air.

Max tensed. It was the weather alert on his phone from the service he and most other storm chasers subscribed to. "Dammit," he breathed out, dropping his hand from Bree's face.

He held her gaze as he pulled out his phone, but then he looked down. He frowned.

"What is it?"

"Thunderstorm headed this way. It's gained strength since the earlier watch was released," he told her. "It was supposed to just be rain, but it's got more power now. High winds. Possible hail. Lightning."

Bree knew what that alert meant for him, so he pocketed the phone and stepped back. "I need to go."

"I'm coming."

"You don't—" But he broke off at the look she gave him. She was coming with him.

"And this conversation isn't over," she added as she turned toward her kitchen. She grabbed a pair of jeans from the basket on the table, quickly shed her shorts, and pulled on the longer pants.

Pending storm or not, nothing could have kept Max's body from tightening at the sight of Bree in her skimpy blue panties.

"By the way, the monthly visits and the weeklong trips," he said as she came back toward him. "Those are definitely going to include sex now, though."

She didn't smile. And she didn't agree. "This isn't over."

But as Max followed her to his truck, he had the definite heavy feeling that *something* was over. And he was pretty sure it was his happily ever after.

CHAPTER TWELVE

"The winds are picking up. Possible hail. Lightning," he said to Jake, his first phone call from the road. Max was practically shouting over the rushing of the wind through his truck window. "We're under a tornado watch, too."

"Watch your asses!" Bree heard Jake shout into the phone.

"Always," Max told him, then disconnected and dialed again. "Storm's coming," he told whomever answered. "We're in a watch, too."

She assumed it was Dillon. Max was one of the first to be notified of a storm because of his storm-chasing network, and he would then pass on the information to those who needed to know. No one worried until Max told them to. And half the time he was the first one to get on the network and initiate the alerts. He typically had his eye on the radar early on.

Of course, today he'd been distracted by telling her he'd rather have Oklahoma than whipped cream and hot fudge.

Bree had thought he would get that the hot fudge was all the stuff that had happened since he'd been home this time—the sweet, hot goodness on top of what they already had.

Clearly she needed to work on her romantic gestures. She'd been cocky after the lightning photograph had gone over so well.

Bree focused on the angry gray sky rather than on her own churning emotions. The clouds were dark, rain imminent, but she could tell they were headed into a thunderstorm, not a tornado. The clouds were churning but not twisting, and, even more, the feel to the air was different.

She might have chuckled at that or shared it with Max, but she was angry. Or maybe it was hurt. Or both. She'd never been truly angry with Max before. Frustrated, exasperated, maybe slightly irritated. But not angry. And never hurt. Max would never do anything to hurt her.

But now that she was in love with him, he was going back to Oklahoma.

Yeah, that hurt.

"Think we're good out here," he said.

It took her a second to realize he was talking to her and not into the phone. "Yeah?"

"There's gonna be a lot of rain—"

A loud clap of lighting cut him off, and as if on cue, the skies opened up. Water poured from the clouds, quickly soaking the gravel road they were on.

"As I was saying," he continued drily, putting both hands on the wheel, "it's going to rain like hell. But I'm not worried about a twister."

"Yeah, I don't feel it either," she said, wondering how he could be scared off by whipped cream. Who didn't want to incorporate whipped cream into sex? Wasn't that kind of a staple? She'd never used it with anyone before, but with Max—oh yeah, she could totally see it being amazing.

"You don't?"

She looked over, realizing he was watching her. She shook her head. "The formations don't look ominous and—"

"You said you *felt* it," he interrupted. His eyes were back on the road, but she could tell his full attention was on her.

Bree wet her lips. "Fine. Yes. This time it feels different than the tornado did. It's more"—she paused, trying to think of the right word—"electric in the air. Last time it was heavy and . . ." She trailed off again, knowing what she'd been about to say sounded silly.

"What? It was heavy and what?" he asked.

"I could feel the twisting," she said. "Like the air was twisting around me. This time doesn't feel like that."

She looked over after three or four seconds of no response. He met her eyes and nodded. "Yeah. That. That's not here this time."

"You know what I mean, then?" she asked.

"Yeah." He looked back to the road, his jaw clenched, gripping the wheel.

She frowned. "What?"

"Nothing."

They turned off the gravel and onto the highway that would take them past Montgomery Farms and back to town.

"Max? What?"

He cleared his throat and shifted on the seat. "It's nothing."

She turned on her seat and gave him a frown. "And, yes, in case you're thinking back to that time when the air was twisting and we were huddled up in a ditch, I *do* want you right now, just as much. No, more. I want you even more now because these past two weeks have been amazing and have showed me what we could have, and it's *everything!*"

Max squeezed the steering wheel and muttered, "Dammit, Bree."

"Dammit, *Bree*?" she asked. "Really? *You're* the one making this difficult! Who gets scared off by whipped cream?"

He scowled at the road. "That is not what happened."

"It *is*," she insisted. "You thought I was trying to spice things up because I was already tired of the same old thing. And you know what?

For about five seconds, I let myself wonder the same thing. You know me best, after all. Why *wouldn't* I believe that's what was going on? But then I remembered that you *don't* know everything about me."

"Stop it." He gave her a stern look. "You're getting all wound up because—"

"Stop telling me what I'm feeling and why I'm feeling it!" she shouted.

He pressed down harder on the gas and clenched the wheel.

"You know the eight-year-old me and the twelve-year-old me and the seventeen-year-old me. Better than anyone. Probably even *me*. You know the adventurous me. But when we were eighteen. you *left*, Max. And it doesn't matter why," she added when he started to reply. "You left, you stopped living here and seeing me every day, and that means that you don't know the twenty-nine-year-old me like you did the eight-year-old me. You don't know the everyday me. You've seen me jumping out of airplanes and diving off boats, but you haven't seen me during a normal workday, or having my regular girls' night out, or my regular meal at the diner, or my regular brunch with my parents on Sundays when they're in town. You haven't seen that I run the same route every time I go running or that my playlist on my iPhone is the same when I go to the shooting range. See, Max, there is *a lot* of *regular* stuff in my life. You just don't know it because you *left*. And up until now, I've been letting you tell me who I am, based on the little bit you see, but not anymore. *I* know me, better than anyone."

All at once, Max cranked the wheel and pulled into a narrow dirt drive that led to the back of a farmhouse. Gigi's farmhouse. They were on the west corner of Montgomery Farms. Gigi's house was about fifty yards away, and the many buildings that occupied the south end of the farm where the entrance was were just beyond that. To the north was the orchard, and stretching out for acres to the east were the pumpkin, strawberry, and watermelon patches.

The farm was getting soaked, and for a brief moment, Bree was thankful the crew had gotten the shingling done on the barn roof that morning.

Then Max jerked her attention back to him when he jammed the truck into park and turned to her.

"Bree." His voice was gruff and his expression pained. "I never meant . . ." But he trailed off.

"Yes, you did," she said, her voice quieter and calmer now. "You did mean to know me best. You wanted to believe that. You wanted to think we were still that close."

He pulled in a long breath. "Yes."

"Well, it doesn't work that way," she told him. "You have to *be here* if you want to be close to me. And you have to quit telling me that I can't commit, because I believed you. But it's not true."

"I just want—"

"I'm going to tell you what *I* want," she interrupted.

She thrust a photograph at him and jabbed it with her finger. "This. This is what I want."

Max looked down.

"That's Maggie," she said, studying the photo as Max did. "Someone brought her scrapbook to me this morning. They found it in the middle of the park and wanted to know if I could get it to her. She told me some stuff the other day when I was with her, and I couldn't help but look through it."

"Stuff like what?" Max asked.

"Stuff about excitement and adventure and . . . life."

She handed him another photo. She'd grabbed these specifically so she could show him and tell him all of this. "This is her traveling through Europe when she was eighteen. See how happy and excited she looks?"

Max nodded.

"I know that look," Bree said. "I've had that look myself a ton of times."

He nodded again. "I know. I love that look on you."

"That's the kind of look I've seen on my brother's face in so many of the pictures we have of him," she said, emotions tightening her throat. "He was an adventurer. A dreamer. But he only got eleven years. He didn't get to see Europe or the Grand Canyon or go skiing. But he explored and played and got excited about learning and trying new things. That look has always been in my mind. I've worked to have that look because I thought that was how to honor him."

Max just swallowed hard at that.

"But this—" She put the first photo back on top. "*This* is what I want for me—and for everyone I love. It's definitely what I would want for Brice if he were still here."

The photo was of Maggie and Gene surrounded by all their children and grandchildren on the front porch of their home with a **HAPPY 50TH ANNIVERSARY** banner over their heads.

She couldn't wait to return the photos to Maggie, but she couldn't help but think that she'd been meant to see them first. At least she was grateful she had. And maybe even to the tornado that had blown it into the park but hadn't damaged it in any way.

"Do you see how happy she looks in both photos?" Bree asked.

Max nodded.

"But do you see how they're different? The first, in Europe, is excited happy. I've had a lot of that. But it comes and goes. That kind of excitement fades over time. This—" She pointed to the family photo. "That's deep, lasting happiness. It's softer, and it gets stronger over time."

Then, as if Mother Nature needed to protect her badass reputation, a powerful *boom* exploded overhead, rattling the truck, and a moment later a bright flash of electricity arced from the sky. There was a loud *crack*, and Bree and Max looked at each other.

"It hit something," she said unnecessarily.

"Yeah," Max agreed.

He looked torn. They weren't done talking, but there was stuff happening outside of the truck that couldn't wait.

"I just—"

He was interrupted again by something hitting the windshield with a big *thunk*.

It was a shingle.

Bree's eyes flew to the main barn just behind Gigi's house, the roof visible over the top of the house. There was a bright blue tarp now flapping in the wind, and as she watched, the wind wrenched another new shingle off the roof and blew it across the yard.

"Son of a bitch." Max threw the truck into drive and barreled down the sloppy mud path.

He drove straight across Gigi's back and side lawn, narrowly missing a garden gnome and a patio chair. He stomped on the brakes in front of the barn.

Bree was already out the door by the time he'd killed the engine. She ran to the barn doors and yanked one open, slipping inside.

It only took a second to realize they had a big problem. It not only sounded like someone had left the bathtub faucet running, but it also *looked* like it. There was a hole in the roof, and water was pouring into the barn. It was the same patch she and Max had inspected the first day here, so for the time being, the water was hitting the loft area. But the supplies that had been re-stored up there were getting wet, and if the rain continued as it was supposed to, the water would eventually seep over the side and run onto the floor in the main part of the barn. One of the first places the Bronsons would want to see tomorrow on their visit.

"Fuck!" Max exclaimed from behind her.

"We have to get up there," she said, starting around him.

He grabbed her upper arm. "We're not going up there. We'll catch the rain in something down here."

"What are you going to haul up to the loft that's big enough? And how are you going to empty it when it fills up before it runs over?" she asked.

He had no answer. She pulled away from his hold. "I have to go up."

"You're not climbing around on a slippery, wet roof in this wind by yourself," he said.

"Then you'd better come with me." Bree made it to the door and out to the truck before he caught her again.

They were both soaked by the time she got to the bottom of the scaffolding that the roofers had been using.

"This is stupid," he said, looking up.

"We can't let the barn get flooded," Bree said. "Besides, I'm the best climber in town, and I have something that guarantees I'll be okay."

"Yeah, what's that?" he asked as he grabbed the bottom railing.

She gave him a smile. "You. I never do exciting, stupid things without you beside me, and they always turn out great."

"Stupid?" he asked. "At least you have climbing gear or a parachute during those times."

She nodded. "But there's always a risk. That's what makes it fun."

He groaned loud enough that she could hear it even over the rain.

Bree turned and put a foot up on the lowest metal pole. "I know how you like when I go up first," she told him over her shoulder. "But watch your step. It's a little slick."

He swatted her ass. "Get moving."

Bree hurried up the scaffolding, feeling Max moving behind her.

At the top, she started to stand but quickly realized the surface was far too slippery for that. She dropped to her hands and knees and crawled toward the flapping blue tarp and the hole.

"Fucking sonofabitch," Max said behind her a moment later.

She looked back. He was likewise crawling on all fours, but he winced when he put his weight on his bad knee.

"I'm going to chew someone's ass so hard," he said as he inspected the area. "What the fuck were they doing?"

"It looks like the shingles that are blowing off were just on those stacks?" Bree asked, pointing to several short columns of remaining shingles. "They weren't attached?"

"Apparently not," Max said grimly. "They covered the opening with the tarp and held it down with the shingles they hadn't used yet. Maybe they had to stop because of the rain, but they were supposed to have this done hours ago."

"But they didn't think about the wind taking the shingles?" Bree asked.

Max wiped a hand over his face. "I guess. Let's just get the tarp back in place. We can't get the shingles on in this."

Bree studied the flapping tarp. It was at least ten by ten and was a thicker plastic than the one Max had in his truck. It was being held in place by only one corner and was flapping in the wind and slapping against the roof with loud smacks. "Okay, great idea."

Max crawled over to her. "I'll steady you. You stretch up and grab for it."

He put his big hands on her hips, and she instantly felt more secure. Still, the moment she got to her feet, the wind hit her directly in the chest, and she wobbled.

"I've got you," Max said over the noise of the storm. "Stretch."

She leaned, letting Max do most of the work of holding her up, and reached. She caught the edge of the tarp, but the slippery plastic quickly slid out of her fingers. She put one foot forward and leaned farther, gritting her teeth. This time she grabbed it in her full fist and pulled it down to where Max could get a grip on it as well. He held the edge of the tarp with one hand and her with the other.

The wind whirled around them, and the raindrops pelted them, making it difficult to see. Bree felt the storm pulling at the tarp, and she grabbed it with her other hand. So did Max. He let go of her completely to fight the tug-of-war with the wind, and Bree felt herself pitch forward. She landed on her knees on top of the tarp.

"Jesus, Bree, are you okay?" he yelled over the wind.

"Yeah. I'm okay." Bruised, but still on the roof, so she was fine. It was hard to remember that she didn't have gear on. She wasn't afraid of heights and didn't worry much about falling when she was up above the earth, but that was because she had ropes and hooks and parachutes.

"We have to secure it somehow!" he yelled.

Exactly. And half the shingles were scattered across Gigi's lawn.

They both looked around, but there was nothing else left up on the roof.

"I'll have to nail it down," Max decided.

"You can't nail it down," Bree said.

"I have stuff in my truck that would weigh it down," he said, staring at his truck. "But you can't hold this by yourself."

Kneeling on it was helping, though. It was easier than trying to hang on to the slick, wet plastic while the relentless fifty-mile-an-hour winds tried to carry it away.

"Sure I can," Bree said, knowing very well she couldn't. "I'll just . . . lay on it." The thought came to her suddenly. Kneeling on it allowed her to put her body weight on it and spread it over a larger area. Lying down would do even more. She weighed a hundred and twenty pounds. That would hold the flapping tarp.

"You'll lay on it," Max repeated. "What? Until the storm blows over? Or tomorrow morning when I get those lazy fuckers back up here to finish?"

"I'll lay on it while you go and get something else to hold it down."

Max glanced at the truck again. It wasn't perfect, but it was the only option. "I'll be right back."

He wasn't. Climbing down the scaffolding, which was basically just narrow metal railings and plywood, wasn't easy to do in these conditions anyway, but added to that was Max's bad knee. The climbing up and down and crawling on the roof would be hard enough on him, but on his return trip he would be carrying something heavy. And he'd probably have to take more than one trip. It wasn't like he could bring a lot up in his arms at once.

For what felt like forever, Bree lay on her stomach on the tarp, her arms and legs extended to hold down as much as she could, while rain bombarded her. She was freezing, her limbs stiff and cold, but that didn't stop her thoughts from whirling. Max couldn't leave her. She would never complain about being bored again as long as she was warm, dry, and not at risk of being blown off a barn roof. And Max couldn't leave her.

Finally, she heard his footsteps on the roof. He plunked a toolbox down a few feet away on top of the tarp and flipped it open. He pulled out several heavy metal tools and distributed them around the tarp, but it wasn't enough to let Bree get up.

He repeated the trip down to his truck and back up twice more before they had enough stuff so that the tarp would stay in place, at least until the wind died down.

Bree got to her feet unsteadily. The wet denim of her jeans, her cold joints, and the wind all combined to make it extremely hard to move gracefully. She stepped forward just as a loud *crack* sounded overhead and a blinding flash of light shot across her peripheral vision. She turned swiftly, just in time to see the streak of lightning hit the weather vane on the peak of the barn. Bree jumped back instinctively, and the heel of her shoe caught the handle of a heavy wrench that was holding down the tarp. She lost her balance, and her feet skidded out from underneath her. She hit her butt and felt herself sliding down the incline of the roof. Scrambling, she grabbed for something to stop her descent but caught only thin air.

"Bree!" she heard Max shout.

"Max!"

She was sliding toward the edge of the roof, and she fought to dig her heels into the shingles. They were slippery, and her momentum was pitching her forward. She saw the green of the grass below come into sight, and she prepared herself to attempt to grab the edge of the roof as she went over.

Suddenly she was jerked to a stop.

She looked over her shoulder to find that Max had grabbed the back of her shirt while hanging onto the edge of the hole they'd been fighting to cover. Grasping the edge of those shingles that surrounded the opening was the only handhold on the roof other than the weather vane that had just been zapped.

"Jesus," Max huffed.

He strained to pull her back, and Bree was finally able to dig in a heel and push to help.

"Thank you," she breathed, wiping her hair away from her face.

He didn't let go, still trying to haul her higher onto the incline of the roof by the back of her shirt. He tried to bend his bad knee to get better purchase, and Bree saw how he winced, then grit his teeth and *made* it bend so that he could use his leg muscles, as well as his arms, to pull her up.

"Holy crap," she panted as she was able to get her hands and both feet under her to also push.

She gave a hard thrust with her feet and felt the hold on her shirt give as she bumped into Max. But too late, she realized that he was pitching backward.

He stumbled, failed to get his leg under him, and fell onto the tarp. Directly over where it was covering the hole.

The toolbox, wrenches, and other items from his truck had been fighting the good fight against the wind, but they were no match for two hundred pounds of falling man.

"Max!" Bree screamed as the tarp molded around him and he went through the hole.

She crawled quickly to the edge and looked in, dreading the sight of him lying on the barn floor. But he had fallen only as far as the loft. True, it was forty feet closer to the roof, which was a good thing. The fall he'd taken was only about twenty feet. Still, major injuries could have occurred.

"Max!" she yelled down at him. The toolbox, thankfully, had landed beside him, and none of the tools had hit him that she could tell. "Say something!"

"Son of a fucking bitch!"

Okay, that worked.

"Where are you hurt?"

"All over."

"Are you bleeding?"

"No." But he sounded majorly pissed off. "My fucking knee!"

Shit. Bree fumbled in her pocket for her phone and dialed 911. "I need an ambulance at Montgomery Farms, main barn," she told the dispatch.

"Hang in there," she called to him. "Someone's coming!"

"Well, at least it stopped raining," he said.

What? Bree looked up. She hadn't even noticed that the pummeling rain had faded into a light drizzle. Not that she would have noticed, considering every single inch of her was wet and cold and felt like it would be for the next ten years.

Twenty minutes later, Max was out of the loft and cleared by the paramedics. He hadn't broken anything and didn't have a concussion. Which was a miracle.

"Just take him home and warm him up," Clay Simons told her. He clapped Max on the back. "He just needs lots of TLC." He gave them both a wink and headed out for the ambulance.

Max and Bree didn't talk as they got into his truck, her in the driver's seat, him on the passenger side.

He pulled out his phone and placed a call. "Get your *asses* to the farm and fix the *fucking* roof right *now* or I swear to God, I'll come over there and nail the shingles to *you*," he told whoever answered.

Bree pressed her lips together and simply drove. Max was hot when he was pissed off and being the big bad boss.

Then again, she thought he was hot most of the time. Even soaking wet and hurt.

At her house, they didn't talk about it, but Max headed straight for her bathroom to shower. He shed his clothes on his way up the stairs. She gathered them for the dryer, catching a glimpse of his bare ass as he disappeared around the corner at the top, but she was much more focused on his pronounced limp. Dammit, he'd been hurt. Saving her. Because she'd been taking another risk. But she'd been right. She was safe as long as he was around.

He came down with a towel around his waist.

He looked so good, so *right* in her house, half-dressed, helping himself to a beer, that for a second she couldn't breathe.

She was in a pair of sweatpants and a T-shirt she'd pulled out of the laundry basket when she'd put their clothes in the dryer. She was 90 percent sure they were clean.

Finally, he came to stand in front of her. He hadn't taken a drink of the beer yet. His golden skin stretched taut over hard muscles. Scratches and scars showed all over his torso—a few from today, several from past days. Bree wanted to kiss every one of them.

"I'm going to Oklahoma City tomorrow."

Her gaze flew from the scar under his right collarbone to his eyes. Her heart fell. He was still planning to leave. Even after what she'd said about him having to be here to really know her. Even after Maggie's photos. Even after . . . everything.

Well, fine. She'd only been to Oklahoma once. But it had seemed nice. "I'm coming with you."

"I was hoping you'd say that."

"I will just—" Then his words sank in. "You were?"

"I'm going to need someone to kick my ass during rehab, and no one has ever pushed me like you do to do more and try harder and go farther."

She blinked at him. "What are you talking about?"

"I'm going to get my knee fixed."

Bree looked down at his knee. "What? Fixed?"

He sighed. "There are no guarantees. The pain won't get better, might get worse, but the mobility should improve, and I need that."

"You don't have to do that for me," she said softly. "I can slow down."

"What do you think this is going to be?" he asked. "Just night after night of cuddling on the couch?"

She saw the smile teasing the corners of his mouth, but she nodded anyway. "I like cuddling on the couch with you."

"Yeah, and I like chasing you around and making sure you don't break your neck," he said. "But if I don't fix this knee, you're going to kill me."

"You idiot," she said with a choked laugh. "You could be in a wheel-chair and I would still love you."

He shrugged.

She stepped close and took his face in her hands. "You're *enough*, Max. You're everything I want and need. You've always been everything I want and need."

He looked into her eyes. "Thank you," he said simply, clearly accepting her words.

Her shoulders slumped in relief.

"But this isn't about that now," he added.

She frowned. "Then what—"

"Bree, my knee was a problem today," he interrupted. "It's not usually. But that's because I'm okay with other people doing the stupid climbing shit. With you—"

"You feel like you have to protect me."

"I thought that's what it was," he agreed. "Now I know it's because I don't want to miss anything. You make everything more fun and exciting, and there isn't anything I love seeing more in this world than your face lighting up. That's why I always want to be right beside you for everything. Not to keep you safe, necessarily, though I'll certainly do that whenever needed, but because you make me live my life fully. And I don't want to miss a minute."

Max felt his heart flip as Bree's eyes welled with tears.

He cupped her face. "So I'm going to Oklahoma City to my knee surgeon, and I'm going to have him fix this thing. And after I'm rehabbed and cleared, I'm going to pack up my house and move home. And I'm going to convince you to marry me, and I promise you won't get bored." He leaned in and kissed her. "After all, we're going to have fourteen kids, three dogs, four cats, and maybe even some alpacas, along with all of our usual adventures."

"Alpacas?"

"That'd be new, right?" he teased.

"Uh . . . yeah."

He grinned at the way her eyebrows rose, then he dipped his head and kissed her again, longer and deeper this time. He started slow, but that didn't last. It only took one little sigh from her to heat his blood and make him drop his hands to her ass and lift her against him.

She seemed to melt, her body molding to his, her mouth soft but hot under his. She sighed against his mouth as he started to slide up her shirt, his hand gliding over her silky skin.

"*This* is the hot fudge."

That made him pause. He lifted his head. "What?"

She opened her eyes and smiled up at him. "*This* is the hot fudge and whipped cream and cherries. It just goes on top of the Sweet Cream Dream."

"What do you mean?"

"I mean, our friendship is the Sweet Cream Dream—it's what I always go back to, what I want regularly, what I know is *always* good. The sex—amazing, hot, and sweet—just adds to that. And the Grand Canyon is like Butterscotch Blitz, and skydiving is like Cinnamon Sin, and skiing is like White Chocolate Whip." She gestured to the coffee table.

For the first time, Max realized there were multiple bowls on the table besides the two with the sundaes from earlier. Of course everything was completely melted, but it was easy to tell that each bowl was filled with a different kind of ice cream.

He let go of her, studying the table. "I don't understand."

"You're not Sweet Cream Dream to me, Max," Bree said, putting her hand on his cheek. "You're *ice cream*."

"I'm ice cream?"

She laughed lightly and nodded. "My favorite thing, the thing that makes me feel the best, the thing that can change up its flavors depending on my mood but is really, underneath, always the same." She rubbed her hand over his jaw. "You're ice cream to me, Max. And I've had ice cream every night for all of my adult life. Over and over again and never once gotten tired of it or wanted something else instead."

Max felt her words rock through him.

She did like something over and over again, in all its many flavors.

It was like her adrenaline addiction. She liked the rush, over and over again. But there were many ways of getting it, and she'd tried them all.

He was her ice cream.

He *wanted* all of that to be true so much that his entire being seemed focused on that—not on keeping him breathing, or his heart beating, or more trivial things like speech. He couldn't speak or move for several long seconds.

"Max?" Bree finally asked, her forehead wrinkling. "Are you okay?"

"You planned this? To have all of this ice cream here?"

She nodded. "I had to go to the store, but I wanted to show you what I'd realized. This is my celebration of you moving home. I get to have *all* of this, all of these kinds, whatever flavor I'm in the mood for, even multiple flavors at once, every day forever. Because it's all *you*." She paused, searching his eyes. "This was supposed to be really romantic."

She was trying to be romantic for him. Again.

Just when he'd realized he'd give up everything to have her, she was giving him everything he'd ever wanted. He'd never been more okay in his life.

"But you think you need hot fudge to make Sweet Cream Dream even better?" he asked.

She gave him a bright, relieved smile. "Hot fudge makes everything better."

"I think I'm going to have to prove you wrong on that."

Before she could process that, he slid his hands up under her shirt and slipped it off over her head. When she'd dressed, she hadn't bothered with a bra. Thank God.

Max's hands went to the waistband of her pants, and he quickly had them off as well. He walked her backward until the backs of her thighs hit the arm of the couch. He gave her a wicked smile and then pushed her gently. She fell back, landing on the cushions with a soft laugh.

He reached for her panties, pulling the pale blue silk down her legs and over her feet, dropping the scrap of material next to the end table.

Then he knelt beside the couch and reached for the bowl of nearly melted Sweet Cream Dream on the coffee table.

"*You* make everything better," he told her, lifting the spoon.

Her eyes got wide—in that *Oh yeah, bring it on* way he loved—as she realized what he was going to do a millisecond before he tipped the spoon, letting a drizzle of ice cream hit her left breast.

Her nipple tightened instantly, and she gasped, but he didn't think it was from the temperature of the ice cream. It was purely because of the heat between them. He held her gaze as he tilted the spoon over her other breast, letting the ice cream drop onto that nipple as well. He dipped into the bowl again, scooping up more of the gooey cream, then letting it dribble over her stomach, into her belly button, and down over her mound.

Bree shifted restlessly. "Max."

He grinned. Hot fudge, indeed. "I might not be able to tell the difference when I lick this ice cream off you," he told her, letting the sticky trail of cream drip onto her clit and then trickle deliciously between her legs. "You already taste pretty damned sweet."

"*Max.*" She arched off the cushion, but Max didn't touch her yet.

He set the bowl back on the table. The sight of her, covered in swirls of Sweet Cream Dream, was the hottest thing he'd ever seen. Mostly because of the desire he saw in her eyes when he met her gaze.

Clearly, lust and romance could, indeed, go together. Cuddling on the couch was great. But *this* was going to go to the top of the list of favorite couch activities.

"What flavor was the sex in the locker room?" he asked, swirling his finger through the ice cream on her stomach.

The question didn't faze her. She smiled. "Peanut Butter Cookie Crush. No question."

He leaned in and licked up the trail of Sweet Cream that surrounded her left nipple. She gasped, her hand going to the back of his head. But he lifted it anyway.

"And what flavor was the other night in my bedroom?"

She was breathing faster now, but she seemed to give that some thought. "It was Sweet Cream," she decided. "With a Snickers bar cut up and mixed in."

At that, Max puffed out a short laugh. She really did know ice cream and everything related to it.

He licked around the other nipple and followed the trail partway down her stomach.

"So what you're saying is that I can have plain Sweet Cream, Sweet Cream with Snickers, Peanut Butter whatever along with regular charades with our friends, family dinners, and three dogs?" he asked, running his finger through the ice cream that led to her belly button and then lower. Before he got to her clit, he lifted his hand and licked his finger.

When he looked up at her, Bree's cheeks were flushed with desire and her breathing was uneven.

She nodded. "Along with Red Velvet Rush, Almond Mocha Madness, and Strawberry Shazam."

He quirked a smile. "Strawberry Shazam? I might have to work up to that one."

She grabbed his wrist, stopping the finger that was circling her belly button lazily. "Practice makes perfect." And she drew his hand between her legs.

Max's smile died as he slid his finger into the hot sweetness that would *always* beat ice cream as his favorite treat.

With his fingers and tongue, he teased her body through a climax that made his body tighten almost painfully.

"Need you," she told him breathlessly, reaching for the front of the towel he wore.

Max got to his feet and dropped the terry cloth, then swept her up, turning so he could sit with her on his lap. With a knee on either side of his thighs, she reached between them to stroke him as he fumbled with the condom. Finally sheathed, he grasped her hips and moved her over him.

"I had some plans for the ice cream and hot fudge, too," she told him.

He looked up into her eyes and gave her a grin that he hoped conveyed even half of the love and happiness he was feeling. "Good thing we have forever, then."

He brought her down as he surged upward, sliding home.

They moved together slowly at first but with heat and speed building quickly. They were soon calling out each other's names and then collapsing together on the cushions.

"So," Bree said a few minutes later, after she'd caught her breath, "this romance thing isn't so bad."

Max laughed and hugged her close, his hand on her butt.

Their laughter died a minute later as Max's phone beeped. It was another weather alert.

He frowned and sat up, rolling Bree to one side and reaching over her to the end table where he'd left his phone.

"Another?"

"Southwest of here," he said, running his thumb over his screen. "Down by McCook."

"Okay." Bree wiggled out from under him and reached for her clothes as well.

Max paused for a moment to appreciate the feel of her body sliding against his, but unlike the feelings of longing he'd had before, he now felt a soul-deep satisfaction in knowing she was going to be sliding and wiggling against him a lot. For the rest of his life.

He still couldn't help grabbing her as she started to stand to pull on her pants. He tugged her back to him and took her mouth in a deep kiss.

When he pulled back, she blinked, slightly dazed. Yep, he loved that.

"What was that for?"

"The fact that you're going out storm chasing still all sticky with ice cream from having sex with me. That's really hot."

She grinned and shook her head. "You get off on some interesting things, Grady."

He swatted her butt as she got to her feet.

Her smile grew sweeter as she pulled on her shirt. "But this all was romantic, wasn't it?"

Max nodded, suddenly feeling like something was stuck in his throat. "I think you've got the romance thing down."

Her face brightened as if he'd just told her she'd won first place at the dirt-bike track.

His phone beeped again, interrupting the moment, then it beeped again and then again as they scrambled to dress. It was going to be a busy night.

"Okay, I'm ready." She reached up and pulled her hair into a ponytail, the holder appearing in her fingers as if by magic.

She'd always been able to produce or make a hair tie in any situation. It was one of the little mysteries about her that he was looking forward to figuring out in the years ahead of them.

He shook his head. "You have no idea how much I want to—"

"Me, too. But you've caught me. We need to go chase another storm right now," she said with the most beautiful smile he'd ever seen.

Max grinned, his heart full. "You are definitely the girl for me."

She gave him a wink as she started for the door. "Always have been."

Seven months later

"Bree!"

Bree turned as Ashley came through the door to the training center. "Hey!" She gave the younger woman a warm hug. "I didn't know if you'd make it."

"Barely did," Ashley said, brushing melting snow from her hair. "It's coming down hard. What can I do?"

A blizzard was bearing down on Chance, and everyone was preparing. Ashley had asked to spend the last two weeks of her winter break in Chance. She was graduating in May and had gotten a job in Dayton, another small Nebraska town, about sixty miles away. The position was emergency community resource manager and was only part-time, but she was also working under a grant for weather study at the university, teaching a couple of classes and helping out with Chance's training center. She wanted to be fully prepared for her new position, so she'd spent time in Chance through all the seasons. Nothing major had happened in Chance since the tornado—at least not with the weather—but she was still on hand to learn and help.

And now they were expecting sixteen inches of snow.

"I think we have a lot done," Bree said. "We've got food stores, generators, people on call for snow removal. Max is out sealing some of the upper windows on the rooms where we're going to put cots and supplies. Let's go see how he's coming along."

She was thrilled for a reason to go see Max, and loved that it was a legit work-related reason versus the pseudo-legit reasons she sometimes had to come up with. But working together in Chance, particularly at the training center, gave her more legit reasons than not. Sleeping with the hot teacher was a definite perk of the job.

She pulled on her coat, hat, and gloves as she and Ashley headed out the front door of city hall. The training center was on the first floor, and Max was working on the second-floor windows on the east side of the building. Outside.

The cold air and swirling snow made her take a sudden breath as they stepped out into the wintry day. The snow had started about an hour ago, but it was accumulating quickly. It was soft and powdery and pretty as it blanketed the ground and covered the evergreen trees. But in her line of work, Bree saw a beautiful wintry scene and a threat all at once.

Even so, a snowy night still made her eager to get the fireplace going and curl up with her favorite heating element: Max. It was true they never knew when they might get called out to help with a problem, but they focused on the moments they were in, appreciated them, and made the most of them. Even ten minutes of sharing body heat with Max was better than nothing.

Bree and Ashley started down the sidewalk that led around the building, and Bree made note of the snowfall amount and the conditions of the road in front of city hall. She was going to need to get out on the streets and highway soon to check them out.

She and Ashley stepped around the corner of the building just as Max was rappelling down the side. Bree felt her heart thump at the sight. It was a familiar feeling now. That same thump happened every time she saw him. Or heard his voice. Or thought of him. But it wasn't getting old. If anything, it was getting stronger.

The rappelling definitely gave her a little extra tingle, though. She watched as he jumped to the ground and unhooked the harness. His knee bent perfectly, and she knew he wasn't hurting. His surgery and rehab had gone amazingly well, and his physical therapist couldn't stop commenting on what great shape he'd been in, even going into all of it.

Bree had taken a lot of the credit for that.

Max shot her a big grin as he strode toward her.

Yep, heart thumping very much intact.

She met him partway.

"Damn glad to see you," he told her. "Parts of me are pretty cold, but seeing you gets my blood pumping to all the parts I *really* don't want to lose to frostbite."

Bree kissed him before grinning up at him. "You know what you climbing around on roofs and in rafters does to me."

"The whole reason I do it, babe. You think I like it up there?"

"I know you like it up there," she said. The snowflakes were clinging to their lashes and hair, and the wind was picking up, but she felt completely warm and happy. "You act like I make you jump out of planes and race dirt bikes, but you love it."

He didn't confirm or deny that. He gave Ashley a big smile instead. "Hey, Ash."

"Hey, Max."

"Hope you're planning to stay for a while. We're going to be snowed in for a bit," he said.

"No safer place to be than Chance," she said with a grin.

They were interrupted by the squawk of Bree's police radio.

"Calling all units. Motor-vehicle collision. Highway 141, three miles east of Chance. Three vehicles. Be advised the driver of one car is in labor."

Bree started for her car that was always parked at the curb. She didn't love accidents or huge snowstorms or mixing the two, but she did love serving and protecting her town. It might be quiet and slow most days, but there was plenty to keep her going. And the thrill of going home to Max at the end of the day couldn't be matched.

"See you later!" she called to Max and Ashley.

"Tell Dillon I'm going to need him to pay up on the beer he owes me," Max said over the wind.

Dillon would, for sure, be on the scene. He was the best physician in the area, but he couldn't stay away from the emergency situations and had become a first responder so he didn't have to.

"Got it," she told him.

"I'll save you dessert," Max said. "It's a great night for hot fudge."

She flashed him a grin. "Hot fudge makes everything better."

Max completely agreed.

She was still feeling warm when she pulled up at the accident scene.

And saw Dillon standing in the snow behind the ambulance clearly arguing with the woman in front of him.

Bree sighed and got out.

"Kit, what are you doing here?" she asked, raising her voice to be heard over the wind as she approached them.

"I was with Avery when she got the call," Kit said. "It's not like she was going to drop me off at home before responding."

Well, she had a point. "So what's going on?" Bree asked.

They were clearly squared off.

"Dr. Derby forgot which end of the body she specializes in," Dillon said crossly.

"Dr. Alexander is just pissed because he didn't get to be the big hero this time."

Bree looked around. Surely someone else could play referee here. But her fellow officers were taking statements, and the firefighters, along with the EMTs, were fixing up the victims.

"What are you talking about?" Bree finally had to ask.

"How would you feel if I were counseling someone with depression?" Dillon asked Kit.

"Like I was glad that person was talking to someone—and someone who was at least marginally qualified. Unless you skipped your psych rotation or something," Kit said.

"I kicked *ass* on my psych rotation," Dillon said.

"Well, I kicked ass on my OB rotation," Kit said. "I do have a medical degree, and at last count, I've delivered more babies than you have."

Of course these two were keeping track of something like that. Still . . .

"Really?" Bree asked. "You've delivered babies?"

"Five. Counting today," Kit confirmed.

Bree's eyes widened. "You delivered a baby *today*?" Bree's eyes went to the ambulance where the new mother and baby must be.

"Yes. I was the first medical person on the scene," Kit said.

The wind was whipping her dark hair around her face, but she looked completely composed. She wasn't even shivering.

Bree, on the other hand, was freezing her ass off.

"And your first thought at an accident scene is to get between a woman's legs and check her cervix?" Dillon asked.

"When her water has already broken and she's screaming that she's in labor?" Kit asked. "Yes."

"You should have waited for the EMTs," Dillon said with a scowl.

"You mean I should have waited for *you*," Kit said.

"I am the *doctor* here."

"You're not the *only* doctor here!"

"You're on my turf, Kit, and you know it."

"Right. Between a woman's legs is your turf. How could I forget?"

Whoa. Kit only ever lost her cool around Dillon, but even when she did, she somehow managed to be composed and sophisticated about it. At least in public. Bree was *really* wondering how things actually went down when it was just Kit and Dillon.

Dillon was staring at her as if he was shocked as well, though.

Bree took a second to enjoy big bad Dillon Alexander being struck dumb.

Then she decided to give Kit the time-out she clearly needed.

"Okay, Dillon," Bree said, pointing to the ambulance. "In there with the patient. Kit," she said to her friend. "Avery's car—go home. And change your shoes."

Kit looked down at her black-leather fashion boots. They were covered in blood and stuff that Bree didn't need to know the name of.

"I haven't dressed for a delivery in a long time," she said.

"Or for the snow, apparently," Dillon said.

"Ambulance," Bree repeated to him, pointing.

He got in, muttering.

Bree turned to Kit. "Wow. You two are something."

"Yeah." Kit was frowning at the departing ambulance. "I couldn't just let the woman go without helping."

Bree rubbed her hands up and down Kit's arms. "Honey, of course not. And even Avery and I are trained in emergency deliveries. I'm freaking glad you were the one here before me."

Kit gave her a small smile.

"Why do you let him get to you?" Bree asked. "Dillon Alexander is the only person in the world who could make you apologetic about what you did out here."

Kit shook her head. "I don't know. I hate it."

"Okay, well, you did good," Bree told her. It was too damned cold out here for a long conversation about Kit and Dillon—that could take days. And required liquor. "Now go home. Get warm."

"But Avery."

"I've got Avery covered," Bree said.

She needed to help with the rest of the scene, but neither she nor Avery was going to be leaving until it was all wrapped up. She was going to be an ice cube by the time she got home. She hoped Max was ready and willing to thaw her out.

She couldn't help but grin at that. Of course he would be.

Bree watched Kit make her way to Avery's car, picking her way carefully over the slick ground in her boots. She'd never say it to Kit, but she agreed with Dillon's opinion of Kit's footwear.

A minute later, Kit drove off, and Bree headed toward the heart of the accident scene, shaking her head.

It was kind of sad that the craziest people in town were the doctor and the shrink.

"Bree!"

She turned toward the familiar voice and felt her smile grow as the warmth spread through her body. Max was coming toward her.

"What are you doing here?" she asked.

He caught her by her upper arms and pulled her in for a long, hot kiss.

When he let her go, Bree had to blink a few times and remember where she was.

"What was *that* for?" she asked, a bit breathless.

"There are lots of parts on *you* I don't want getting too cold out here, either," he told her with a grin.

That grin. It was almost the one he wore before bailing out of a plane. It was almost the one he gave a roomful of students before launching into a lesson about the weather or emergency management. It was *almost* the one he gave Jake and Dillon and his mom and dad.

But it was even more than all of those. It was the grin he saved just for her. The one that said he'd never been happier.

There was absolutely no fear of her getting too cold out here. She could just conjure up that look on his face and she warmed right up.

But she was really glad he was here. "I'm nice and warm now," she assured him.

He gave her a wink. "I know."

"You sticking around?" she asked, knowing his answer would be "Of course."

"Of course."

That also warmed her. Max would always be there beside her when she was hang gliding or hiking or snorkeling. But he'd also always be there beside her protecting the people they loved and making the place they lived better.

"Awesome. Let's get to work, then," she told him, taking his hand and heading right for the middle of the excitement.

"Right beside you, babe."

She knew he was.

And the best part of all, it was never too cold for ice cream with Max around.

ACKNOWLEDGMENTS

I grew up in Tornado Alley. Going to the basement and spending the night there because of severe weather was a regular occurrence for us in the summer months. I was just a kid, living thirteen miles from Grand Island, Nebraska, on June 3, 1980, a night that would become known as the Night of the Twisters. That evening a tornado outbreak produced a series of seven slow-moving tornadoes in Grand Island over the course of only a few hours. It's been called an "unparalleled event in meteorological history."

There's no doubt that the seed for this series was planted way back then. I still remember that night. The days after. The fear and the sadness, yes, but I mostly remember the stories of bravery and hope and recovery.

To all the people who helped Grand Island recover after that night, thank you.

There are some really amazing resources out there about weather and tornadoes, including safety, spotting, recovery, and more. Knowing how to be safe in the event of a tornado, and the people who are dedicated to storm spotting and tracking, are the two things that stand between these destructive storms and people's lives.

Some of the websites that were instrumental in the writing of this book include:

Grand Island Tornado National Weather Service page: www.weather.gov/gid/53032

National Weather Service: www.weather.gov

National Severe Storms Laboratory: www.nssl.noaa.gov/education/svrwx101/tornadoes/

Federal Emergency Management Agency: www.fema.gov/

Weather Underground: www.wunderground.com/resources/severe/tornadoFAQ.asp

The Tornado Project: www.tornadoproject.com/index.html

ABOUT THE AUTHOR

New York Times and *USA Today* bestselling author Erin Nicholas loves reluctant heroes, imperfect heroines, and happily ever afters. She's written more than thirty sexy, contemporary romances, which have been described as "toe-curling," "enchanting," "steamy," and "fun."

Erin lives in the Midwest, where she enjoys spending time with her husband (who wants to read only the sex scenes in her books), her kids (who will *never* read the sex scenes in her books), and her family and friends (who claim to be "shocked" by the sex scenes in her books).